WHY THE COYOTE CRIES

Pamela Shelton

WHY THE COYOTE CRIES

Copyright © 2016 Pamela Shelton.

All rights reserved. No part of this book may be used or reproduced by any means, graphic, electronic, or mechanical, including photocopying, recording, taping or by any information storage retrieval system without the written permission of the author except in the case of brief quotations embodied in critical articles and reviews.

This is a work of fiction. All of the characters, names, incidents, organizations, and dialogue in this novel are either the products of the author's imagination or are used fictitiously.

iUniverse books may be ordered through booksellers or by contacting:

iUniverse
1663 Liberty Drive
Bloomington, IN 47403
www.iuniverse.com
1-800-Authors (1-800-288-4677)

Because of the dynamic nature of the Internet, any web addresses or links contained in this book may have changed since publication and may no longer be valid. The views expressed in this work are solely those of the author and do not necessarily reflect the views of the publisher, and the publisher hereby disclaims any responsibility for them.

Any people depicted in stock imagery provided by Thinkstock are models, and such images are being used for illustrative purposes only.
Certain stock imagery © Thinkstock.

ISBN: 978-1-4917-8800-4 (sc)
ISBN: 978-1-4917-8801-1 (e)

Library of Congress Control Number: 2016902227

Print information available on the last page.

iUniverse rev. date: 5/10/2016

All the Pretty Little Horses

Hush-a-bye, don't you cry,
Go to sleepy, little baby.
When you wake, you shall have,
All the pretty little horses.

Blacks and bays, dapples and grays,
Go to sleepy, you little baby,

Hush-a-bye, don't you cry,
Go to sleepy, little baby.
Hush-a-bye, don't you cry,
Go to sleepy, little baby,
When you wake, you shall have,
All the pretty little horses.

Way down yonder, down in the meadow,
There's a poor wee little lambie.
The bees and the butterflies pickin' at its eyes,
The poor wee thing cried for her mammy.

Hush-a-bye, don't you cry,
Go to sleepy, little baby.
When you wake, you shall have,
All the pretty little horses.

—old African American lullaby

CHAPTER 1

The mother rabbit struck with vicious speed. One swift thump from her hind foot and the blind newborn lay alone against the cage wire. Allowing the victim's sibling to suckle, the dam focused an alert eye on the reject and kept her leg at the ready to kick again.

Kathleen yanked open the cage door and slid her hand inside. It curdled her stomach how any mother could pick and choose between her babes. In all her twenty-two years, Kathleen Egan's mother and father had treated her no differently than any of her three older brothers, except for her mother's constant but futile attempts to get her only daughter into frilly dresses.

Life was different at the Brennan farm though. All those years, she and Sam had spent looking out for Casey, feeding him when their mother locked him in his room, day after day, weeks at times, placating her so she'd forget about Casey for a while, and he could escape to the barn or the stable where he would be safe. Mrs. Brennan hardly ever went out to the barn. So many times Kathleen had wanted to be honest when her mother asked her what was going on, why Casey was missing so much school, why he was often bruised and overly quiet. The boys had instructed Kathleen time and again that if she told, their mother would take them away, so Kathleen had helped Sam to keep Casey safe and right where they were. She'd remained quiet.

"No, Bunny! Stop that!" Kathleen scooped up the tiny rabbit and placed it next to its mother that now, with her hand dangling there as a warning, seemed not quite so eager to push the kit away. She closed the cage door and, removing her wet parka, hung it on the coat rack.

"You have to love both of them, Bunny," she said. It didn't help that Bunny was her prize rabbit. The dam had taken first place at the 1987

Killkenny County Fair the summer before. Bunny might have the softest fur around, but she fell short in the loving genes. Even Mr. Bunny was afraid to be near her. He would hide in the opposite corner of their cage, so Kathleen had to remove him and put him in a cage of his own. Maybe she'd enter Mr. Bunny in the fair this year. She'd raised a couple of great rabbits that could very well take the 1988 First Prize, not to mention her pedigree chickens, best egg layers around.

Kathleen had taken top prize in the women's bale-throwing competition at the 1986 Maine State Fair, the same year she became the first girl to nail the spike-driving contest at the Rome Plowing Match. At five foot, one hundred ten pounds, she liked to think she could pin any one of the guys in Killkenny County. Sam was right when he said that Kathleen fought dirty. Only Sam ever beat her, because he fought dirty too.

Kathleen tugged at her icing-covered apron, "The Donut Hole" embroidered in gold across the left breast pocket. She tossed it into the washing machine and closed the lid, once more hating her uniform. Sure, the orange and brown colors worked for the rest of the servers. Her uncle always hired redheads at the Hole, girls with hair the color of ember flash and skin like ripe peaches. He only hired girls with hair the color of coal when they were relatives. Kathleen knew hers was a pity employment, a favor from her uncle to her mother, a she-has-to-do-something job.

She'd been the last to leave the Hole that night. She'd offered to stay, to let the other girls go, mostly because she didn't want to go back to an empty house, not with the ice storm that was just starting. Besides, someone had to keep the coffee flowing for the half-frozen travelers stranded on the roadways and those who just had to have a dozen mixed or chocolate glazed or perhaps a fritter or two. It had become apparent after a while, though, that no one else would be crazy enough to be out in the storm, so she'd closed up and headed home. Usually a fifteen-minute drive up and down the hills of Killkenny County, she'd spent an hour getting from Saint Jude to her house. The road had turned into a rink, and her eldest brother Frank's 1976 black-and-silver Mustang had spun around the curves like the last skater in an ice-circus conga line.

Mother Bunny, having fallen asleep, and both the kits happily feeding, Kathleen picked up her bag and sketchbook from the hood of the car and went into the kitchen, closing the garage door behind her.

The kitchen light flickered before it came on. The power wouldn't last long. *Great*, she thought as she looked around the room at its linoleum floor, imitation brick, the walls, robin's-egg blue with Aztec-brown circles. Her mother's decorating style was groovy city chic in a small rural bungalow. Kathleen had always preferred the comfort of an oversize country rocking chair.

Kathleen plopped her bag and sketchbook onto the table. She ached for her mother and father, for Sam. Sam would make a night like this fun. He'd have Casey and her out on flattened cardboard boxes, sliding on the ice as if they were kids again. But he had another three weeks at Concordia before he'd be home for good.

As for her mother and father, Kathleen didn't know when they'd be returning. They'd told her that they were going to Boston to visit Frank and Laura and their babies, twin boys. Her mother beamed when she used the word "Grandma," and Kathleen had to admit, when looking at the photos Frank had sent them, they were the cutest babies she'd ever seen.

That wasn't the only reason her mother and father were in Boston though. They were doing what they'd always planned.

"This isn't new," her mother had said over the phone, just the week before. "We always said that once your father retired, we were moving back."

"But this is my home, Mum," Kathleen had said.

"Boston's where you were born."

Like that made a difference. "I've lived here almost eighteen years, right here, and suddenly you want me to give up everything and move to the city."

Her mother had become very quiet, and Kathleen had known she was upset. But Kathleen had been upset too.

"I can't move a horse to the city. What about my chickens and Bunny?"

"What about your education, Kathleen? You can't spend the rest of your life working in a doughnut shop, dreaming of being an artist."

Angry tears had stung her eyes. "For the last time, I'm not taking accounting, Mum."

She had heard her mother sigh. "We could look into an art school. I have some connections here. Look, Kathleen, I want to be reasonable. I'm sorry, sweetheart; you know how much I want this." Her mother had hesitated. "We're looking at houses down here, houses with lots of bedrooms, what with your brothers in and out all the time, and we'll look for maybe a room where you can paint, one with good lighting."

Kathleen had never planned past living right where she was, being a part of the Brennan farm and selling paintings until she was old and famous.

"My life is here, Mum," Kathleen had said, already knowing her parents had made up their minds.

"You're overreacting, sweetheart," her mother had said quietly. "I know you don't want to work in a doughnut shop for the rest of your life. The move won't happen overnight, Kathleen. You have time."

She had time. Time to get used to it. Time to grow up. The kitchen clock clunked out the minutes. Its worn, tarnished chrome looked as old as Kathleen felt. She wiped away tears and pushed her dilemma into the background. She'd think about it later. She had more important things to worry about. She had to get ready for the storm.

Peridot eyes peeked up at her from below the rosebud-embroidered tablecloth she'd made for her mother the Christmas before.

"There you are, Penelope Puss."

A large black-and-white cat purred a saw-buzz hello, sticking out a paw to catch her. One claw snagged Kathleen, and she grinned as she untangled the cat's claw from her skirt. She rumpled its head, and static sparks snapped off the animal.

She crossed her arms and rubbed them warm. "It's really coming down out there." Stretching up on tiptoes, Kathleen leaned across the sink and looked out the window and up at the farm on the top of the hill. The Brennan farm shone as it usually did—the barn, beacon bright; the house, darker than a boneyard. She shivered and then jumped up when the lights flickered again.

"Frig. I have to get a move on."

Pushing the toaster aside, she grabbed a flashlight magnetically stuck to the side of the fridge. The flashlight came on but quickly faded.

"This won't last long."

The cat, now curled up like a fluffy yin and yang, yawned.

"We're screwed if the power goes off, Penelope. Well, I'm screwed. You can see in the dark." The lights flickered again, a cautionary spark, a get-going spark, a we're-not-going-to-last-stupid spark!

"Maybe I'll go up to the barn tonight." Casey would be looking for her, worrying about her. "Right. Candles."

She was furious at herself for being so spooked. She had no reason to be nervous, just because her parents weren't there, just because she'd seen strange people on the road, studying her house, just because she wasn't sleeping all that well. She jumped when a branch from the apple tree outside whipped the kitchen window. Even the trees were distressed that night, buffeted by winds from every direction. She should have been used to that too, to the branches hitting the house. Kathleen would never admit to anyone that some of the trees around her home were downright spooky. They were orchard trees, all bent and menacing without their leaves. She often thought it odd how spidery tree shadows could be spooky, but some ghosts could be just sad and lonely shadows of lost love.

After a short search, she realized there were no candles. She wasn't surprised. She was almost positive they had no matches anyway.

Penelope Puss pushed herself up, hopped onto the tabletop, then jumped to the counter, and padded over to Kathleen.

Kathleen froze. Tilting her head, uncertain, she stared down the hallway to the front door. What was that? Had she heard that? It was a thump from the front of the house.

Must have been another branch. But it wasn't the scratch of a limb against the siding. It was definitely a heavy thump. Her stomach knotted.

The doorbell ring ripped throughout the silent house. The ring zinged through every nerve from the base of her skull and down her back, and she felt it burst out from her fingertips. Her flashlight went sailing out of her hand, tumbling through the air, then hit the floor, and spun under the table. Fur flying, tail like a bottle brush, Penelope hissed and leaped a good three feet straight up and then down to the floor, scrambling from the kitchen, claws scratching and scraping on the linoleum. Every hair on Kathleen's arms stood on end. She bent down and grabbed the greasy flashlight.

The doorbell?

Another ring tore through the house. Kathleen jerked at the unaccustomed assault. No one rings the doorbell in the country.

"Frig." She froze, not daring to breathe. "Who in the hell is that?"

Her heart raced as she fought an embarrassing urge to hide in a closet. No. She wouldn't panic. She could handle it. She inched forward.

Kathleen's world turned black as the power gave in and went out.

"Penelope?" Her voice broke as she looked through the darkness for the cat. Think, Kathleen. "Maybe someone's gone off the road, Puss." She saw the shadow of the cat, now crouched, transfixed, staring down the hallway to the front door.

"Gran!" *What if Gran—no!* Her heart squeezed at the thought of anything happening to Sam and Casey's grandmother. Casey would just come in if Gran was sick. "Sam?" She shook the thought away as soon as it leapt into her head. He was in the middle of exams, and he'd just walk in too. She'd spoken to her mother earlier that morning, and Kathleen knew they were in Boston.

Now, pounding rattled through the house like thunder. She inched forward, out of the kitchen and into the hallway. Kathleen tightened her fist around the flashlight, lifted it, shook it hard, and turned it on. She crept farther into the shadows. Wanting to hide, feeling disgusted at herself for it, she went over the self-defense instructions she'd learned from her brothers.

Stay in the dark. No problem there, although she was sweeping the flashlight throughout the house like a weak runway beacon. Not too smart. Keep the intruder in the porch light. They had no power. That advantage was gone. Don't open the door unless you know who's there. She had no idea who was out there, but they could be dangerous or simply in trouble.

She struggled to remain calm. Half crouched, she stumbled forward as a ghostly apparition shimmered and undulated through the crackled glass of the front door.

Hey! Her gun. She should have brought the gun inside, but no, she didn't like guns, and when Frank had insisted she keep it, she'd told him to shove it. Frank had been way too protective. As if she'd need a gun, she'd told him, hands on her hips. He'd compromised and left it loaded up on a beam in the garage. She was not about to run back and get it.

Kathleen's pulse roared in her ears as the specter hovered. She gave a startled gasp and stared harder. The figure appeared to have a medieval mace in its hand.

A mace? Kathleen stopped short. She straightened up a little and rolled her eyes.

"For the love of God, Kathleen! Grow up. A rapist with a medieval mace wouldn't ring the damned doorbell."

Taking hold of her common sense as well as her courage, she strangled the flashlight-cum-weapon, stepped forward, and opened the door.

"Oh, hello, dear," the woman said to Kathleen.

Kathleen stared at the weapon in the woman's hand. It wasn't a medieval mace. It was a rubber hammer. Just as dangerous—Kathleen tried to justify her panic—in essence, a more modern medieval mace. She felt somewhat let down and stupid—very stupid.

The woman, sodden, silver-blue hair under an inadequate scarf, wore a trendy trench coat that wasn't up to the ice and, in place of serviceable boots, three-inch heel pumps.

Kathleen stared at the heels and then back up. The woman was rifling through her overpolished, patent leather purse.

"Is your mother or father in?"

"No. Afraid not." *Oh no.* She wasn't supposed to say that.

Kathleen felt a sense of relief when she recognized the woman then—Leena Schmiester, real estate agent extraordinaire, winner of the 1978 Saint Jude Chamber of Commerce Award for Excellence. She was one of many faces magnetically stuck to the front of the Egan's fridge.

Saint Jude, the tiny town closest to the Egan home, didn't have much to choose from for awards such as that. There was one realtor, one independent grocery store, one hair salon, one hardware store that specialized in hunting gear, one drug store that ran the local post office, a jewelry store, and the newest thing, a nail salon. There was one liquor store situated right next to the graveyard and four churches, lined up like soldiers along the highway next to the Saint Jude River.

Schmiester looked away. "That's all right, dear." She grabbed her car keys with her frosted silver nails and closed up her bag with a harsh snap. "Nasty weather, this. Maine, we should expect it."

Kathleen put her hands on her hips. "May I help you?"

"I know I'm a day early." Schmiester shivered and pulled her coat closer around her. "I'm on my way home. Thought I might pound the sign in, but with this ice, it's impossible." She gestured to a placard behind her, propped up against the railing on the deck. "This is your key. It's going right into this box here." She closed up the lockbox that was now hanging on the doorknob, rapidly freezing in the sleet. "Here's the key your parents gave me. I made an extra copy. Here's their copy of the contract and my cards. You put them on the counter so the buyers can pick them up. That's it. That's all. She's officially listed."

Kathleen's heart stopped. She stepped back as she felt the pain from the bullets of sleet that the wind shot at her. "Pardon me?"

"The house, dear. Your parents listed it."

For a second, Schmiester stared like a raccoon caught in a garbage can.

"Oh no. They didn't tell you." She shrugged and then smiled condescendingly. "I wasn't supposed to come until tomorrow. They'll probably call tonight. Let's hope your line doesn't come down," Schmiester said. "I'm sure they'll phone. Now your parents may have some questions. Tell them to call me."

Kathleen looked at the phone line. The line was already low and heavy with ice.

Kathleen watched Schmiester's nose lift a little as she looked down at the railing covered by the eaves of the house and flaked off a piece of peeling paint. It blew away into the storm.

"These stairs could use a touch up," Schmiester said, and then looking back up, she pushed a wrinkled envelope into Kathleen's hand and started down the stairs, holding tightly to the glassy railing.

Kathleen watched her slip and slide under the branches of the icy plum trees and over to her vehicle, leaving Kathleen, dimming flashlight and manila envelope in hand, gawking at the ugly sign shining in the rain, mocking her—"For Sale."

CHAPTER 2

"Door!" his mother wailed at him like a drill sergeant.

If Casey hadn't expected it, he might have fallen backward from the force. He waited for the rest.

"You're letting the warmth out!" his mother said.

Yup. There it was. He shut the mudroom door behind him. The rose-of-the-month calendar, a rather fake, red Lincoln rose printed on the top half, April 1988 on the bottom, swung back and forth. His mother always checked off every day, like a prison guard, making certain he knew she was still in control.

He patted down his straw-like hair. It wouldn't do to have one strand out of place.

Christ! The room was so warm. Steam from the boiling pots on the stovetop glistened on the walls and dripped down the kitchen window above the sink. He'd like to think his mother was making certain there would be heat upstairs, should the power go out, but she probably just wanted the heat, needed the heat. His mother was always cold. She had wiped the condensation off the window, giving her a good view of the stable and the barn. He knew that she was still watching his every move. He looked away from her to hide the painful disdain he felt.

The earthy scent of pot roast, the sweetness of the carrots and onions, made his stomach growl. His mother might be mean, but she could cook, and he could never get enough of her cooking. Casey wondered if she'd feed him tonight. It changed meal to meal, depending on how angry his mother became. Of course, it was somewhat better now that he'd grown, but it had been very different when he was a kid. Often, he had gone weeks eating chocolate bars and apples that Sam and Kathleen had snuck into him. Sometimes Gran would let him out of his bedroom and feed him some meat and potatoes. But it was right back into the room after his mother came home from one of her socials. Casey still kept a stash of chips and doughnuts under a floorboard in his room. His mother had never found his stash. Maybe if his mother had fed him more as a kid, he'd have been able to put on some weight, but now, no matter how much he ate, he was still a skinny, scrawny pole of a guy.

Casey removed his sweater and put it on the back of the chair closest to the stove to warm.

Crossing the dismal room, trying his utmost to stay out of his mother's way, he opened the cupboard and removed one of the faded blue-and-cream ironstone mugs meant for family, not company.

"You're late." His mother's voice rose. "Not my fault your cocoa's burned."

Casey couldn't remember any other kind.

He used to shake, terrified, when he was a kid, expecting the back of his mother's hand on his face just for entering the room, just for smelling like the barn. But he was young then. His mother couldn't really hurt him physically anymore. Her weapon was her tongue now and the way she hovered like a winged devil around Gran. Lately, he'd been seeing bruises on Gran's arms. Gran had told him she was getting old and was bumping into things more, but Casey was suspicious.

"You stink," his mother said, her voice now taking on a harsher edge as she scrubbed away at pots in the dishwater.

"Rachel, dear," his grandmother said from her chair at the table. "Leave him alone. He's tired. Did Billy make you lunch, darling?"

He nodded. "A sandwich. There are no lights on down at the Egan's," Casey said. Ignoring the chip in his cup, he pulled out a drawer and picked up a teaspoon. "I hope Kathleen stayed with one of the girls in town. It's safer than driving around in Frank's old piece of crap." Kathleen's oldest brother, Frank, had reluctantly passed the car down to Kathleen when he and his wife purchased a more practical family sedan.

"Thomas says she's down there, darling." Gran's eyes were clouded with concern. "She'll probably come up tonight, Rachel. Best get Sam's room ready for her."

His mother grunted. "She can sleep in the barn. I'm sure it will be nice and toasty in there with all the animals and those new generators."

Casey ignored his mother. "If she doesn't come up, I'll go get her," Casey said quietly to Gran. He knew Gran would worry about Kathleen. He would worry about Kathleen.

Kathleen was just as much a part of their farm as they were. Folks in town always figured she was Sam and Casey's sister. Growing up, they ran together, rode their horses together, bounced along the roads in the back of her dad's rusted out '65 Ford truck together. They smelled badly of barn, cattle, and sweet hay, and they played at being farmers, cattle barons with ten cows. They even looked the same, their jeans practical and unfashionable, their T-shirts emblazoned with Massey Ferguson tractors, and flannel plaid was their shirt of choice. Sam and he had never thought of Kathleen as a girl. She was their sister.

Casey could sit and watch Gran and Kathleen together all day. They were so much alike it was uncanny. Distant cousins about four generations apart on Gran's mother's side, Gran's eyes differed from Kathleen's only in color. Gran's were the blue of the misty morning sky, Kathleen's the color of a July cornfield, green with flecks of gold. Sam said that when standing side by side, Kathleen and Gran were a panorama.

To Casey, Gran was a pale, fragile beauty, a cameo. Kathleen told him it was Gran's hair, the drifts of snow-white curls, soft tendrils held back with antique clips. She wore simple clothes, dresses from the five-and-dime and polyester slacks, though she preferred cotton. She had a considerable knowledge of science, literature, and math, but her specialty was history. For years, she had put her skills as a librarian to work by carefully preserving the heritage and lore of Killkenny County, a history of the region that she'd passed on to both her grandsons and Kathleen. Casey had no idea how she put up with her daughter-in-law.

"Sit down by the stove, darling," Gran said. "Your poor hands are so red. Thomas says you fell out there." She reached for his hand. "More than once."

His grandmother's smile was slightly off kilter as she tilted somewhat precariously to one side of her chair, as if she was leaning against someone. He shuddered at how easily she could fall and break another bone. Since her fall the September before, Casey had worried, but Kathleen constantly reminded him of Gran's strength, and Kathleen was usually right when it came to Gran.

Casey took Gran's hand, bent down, and kissed her cheek. Then he noticed that the knitting needles she held were empty. Putting down his cup, he squatted. Six foot two, there wasn't much room for his legs between the rocker and the woodstove, so he scrunched up as best he could and pulled out a woven basket, overflowing with assorted yarns.

"What color, Gran?"

"You know, Thomas and I were just talking about that. Thomas wanted the blue because it matches your eyes, but I'm saving that. The purple strikes my fancy, darling." The older woman leaned over to the empty chair beside her. "Don't you think, Thomas? The purple?" She paused for a second, staring at nothing more, Casey thought, than the shimmering heat from the stove.

A familiar ache rushed through Casey's heart as once again he struggled to see the ghost of Gran's husband, but Thomas had never been more than the shimmer of heat behind the stove or a faint movement always just behind him, out of sight, never there when Casey looked.

Thomas Brennan had been haunting them for a long time, having died in 1943, crop-dusting in his biplane, just before the Second World War. He left his wife, a widow at twenty-seven, and two boys behind; their father had been four, their Uncle Billy, only two.

Casey's uncle Billy loved to tell the story.

"Hell. Thomas was up in his plane, and his buddy was flying the other one, and they were fooling around, I guess. Seems his friend's plane came down right on top of Thomas." Billy would always smile softly at that point. "Your gran never accepted it. She tells me that Thomas showed up back in her bedroom about two days later. According to her, he walked all the way back from the crash site. It was a long walk, Thomas told her. He's been here ever since. Waiting for your gran, I guess."

Casey figured that had to be true, at least for Gran. Thomas hardly left her side. It had to be wonderful for her, having had him all those years, but Thomas had never been there for Casey.

Thomas had always been there for Sam and Kathleen too. Maybe they were more gullible, or maybe he was just too cynical.

"I can almost feel him, you know," Kathleen had said once, a long time ago. "Maybe a cool breeze in the summer or a warm one in winter, sometimes his hand on my shoulder."

"Sometimes a curtain will move, and Gran will speak to Thomas, and I can almost hear his answer," Sam had chimed in, more than once.

"It's true," he'd insist when Casey scoffed. "Sometimes he talks to me in my dreams too."

How Casey had wanted to be part of those conversations or even to have Thomas speak to him in his dreams. But no matter how he tried, he never saw the ghost of his long-dead grandfather.

Gran put her finger up to hush an unseen husband. She smiled back at Casey. "Shush, Thomas. Purple is the perfect color for a raffle afghan. I'll use the blue for a sweater for Casey." She touched Casey's head, tenderly moving a lock of his hair. "The bittersweet nightshade matches his eyes perfectly."

His mother had always told Casey that he had his father's eyes, a dim blue. She called Sam's eyes, the eyes his brother had inherited from their Uncle Billy, blueberry-blue. Casey had none of Sam's good looks. Sam's features were chiseled like their uncle Billy's features. Casey had what he considered a plain nose, an easy-to-forget mouth. Thinking himself unremarkable was far better than being anything like his deadbeat, runaway father.

"Purple, it is," Casey said. He rummaged around in the basket until he found a purple skein. He ran his fingers over the wool before he handed it to Gran. "There are about four or five balls."

"That's fine, darling," Gran said, smiling softly at him. "If I run out, I'll ask Kathleen to pick up a few skeins in town."

He rose, grunting quietly at the familiar course of pain that shot up his back. If he hadn't fallen out there on the ice, it wouldn't be too bad, but he'd jarred his spine again, and that meant pain for a while.

Over at the stove, the kettle began its angry whistle.

He glanced at the table. Sure enough, there was the teapot with two teabags beside it. He reached for the kettle.

"Don't touch that!" his mother barked. "I'll do that!"

He stared back at the kettle for a moment and then picked the boiling water off the heat. He should pour it into the teapot himself, eliminating the possibility that the cauldron of pain could become a weapon. How many times had his mother reached a rage where she'd thrown the boiling kettle just because the whistling interrupted her fury? Casey had the scars to prove it.

"I said don't touch it!" his mother said, glowering at him from the sink.

He placed it on the mantel above the stove.

"Do you listen? Oh no! Oh no, no, no!"

There it was, Casey thought. The Klugg, Klugg, Klugg, Klugg.

His mother came from a long line of Kluggs before she became a Brennan. She looked, acted, and sounded like what a Klugg should be. She'd inherited the Klugg family looks—a tight, upturned nose, and hair that she dyed to the texture and color of kinked copper wire. She had a false smile, always painted up larger than it really was, and hawk-brown eyes. Even her ears—her hair was always harshly pulled back—appeared surprisingly small for her head, ironically small to hear anything with acuity. She was a long woman, svelte when younger, heavy in weight now, and she brought her fist down fast and hard when she felt the need to convince anyone that the Klugg way was the only way. She hated that she came from the poor side of the Klugg clan and spent day after day trying to prove to them that she was worthy of the name. She was president of the Women's Institute in the Saint Jude Baptist Church, the church most often attended by the Kluggs. She worked in the local elections, endorsing Henry Klugg for mayor and Ronald Klugg for sheriff. She took top prizes for her roses under the name of Rachel Klugg-Brennan so that she could brag that her father—the town drunk—had taught her everything about gardening.

It was no secret in town that the Kluggs had always wanted the Brennan acreage, the best farmland in Killkenny County. The long-standing feud had gone on since the mid-1800s when James Brennan won it from Dedrick Klugg in an all-night, drunken poker game. Even now, a Brennan could never go to a plowing match or the sales barn without some bitter Klugg bringing it up.

Casey figured that was what his mother had wanted the land from the beginning—to reclaim it for the Kluggs. Sam disagreed.

"She'd no more give it to a Klugg than back to a Brennan," Sam had often said. "She'd sell it to a developer."

Casey poured himself some cocoa and then noticed the bottle of Hotter 'n Hell Sauce. It was sitting on the shelf next to the stove. He sniffed the cocoa. It definitely smelled burned, but he'd never complain about that. He was used to his mother burning his food. It was the hot sauce that bothered him. There was no reason it should be there, right next to the stove. Casey spooned out a teaspoon of the steaming cocoa, blew on it to lower the temperature, and tasted it. The burn was strong enough to conceal the bitterness, but there was no sign of hot sauce. She hadn't laced it. Still. He looked back at the tiny bottle of pain. Had she forgotten to lace the cocoa with the hot sauce, or had she just put it there to remind him that she could? She was watching him when he looked over.

Pulling out a chair, he sat back down next to Gran and the heat. The cheap feed-store clock, bent hands on a faded pastoral scene, clunked out the minutes of the night. He thought of the things he still had to do. The lights would never last in the house with the ice storm. He'd have to get the gas lanterns out. Sure, they had the generators at the barn and the stable, but they used the stove for heat in the house, and if the lights went out, they'd be in the dark. Casey picked up a new tapered candle, one of many that his mother had placed on the table, rose colored with pink plastic over them. His mother never bought safety candles or storm candles, only useless and decorative candles, candles she never lit, candles that matched the décor. Casey didn't take much notice of the overdone décor. He'd grown up with it. The plastic-covered candles on the table always matched the wallpaper, the knickknacks matched the pristine place mats, and the curtains matched everything. All to impress the other Kluggs.

His mother lumbered over to the stove. She picked up the kettle, still steaming, and carried it over to the table, stopping next to Gran. The kettle just inches from Gran's head, his mother eyeballed Casey as she leaned over and pulled the teapot over to her.

"Careful, Gran," Casey said. "Watch it." Jumping up, he reached over and placed his hand between his grandmother's head and the heat.

Would his mother hurt Gran, or was she simply tormenting him? He wasn't certain, but he thought he saw his mother swirl the water a little before she tossed the teabags into the pot and then dumped in the hot water.

"I'm not the klutz in this family," she said quietly, smiling innocently at him.

She pulled the kettle back and headed to the sink, a wicked grin on her face.

Gran gave him a calming glance. "I'm all right, darling. Don't fuss," she said quietly.

Don't fuss? Christ! He felt the throb of a years-old burn on the back of his arm.

Wiping her hands on a rose-covered tea towel, his mother came back and placed two cups on the table. She landed in her chair and pushed a rose-colored candlestick out of the way in order to drag the teapot over to her. "Get the cream."

Casey did as he was told and headed for the fridge.

"I told you to leave the cattle outside, but no," she said, staring at him, her eyes glaring. She stirred, her spoon clanking and scraping, and then placed the top back on the teapot. "Putting those animals in the barn. We're a laughingstock in town, with that bunch of spoiled, pampered, money-wasting cows."

She poured the tea into the two cups. "They're just animals," Rachel said. "Uh, uh. No. It's all about that fancy heifer. That heifer has been nothing but money spent badly. Two thousand bucks! But no, oh no, no, no, no"—her voice grew more strident—"you go behind my back and buy her anyway."

Casey watched as his mother laid a napkin over her heavy chest to catch any errant drops from her tea.

"You can't keep things like that from me. I saw her when Billy snuck her into the barn. She's too small for calving, especially with our bulls. Our bulls are big. They give big calves, every time. Big! Big! Big!"

"We want small calves, Mum, fast growers. The birthing mortality rate drops. Profits increase. That's where the market's headed," he said.

Gran didn't look up at her from her needles. "Zero loss, Thomas says. That's what we're after."

"We don't want any one of the cattle falling on the ice out there," Casey said, coming back with the milk to the table. He knew he was wasting his breath. His mother didn't believe in fancy breeding or purebred cattle, and this was the first time Casey had stood up to her, ever, in twenty-three years. He'd try to make her understand again, reason, like Sam was so good at doing.

"There is no protection out there. They could easily fall on the ice and freeze to death. We have three, besides Libby, that could drop a calf tonight, and if we left them out in the storm, they'd be dead by morning. Every calf counts, Mum."

That's what Sam would say. Then he remembered that his mother didn't really listen when Sam tried to talk about upgrading the farm, even when he mentioned the money they could make in artificial insemination and breeding show animals. He sat down.

"Big calves endanger the cow. We want smaller calves that index faster," he said and then realized his mother wouldn't understand. "Grow faster from birth weight to feed-yard weight." Casey didn't look at his mother but down into his congealing cocoa. He wanted to say that none of it was coming from her budget, and she had nothing to say about the farm business. But that could set her off, and no one wanted that. Besides, she would hate Casey no matter what he said.

Twenty-three years old and that had never changed. Casey had no idea why his mother hated him, but she had always been out to punish him. Maybe it was because he couldn't entertain her like Sam. Maybe it was because he couldn't impress her friends like Sam. Maybe it was because he didn't look like Sam but more like his no-good father.

Sam had told him it was none of those reasons, that she was just crazy. Kathleen always said that his mother tortured Sam just as much, but in a different way. When he asked Kathleen to explain it, she would get tears in her eyes and change the subject.

Gran had done nothing but tell him when to hide. His uncle Billy had done nothing but give him places to hide. For years, he'd wanted to run away, but Sam would always stop him. We have our dream, Sam had always said.

And now they'd made it. All their plans were about to come true. They had a little money in the bank, Sam's degree to prove they knew what they were doing, and they were going to breed the best meat cattle in New England. They'd show the old farmers who told them they were wasting their money. They'd take the first prizes at the major fairs and make top dollar for each cow/calf or bull they sold. He, Sam, and Kathleen were going to bring back their farm to what it was before Thomas died.

"There's a recession going, on or are you too stupid to know that! We'd be better off mining the quarry. The quarry, that's where the money is," she said. "I was talking just the other day to Judge Klugg."

Christ, Casey thought. Why couldn't she call him *Walt*? Everyone in town called him *Walt*.

"He thinks all this fancy breeding is a waste of money. He says Limousin cattle don't produce enough eggs."

"That's ridiculous, Rachel." Gran chuckled. "Chickens produce eggs. Cows produce calves."

His mother scowled. "Embryos then! Judge Klugg says that we'd be better off with a dairy herd for that." She leaned forward and leered at him again. "Our money's in the mineral rights here."

How many times had he heard that?

"Yes, I know, Thomas," Gran said, laying her knitting on her lap. "Thomas says the heifer is pedigree, Rachel. She's a perfect start to a better herd, and a better herd is more money in the bank."

"So Thomas agrees? Do you agree, Thomas?" His mother taunted. "The illusive Thomas." Rachel snorted and glanced back at Casey.

His mother knew that first time heifers often had problems calving, but this time he wasn't going to let his mother stop him. He did what Sam would do. Rising, he went over to the phone on the wall by the door and pressed out a familiar number.

"Who the hell are you calling?" His mother said, twisting in her seat. "Are you calling that vet again?"

He waited for someone to pick up at the vet's office, but no one was answering. He waited until he heard the message machine kick in, and he hung up again.

"Goddamned answering machines." He came back to the table, sat down, and looked at Gran, realizing he'd sworn out loud. "Sorry, Gran."

"You called the vet? Again!" His mother's voice lowered, and she almost snarled.

"Yes, Mum," he said cautiously to his mother. "I got through earlier. They should be calling back."

She laughed at him. "They already did. I told them they had the wrong number. They won't be coming."

Casey tightened his fist, trying his best to hide his anger.

She leaned back, and her sneer disappeared. "More money wasted? I don't think so. I could use that money for my roses."

He wanted to say to her, *This is none of your business. Your* house and *your* garden and *your* damned roses come out of *your* budget. You have no business in the running of the farm. That was the agreement, but he didn't dare say it. It would only make her mad, furious maybe, what with the weather and Libby.

"Calling the vet in for one cow. Waste, I tell you." Rachel began rocking in her chair, as she always did just before she got mean. She began to scrape her finger along the gouge in the grain of the table, the gouge she had worn deep into the wood for as long as he could remember.

"The vet won't get here anyway, not with the ice." *There*, Casey thought. *That's what Sam would say.*

"Wherever did you get the space, darling? Thomas says there wasn't enough room in the barn for the whole herd." Gran looked over at an empty chair, smiled, and then looked back at Casey. "Did you put the bulls in the stable?"

"And Kathleen's chickens," he said. "The coop may not make it through the storm." He leaned toward his grandmother. "They're all crammed in pretty tight. The horses don't care for it one bit." His stomach growled again, and he wanted to change the subject, maybe try using Sam's tool of flattery. "The pot roast smells good, Mum."

"Pedigree," his mother muttered. "Bet she won't last till morning. More money lost." Again, his mother ran her right index finger over the grain of the maple table, digging into it with painful abandon, seemingly unaware of the possibility of splinters, unaware of the gouge she'd made over the years. Her fingers revealed the truth though. Her right index fingernail was worn down to the quick, swollen and bruised, raw.

Looking like a wolverine that's cornered her prey, she stared over at him. "You didn't bring in extra wood."

Casey closed his eyes and silently groaned. He'd forgotten the wood. He looked over at the pile, knowing they had plenty.

"You'll do anything to get out of bringing in wood. And that back door! Why can't you come in without losing it to the wind? Why? Tell me why," his mother said, her eyes boring holes into his head. "You waste half the heat in the kitchen each time you do it. It's just more wood for you to bring in, you know."

He winced, remembering how the wind had ripped the storm door from his grip. "Sorry, Mum. We should get that handle fixed. The whole door needs replacing."

Her voice rose to an almost shriek. "That handle works just fine. You're not taking the money out of my budget."

"We'll take it out of the farm budget. They don't cost that much, Mum. Sam said—"

She slammed her hand down on the tabletop, and the dishes shook, tea sloshing over the cups. "Are you talking back to me?" She slammed her hand down again. "Sam can come in the door without losing it. Why can't you?"

He knew she'd be throwing the china next. How many teacups and plates had his mother broken over the years, simply because she didn't like what she was hearing?

Casey pushed his chair out and got up. He grabbed his sweater and pulled it over his head. "Forget supper. I have to get back to the barn." He started for the sink with his cup.

"Casey, no," Gran said, pointing at the stove. "Rachel, plate him up some dinner."

"It's not done yet. If he wants some later, he can join us," his mother said without any emotion.

"Rachel." Gran put her hands on the table and tried to rise.

Casey looked back over to his grandmother. "Don't, Gran," he said, tossing the remains of his cocoa into the sink. "It's okay." He grabbed a banana from the fruit bowl on the counter and wobbled it at her. "This will do for now. I'll get something when I come back," he said.

"Door!" His mother wailed at Casey as he grabbed a dry coat from the coat rack. "Close it well this time. You're letting the warmth out!"

"There is no warmth in here," Casey said under his breath and closed the door behind him.

CHAPTER 3

"Sammy?" Missy called from beyond his door.

Sam snapped the pencil he was holding in two as his eyes jerked away from his calculus book. He moved the notebook, placing it on top of his copy of *Artificial Insemination—The New Method of Cattle Breeding* that he read in order to relax when working on calculus. He stared out his window into the same storm that he knew was just starting over the farm. The ice had hardly touched Ithaca, but it would hit Killkenny dead on.

He wondered if he kept perfectly still Missy might think he was asleep and go away. He looked down at the broken pencil in his fingers and felt a pain begin to form in his jaw. He placed the pencil pieces down between his calculus book and the framed photo he kept of Casey and Kathleen.

"Sammy?" Missy called again from the other side of his dorm-room door.

Why was she still calling him Sammy? His name was Sam, even Samuel when Gran used it or he was being given an award or renewing his driver's license. But Sammy? Never. In the short time he'd known Missy, he'd corrected her more than an English teacher in grammar class. It was as if Missy relished calling him Sammy each time, as if she were addressing a child.

Samuel Brennan, with his black curls and violet eyes, had inherited the same strong features as Billy, features that came from Gran and her family, the Kennedy side. Unlike Casey, Sam had stopped growing in height when he reached five feet seven inches, but he never felt smaller than his older brother was. He used his height as an ice-cracking joke with the ladies. He compared himself to his Arabian stallion, Charger—to Charger's size, his fire, his strength.

Missy had told him she liked short men—men she could look down on, she'd kidded. At least he thought she was kidding. She told him he was a regular Sir Walter Raleigh, with his compassionate smile and carefree, seductive bedroom eyes. Of course, he had bedroom eyes. Lack of sleep will do that to a guy. And as for the smile, he had practiced it for years in front of his mirror. Kathleen said he used his smile like the laser she used to play with her cat. All Sam had to do was shine his laser smile and the girls would follow him anywhere.

Except Kathleen. She never followed. She was always right there next to him. What would she think if she ever met Missy?

"Are you sleeping? Are you sleeping?" Missy sang through the door.

Oh God! She was singing.

He wanted to sing back, "Yes, I am," and see what she'd do. Instead, not wanting her standing outside his dorm room, possibly in her clown costume, singing through his door, Sam rotated his shoulders and braced for what he knew was coming. He pushed himself out of his chair and, stepping to the door, opened it for her.

"Hi, Missy," he said, thankful she wasn't in her costume.

Missy's guitar case banged into his leg, and the guitar inside thrummed out a muted discordant chord as she strutted by him into his room. Missy never walked. When she wasn't skipping or dancing like a clown, she was strutting like a model. It was a model night, no clown makeup, no costume. She stood there in her leather skirt, undoing her coat as if expecting him to take it.

"I hope I didn't come at a bad time." Missy looked over at his desktop and fanned her face. "Gee, it's warm in here."

Still refusing to take her leather jacket, he closed the door behind her and pinched the bridge of his nose, hoping his headache would go away.

She batted her eyelashes at him. *Did that work on any man? Of course it did.* It had worked on him.

"You look tired," she said without compassion.

Sam rubbed the back of his neck. "Just the storm, I think. Plus, I have my calculus exam for breakfast Monday morning."

She looked back at him. "Have you heard about that fancy new calf yet? What's her name?"

She'd remembered. He smiled, hesitantly. She was being so nice, too nice.

"Libby. She's in labor, so it'll be sometime tonight," Sam said. "Where did I put those juggling balls?" He turned away from her quickly. Guitar strings, juggling balls, and a honk-honk nose ball, that's what he'd found. He had no idea why she'd left them, but then he didn't remember much about that night when he brought her back to his room and made love to her.

She gazed around his dorm room. All the girls he brought there did.

His room would have been gray, but he had littered every inch of space with posters—cattleman posters, prize bulls, cow/calf, quality Limousin cattle. He had Arabian horses and prizewinning quarter horses. John Deer, Massey Ferguson, and Fendt and Case combiners and tractors cut furrows across green pastures of rye and wheat, golden timothy, and cornfields.

Missy turned her head and focused on the ceiling.

Most guys his age had half-naked models on their ceilings. A few were into J. R. R. Tolkien or *Dungeons and Dragons.* Sam had always read *The Sword of Stone Mountain* by a lesser-known author. He had begun reading when he was sixteen, his way of forgetting his mother.

Sam saw himself as Becket, the Celtic prince, the hero of *The Sword of Stone Mountain.* Becket had been sent off to save his world, as Sam had been sent off to university. The parallel didn't end there. Becket took care of those he loved, suffered greatly for it, and wasn't much taller than Sam. Becket never grew weary or lost faith. Becket only had one princess, and he'd do anything to keep her.

"These are interesting. I didn't really pay attention before." She smiled at him like a patronizing psychiatrist. "You can certainly tell where your head's at."

He couldn't help the smile. He had no idea where his head was anymore. He could hear his grandmother's voice. *What is it that you want, Sam?* Finally, he was getting it. He wanted to work the farm with Casey. He didn't want to be an accountant. He didn't want to sell the farm and go work in the city. He wanted Kathleen.

Sam knew his mother would be more than furious when she discovered he'd changed his major from accounting to the economics of agriculture, the degree he needed for the banks to invest. But he was going to tell her as soon as he got home. If his mother wanted to move to the city, he was more than eager to help her on her way, but he was not going with her.

Missy turned and looked at his desk again, and he realized she was staring at the photo.

"This is nice," she said, picking it up. "I don't remember this when I was here before." She emphasized the *before*, he knew to make sure he got it. The night we slept together—the one night—*before. Before* you made love to me. *Before* you dumped me.

The photo was a shot Billy had taken of Casey, Kathleen, and him on their horses, looking all excited for the upcoming ride, happy, carefree.

"That's Casey?" She pointed. She ran her finger over his face. "He looks like his father."

Sam stopped and stared at her. "How do you know that?"

"Oh," she said, smiling. "You told me. We might have only had one night, Sammy, but we made use of the time we had."

He didn't remember telling her anything like that, but then he didn't remember much after he brought her into his room. Strange, though, he usually managed to keep his family to himself, no matter how drunk he was.

"And that must be MyKate," Missy said.

The ground under him seemed to move. He reached over, grabbed the photo, and placed it face down on his desk.

"Strange name, MyKate," she said with a laugh. She leaned over and touched his arm. "You talk about her a lot. It's a real turnoff." She looked at the back of the photo. "Kathleen's really quite pretty for a farm girl."

He felt anger percolate in his stomach. No one else called Kathleen "MyKate," not even Casey. Sam had called her that since their first day in kindergarten when he'd rescued her runaway red crayon and reached out to return it. She, of course, figured he wanted to pull her hair, as her brothers were known to do when their mother wasn't looking.

"Pull it and I'll slug ya!" Kathleen had said.

"Wasn't gonna!" he'd replied.

"If ya do, I'll slug ya!" she'd said again, accepting her red crayon.

He'd never forget how her eyes narrowed dangerously as she'd tugged on the frilly dress her mother, she told him later, had made her wear.

"I'm Kathleen," she'd said, "but my brothers call me Kate."

"Can you be my Kate too?" he'd asked, and she'd become his MyKate from that day on.

While Sam was saving Casey or some cheerleader who'd been dumped by a football player or maybe a nerdy girl who needed to be loved, he'd never had to save MyKate.

"You're a sucker for a needy lady," MyKate had often said. "A knight-in-not-so-shining-armor, meant to rescue and set free. You should be a fireman."

She'd always been there for him—to kid him and make him laugh, to innocently run her fingers through his hair, for the hug she'd give him and her lap for his head. Kathleen had never been more than a friend, and she was still just a friend, thanks to his inattention and stupidity. He'd dated others. Kathleen had dated others. He told her and Casey all about his conquests. He knew he'd never tell Kathleen about Missy. He could hear MyKate's voice: *You're screwing a* clown*?*

That's exactly what Sam had done with Missy.

Sam had met Missy in a bar off campus only four months before when, after having dropped her guitar on her expensive stand, she'd finished her very first set of her very first barroom gig. For shows, she kept her hair, mousy blonde with streaks of sunshine bleached into it, tightly hidden beneath a rosy rope wig. Black suspenders held her rainbow clothes together and accentuated her small breasts. Her mouth was painted into a pink heart-shaped smile. Sitting there in her rainbow costume that first night, she had not been downing beer or children's lemonade but expensive champagne.

The patrons had sat on their hands, obviously confused by the sight of a clown singing kiddie songs in an off-campus bar. As usual, Sam had felt it necessary to rescue a damsel in distress.

Missy had snagged him faster than she could twist out a dachshund balloon.

Sam had never really thought about clowns before, except the scary ones in horror paperbacks, but as they'd talked, she had made clowns sound interesting. Missy could rattle off the litany of clown history from the grand-master clown, Italy's white-faced Grimaldi and the Great Pierrot of France to Red Skelton and Bozo, and she cried when she told him how her father never found her funny. That had caught his attention. Sam knew all about bad fathers and had told her about his, how his father had run off years before, leaving Sam and his brother with their abusive mother. He'd told Missy how his mother had treated Casey, how she'd starved him and beaten him, things he'd never told anyone, except Kathleen. She had asked why they didn't kick his mother out. Sam had sighed and sat back with his beer. He had no idea.

Missy had asked about their farm, what his plans were, and how he treated the land. He'd told her what they'd planted and about the newest electrical fencing and how it improved grazing. He hadn't been able to help bragging when she'd asked about the cattle and his horses, and she'd told him how she loved to ride.

She had told him about her sister, who had died five years before, despite the bone marrow Missy had donated, and she'd told him she didn't know which hurt more, the physical pain or the emotional pain.

She had seemed so sensitive and vulnerable that night, even crying when she'd sung "Puff the Magic Dragon," and Sam had found her voice pleasant as she'd trilled out "The Farmer in the Dell," and "Row, Row, Row Your Boat." She had a song for most conversation.

"Don't you sing any adult songs?" he'd asked.

"Yellow Submarine," she had said and then had resumed singing.

The next morning, when she'd leaned over and kissed him, Sam had said, "I like you, Missy. I'm not into long-term relationships though." She must not have heard him, because she had asked what he was doing the next day. When he'd repeated that it was over, she had picked up her guitar, and she'd started into "Send in the Clowns."

"Do you think I should work this into my routine?" she had asked as her strumming had become more forceful.

"The kids probably won't get it." His jaw had clenched. "How about 'Happy Trails to You'?"

She'd laughed and had launched into "High Hopes," and Sam had known then—he was in serious trouble.

He had begun avoiding her in the hallways, but it had been difficult as she was taking some of the same classes he was—agriculture in New England and business law. She had always made sure to sit across from him and cross her bare legs to tease him, he'd realized.

She had begun showing up at his door, hanging out in front of his classrooms and sitting with his friends in the cafeteria. It had gotten worse. He'd tried hiding in the library. She had followed him to the library. He had thought about getting his phone number changed, because she'd called him so much. He had stopped going out to the nearby pubs and had started hiding out at various Denny's and Burger King in Ithaca, but he found it difficult to study at fast-serve restaurants. And finally, three days before, reluctantly, she'd told him she'd be over to collect the few things she might have left behind. He'd offered to bring them to her, but no, she'd insisted, and there she was, doing her best to make him feel guilty, again.

"I looked around." Sam held up a package of guitar strings to Missy. "You can't play without these." He waved them in front of her face and gave her his best attagirl-smile. "Oh"—he moved over to his desk and reached behind his book—"here are your juggling balls." He laughed in a teasing way. "I hate to give them back. I'm getting quite good at juggling." One by one, Sam tossed Missy her fluorescent green, juggling balls.

"I have others." She looked up and stepped over to him. She touched him gently on his face. The catch in her voice made Sam realize his worst fear. She was going to cry. "You can keep them." Tears welled up in her eyes.

"Lookit, Missy." He lifted her chin, but his charm wasn't working. Tears were running down her cheeks. "There are other guys out there. Some are even taller than me." He raised his eyes in jest, trying for the cheap joke at the expense of his height, and then he pulled her closer. "Ah, Missy. Don't cry."

She sniffled on his shoulder. "A fling." Her sniffles turned into a sob. "That's all it was, I suppose. I just don't want it to end. I've fallen in love with you, Sammy."

Sam looked away. How could he have let this happen? He'd been so careful to make the girls know he was not interested in anything but casual relationships. The muscle in his jaw twitched. When had she the time to fall in love? He'd spent less than thirty-six hours with her. He'd never once told her he loved her. He should have known better.

He leaned over and grabbed the last item he'd found, a plumlike ball from the shelf behind her. He opened his hand to her as if presenting a gift. "You'll make your nose all red." He gave it a squeeze, and it blasted out a honk-honk.

She sniffed, wiped her eyes, and smiled slightly as she rammed the clown's nose over hers and then stepped back and picked up her guitar case. "So … I guess that's it then." She looked away as a new wave of tears overflowed.

"Well, I should go." She pulled her jacket closed and grabbed her guitar case.

Sam didn't argue.

She pulled the guitar case on as Sam opened the door.

"Hey." She turned around at the doorway, thrumming out another discord. "I have a gig."

Sam's world brightened a little. He wasn't sure whether it was because she finally had her second singing job or because he didn't have to feel so guilty any longer. "Where?"

"In town. The Pig and Crown."

He leaned back against his door jam, trying not to show his amazement. "Wow." That was one of the best pubs near the university. "Nice place, Missy. You'll knock 'em dead."

"I hope so." Her face turned the color of her clown nose. She leaned closer to him. "Kiss for luck?"

He hesitated, hoping she'd take off the clown nose, and then gave her a quick peck on the cheek. She opened her eyes, a hurt expression flitting across her face. It had been a rather lackluster kiss, he thought, as she walked past him down the hallway.

"Break a leg," he called after her.

She wailed, throwing her hand over her mouth. "Oh no! What have you done?"

He hit his head against the door, realizing his mistake. "Sorry. Bump a nose! That's it, isn't it? Not good luck—bump a nose!" Actors break a leg. Clowns bump a nose.

He waved as the elevator doors closed on her. Leaning back on the doorjamb, he banged his head against it. "My own fault. My own fault." Rubbing his eyes, he went back inside. Closing his door, he listened to the storm beat against his window. He shouldn't be in New York. He needed to be at the barn.

CHAPTER 4

"Christ. It's April already," Casey said as he closed the door against the storm, knocked the ice off his jacket, and looked around the barn.

The barn was a one-hundred-year-old warhorse of oak, hard maple, and ash, decorated up with a new blanket of red paint and silver trappings, rotten wood replaced with pressure treated, and wiring done up past standards. To Casey, the barn was the closest place to heaven.

Billy must have been testing the generator, because he heard it humming in the background as he started down the center throughway. The pipes would hold up too, as the heating tape was doing its job. Water was running to each water bowl.

The mournful heads took turns looking slowly up and over at Casey as he sauntered past the stanchions to his right and the pens to his left. He checked over the cows as he went, their steam giving the barn ethereal warmth, softening the boards, concrete, and brick. The smell of sweet grain, the grassy haylage, and the curly wood shavings were perfume to him, and the cow droppings, musk. Every now and then, a cow would bellow as if complaining about being locked inside. *Not the smartest cows in the barn*, he thought. Casey wasn't thinking too much of the herd though. He was concentrating on Libby, as she glowed from the yellow lamplight in the small calving stall closest to the milk house, the warmest place in the barn.

"You in there?" Casey called into Billy's trailer.

Billy's trailer was adjoined to the milk house outside of the barn's northwest corner. The doorway, aligned with the barn wall about ten feet west from the barn's middle throughway, allowed Billy to sit at his kitchen table and look out over some of the stations and the ladder to the back hayloft. Not a great view, but Billy seemed to like it. Billy's doorway was the only way in and out of his trailer. When the boys worried about a barn fire, Billy always pointed to the back double-wide barn doors and then to the smaller door just in the corner. Casey wasn't so sure his uncle could open the double doors fast enough in a fire, as they were used only when they had to bring in the haying wagons and the tractors for cleaning the barn out. In the winter months, they iced up pretty solid, and it took some time to free them up. Of course, there was always the single door, but even then, in the winter, Billy kept hay bales in front of it to cut the draft down. Billy said his arthritis played up in the cold.

"Over here," his uncle called from the east side of the barn, somewhere in the middle of the cattle.

"Bitter out there, Billy," Casey said, removing his coat, once again surprised by the heat given off by almost twenty-five head of cattle.

"Cripes!" Billy said, his head appearing from the middle row of stanchions as the occasional cow bellowed for her calf. "Did you fall out there?" Hooking the last cow's head in snuggly between the iron bars, mother cow would stay safely in place and not stomp on her baby. The calf sucked away on her back teat, happy to be inside while the mother ate the molasses grain in front of her.

Craggy, desolate, his uncle Billy had a guarded smile, a determined jaw, and a scar on his nose he'd taken from a wild puck in a youthful hockey game. Despite niggling arthritis in his fingers, he could take either of the lads in arm wrestling, and there was no dad for Casey and Sam. Billy had taken on that job. Billy lifted them up and kept them there. Billy went to parents' night at the school and Christmas concerts. He did the 4-H clubs and educated them on farming. Billy taught them how to handle the guns, when to shoot, when not to shoot. The lads didn't like Billy's living in a trailer attached to the barn, but no amount of arguing could change Billy's mind. Nothing would get him anywhere close to his brother's wife, and Casey envied his uncle's choice in the matter.

"Sorry, son. I thought you'd be longer. I should have got the sand out there first."

"I'm fine," Casey said automatically. "I landed on my butt. Putting the sand out wouldn't matter, what with that crap still falling, Billy. The freeze isn't going to stop soon. Are the cows all okay?" Casey stared around the crowded barn.

"Yup. Looks like a few are ready to drop, so the calves will probably make it. Don't know how many could break a leg out in that shit. It just keeps coming. We'll have to throw some salt out a couple of times tonight," Billy said. "Should sprinkle lots around the house. Your gran ain't getting younger."

Casey knew that if there was an emergency with Gran, they'd never get an ambulance out to the house, despite all the sand they scattered around.

"You were right." Casey pulled off his hat, leaving his straight hair sticking out in shards once again. "Was Mum ever pissed off!"

"Eh, yup. I saw her on my way past in from town, earlier, eh. The way she slammed the postbox closed? Cripes." Billy grinned as he stepped past the rest of the herd and started over to his nephew. "Rachel just don't understand the business, Casey."

"Don't care's more like it. It was hotter than hell in the house." Casey pushed aside the weather and the pain in his back as he put his leg up on the bottom rail and stared in at the young cow inside the stall. Sad honey eyes looked back.

"Jeez, you're a pretty girl, Libby." Casey held out his hand and grabbed her harness. The heifer gave her tail a swish.

Libby, not too long or boxy, but sturdy and feminine, with good form and a lovely beefy behind, was just what they'd wanted in a breeder cow. Sam and he had spent years studying and saving for the best, and Casey knew Libby was perfect. After years of reading and watching the markets, after saving up their meager chore money and odd-job payments, he and Sam had handed their two thousand dollars to Billy, and he'd come back with Libby, the prettiest pregnant Limousin heifer he could buy. An animal of her quality, bloodlines, and temperament, bred the way she was, show quality, cost more than their mere two thousand. Billy had told him he'd got a deal, a going-out-of-business sale, and he knew the guy. Billy always knew a guy. The lads hadn't argued. Why argue a good deal?

Casey leaned down to the dusty bag on the floor next to him and scooped up some grain—fresh, sweet, and strong in molasses. He poured it into a plastic pail and then lifted it up to Libby's polished nose. She sniffed at it and then swooped in her conger eel tongue and tasted. Looking up at him dolefully, she turned away and resumed circling the stall, the top of her tail lifted in pain.

"Ah shit." Casey expelled the curse as he sighed slowly. "Not good." He kicked his foot against the support post and bit his lip. "Mum told the vet he had the wrong number." He looked at his watch and leaned against the railing as Billy walked up to him.

"The vet's not going to get out here on a night like this. That's no problem though. We can handle it," Billy said.

Casey put the bucket down and waited for Libby to come back to him. He reached over and rubbed her above the nose. "No. Not good."

Billy eyed him suspiciously. "I suppose your mother didn't feed you."

"She said it wasn't done." Casey took another long deep breath in and let it slowly go, ending with a snort and a shiver. "It sure smelled done." He grinned and pulled up the arm of his sweater, revealing the banana he'd taken from the kitchen.

"Want a banana?" Casey said. He handed it to Billy.

"Come on. I have plenty of beans and bread," Billy said, heading to his trailer.

* * *

Sad and easy country music drifted around Billy's trailer all the time, except hockey nights. Billy's favorites were melancholy ballads, and the boys could sing those songs in their sleep. Billy's caps lined one wall in the trailer, a collection of oil-company caps, mining caps, farm-equipment caps, and cattle-breed caps in the middle, and he had an odd assortment of caps from Brazil. The boys didn't get those at all. Maybe Billy dreamed of going to Brazil. Maybe he knew a guy there. On the back wall, under Billy's old Remington rifle, there was a collection of pictures from all over the world, places Billy said he'd visit should he win the lottery.

Stepping around avocado-green chairs, Casey made his way across the faded oilcloth and smiled, his eyebrows rising when he saw the money on the table, five one-hundred dollar bills, half hidden under the cutlery. Billy must have been too tired or worried about Libby because he rarely left his money out to be seen.

All his life, Casey had wondered how Billy found his bargains. Billy was a farmer, not a crook and never, ever a gambler. More than once, Casey had feared the police would show up and drag enigmatic Billy off to jail, and they would never know why. Casey touched the top bill. He grinned and sat down. Then he spotted something else, something new—a five-by-seven faded black-and-white framed photo of a young man. The man in the flying suit stood in front of an old twin prop. Leaning over, Casey carefully removed it from the wall.

"You getting into genealogy, Billy?" Casey said, his interest peaked as he rose and stepped over to his uncle. Billy's fingers stopped drumming out in time to the music. He turned on the larger burner of his hot plate to heat up the canned beans he'd opened and poured into a pot.

"When was this taken?" Casey examined it, trying to make the most use of the dim light behind the square glass shade above them.

"Oh, 1941. Thereabouts. Just before he died." Billy leaned over and pointed. "Dad had to be all of twenty-five. That would make me—oh, two, almost three at the time." He kept stirring, without looking up and then put a kettle on the other burner. "Never thought I'd make it this long."

Casey grinned. "Forty-eight isn't old, Billy."

"Yeah? Tell that to my knees. You hear from Kathleen tonight?"

"I haven't spoken to her. The lights are off down there. She'd have been smart to stay at a friend's." Casey touched the face in the picture. "Thought I'd go down later and check on her. Jeez, Billy. He really does look like me."

"He looks like your dad too, eh?" Billy rubbed his chin.

All the photos Casey had seen of his long-dead grandfather, Thomas, had been old and fuzzy, but this one was perfectly clear and more than a little illuminating. He could see the man his grandmother still talked to—the man he'd been told looked just like him, Casey's own chin, his hair, but mainly the mouth. He saw only one difference. His grandfather had carefree eyes, lady-killer eyes, Sam's eyes.

"Is this the plane Thomas was in when he died?" Casey asked.

Billy grunted out a yes.

"Could I get a copy of this, Billy?"

"Take it." Billy pulled the salt and pepper down and placed them on the table.

"Oh no." Casey quickly placed the photo down on the counter. "I'll take it to the photo shop."

"For cripes sake, Casey! Your gran would want you to have that." He peered over at Casey slowly as he reached up to the ledge of condiments for the bottled relish.

Casey nodded thanks to his uncle and then took a whiff of the beans and reached for a couple of Melmac plates from the shelf above the burners. He tried his best to seem disinterested. Some things they just didn't talk about, and his grandmother's conversations with her dead husband were top of the list. Casey worried that Gran was a little crazy from grief or maybe had some sort of cancer in her head, the early stages of dementia perhaps, when it came to Thomas, but he was alone in that belief. Sam, Billy, and Kathleen all talked about Thomas as if he'd just stepped outside for a smoke.

"You don't remember your father?" Casey said, looking over at his uncle as he edged into new territory. "I feel I know him. The way Gran talks about him."

"Talks *to* him." Billy plated up the beans as Casey reached for the instant coffee and then grabbed the bubbling kettle.

"Yeah." Casey grinned as he sat down and took a fork out of the many in the mason jar on the table. Casey's right eyebrow rose as he looked at the tabletop. The money had disappeared. "I love Gran but … well …"

Billy looked up, his slight smile all but gone. "Sam believes." He turned, put the coffee down, and then sat with his plate. "Katie too." He spooned the sugared green hot dog relish onto his beans as Casey made the coffee.

Conversation died back as they went through the mechanics of eating the food from their plates while Casey digested his uncle's comment. Thomas had always been there for Sam and Kathleen. Maybe they were just more gullible, or maybe he was just too cynical, but it had never happened to him. Ghosts? No more real than guardian angels.

"How about you, Billy? You believe Thomas hangs around here?"

Billy didn't say anything for a minute or two, just ate and then had a sip of the coffee, savoring it before he put it back down. He leaned over and almost whispered, "I've never seen him, Casey. But then, you don't see the wind."

Casey grinned, pointing his spoon at his uncle. "Fine. You ever feel Thomas then?"

"Nope." Billy picked up his coffee again. "But your grandmother … she does"—he dug his fork into his beans once more—"and that's good enough for me."

Libby lowed from the barn, and Casey scraped his plate clean with a sudden urgency. "Yeah," he said with his mouth full. "Bottom line, I guess."

He swallowed and rising, tossed the dirty dish into the sink, and gave it a quick rinse. Stepping out of Billy's trailer, he rubbed his arms, feeling the freezing wind blowing through the cracks of the back door. Casey felt cold air blow through the door now that they'd moved the huge hay bales out to the pasture.

"Christ, Billy! That's some draft there."

Billy raised one eyebrow. "That ain't no draft, son. That's fresh air." Billy stepped out into the barn. "Wind's shifted spring-side."

"Still. We should find some rags and plug her up. Maybe a few more bales in front." Casey put his hands up to the crack in the door and shuddered at the cold. "I'm going to move just a few over to cut that wind."

"Leave it be, Casey. You never know when you might need a back door to run through."

Again, Casey thought of the money on his uncle's table. He wanted to ask about it, but Libby moaned and all other thoughts vanished.

"I'll put some sand out. Test that generator in the stable," Billy said, stepping out next to Casey, starting to the front of the barn. Billy stopped, and without looking back, he said, "The calf pull's in the loft."

Casey's head jerked up and turned to the corner of the stall where the pull would usually be. Then his eyes darted up the rickety ladder to the darkness above him. His heart began to pound too quickly, his palms began to sweat, and he looked halfheartedly at his uncle. "I'll get it."

Billy hesitated, looking back at him. "No. I'll get it when I come back in. Leave it be, Casey."

"I put it there," Casey said. "I'll get it." Squaring his shoulders, he walked over to the hayloft ladder and staring up, he wondered if there was an official name for his private struggle, his fear of haylofts.

"I can get it," he muttered as he heard his uncle's footsteps fade into the distance. That's why he'd put it up there. So that he'd have to go up to the hayloft, a feat that still paralyzed him. "I can get it. I can."

Casey's hand felt like rubber as he gripped the worn rung of the ladder and began his slow ascent into the loft. Foot forced on board, hand tight against any possible splinter, next foot forward. *Don't look up or down—only straight ahead.* He didn't look down, but concentrated only on the wooden slats directly in front of his face and the firm feel of his flat boot against the board below. Trickles of sweat ran in rivulets down his forehead. He should have thought of his back before he'd started up, because it was pounding now.

Don't think about it. Just keep climbing. He let go of the last rung, stepped up, lunged for the bar inside the black hole, and then leaned over to the light switch, flicking it on as he gave into his final heave and landed in the straw on the loft floor.

He'd done it, he thought with a giddy laugh. But that was the whole point. He'd made up his mind to get over this fear, and he'd done it. After all, he'd made it up with no problem. Sort of. Now he had to find the winch and get back down.

Despite the efforts of one hazy bulb to illuminate, the mow was darker than a January midnight. Sam could scale these ladders like a spider, jump the highest fences when riding, and take the stairs in the house in one leap. Casey had never seen his younger brother fall. Ever. Casey's stomach heaved as the bottom swirled below him.

Libby. Think of Libby and get the damned winch.

Twisting, he pushed farther back away from the hole, his heart pounding too hard and too fast. He raised his wobbly legs up through the entrance. The familiar sweetness of dusty air overcame him as he looked to the far corner of the bales, searching for the pull without moving from the safety of where he sat.

The calf pull was leaning against a post, right next to the double-barreled shotgun and a pitchfork. It seemed to be almost looking back at him—hard, glowing, and laughing at him.

An archaic mechanism of pain, the calf pull used a steel winch and chain to pull a difficult calf from a cow. Its long, yellow handle, now chipped and sharp, yawned out to a huge *U* shape. Farmers had used them for years, placing the metal, U-stirrup around the back end of the cow, attaching the chain to the legs of the calf and pulling away with the help of the winches. The sound the chain made when it hit the metal caused

Casey's teeth to hurt every time. He hated the calf pull more than the hayloft.

"Goddammed thing."

His eyes adjusted to the black. Brushing off the dust from his sweater, he stood up and maneuvered cautiously over the straw-covered planks. He grabbed the heavy winch and lugged it back to the exit, dragging the pull behind him, thumping it over every beam. Inching closer to the hole, he grabbed one end, lifted the other, and lowered it through. He dropped it when the tip touched the concrete. The winch hit hard, and for a few moments, the rattle cut through the peace of the barn as the cows bellowed out an alarm. Casey stared through the hole to the brightness below. It would be worse going back down.

It was always worse in the hayloft and damned if he could figure out why. *One fall, that's all*, he thought as he swung his legs over, grabbed the rail once more, and began his descent. He could still feel his fall into darkness. He hadn't felt anything when he'd hit the hard earthen floor of the cellar, not until he'd woken up in the hospital, and then he'd had sixteen years of back pain to remind him.

"He hit the ground hard. Almost like he was thrown," he'd heard the doctor say to his uncle Billy in the hospital. "He has a major concussion, and he's cracked two vertebrae in his back. He'll be in a cast for a while." Casey had heard the anger as the doctor talked to his uncle. Casey had wanted to hide. "Where did you say his father is?"

"Lester has nothing to do with this," he'd heard Billy reply.

That had confused Casey as he could still feel his father's hands on his back. He could remember his mother's screeching and his brother Sam's wailing. Billy hadn't even been there. But his uncle was his father's brother after all. Brothers protect one another. Casey knew this to be true. Sam looked out for him all the time.

"Take a look at these X-rays! This child has been tortured," the doctor had said, while Casey'd kept his eyes closed, wanting them to go away.

After a while, they had. The head of the hospital had been a Klugg, and back in 1972, in rural Killkenny County, the Kluggs could have made anything go away. Anything but his mother.

Pushing the memories away, he began his descent, concentrating only on the rungs, trying to keep the pain under control.

Libby gave a long, pained low as Casey felt the floor once more beneath him. Letting go of the ladder, he told himself to breathe again, his heart still beating out of his chest. Then he opened his eyes and stared down at the calf pull. He picked it up and pulled it over to the cow. He gave Libby a weak smile.

"We might not need it, Libby." *No sense in worrying about it, at least not yet.* "You're going be just fine." Casey ran his hand down her side and felt the gentle thump of a kick. "You see? You're baby's still kicking. Now, I'm going have a feel inside." He smiled kindly into her huge, somber eyes. "Let's just see how big your baby is."

Casey walked over to the supplies he'd gotten together earlier and had left by the rail. Pulling an opaque glove from a plastic box, he removed his sweater and rolled up his right shirtsleeve. Rolling the serpentine glove up and over his lower arm and then his elbow, he stopped when it finished halfway from his elbow to his shoulder. He'd had training, taken courses in calving problems. He'd passed the courses with As. According to the teachers, he could handle any situation, short of cesarean. So he'd practiced on a fake cow. He'd done okay. He glanced back at the barn door. Still no vet, but he could handle it. He'd have to.

The rest of the cattle became strangely still, as if they knew he needed to concentrate, or perhaps they recognized the pull. Casey smiled a little at their worried faces staring back at him. "It's okay, ladies. Not your turn yet."

The air in the barn closed in around him as with his left hand holding her tail, as gently but as tightly as he could, he twisted the tail up around and back. He then leaned against Libby's caramel end and gingerly inserted his gloved right arm into the heifer.

Casey worked blind, concentrating on touch, concentrating on the tips of his fingers. He could feel Libby's cervix, fully open and soft so dilation wasn't the problem. But no matter where he reached, he could find no sign of legs, no reassuring head. He couldn't find anything to grab. The calf was positioned sideways, completely breach.

"No. Not good." Slowly, he removed his arm. He stood there, gloved arm now hanging at his side, watching Libby strain, knowing that each contraction put the calf further and further in danger. They could lose not only the calf but Libby as well, and it was hard for him to feel anything but guilt. He should have called the vet earlier, if only to let them know there could be problems. "Dammit! I'm sorry, Libby."

The barn interior lit up with beams of brilliant lights, moving fast, arcing from one side of the barn to the other. Someone had arrived. No one else would be out on the roads but the vet.

"Yes!" He started out of the stall, almost running across the concrete, past the stanchions, past the other bemused cows to the barn door.

"Yes!" He reached the handle just as Billy, grinning, carrying a vet box between his hands, blew in with the sleet.

"You made it!" Casey smiled madly as the vet, covered almost from head to toe in rescue-yellow, all-weather gear, stepped through the doorway. Casey grabbed the vet's bare hand and shook wildly, pumping it up and down, already looking back toward Libby, while Billy stammered.

"Thank you! God! I can't believe you made it! Thank you!" Casey pumped away at the hand.

"Casey." Billy closed the door behind them and grabbed for Casey's gloved arm, muck-covered, still steaming in the cold of the barn.

"Oh! Sorry!" Casey's eyes widened as he looked down. He dropped the vet's hand. "Sorry."

Wasting no time, he started back to Libby, pulling the vet's icy coat with his clean hand as he went. "She's down at the back. I didn't think you'd get here. She's been in labor too long. I've seen it before. She's special though." He looked back to make sure they were still with him. "And she's pushing, but the calf's breach."

He stopped at the gate and opened it, still staring at Libby, his arms flying about as he continued on about Libby's heritage. The vet said nothing but moved past Casey into the stall and over to Libby. "She's really special. We had her inseminated, eh? Her line goes all the way back to Prince Pompadour in France. She's our first full-blood and Sam—that's my brother—and I put a lot of money on her."

The vet studied the young cow and then turned around, finally looking at Casey full in the face.

"You must be Casey." She grinned and pulled down her hood. "I'm Sadie Parker."

"I ... ah ... uh," Casey spluttered, feeling his face grow hot. He tried to shake himself together. "You made it." The new vet was a woman, a young woman with pretty blonde hair.

Dr. Sadie Parker smiled broadly, picked up a clean rag from the bedding, wiped her hands off, and, looking around the stall, began removing her weather suit. "I suppose a section is the last thing you want," she said, pulling her blonde hair back into a knot.

"Ah ... yeah. Sorry about the ... glove ... ah ... sorry."

She laughed and Casey tingled.

"You were on my way home. I called, but ..." she said as she hung her gear on the rail of the pen and walked to the heifer. Sadie's hands moved deftly as she examined Libby. "Some woman told me I had it wrong." She looked up at him. Her eyes were a color he couldn't discern, gray or blue, but maybe they were green. "I figured I had the wrong number, and you were on my way home so I'd stop by."

He nodded and pulled the glove off his arm, feeling the embarrassment burn his face.

"Libby's big for having a first calf." Straightening up, Sadie studied Libby from another angle. "I'm going to try to turn the calf around." Sadie looked straight at Casey. "Try. I'm not making any promises."

He nodded again.

"You just keep talking to Libby." She began donning latex gloves. "Billy, you come back here and give me a hand. Get that chain off the pull. Hopefully we'll only need the chain."

Casey's heart began to beat too quickly as he moved over to Libby's head. No pull? She didn't like the pull either. This new vet was not only beautiful, but also she was smart and kind.

Sadie Parker stood almost as tall as Billy, taller than Kathleen was and, though willowy, sturdy. She was vaguely familiar. Parker. Which Parker? He looked back at Libby, trying to concentrate, his hand stroking the cow's jowl, mumbling quietly to her. Casey tried to think of where he might have met Sadie while he watched everything she was doing.

"You know there are courses you can take to learn how to do this," she said from behind Libby. She leaned over and looked Casey squarely in the face.

"I ... ah ..." He decided not to admit that he had taken one.

She disappeared back behind the heifer. "The state offers them." She groaned a little as she worked. "They're well worth the money, especially with animals like this one. Most guys are scared of the cow breaking their arm, but if you know what—" She cursed and shifted to get a new angle, and the talking stopped. "No. The classes wouldn't help with this one. It's really twisted."

Within minutes, a small smile formed on Sadie's face as she whistled in relief. She looked up from behind Libby again and announced that she had the chain around the calf's back feet. Sadie waited for the next contraction, when she and Billy would pull. Casey felt almost light-headed at the thought that it might work out, that they might have a healthy calf.

"Here it comes, Billy. That's it, baby. Come to mama," Sadie said, chain wrapped around her hands, her voice soft despite the exertion being used by both Billy and her to pull the tiny, wet form free from its dark cocoon. Libby's miracle slipped out then, down to the straw, glistening amber swirls of wet fur and legs. Sadie cleaned out the calf's airway.

Sadie removed the chain link, wrapped straw around her hands, and pulled the calf immediately over to Libby's head as Casey removed the harness.

"Let Libby smell her," Sadie said, smiling now as she moved back over to Libby and then ran her hand along the cow's side again as if searching for something.

"Holy Mother of God! Doc?" Billy poked his head past Libby's back end to the front. Both Casey and Sadie swung around.

"I thought so!" Sadie's mouth formed a large grin. "There's another one, isn't there?" She leaped over to Libby's behind almost as excited as Casey was. "Well, look at you." Her face bloomed into a peony smile as she stared. "Come on, darlin'."

Sadie caught it as the second fell into her arms and then slid down to the floor.

She bent down and examined the second calf. "A bull. He's fine, not at all stressed, Casey." She smiled over at him as Casey gaped at his second miracle. "Do you have a nurse cow if we need one?"

"Eh, yup," Billy said as he stared at the new family. "I'm betting we won't need one though."

Casey felt weightless as he watched the scene. His new vet was indeed, a for-real guardian angel, turning his sorry world upside down.

As she gathered up her equipment, Sadie told them what to do should Libby not want to suckle both calves. "Odds are Libby won't let both suck, but let's get this stuff out of here and see what happens," Sadie said.

"She'll nurse them both. Sure, she will," Casey said leaning over to get a good look at the bull calf. "Won't you, Libby?" Casey peered at his watch and then over at the barn phone as they stepped out of the pen. Sam. "Billy, I should ..."

Billy nodded. "Go ahead. He's probably pacing a rut in the floor." He pointed to his trailer. "Coffee, Doc?"

"I'd love one. You coming, Casey?" She picked up her box and glanced over at Casey.

He felt his skin burn. "I ... I have to make a call, ah, my brother ..." he stammered as Billy closed the gate.

"Come on, Doc. I'll show you some of our trophies." He placed his hand on Sadie's back and eased her toward the warmth of the trailer while Casey made for the phone.

CHAPTER 5

Sam's phone only rang once before Casey heard his brother's voice on the other end.

"Casey?"

Casey told him step by step what had happened in the barn. He had to take the phone away from his ear as he laughed at Sam's yelling.

"Didn't see that coming!" Sam said, repeating "twins" over and over again.

"I'm taking photos. I'll send them." Casey's jaw hurt from the smile. Sam listened quietly until Casey mentioned Sadie.

"A woman?" Sam said. "We've never had a woman. Bet the old timers like that."

Casey didn't miss Sam's sarcasm. "Their problem. She had those babies out in ten minutes, Sam. Damned near breathed the life into them. Libby's a born mother. She's cleaning one, the bull, I think. The heifer's already looking for the teat." Casey bobbed up and down to try to get a better look at the trio through the rails.

"Who is she?"

Casey knew he was still hung up on the fact that there was a female large-animal vet in Killkenny County.

"She's Hank Parker's daughter, you know, the contractor over Forton way." Hank Parker did their combining when years were kind to them and they had more to harvest than their equipment could handle. Usually the contract combiners only took the large jobs, but Hank always came out to do their small job. "Sadie's her name."

"Is she a big gal?"

"Not your type," Casey said. "Too wholesome."

"Hey, that's not true."

Casey recognized a sadness in Sam's voice. "Is MyKate there?" Sam asked, his voice a little distant.

"No. The lights are off at her place. I'll go down later." Casey wished Kathleen had been there just a half an hour before.

"You should. Knowing MyKate, she'll try to stick it out on her own."

"Don't worry. I'll bring her up."

There was a long pause. "Casey? I'm coming home tomorrow. I'll call you from the Hole. And Casey?"

Casey laughed quietly. "What?"

"Good job."

Casey looked down at his feet. "I didn't do anything."

Sam laughed. "Bull crap! See you at the Hole tomorrow."

Casey grinned as he hung up the phone. He had done a good job, he guessed, but the compliment was a surprise. The twin was a surprise. The vet was a surprise. Casey couldn't remember the last time he'd had a surprise. The Brennan boys didn't bank on surprises. They planned everything and executed their plans with precision. It had to be like that. If his mother discovered any surprise, she'd ruin it—like the time Kathleen gave Gran a kitten. His mother strangled it for no good reason and then threw it out in the backyard so they would find it there. Their mother didn't believe in house pets. Dirty, she'd told them.

Then there was the surprise bicycle Gran had given Casey for his ninth birthday. His mother backed over it with her car. Casey could still remember those two white reverse lights headed right for him, could feel the heat from the exhaust pipe as he scrambled away as fast as he could. He watched as his mother drove squarely over his bike, then laughed as she threw the car into drive and pulled forward, and then reversed and drove over it again. Only Sam was there to witness the end to Casey's red bicycle. He washed off Casey's scraped hands and knees, applied ointment on them, and told Casey they could take turns on Sam's bike. Of course, his mother blamed Casey. Only an idiot would be stupid enough to ride behind a car.

Or the time his mother had told him that despite his scholarship to Concordia, he wouldn't be going, that Sam would go when the time came. She told them that they needed Casey's hard work on the farm, and they had no extra money for boarding or supplies. Casey knew the farm couldn't afford it, so Casey had accepted her verdict. Casey would not let the Beast destroy this surprise.

Casey looked over as the barn door crackled and opened. Another angel in from the cold. Kathleen slipped in, balanced precisely on her ice cleats and bundled up in her worn white parka, the rabbit trim frozen around her face like crystal filigree.

"Katie," Casey swung around the barn posts and then ran to Kathleen.

"I saw the vet drive by." She grinned up at him, as he closed the door behind her. Grabbing his arms and leaning against him, she removed the ice picks from her boots. "Libby can't give birth without me here."

Casey took the picks from her. "Dammit, Kate! You just missed Sam." He picked her up and twirled her around before putting her down again. "Wait till you see!" He hustled her farther into his ark. For the second time that night, Casey was dragging an attractive female to the back of his barn, and he was getting to like it.

"Oh!" Kathleen slowed as she spotted them. Then she stopped and stared as if witnessing a miracle. "Oh, Casey."

"Somethin', eh?" He looked down at her soft smile.

Kathleen's eyes filled with tears as she walked up to the rail. "Oh, Casey. Two."

He saw the tears spill over and put his arm around her waist. "You're not supposed to cry."

"They're so beautiful." She wiped the tears away. "I wish—"

"Four weeks. He'll be home for good in four weeks." Casey wasn't going to say a word about Sam catching the next bus. Kathleen deserved a surprise too.

Kathleen swallowed hard and turned back to the babies. "Sam must have been so happy."

"Over … the … moon!" Each syllable defined and distinct.

She nodded, wiping the tears away and studied him. "Four weeks." She looked around. "Where's Billy?"

Casey realized then. "You haven't met the new vet."

Kathleen laughed again when the female calf took Libby's teat, her long tongue lolling around the nipple, enjoying the first taste of her mother.

"Come on." Casey pulled her forward.

"New vet?" Kathleen grinned up at him as he pulled her along and then pushed her into the trailer.

"Kathleen!" Billy grinned as they came in. "I would have bet the barn you'd show up. You should have come up sooner." He handed a mug to her. "There's a coffee for you. I'll get another for him, eh."

Kathleen took it in both hands and studied the young woman standing slightly behind Billy. "I only managed to get home. The power's off down at our place. I saw the lights on up here." She blew on the hot coffee, and a cloud of steam rose from the cup. "Don't know how long you're going to have them though. The ice is solid now." She stared down into the coffee clouds. "Should be pretty tomorrow." Her eyes filmed over.

Casey tightened his arm around her, worried now. "You okay?"

"Oh yeah. Only madmen and real estate agents on the roads." She blinked a few times and then looked over at Sadie. "And apparently vets."

"You did the right thing, Kathleen," Billy said. "Your place will be colder than a penguin's flipper tips."

"Kathleen Egan," Casey said, moving her forward, "this is Dr. Sadie—"

"Sadie," the vet stressed. "Sadie Parker." Putting her hand out, she shook Kathleen's hand. "I'm just an intern. I don't go by 'Doctor.' I've seen you before."

Kathleen laughed with a grimace. "Probably." She nodded. "I work at the Donut Hole."

"That's it," Sadie said, her eyes sparkling. "You're the smart one."

Kathleen's eyes widened at the remark, and Sadie's mouth clamped shut, her cheeks taking on a hint of red. "I'll just go gather up my things." Sadie disappeared out the door.

Casey leaned over and accepted a cup of coffee from Billy. He didn't know why, but a cup of coffee from the Hole could never measure up to one in Billy's trailer.

"The smart one?" Kathleen looked up at Casey, her eyebrows raised.

"What?" He saw amusement cross her face. "Don't look at me like that. You are the smart one. The prettiest too."

She shoved him. "Did you tell Sam about her?"

"Of course." He watched her eyes lit up in amusement.

"Bet he was curious."

Casey leaned closer to her. "He was more concerned about you."

"Yeah. Right. Did you know he doesn't want to go to his graduation ceremony? Says it's a waste of time," Kathleen said.

"Yeah. He told me too," Casey said.

"It's not that long a drive," Kathleen glanced over at the vet and then back. "I looked it up. The Mustang can handle three hundred fifty miles."

Casey laughed. "Ah yeah. But can it make it back?"

"It would last longer than that heap of yours."

Casey had to admit that he was constantly under the hood of his old Chevy truck, fixing it. Kathleen always laughed when he called it tinkering.

"He's leaving for home right after his last exam," she said.

"The sooner he's home, the better."

Kathleen poked Casey.

"I have almost everything planned for his party. He has no idea. Right? You didn't say anything. Right?"

Casey felt his face burn.

Kathleen tilted her head and stared hard at him. "Oh no, Casey. Tell me you didn't. You told him."

Casey cleared his throat. "It sort of slipped out."

"After all the work I did to keep it quiet. All the organizing."

Again Casey laughed. "Ah-yup. I'm sure you'll have it all organized, Kathleen."

She did her best to fake a scowl.

"Have you heard from your folks?" Billy asked. Casey had noticed how quiet he'd become.

"They're fine. They can't get enough of their grandsons." Her laugh bubbled over despite her blue mood. "They call me *Nauntie* Kate. I'm a *naunt*, according to them."

"Naunt*?*" Casey put his arm around her shoulders. "Nice."

Billy grinned. "I used to be a *nuncle* once, a long time ago."

Kathleen put her arm around him. "You'll always be a *nuncle* to me, Billy."

"Looks like I'm ready," Sadie said as she came back to the trailer, chin a little down, eyes a little hooded.

Kathleen leaned against the counter. "I don't know, Doc. I don't think you'll be going far."

They all stared at Kathleen. "Cops came by on snowmobiles. Salt truck went off the road right at the bridge. No getting around it, in or out."

"Oh." Sadie bit her lip. "I have a problem then."

"No! Ah … no," Casey said with an embarrassed laugh. "Not after what you did in there tonight." He knew he was laughing a little too much.

"Oh, I think it's a problem." Sadie cleared her throat.

"You can't get back to the clinic; you can't get home," Kathleen said, sipping her coffee. "Even with four-wheel drive, you wouldn't make it out of here, not on those hills. Not now." Kathleen smiled. "There's always my place, but the power is gone, and it'll get chilly. We're electric. No woodstove."

"No," Casey assured her once again. "We have a room in the house."

"No!" Sadie put her hand up. "That's fine really. I can just bunk down on the hay until it blows over. God knows I've done it before."

Kathleen looped one arm in Casey's arm, the other in Sadie's arm. Casey winked at her, as he already knew what Kathleen was thinking.

"That works," he said to Kathleen.

Kathleen let go of Casey and put her hand on the vet's hand. "I've always stayed over at their place. I'd take Sam's bed, and they'd camp out on the floor. We'll do that tonight. What do you say?" She looked at Sadie, pleading, as if needing to have fun. "We'll have a sleepover."

Sadie's head wobbled a little as she thought about the invitation. "Fine. I'll call my dad before these lines go down." She headed to the barn phone.

"Yes!" Kathleen leapt. "Hope you're good at sliding, because it's a rink out there."

CHAPTER 6

Lester Brennan, CEO and owner of LWB Mining Inc., straightened up and stared through the patio doors of his Brazilian penthouse, studying the night outside. The lights inside were off. He liked them off, as he could better see the vista of Brazilian glitter, the stars converging with the lights of the city, and the skirt of Sugarloaf Mountain sparkling like the emeralds and gold from which it had risen. They hid his reflection as he stared back.

He didn't much like who he'd become. His strong forehead—regal, he'd called it as a young man—was now creased with the lines of middle age. His nutmeg hair, graying at his temples, was thinning at his crown. Women told him his eyes hadn't aged much, maybe a more melancholy blue, but he didn't take women too seriously anymore. The young ones found him boring and were more than disappointed when they discovered he had better things to spend his money on than them. Older women felt the need to protect him, as if he needed saving, until they got to know him, and then his anger generally scared them away.

With two fingers, he slowly twirled the Corona cigar he'd been enjoying. Its wood-and-fruit essence circled and drifted around him. He strangled the neck of the decanter with his thumb and index finger. He poured himself a drink from the decanter into his glass. The deeply cut crystal never felt right in his hand, his hand too rough, too large for the fancy Waterford glass. Stepping past the statuary of horses and cattle, he made his way over to the leather sofa. Gaunt shadows played over the expensive, tiled walls of the room as he sat down on the leather sofa and took a long, slow drink, savored the liquor, and then swallowed. As usual, he wondered what Billy would think of all this. Billy had always been the one who dreamed of making it big, living high on the hog. Big wasn't all that great. Sure, the rooms were all larger than they needed to be, the ceilings too high even for him, but the penthouse made Lester feel small.

He poured himself another cognac, draining the last of it into the glass, decanter empty. *Fine vintage, gone too soon*, he thought. With no hesitation, he threw the decanter across the room. It shattered against the fireplace. Bits of small crystal scattered all over the hearth, his very own tiny ice storm.

Lester had felt happy for a while. Billy had found an Arabian that would make a good brood mare, and though the heifer had given them a scare, it had worked out—twins. Fantastic. But the inevitable loneliness had quickly shattered any happiness he'd had. So many years—almost fifteen years—he'd stayed in exile. How he envied Billy being there, watching his boys grow up, but if he went back, God knows what Rachel would do.

How many more years would he have to pretend he didn't love his family, send them everything he could to make up for the fact that he'd run away? Would they ever understand? Would they ever forgive him? If he could just talk to the boys, explain what had happened and why, maybe they would understand.

Maybe it was time to go home. Maybe it wouldn't be too bad, now that they were grown. Maybe he could buy Rachel off, tell her it was over, that Casey was a man now and able to take care of himself. Thing was he knew Rachel was more than capable of carrying out her threat to kill Casey. Yes. Perhaps they could finally buy Rachel off. Everyone has a price.

Lester Brennan stretched his legs, long and lean, and put his drink down on one of the many magazines about mining and agriculture that littered the mahogany coffee table in front of him. He slid down onto the Brazilian cherry hardwood floor, as if he belonged there, the spot where he was most comfortable. Pulling his legs into a crossed position, his back against the sofa, he took a shiny harmonica out of his pocket.

It was one of his best, having cost over $700, and was well worth it. A chromatic that could belt out the blues and haunting Irish folk songs was far better than most. The mouth harp always came out when he was depressed—for his wailin' blues. He'd break into song now and then with his shattered voice as he played. Not many ever heard him sing, not since

Casey fell down the cellar stairs. Not since he sang little lullabies to his boys.

After a few songs, he dropped the harp and let his head fall against the cushion of the sofa. He closed his eyes. "To the twins, fine cognac, and the blues." Lifting his glass, he twirled the drink and then drank it down. It didn't burn his throat so much as numb it. Then, with nowhere else to go, nothing else that could be done, he went to bed.

CHAPTER 7

Sliding and gliding on the ice while the sleet did its best to hold them to one place, the wind did its best to blow them away. Kathleen didn't notice that it took fifteen minutes for the three of them to work their way over from the barn to the door of the Brennan house. Even Kathleen, wearing her cleats, took the occasional freefall on the glassy rink, mostly trying to keep Sadie and Casey on their feet.

The house, as always, stood hard against the oncoming night, its shaded windows cracked here and there, its brick, dilapidated, chipped, and frozen. Kathleen watched as Casey knocked the ice off the frozen handle of the warped screen door, knowing that, as always, the wind would take it from him.

Casey never could get a grip on the broken handle. There was nothing left but a tiny hook, hard to hold onto in the best conditions, impossible in these. As if practiced, the screen door blew out of his hand and flew back, banging against the bricks. He pushed open the weathered inside door and let Kathleen and Sadie inside.

The mudroom was dank and dim, a chamber lock between outside and in. The weak light through the shaded glass of the kitchen door did nothing but muddy the waves of grime and salt.

Casey grabbed the storm door, pulled it, and then stopped dead, half in, half out, the wind whipping his jacket.

"Aren't you coming in?" Kathleen asked, and then she noticed his hand still on the knob, stuck solidly. She covered her mouth with her hand, trying her best not to laugh at the abashed expression on his face. Kathleen thought of her old hound puppy, the many times she'd caught him chewing on the metal flagpole in the freezing rain. The dog never did learn. They'd freed that dog's tongue from the metal so many times he barked with metallic whine.

"I … ah …" He stuttered as he painfully looked down. Sadie glanced back.

Casey grimaced and tried to smile as he looked up at Sadie. "My hand's kinda frozen to the door."

"Oh my God!" Sadie said. She dropped her coat and made through the mudroom door, straight into the kitchen.

Leaning over, Kathleen placed her hand on Casey's shoulder, balancing herself on him, removing her cleats, first one foot, and then the other while he squirmed.

Kathleen giggled and blew on his hand. "She's not bad, the vet, eh?"

"Would you be quiet?"

"No. Really, Casey. She must go for the strong, silent type."

"Quiet."

Sadie rushed back into the mudroom, balancing the water carefully in a cup. She poured it out slowly over his fist. As the water trickled over his hand, it slid down the crevices between his flesh and the metal, melting the ice and freeing him from the door.

Kathleen grabbed the storm door, closing it tightly behind him. She gave it an extra tug and then moved the safety latch to ensure it was secured, once again impressed how such a little piece of metal could hold a door so tightly to the house.

He raised his palm and stared. "It doesn't hurt," he said.

"It will. You're freezing. Let's see the other one," Sadie said, inspecting his hand. Then she lay both of her hands on his hands, not rubbing, just holding them. "You shouldn't bite your nails." She smiled straight at him, teasing.

"They'll … ah … be okay." He glanced up into Sadie's eyes. Then he looked over to Kathleen. Kathleen couldn't help the grin. He looked away. "We're making too much noise in here." He nodded over at the stairs to the second floor.

"No, we certainly wouldn't want to wake her," Kathleen said, hanging up her parka. She stepped out of her snow boots, lining them up with the others, close to the kitchen door for warmth. They smelled strongly of barn. Mrs. Brennan wouldn't like that. She watched the heat pass to Casey from his new lady vet. This night was just getting better and better. "Did he lose any skin?"

"Doesn't look like it." Sadie pulled Kathleen over to him. "He's freezing though. You take over, Kathleen, while I get out of my things. Don't rub, just hold. We'll get him next to the woodstove, and he can sit on his hands."

Sadie paused and looked down at his trousers, and then she turned him by his belt loop and studied his backside. "Forget that. It's probably frozen too." She leaned over and whispered to Kathleen. "Nice butt though."

Grinning, Kathleen ushered Casey into the kitchen and pulled a chair closer to the woodstove.

"That damned door hates me," Casey said.

"Not too close to that stove," Sadie called over to them. "You had gloves on when we left the barn, Casey."

"They stuck to the ice when I fell the first time." He glanced over at the stairs.

"Wait," Sadie said, her hand stretched out in front of her in a stop sign. She paused as if thinking and then leaned over and grabbed his wrists. "Place your right hand in your left armpit and vice versa. Let your own body heat warm them. That's better. If you put them too close to the stove, you could burn them." She beamed and then grimaced playfully. "I'm only a vet. Not so great at first aid."

Kathleen giggled, grabbed a knitted blanket, and wrapped it around Casey. "You're doing fine, Doc." She reached into the fridge. "I never would have thought of the armpits." She grabbed a plate. "I'll just make a few sandwiches, and we'll get upstairs." She glanced over at Casey. "We'll use Sam's room. He has the double bed, Sadie. We used to use Casey's, and I got the bed—it's a single—that way there was more room on the floor for the boys." She grinned and looked at Sadie, who was now sinking down into a chair and staring around the kitchen, her legs crossed at the ankles, her hands clasped in front of her like a hesitant child. Kathleen could tell the vet was suddenly very unsure if she'd made the right decision in staying.

"Ham and cheese?" Kathleen grabbed the bread. "And peanut butter for me."

It had only been the year before that Kathleen had informed the boys she'd become a vegetarian.

"No way!" Sam had spluttered out as they'd watched her chow down on a salad.

"You don't have to kill the cattle," she'd replied puffing up, meaning business, unwilling to take any of their guff. "Grow soybeans. That's where the future is. Soybeans. I read it in one of your books. Gonna be big. Soybeans!"

They had gawked at her.

"Why not?" She'd pushed her salad over to them, tempting them. "Taste."

"We're cattlemen!" Sam had said, his nose in the air, his eyes horrified, pushing it back at her. Even Casey had snorted.

"Well, you could at least treat the cows better." She stuck her chin out. "They do in Japan!"

"Do you know the cost of Kobe beef!" Sam had jumped up, folks in the diner turning and looking. "We'd need to employ massagers."

"Masseurs!" She'd shoved him. "Frig! Sam! You're the college student." Kathleen had grinned and taken a bite out of a chunky tomato. "Well then, let's go with all show cattle. You don't kill show cattle. You just breed them. They're okay. Or alpacas! Think of the wool market. Or we could breed emus. Everyone's getting into emus."

"They're bred for meat too," Sam had blurted out, his chin out, his eyes snapping with superiority.

"The eggs!" Kathleen had retorted. "I could decorate the eggs, and sell them at craft shows. We'd have the market cornered. Yup. Soybeans are a good start."

It had all seemed so simple back then, before Sam had to go away, before her parents wanted to sell her home.

"We'll take the sandwiches upstairs." Casey glanced once more at the stairway.

"Okay." Sadie reached over and touched a tiny pipe cleaner bumblebee, one of three wrapped around a plastic-covered tapered candle that precisely matched the tablecloth. A line of thin ribbon had been added, and it ran in candy cane fashion around each candle. Kathleen watched Sadie stare at it for a moment and then look up at the curtains.

Kathleen wasn't sure when Mrs. Brennan acquired her curtain fetish, but she'd never seen anything like it. No one had. Sure, Casey and Sam's mother had a rough childhood, and it was terrible, she'd told them, to grow up with plastic curtains, but Mrs. Brennan had taken overcompensating to the extreme. Curtains bedecked everything, curtains in every room: rose-colored sheer ruffles over the window, over the sink, over the fridge, over the doorway to the rest of the house, even over the doorway to the mudroom. Behind the rose-colored ruffles, Mrs. Brennan had hung white-ruffled curtains to separate the different colors from room to room. The hallway to the rest of the house was blue, so she'd hung blue ruffles on the hallway side that, of course, matched the color of the hallway precisely. She had overrun their entire house with layers of ruffled curtains, Kathleen thought, to hide the truth—that a joyless home has no real color.

"Bizarre, isn't it?" Casey said as Sadie looked up at the curtains.

"No. No." Sadie smiled politely. "It's very … ah … whimsical."

He smiled grimly. "Whimsical?" Casey stared around him. "In a freakish way, I suppose."

Sadie nodded then ran her index finger in the gouge that Mrs. Brennan had scraped into the tabletop over the years.

"Ouch." She pulled her finger up, studied it, and then stuck it in her mouth.

Casey reached over for her and then pulled his hand back.

"Did you get a splinter?" Kathleen asked.

"No." Sadie said, pulling her finger out and studying it. "No, no splinter. Stopped in time, I guess." She went back to studying the gouge. "So what's Sam studying?"

"Agriculture and business," Casey said. "Concordia."

"Ah. My alma mater. You didn't go?" Sadie asked Casey.

He twisted down a bit in the chair a little. "I'm better with the machinery."

"Bull," Kathleen said, giving him a hard stare as she slathered peanut butter on the bread. "You have the business mind, Casey, not Sam. Saddle or tractor seat, Sam's never lost in the cornfields." She turned to Sadie. "They had it all planned. Casey would go—"

"That's enough," Casey said, staring down at his chapped hands. "What's Sam say? Dreams ain't no more than ripples in the quarry."

He shrugged. "The plan might have changed a bit, but it is working." He nodded at Kathleen. "She should have gone to the College of Art in Boston. Her parents would pay for a business degree but not art."

Kathleen closed her eyes for a moment, wanting now to change the subject, trying not to think of the sign propped up in her front yard. "You chose a rough path, Sadie. There aren't that many women big-animal vets around yet."

Sadie's mouth formed a warm smile. "I like the country. Love the animals—the bigger, the better. It's the old guard; that's what's rough." She uncrossed her ankles and crossed her legs, leaning back and letting go. "Tonight, I was out at a hog farm out past Parkland. The place was a mess. The sows were riddled with infection. Do you know what the farmer said to me? 'That was a good bit of hog vettin', fer a girl.' That's what he said. I couldn't believe it. It's 1988, for the love of God."

Kathleen didn't mean to choke. She reached for a mug and turned on the water.

"That's not the worst of it." Sadie slumped lower. "He said how great it was to have 'sumpthin' better than a sow's butt to stare at.'"

Casey groaned. "He's a creep."

Sadie didn't answer for a second. "I was third in my graduating class. I should have been first. I was smarter than the two guys in front of me." She sighed. "Now I'm better than a sow's butt. Maybe it will change when I'm past interning."

"Interning?" Kathleen asked, holding the peanut butter in her hand.

"Uh-huh. I have to intern for a year before I get paid the wages of a real vet."

Casey leaned forward. "You don't get full wages? For what you did tonight?"

"Nope."

Kathleen noticed Sadie's voice become suddenly strong. "But if I can get some copies, those photos you took are going straight up on the clinic wall with my name written all over them." She grinned.

Kathleen plated up the sandwiches, and Casey grabbed the beers.

"Come on, ladies," Casey said. "Let's get you upstairs to Sam's room, safe and sound, before my mother wakes up."

* * *

Sadie followed Kathleen and Casey up the creaking stairs.

The hallway surprised her. Old and faded wallpaper ran down the length of it, but the wainscoting and tin ceiling showed the true beauty of the home. Though it was lit by two cheap ceiling lamps, Sadie knew it would be beautiful if the paper was replaced and the lighting came from flickering gas or candlelight. The floor seemed to be the original wood, and it creaked and groaned underfoot. The creaking, however, was hidden by the noise coming from down the hallway.

Severe snoring, like elephant cries, emanated from the end bedroom.

It stopped.

Kathleen and Casey stopped.

Within thirty seconds, the snoring began once more. Casey continued on, and Kathleen and she followed behind until he opened the door into what Sadie assumed was Sam's room. As soon as they were in, Casey disappeared into the room just across from them, his room. He reappeared with oversize flannelette shirts, handing them to Kathleen and Sadie. Sadie knew that the one, gray with turquoise highlights matching precisely the color of her eyes, was probably for her. The other shirt, emerald with yellow and gold, edged with black, had to be for Kathleen.

"Quick. Get undressed," Kathleen said. She began disrobing, seemingly unaware of embarrassment.

Sadie thought about turning away and then thought, *What the hell*, and commenced changing too. As she did, she stared at the posters that covered every inch of wall space in Sam's room—*The Sword of Stone Mountain* with its hero, Becket. She knew them well as she'd read the series as a teenager.

"Has he been collecting long?" Sadie said, hiding her surprise behind her hand. Sadie pointed to one that stood out from the others, a framed watercolor of a medieval man under a tree with book in hand, daydreaming.

"Sam likes to think he's Becket. Do you know the series?" Kathleen finished buttoning her shirt as Sadie nodded. "He's read all the books. I think he's grown out of it now. He hardly ever talks about them." Kathleen grinned. "It used to be awful. He'd want to read passages from one or another of the series, and Casey and I would take off running. He talks about Limousin bloodlines now."

"I like this one best," Sadie said. "It's beautiful. So very sad, you know, despite the colors."

Kathleen's eyes suddenly glistened as she straightened up. "That's exactly what I wanted the picture to do. It isn't a real poster, just painted poster board with a spray glaze to make it fit in with his others." Sadie watched Kathleen unconsciously place her hands over her heart. "Not too many people see that."

Sadie leaned closer and stared up at the corner of the poster. "I can't believe you did this!"

Kathleen nodded. "Gave it to him for Christmas, two years back. He wouldn't take it to school with him for fear of hurting it."

"It's beautiful!" Sadie said. She reached out and touched her. "You have real talent."

Kathleen stared at the poster, sadly, as it hung above them all dreamy and blue. "It doesn't pay the bills. My folks think it's time for me to check into reality, cut out the art, and study something that's a 'career.'" She gestured quotation marks in the air.

Sadie sat staring at the poster.

"Is there something special between you and Sam?" Sadie felt herself turn a little red. She wasn't used to being so brash, but these people made her feel so welcome. "I don't mean to pry but—well—you get this kind of look, you know, when you talk about him."

Kathleen turned away. How had Sadie known it so fast? Did other people see it—her mother, the girls at the Hole?

"We're all friends. That's all."

Sure, Sadie thought. "Casey thinks of you like a sister. I can tell."

"You have that one right. Casey has always been my friend, just like all my brothers, but so has Sam … kind of. There's nothing between Sam and me. Preposterous."

Sadie smiled. "Right."

Sadie nodded then leaned her ear against the door and listened to the bearlike growls coming from down the hall.

"Is that Casey's mother? Does she always snore like that?" Sadie said, her eyebrows arched in dismay.

"The Beast roars—always." Kathleen shrugged.

"The Beast?" Sadie turned back to Kathleen.

Kathleen giggled. "You'll find out tomorrow morning."

"That kind of snoring's not healthy." Sadie leaned closer to the door once more.

"She's always snored."

Sadie's did up her flannel top and dropped her jeans around her feet.

"So. What do you think? How 'bout those curtains?" Kathleen asked.

Sadie's chewed on her lip and then nodded a little. "Are they like this all over the house?"

"Yup." Kathleen reached out and touched the periwinkle-blue sheers above Sam's door. "Sam hates them. They do nothing to block the draft. The cold blows right through the windows and the doors." She raised her right shoulder in what Sadie knew was exasperation. "What can Casey and Sam do?" Kathleen's smile disappeared. "Sam would love a night like this."

Sadie grimaced. "I can't believe I'm doing it."

"Don't worry." Kathleen took her arm. "Casey's a gentleman. He'll only stay until we get tired, he gets tired, or the lights go out. He's got a perfectly good bed in his room. Only an idiot would sleep on the floor."

"You three did this all the time?"

"We skinny-dipped at the quarry too, but that was ages ago."

Sadie watched Kathleen struggle not to cry.

"I can't remember the last time we went skinny-dipping." She sighed. "It's all gone now. Time to grow up, make decisions." Grabbing the plate of sandwiches she'd made, Kathleen pulled the covers down on Sam's bed and climbed in. "I'll take the side by the wall."

Casey's knock on the door was softer than the blankets. Quickly Sadie hopped into the bed and under the covers next to Kathleen. Kathleen rolled her eyes, giggling as an arm waving a spotless, white handkerchief appeared through the door—a surrender flag, flapping around, dangling from his fingers.

"Parley?" He stuck his head through.

Sadie laughed out loud at the sight of him, bare feet, dry jeans, and a blue flannel pajama top, a pillow and a blanket, the look topped off with a raggedy, old stuffed teddy bear. He closed the door gently and dragged his cargo over to the side of the bed.

"Look what I had hidden in my room." He held up a bag of cookies.

Kathleen leaned over and whispered into Sadie's ear. "He probably has half the bakery section at the IGA hidden in his room."

"Amazing," Casey said as softly as he could, his shy grin melting Sadie's heart. "I should take a picture. Sam is never going to believe this." Casey grabbed two beers from the six-pack on the table and handed them to the women.

Sadie helped herself to a sandwich and passed the plate to Kathleen. "Love the bear," she said to Casey.

"Mr. Rumples." He waved the toy proudly at her, the floppy brown bear clad in denim overalls, a red-checkered scarf around its neck. "Got him from my grandmother when I was seven." Casey slid down, nestling his back into the pillow against the wall as he grabbed a ham and cheese, biting into it as if he hadn't eaten all day.

"He fell down the cellar stairs," Kathleen said with dramatic emphasis.

Sadie stopped chewing. "Oh no!"

He looked down at his beer. "I bounced."

"Right. You didn't bounce for a while." Kathleen sat up in the bed. "He ended up in the hospital for a week. Hurt his back really bad. Whenever he falls or when the weather's bad like this, it plays up. Anyway, we never had these sleepovers at my place. Too many brothers and not enough spooks at my house. This place has ghosts inside and out, hidden passages and"—Kathleen leaned closer to Sadie—"secrets."

Sadie's mouth turned up at the corners. "Spooks? Right!"

Kathleen laughed. "Spooks. Right. They're the ones that haunt Mrs. Brennan. Mean and scary. I think she's a schizoid, probably just imagining them. They only bother her in her bedroom. She swears we're playing horrible games on her, but we aren't. She says it's a bad house. It's not a bad house. It just has a lot of secrets."

"I'll give you that. You can't beat an old farmhouse for secrets. But not spooks," Sadie said, enjoying the sandwich more than she thought she would. Then she remembered she hadn't had dinner.

"No! Really!" Kathleen said, her eyes widening at Sadie's obvious disregard of the truth. Kathleen turned to Casey. "Tell her."

He shrugged and looked around the room as he popped the crusts of his sandwich in his mouth. "Did you notice that the rooms seem small for the size of the house?"

"Ah … no." Sadie relaxed back into her pillow, staring around her, trying to take it in.

"They've been made smaller over the years. You know, a pantry where the back staircase used to be, walls knocked down and replaced with plasterboard. The original lathe and plaster walls are still there, behind. You can get to almost any room through the corridors behind the walls," Casey said with a grin. "If you like the dark and spiders, the passageways can be fun."

"Really?" Sadie sat up in the bed.

Kathleen pushed the blankets away and crawled over the bed, headed to Sam's closet. She yanked open the door and began rummaging, pushing clothes and shoes out of the way. "Back here." She reached up for the string to turn on the light above her. "We used to go through here all the time. We needed the passageways to smuggle food to Casey when …" She then sharply looked back over to Casey and then quickly at Sadie as if she were five years old and caught telling a lie to her teacher.

Sadie stared at Casey who was looking at his hands.

"Smuggle food to you, when?" Sadie asked. "Holding food from a child is against the law."

A pause hung in the air like a black cloud about to release its deluge.

"You have to prove it," Kathleen blurted out. "No one around here would believe us." She seemed to slow down. "And they would have taken Sam and Casey away."

No. Sadie stared at Casey's thin frame. "Do you want to run that past me again?" Sadie said.

"It's not what it seems. I got plenty to eat," Casey said, staring numbly at her with eyes like those of rescued dogs that came through the vet clinics.

She could tell by the wounded look in his eyes that the conversation was over. They weren't going to say another word.

When she looked back, all she could see was Kathleen's panty-covered bottom as she rummaged through the closet. Looking over at Casey again, he was focused on his sandwich, a disinterested brotherly look on his face, undisturbed by Kathleen's bare legs and panty-covered bottom staring back at them.

Sadie looked down at her hands, as embarrassment burned into her face.

"Ah," Kathleen said, suddenly standing upright and putting her hands over her buttocks. "It's okay, Sadie. Casey isn't seeing anything he hasn't seen before." Kathleen let go of her butt and grabbed the hangers. She pushed them as far back as they'd go. They scraped and creaked in outrage.

"There's a lever"—she reached up and rattled it—"and you give it a pull and then push." She popped back out, her hair now everywhere around her head. "I swear, Sadie, you can go anywhere in this old place if you have a good flashlight. We've had hours of fun in these old passageways."

Sadie felt Casey's eyes on her for a moment.

"Nothing malicious. Just, you know … pranks," Casey said.

Stepping away from the closet, Kathleen closed the door. "You can smell Thomas's tobacco in there. Sometimes you can see Thomas."

Casey snorted. "You see Thomas anytime someone lights a pipe."

Kathleen grunted and threw herself onto the bed once more, snuggling under the covers.

Sadie stared at her. "And Thomas is?"

"Casey and Sam's grandfather." Kathleen said. "He's not what you should be afraid of though, Sadie."

"He died in a plane crash. Crop-dusting. Billy says he loved to fly."

Sadie sat up straighter. "What happened?"

"From what Billy says, Thomas and another flyer were up, fooling around, and his friend's plane came down right on top of Thomas's plane," Casey said.

"They collided in the air?"

"Seems like it. Billy says Thomas probably never knew what hit him." Casey said, staring romantically into space. "What a way to go!" Casey bit into a cookie.

"It's horrible." Kathleen snorted. "There's nothing glorious about death."

Casey nodded as if thinking about it. "Yeah, but if you're gonna go, that's the way."

"How old were Billy and your father?" Sadie said.

"Preschoolers." Casey paused, took a deep breath, and Kathleen knew how hard it was for him to say what he was about to say. "When we were young, Thomas ... he would come and talk to Sam." His eyes moved over to Kathleen as if expecting ridicule. "He said he could almost feel him, you know? Maybe a cool breeze in the summer or a warm one in winter. Sometimes his hand on Sam's shoulder. Sometimes a curtain would move, or Gran would speak to Thomas, and Sam swore he could almost hear his answer. Sometimes he'd answer Thomas—at least he said it was Thomas—and Gran would look at him as if he were part of the conversation." He looked down at his hands. "I wanted to be part of the conversation." He smiled sheepishly. "Thomas talks to Sam in dreams. At least he used to. Sam hasn't spoken to him for some time." He turned to Sadie. "Sounds nuts, eh?"

"No. What did they talk about?" Sadie asked, her sandwich seemingly forgotten.

"Farming mostly," Kathleen nodded enthusiastically. "Gran, a lot."

"What does he look like when he appears," Sadie said. "Is he fully there or just sort of wispy."

Kathleen put her sandwich down and leaned into the conversation as if telling a very special secret. "Kind of like Casey. Yeah. Casey in a kind of fog."

Kathleen shook her head, an ache in her throat. "Thomas is sort of stuck here. I think he's hanging around for Gran."

"I'm the only one who hasn't seen him," Casey said, reaching for another oatmeal cookie. "For some reason, I've never had that feeling they get."

"Sam doesn't see him anymore," Kathleen said. "It all stopped when he went to university. His own fault. Nothing's changed. Thomas is still everywhere in the house. He doesn't have to jump out and yell boo, you know," she said, popping the last of the sandwich in her mouth. "You two are the ones who've stopped believing. You've even stopped talking to Gran about it." She looked over at Sadie. "There's nothing to be afraid of when it comes to Thomas, Sadie."

Sadie grinned and nodded, but the hair on her arms and the back of her neck was standing up. "Oh. Okay. I won't be afraid of the ghost or the spooks."

"No. I'm serious," Kathleen said. "Thomas isn't dangerous. The Beast is dangerous."

Sadie's heart began to beat too hard. What was it with this *beast*? She couldn't be that bad.

"If she wiggles the doorknob, you'll hear her. Don't worry. I'll get you into the closet," Kathleen said, with a wicked smile.

Sadie leaned back a little. The barn was now sounding like a better sleepover place. Beasts and ghosts. No one had said anything like this in the barn. And she'd thought this was just another county home. She was surrounded by crazy.

Casey reached over and touched her arm. His hand felt warm and comforting. "She won't touch you. I promise."

"Right," Sadie said.

"Don't worry," Kathleen said. "I can usually handle her. It's best to be quiet, and let me do the talking. She usually disappears when I start chatting to her. She can't stand it. Says I make her head hurt." Kathleen giggled. "It's worked for years, and besides, she generally stays in her room until light, which won't be early tomorrow."

"What exactly does she do? Is she violent?" Sadie thought about Billy and the safety of the barn. Maybe they could make it back.

"No, no," Kathleen said with a slight hesitation. "Like I said. She's just big and loud. Kind of like a gorilla. She beats her breast a lot and yells but is only really dangerous if cornered. We can handle her, can't we, Casey?"

He nodded as he rose, but Sadie recognized a deep fear in his eyes.

"I'm locking your door from the inside," he said as he twisted the lock. Wishing them a good sleep, Casey closed the door behind him.

Suddenly all Sadie wanted was to take on this Beast. She couldn't wait until morning to see what she was up against.

CHAPTER 8

Rachel woke to a black room. Why wasn't her bedside light on? She heard the sleet on her window and remembered the storm. Throughout the night, she had tossed and turned under her white quilt like a dory floundering in a frothy sea. The blankets pulled at her, trapping her feet, bunching up under her back, and no matter how she tugged at them, they would not flatten out. But she'd be dammed if she got out of the bed in the dark to smooth them away.

Rachel's head pounded. This was a bad one, as headaches went. It felt as someone had taken a vice, wrapped it around her head, and was squeezing, squeezing. She knew it would not go away anytime soon.

She was almost sure she had been asleep, but with the power now off, she didn't know how long or what time it was. She wanted to forget the sound of the sleet on the window, but every time she felt herself just about to drift off into oblivion, a leg would jerk or a knee twitch, and she'd feel what seemed like a million ants crawling beneath her skin. Why the doctor in town refused to believe that her legs came alive and attacked her every night maddened Rachel even more. He'd looked at her as if she was crazy, but then she never expected much from a Dutchman. He was the crazy one. Not her. Oh no!

Rachel didn't like many men, her father's fault, she supposed as she tried her best to slowly scan the shadowed room. Her father, the town drunk, the town crazy, ran a barbershop for money to buy his booze. She spent most of her school days hiding from the other children who taunted her with insults and jibes about how they'd seen her father blubbering outside town hall over the cost of fishing licenses or dancing up on a hay wagon, butt naked after the summer solstice celebrations.

Rachel learned early on how to hide the marks of her father's anger, the welts of the strap, the bruises on her body. She learned how to steer her father away from her mother, when Daddy was in one of his moods. She became very good at manipulating men. Rachel figured that beneath the belt, they were all the same. For a short while, she had thought Billy was different, but before long, she realized that he was no better than his brother Lester was, and Casey was worse than either of them. Rachel would be goddamned if she allowed Sam to become like them. Oh no. Not her Sam.

Rachel needed to sleep, to dream of how it could have been, how it might be. Oh yes. She'd had dreams, long since engulfed by the snowbanks of Killkenny County, and her demons whipped at her harder than the winds outside the house. It wasn't playing out as she had imagined.

Casey, for instance. Casey was defying her, and it would a cold day in hell when Casey told her what to do. Casey didn't deserve the farm. Sam did. She did. And now Casey was spending money faster than they were bringing it in. He had to be. The horses, the cattle, where was it all coming from?

Rachel Brennan tightened her fists as another wave of sleet whipped at her window.

And then, her worst fear, she smelled a whiff of pipe tobacco in the clammy air.

The sound started out so low that at first Rachel wasn't sure she heard it at all. It disappeared. No. There it was again, something crawling, creeping behind the walls. Faintly, it almost seemed normal, just one more noise in the night, and the patter of ice on the frozen glass, the moan of the wind coming through the cracks of her window, the creak of the old pipes as they rattled around her. There. She heard it again. Her heart tightened. Her stomach clenched. It was under the bed.

Squirrels. There had to be squirrels in the attic again. That was it.

No. She knew squirrels. That wasn't the sound.

Bats! Not bats! She couldn't bear bats!

It grew louder. She rammed both hands over her ears and held them there, but she couldn't block it out no matter how hard she tried. No. She wouldn't look!

Across the room, her empty rocking chair creaked. Stop it, she thought. It's just the whistling wind that always came through her window.

She tried to breathe evenly. Creak, sigh, creak, sigh, it went.

The chair was definitely rocking by itself again, so slowly, as if someone was in it. So often, she'd awakened to the creaking of her rocker. Only when she was off her rocker. Off her rocker. Hah! She shivered and the vice tightened around her head.

It wasn't a scrabbly squirrel noise any longer. No. It had become a moan. Disembodied, it seemed to come from nowhere; yet it was coming from all around her. Her heart pounded in her chest, so fast she could hardly breathe. She yanked open the table drawer and grabbed her flashlight.

Beaming it around the room, she saw nothing but shadows.

"No!" She pulled the covers over her head, the flashlight illuminating from beneath the blankets. "No! Not tonight! Go away!" The wind screamed. Her room was blacker than the cast-iron pan she kept so carefully hidden under her bed table. "Go away!"

The disembodied voice undulated, one moment from far away, the next from farther on, drifting in waves, closer, more distant, and then even closer.

She shrank beneath the covers. "I said go away! Don't come any closer!"

She knew it wanted her out. They all did, but she wasn't going anywhere. She deserved this land as much as any of the Kluggs did, and she was going to whip it right out of their superior Klugg fingers. She deserved the quarry and what lay beneath the surface. After all the years she'd spent cooking and cleaning for them, after lowering herself to marry Lester when she wanted Billy, she wasn't going anywhere. After all those years she put up with that old woman, only to be told the property was being jointly willed in trust, to Casey and Sam. She never let on just how much it hurt her when she discovered that she was nowhere in the will. All that potential money from the quarry and it was all going to Sam and that good for nothing brother of his. It should all be going to Sam.

She'd put up with Casey for so long. She'd promised Lester she wouldn't kill Casey as long as Lester left. As long as Lester stayed away, she could convince Billy to move into the house and love her. She hadn't cared if he didn't love her. She could make him. She'd never dreamed Billy would stay as far away as possible, hiding in that disgusting barn. All Billy did was protect Casey and turn Sam against her.

It wasn't really Billy's fault though. Casey was the source of all her problems. Getting pregnant by Lester got her into the Brennan family, but it was Billy's child she wanted. Casey had been a burden since the day he was born. And now he was defying her, and Sam was buying into Casey's dream of better cattle. Useless cattle.

The disembodied noise grew louder. It was a hiss of steam, a whiff of breeze, probably from the window, but the window was sealed, and the storm should have been outside and not inside to haunt her.

"Stay away from me!" She shivered at the sudden chill in the room.

Rachel sobbed as she clenched the flashlight to her, blocking her ears at the same time, making her head ache more as she screwed her hands into her temples. She couldn't fight it anymore. She peered up from her covers, hoping to see even a shadow in the void, at the same time, not wanting to see anything. She waved the flashlight around the room. Maybe it was gone. Then she caught the scent of pipe tobacco. Her stomach lurched, and she pulled the pillow over her head once more.

"No. Oh no, no, no." She waited, shivering. The voice was louder than before, angry, desperate, the words indistinguishable. She didn't need words. The voice wanted her gone. She lay there with the diffused beam from the flashlight to keep her safe. It sounded like Lester. It was Lester, she knew. It had to be him. He had to be dead, because he was haunting her, and she wanted him to stop.

CHAPTER 9

A sharp ring tore into his head at the temple. He opened his eyes and stared at the ceiling. The phone rang again. Lester didn't move, hoping it would stop. He wanted to sleep, but it all came back to him, the night before. There'd been no ice storm in Rio de Janeiro. The ice storm was happening so far away.

His personal assistant, Dirk Rutger, knew enough not to call unless it was an emergency, so without opening his eyes, he pulled the phone to his ear.

"Morning, Dirk. What's up?"

"Sorry to wake you, Les, but Miss King is calling again."

Lester's arm dropped, carrying the phone with it. Bringing the phone back to his ear, he put his other arm behind his head. "I'm assuming this is urgent?" He glanced over at the clock beside his bed. "Kind of early for her, isn't it? Where is she?" He listened for the familiar voice.

"That's why I woke you. The call's coming from Ithica," Dirk said.

Lester yawned and shook the sleep off. "New York?" He rubbed the stubble on his chin. "She should be in Paris. Put her on."

Dirk apologized once more, and then the phone lines changed.

Lester hadn't fired her, and he'd never promised her anything. He hadn't threatened to send her naked out the door. He'd given her good references as he would any student trainee. Melissa was a smart one, working summers and getting paid well for it. So she was an intern. That hadn't stopped him from bedding Melissa Anne King when she made a pass at him.

She'd told him right from the start that she wasn't looking for a relationship, just a bit of company. She'd seemed quite happy to have summer affairs and leave for school in France each September—until this last year when she'd started showing up on long weekends and her birthday and Christmas. Les had told her again, just four weeks before that he was through, that it was finished, and he had sent her packing back to her parents in France. And now she wasn't in France, but New York.

It was true she had this vulnerable beauty, but she didn't make sense. That ridiculous clown getup she used to get attention, the singing instead of talking. There was something terribly wrong with her. She had all the drive and vision an environmentalist needs to push a cause; she could be a sterling asset to any mining operation. Good public relations at a time when mining was under scrutiny was paramount for LWB Mining, and Missy had the legal mind to get where she was going, to fight for those causes of hers. Yet she seemed so lost. At least she did in the beginning. Now she was after something.

"Les?" Her voice had a bereft cadence.

"Melissa. Those airline tickets were for Paris. Weren't you supposed to be studying in Paris this year?"

"I had thought of that but changed my mind. I'm doing research. That's why I called."

"In New York?"

He thought he could smell the aroma of coffee coming from the kitchen. He took in a deep breath.

"You know those maps you had in your office, the ones I wasn't supposed to see." She tittered as if it was a cute little secret.

Lester felt dread suddenly envelope him. He knew full well which maps she'd seen. She shouldn't have been in his office at all. She'd been snooping. He'd found the framed photo that Billy had sent him of the boys and Kathleen, all of them so cocky and innocent as they sat in their saddles on the horses he'd bought for them. The photo had been moved from where he'd kept it, knocked over by the maps she'd pulled out.

"I'm doing a paper on mining and the effects past and present on the ecosystems of Maine's north counties, and I was wondering if you had any geological papers I could use for references."

"You told me you were doing your work on the Brazilian rain forest. That's why I hired you."

She laughed lightly. "Oh, I don't think that's the only reason you hired me, Lester. With the ties I have here, I thought I'd have a more personal take on the paper, a better way to a better thesis. Don't you think? I'm more likely to get a job offer in Augusta or Boston even. 'For I've got high hopes,'" she sang. Melissa paused as if waiting for him to say something. "I have to broaden my horizons. You said so yourself, Les."

He pinched his nose between his eyes. How he hated it when she sang. What in the hell had he ever seen in her! "Give me your address, and I'll send you something."

"No. Just send them to my folks in France. You have their address."

He stopped to think about that. "Why should I send them to France, Melissa? You're in New York."

"I'll be moving about in the next few weeks—clown stuff—but Mother can send them to me once I get a permanent address. 'I get by with a little help from my friends,'" she sang.

There was a long pause on the other end. Lester stared up at the ceiling.

"Really. Send them to France. There's no rush," she said.

Something stank.

"About your job this summer, Melissa. I really tried." He sat up in the bed, lying to her. "I can't hire you." He waited for her reaction. She said nothing. *Okay.* "The Brazilian government has really been cracking down about hiring locals." He waited once more for the crying to start. Nothing. She had cried every time she'd left for school and had to "leave him behind."

"I'm sorry, Melissa."

"Things change, Les. I wasn't planning on coming back. I already have other plans for the summer."

Lester let out a long, slow breath. That would be the best thing in the world for both of them. Still, he thought, a slow ball of worry growing in his gut, something wasn't right.

CHAPTER 10

"Open up! Casey! What in the hell are you doing in there? Casey!"

Casey's eyes fluttered opened to darkness as he heard his mother's voice booming from the other side of his bedroom door and the banging of her heavy fist. She was yelling about Sam's door being locked.

The floor, when he jumped up, felt like ice beneath his bare skin, and the hairs on his flesh rose angrily at the cold. Turning the knob, he yanked open his door and then tried his best to get out of the way of the beam from his mother's flashlight as it shone into his eyes, a yellow-green glare blinding him.

"Shh!" he said and rubbed at his closed eyes, trying to get rid of the florescent circle now cutting through to the back of his brain. "What?"

"The power's out," Rachel said in a voice stronger than the wind the night before.

All this over the damned power being off? "Uh ... yeah."

"Don't you use that tone with me. Sam's door's shut. Who's in there?" His mother's finger found its mark as she poked him hard in the shoulder.

Casey's hand moved from his eyes to the pain in his shoulder. Anger coiled around his stomach like a python. "The vet got stuck here overnight." His mother's flashlight turned toward Sam's door. "Let them get some sleep. For chrissake!"

"That's Sam's room!" She paused and swiveled back toward him, her hand poised, about to pound again. "The vet's in there?"

"Mum, please, it was a rough night, and Kathleen's in there too. Let them sleep."

"Kathleen? With the vet?"

Before he had a chance to explain, Sam's bedroom door banged open. Rachel Brennan gasped and her mouth dropped open as she turned her light toward the figure in the doorway. Casey's eyes grew wide as Sadie's striking figure exploded into the spotlight.

The blinding beam from Rachel Brennan's flashlight didn't appear to faze Sadie. She was looking beyond it, directly at Casey, smiling, wearing only the flannel shirt that he had loaned her just hours before. Casey, his mouth forming a small grin, was no longer concerned about his mother. He was far too busy appreciating his new vet's long legs as the light from his mother's torch washed up over her ankles, past her knees and the curve of her hips, and back up past her breasts to her smile.

"I'm Dr. Parker, Mrs. Brennan," Sadie said.

Casey grinned. Dr. Sadie Parker did not say, "Call me Sadie."

His mother, her shoulders tightening, twirled the light back, and he drew away from it.

"Casey, get dressed and come downstairs." Rachel swung the light back at Sadie, giving her one more terse perusal, and then she barreled down the hallway, her dark form a fading storm as her shadow disappeared, rolling thunder banging and booming over the valley and heat lightning bouncing off the heavens. Casey felt the muscles in his face relax while they watched the Beast retreat. He looked back through the darkness to where Sadie's eyes would be.

"I'm sorry," Casey said.

"What for?" Sadie laughed, and he melted as he realized she hadn't been the least upset.

"Mornin', Casey." The salutation was followed by a little giggle.

"Mornin', Kathleen."

"The Beast's in a good mood, eh?" Kathleen said laughing. "I think she likes you, Sadie."

Casey shivered, suddenly aware that he was standing there in his briefs, and if he could see their outlines in the dark, they could see his.

"You'd better get dressed, Casey," Kathleen said. "I can hear your teeth chattering over here."

Casey muttered his agreement and stepped back into the darkness of his room.

Usually he grabbed the first flannel shirt or sweater he saw, but not that day. That day, he wanted to look good. That day, he took his flashlight and searching through his clothing with the dim beam, found clean jeans, a shirt that appeared navy in the light and a pale blue sweater that Gran knitted for him one day when she said she'd found wool the same color as his eyes. He would have tried for matching socks, but he was running out of time, hearing the ladies stumble down to the bathroom and then back. The chatter of the girls made him wonder if perhaps it wasn't real. Something this good couldn't be real.

He flung open his door, holding his flashlight pointed down. The door to Sam's room was already open, and the ladies were ready to go, so he led the way.

"How beautiful this hallway must be in candlelight," Sadie said as they headed downstairs. "That's why these old places were built—to glow."

Sadie liked his house. He'd never really thought of it as his home. The barn was more *home* to him than the house, but when Sadie saw the place, she saw it with appreciation, and he realized that must be how Gran saw the house. Casey rubbed his jaw and realized that for the first time ever, he wasn't rubbing it because of a stress-induced aching jaw. He was rubbing it because he needed to shave.

* * *

"Mornin', Gran." Kathleen leaned down to kiss Gran's cheek. "You're cold." She squeezed Gran's hand a little while she searched around the kitchen chairs for a blanket.

"Katie, darling," Gran said, her smile as warm as a summer day.

"There you go," Kathleen said pulling a blanket from the back of another chair and placing it around Gran's shoulders. The light from the lanterns made Gran's face as beautiful as an antique painting.

Gran placed her hand on Kathleen's hand. "Thomas told me you were here. That was a wild night, wasn't it?"

"It sure was, Gran. We'll warm you up. How about some hot tea and my French toast."

"There's none like it in the county," Gran said with a soft smile.

"Where's the Bea—," Kathleen stopped, catching herself in time. Gran didn't approve of them calling Mrs. Brennan the Beast. "Mrs. Brennan."

Gran squeezed her hand. "She's having one of her spells, dear. She won't be joining us for breakfast."

Gran glanced over at Casey, who was standing almost in front of Sadie. Kathleen walked past him and gave him a poke. He jerked and then recovered.

"Gran?" Casey said with a bashful smile. "This is Sadie Parker, our new vet."

Kathleen studied Gran as Gran placed her knitting on her lap and rocked gently.

"Oh, Thomas," Gran said, casting a glance over her shoulder with a pleased smile, "you didn't say a word to me." Gran held her hand out to Sadie, who graciously took it. "You've made an excellent choice, Casey."

Kathleen snorted out a laugh and then covered her mouth with her hand. Casey staring over at her with mortified eyes. She pulled on the fridge door. "You can't make French toast without eggs," she said and pretended to be busy.

"No—ah—Gran," Casey stammered. "Sadie came out for Libby. She's the new vet—ah—it's not …"

Kathleen saw that Sadie was smiling kindly, seemingly enjoying it as much as Kathleen was, not in a mean way at all. Sadie's face was filled with a humble acceptance, as if she'd been there with them forever. Kathleen sighed, keeping her smile bright but sinking inside. Casey had found someone. Sadie would be there now, to look after him. Kathleen looked down at the bread, picked up a slice, and cut a small circle in the middle of it. If only Sam … No. She had other things to worry about.

Casey shot past them and headed for the woodstove.

Opening the firebox, he peered in at the coals. "We had twins last night, Gran."

"You didn't have twins," Gran corrected him, patting Sadie's hand. "Your heifer must have had the twins."

"That she did," Sadie said. "She was nursing both of them when we left the barn. She had a bull and a heifer, Mrs. Brennan."

Gran cocked her head. "You must call me, Gran, Sadie. My goodness, Casey. You and Sam have a herd," she said, without really looking at him. Instead, she took Sadie's hand. "Yes. You certainly have made an excellent choice, Casey. She's perfect and I can see from the look on Thomas's face that he approves too."

Kathleen wanted to give Casey a good kick as he stood planted, more frozen than the trees outside, seeming unable to breathe, let alone say something.

"Thomas approves," Sadie said, smiling hesitantly at him. She didn't say it in a sarcastic way, or confused or upset. Sadie surveyed the room.

"Just wait until you taste Kathleen's French toast," Casey said as he leaned over to the pots and pans and came up with a frypan. "She doesn't make it like regular French toast. She makes a hole in the bread and drops the egg in it and then adds maple syrup. I swear, Sadie. There's nothing better."

"Stop, Casey," Kathleen said, feeling her face burn. "It's just egg in a hole. My brothers kidded me when I made it. They always said it was the best I'd ever do."

Gran's eyes lit up as she let go of Sadie, and looking over at Casey, she studied him. "And you look so handsome today." Gran studied Kathleen. "You don't seem yourself, Kathleen."

Kathleen took a long deep breath and then dipped into the pantry. "I'm fine," she called back.

"Kathleen Abigail Egan. You're going to make me come in there ..."

"No!" Kathleen stepped out and went straight over to Gran. "I'll tell you. Just sit. Please, Gran. Don't get up. We don't need for you to fall again."

"Well then?" Gran settled back into the chair and waited.

"Mom and Dad put the house up for sale." She watched Casey's mouth drop.

He looked quickly away and grabbed a log. "Don't worry." He threw the dry wood into the embers. "We have time," he said. "It won't sell soon."

"Gee. Thanks."

"That's not what I meant, Kathleen, and you know it."

"It's not that simple now, is it, Casey? Maybe they're right. Maybe I should go to school. Face it! I don't see much of a future here."

"You're wrong, Katie." Gran put her hand on Kathleen's hand. "We'll work something out."

Kathleen glanced over at Sadie, who was watching the tableau unveil. "I know. Really." She took another gasp of air as if there weren't enough in the room. "It'll work out. Now! Breakfast!" Kathleen forced a laugh, rubbing her hands together with bravado.

"The wood's caught." Casey stepped back around Kathleen and over to the woodpile.

"This stove is amazing." Sadie pulled open the door to the antique oven, and she examined it in the dim light of the lanterns. "I noticed it last night, but with your hands and the storm …"

It was a big, cast-iron stovetop: heavy stovepipe, smaller oven compared to those of today, the circular burners with wedged notches in each to allow for the handle, enabling the cook to lift each burner and check the fire when needed. It almost looked like a baroque dresser, standing on its curved legs, its decorative swirls and knobs like icing. It had a firebox directly under the oven, where the wood was stored to keep it warm and dry for easy ignition, and a shelf above the stovetop to hold containers and utensils, all wrapped up in pretty, pastel enamel, mint green and cream.

"My mother said that these are the best way to go for cooking, that they cook the food much better by sealing in flavors and moisture. Hot though. The amount of heat these cast-iron stoves give off is wicked. It's great in the winter, but it's my guess you don't cook a whole lot of heavy meals in the summer." Sadie stopped and, blushing, looked over at Gran. "Sorry. Sometimes I get carried away. I've never seen a real Kitchen Queen Green and Cream wood cookstove before, except in the magazines." She bent down and examined the curved feet of the antique that kept the fire from the floor. "This has to be sixty years old."

"Closer to seventy, dear," Gran said. "That stove belonged to Thomas's mother. It's like me—another Brennan relic." Gran's head tilted a little. "Parker? Who is your father, Sadie?"

"Hank Parker. You must know him."

"I most certainly do know him. A very nice man." Gran's eyes darkened. "I'm sorry about your mother, dear. It's always hardest on those left behind."

Kathleen stared over at Sadie with concern. She'd said nothing about her mother having died, and she'd talked a lot about her mother the night before. Sadie caught her eyes and looked away.

"My mother died last year of ovarian cancer. She was sick for a long time." Sadie ran her hand over the table next to her and then stared back at the fire. Kathleen knew Sadie was doing her best not to crumble as Casey mumbled out an apology.

Sadie stiffened a bit. "Mom didn't want sadness around her then, and I know she wouldn't want it now," she said, smiling slightly.

Kathleen nudged him as she reached over his head and picked up the teapot from the stove mantel. *Change the subject for now*, she tried to tell him.

"Breakfast. You bet," Kathleen said. "Let's break a few eggs."

Chapter 11

As Casey knew it would, the farm was a picture of icy perfection. The wires hung like Christmas garland and sparkled on the trees like Christmas cards. Though the ice was still there, Casey knew that, by noon, it would be gone.

He caught Sadie's look of appreciation as they carefully made their way over to the stable, and he beamed as she studied the barn. The post-and-beam stable was far from grandiose, but though it was an aged barn, it had been kept in good shape and refurbished over the years. The beams were solid, and the posts, though chewed in places, were sturdy. The interior, usually bathed in sunlight from the five skylights cut into its roof, had a silver glow that highlighted the polished oak of the stall doors. Some folks stuck their horses just anywhere, but Casey knew they deserved a special home.

Sixteen stalls were lined along the central aisle. Casey knew the stall doors were the prettiest around. Double doors, the bottom doors were made with finished hardwood, glossy and bright, and the top doors had open white bars, not at all like prison bars, more like garden fencing. Every horse had the space to stick his or her nose out and sniff around at whoever might be visiting, and nine of the sixteen stalls had exactly that, a head poking out through the headspace. The racket raised was louder than the barn the night before.

The horses usually occupied the stalls closest to the paddock entrance to make use of the sun and fresh air, but that morning the bulls had the honor, and the horses seemed not at all happy about it. How could they be happy, staring across at the bulls?

The concrete floor slewed down to a drain at the far end, down past the tack room that was situated halfway, close to the middle on the left and across from a cleaning station. Behind the bulls, double Dutch doors at the far end could be opened fully, top and bottom, to allow the tractors in or only at the top, depending on the day or necessity.

The chickens were making the most noise, clucking and cackling, upset with the fact that they'd been tossed into the shavings stall.

Casey shot a quick glance over to Sadie to see if she was taking it all in. He knew she couldn't help it. The horses had started calling him as soon as they heard them outside. Their heads were bobbing, and they were whinnying, their eyes bulging out as if it was his fault the chickens and bulls were messing up their stable.

"Billy," Casey called out. "Sure does stink in here."

Billy was seated at the desk in the office, wrapping insulating tape around a piece of pipe. "Uh-yup," he said.

"Careful! Don't trip, Sadie. There's a chicken loose, Billy," Kathleen said, shooing a speckled hen that was hissing and clucking as it spread its wings and taxied haphazardly, a tiny spluttering float plane under their feet. "Shoo, Hilda. I could have guessed it would be Hilda Hen. She never stays put."

Sadie stopped and turned to Kathleen. "Don't tell me you named them all."

Kathleen seemed not at all fazed by the question. "We try to get all names that start with *H*, but sometimes"—she scooted over to Billy—"if they have outstanding personalities, you know the type, crazy or persnickety, then those ones require special names. The roosters?" She pointed to a large, mahogany Rhode Island Red surrounded by hens. "Well, that one is named Randy."

Sadie grinned as if that made complete sense.

"Breakfast," Casey said, trying his best not to laugh as he handed Billy a towel-covered dish.

"The bottom of the inside towel is hot, so that's a good sign. Sit!" Kathleen told Billy, pushing the paperwork aside and placing it on the desk. "Hilda is just an average chicken, but she cackles with a slight Swiss accent."

Sadie exploded into laughter.

"No, really," Kathleen continues as if she was used to the reaction. Sam had played a pivotal role in the naming of the animals. Casey liked the short commonsense names: Ronnie Rooster, Reggie. Kathleen called him Reginald, Sir Reginald in front of the hens. His favorite was a big speckled beauty, a mass producer he'd named Eggbert the Eggspert. Even Kathleen had liked that one, though Sam felt it was more a more a title than a name.

"Open it up and eat. It doesn't bite," Sadie said to Billy, not quite in the tack room, still laughing and studying the horses.

"Holy jumping Jesus!" Billy said as he took the foil off, seeing the scrambled eggs, bacon, sausages, baked beans, and toast.

Kathleen prodded him then leaned over to remove the ice picks as the others were removing their jackets. "Eat it before it gets cold."

"Just enjoying the smell, Katie," he said with a long smile, and then he did as he was told and dug in. "Cripes! This is great!"

Casey grinned. "I thought the Beast could cook until this morning." He noticed Sadie studying the stable. "It's a mess in here what with overnight guests," he said to her. The whinnies of horses were coming from every stall, protesting the rabble of chickens and the bellowing of the bulls.

"Let Billy get to it. You two show me around," Sadie said, reaching for Casey's hand. He didn't hesitate, despite Kathleen's giggle as she slipped off her parka.

While Billy ate, they stepped warily from one stall to another, gently talking to horse after horse, giving each a handful of grain. One or two of the horses kicked at the rails in frustration or anticipation, but eventually they all quieted down, nuzzling and bumping against him.

"Not bad. Seven quarter horses and two Arabs. You're breeding them?" Sadie leaned closer to a bay mare.

Casey nodded. "Some. The white Arabian there is Sam's." He nodded at Kathleen, standing in front of the ebony Arabian mare. "She belongs to Kate. We're hoping for a foal from them."

Kathleen smiled up from under the horse's muzzle. "This is Kahlall. It's Arabic for 'dark eyes.' She doesn't really belong to me, but she's been kind of my favorite since they brought her here." A curtain of sadness dropped over her face. "I'll never leave you, sweetie." She leaned her cheek down on Kahlall's head.

"I can picture you on an Arabian," Sadie said, walking over to the mare. "You have the fire for it."

"She's a pussycat." Kathleen giggled, sniffling and hiding her face in Kahlall's mane. "Aren't you, sweetie? You're a pussycat."

Sadie looked quickly away. "They're magnificent. How are their temperaments?" Sadie asked as her eyes moved across their backs and their legs for any sign of imperfection.

"Depends who's on them," Casey said, obviously staring at Sadie for her approval. "Charger's a bit high-strung. No one rides him but Sam." He ran his hand down the stallion's glistening winter-white neck, and then he nudged Kahlall under her ebony nose. "She's easier." He had his other arm out now, enticing her with a bit of sugar from his pocket. He grinned shyly. "Have a look at the quarter horses."

"I have been," Sadie said, studying them, each one a beauty. "How could you afford these?" She seemed to choke as soon as she said it. "Oh God! I'm sorry! I didn't mean it that way. It's just that they're perfect. I haven't seen the likes of them around here. They're pedigree too, aren't they?"

Casey, clearly having fun, was grinning from ear to ear. "Billy swears he gets them for horsemeat prices."

Kathleen laughed out loud as she grabbed up the vagabond hen and placed it back in with the others. "A friend of a friend, right, Billy?" she called over to the tack room.

He nodded—too busy eating, Casey knew, to waste time talking foolishness.

Sadie went from horse to horse and then walked over to the middle one, a chestnut mare with a plaque on the stall door. "Casey's Bob?" Sadie said and smiled broadly. "Bob?"

"Her registered name is longer than her tail. There's a Bob in there somewhere. I liked it." Casey shrugged and smiled, and she laughed.

Kathleen pulled her cleats out of her pocket and grabbed her coat. "Well, folks, as much fun as this has been, I think I'll put these on and pick my way home. I might have to work."

"No!" Casey was up. "You're not driving to town in that bucket of bolts your brother calls a car. I'll take you."

Kathleen bounced up to his cheek with a quick kiss. "I have to check the house. I'm sure Uncle Dick will be opening up." She looked away. "And … I have to call Mum and Dad." She pulled up her hood, her face disappearing in the fur around the edge. "Besides, with the lines down, I have to do that from work. Don't worry." She started for the door, her parka swooshing, and then she turned. "You'll be back, right, Doc?"

Sadie nodded. "Sure will."

"Great." Kathleen pushed the door open and scooted out. "See ya', Billy. Later," she called back.

"Is she okay?" Billy asked as he came out of the tack room, wiping his mouth off with a huge handkerchief.

"No. The generator kicked in okay?" Casey reached over to the water bucket and turned the water on and off again. "We have a problem." He grunted and stood up. "Her folks put their place up for sale."

"Does Sam know?"

"I doubt it."

Billy nodded and swallowed. "It'll take some time to sell her place off."

"I already told her that. I think I insulted her."

Billy walked over to Sadie in front of Bob's stall, running her hand down the horse's neck. "Do you ride, Doc?"

"Used to, long time ago. Mom had one or two horses around all the time. After she died, Dad sold them. He couldn't bear to look at them."

Billy started toward the back, picking up a shovel as he went. "You, Doc, have your pick." He swung the shovel as he walked. "You probably ride like a pro."

"You should … come over … anytime," Casey said, nodding, his heart beating too quickly again.

"I'd love to."

Everything seemed to fade for Casey as he stood there. Maybe it was her eyes. They were hypnotic, and he could almost see himself in them. Maybe it was her touch, so light yet strong, her hand burning into his. Maybe it was her voice and how she so calmly found the truth and beauty in the place around him. She caught him staring.

"Sorry." He jerked his head back down.

"Why?"

"Why what?" he said, feeling like an idiot.

A gentle squeeze of her hand on his pulled him back to her. "Why do you always say sorry, Casey? You apologize for everything, even if it has nothing to do with you, even if it's something good. You don't have to … you know … say sorry. You've done nothing wrong."

For the first time in twenty-three years—Casey realized—he hadn't. He'd done nothing to screw up the works, hadn't hurt anyone's feelings, and had even stood up to the Beast. Sadie had stepped in and changed everything, and he wasn't sorry, not one little bit.

CHAPTER 12

The bell jingled the arrival of yet another customer when Casey walked through the door of the Hole, but no one in the exasperated crowd seemed to notice. The Hole was loud with an undercurrent of complaint as they tried to step around the shoddy "Caution! Wet Floor" signs that warned of the grimy water. The thin afternoon sun was doing its best to break through the clouds, but folks were too busy looking out the steamed windows for the bus, too busy complaining. Killkenny bus number 317 was late, stuck in the ice somewhere between Boston and the Hole, and Casey seemed to be the only one not grumbling about the weather and the remaining piles of gritty snow.

He stomped his boots on the mat, splashing liquid salt over the worn tile, and then wove his way past Wanda, the eldest waitress, through the throng to the counter of the dingy diner to the one empty stool, the one wobbly seat, deserted except for someone's leftover newspaper. He sat down to wait before noticing that the counter was sticky and he'd have to wave over the top of two six-foot Hydro workers to catch Kathleen's eyes. The coffee smelled inviting, and the scent of baked goods almost tickled the inside of his nose.

Kathleen was in the far corner, pouring smiles into customers' cups. That single fact made Casey's heart hurt. Kathleen didn't deserve the Hole. She didn't deserve having to move. He didn't deserve to be this happy, as he'd spent the entire morning and most of the afternoon with Sadie and Billy in the barns.

"Casey!" Kathleen spotted him. She stood up straight, and she was prettier than the painting that hung behind her. It was one of four hanging on the wall next to the washroom sign, and like the others, it had a little For Sale ticket stuck in the bottom corner of the frame. Like the others, it was a Kathleen Egan original, on consignment, crying out for a buyer who might realize its worth. He grinned at the sound of her voice and looked over at her.

"What the hell you doing here?" Kathleen called over to him.

"Doughnut!" he called back.

"What?" she yelled over the cackling laughter of a group of old men.

"I want a doughnut," Casey said, cupping his hands around his mouth.

"You can have mine," an old guy—Arnie of Arnie's Towing & Salvage—called over to him. "I've had my fill." The crowd tittered.

Kathleen, empty coffeepots in hand, eased past a woman with a screaming toddler. The child was holding half a soggy chocolate-glazed in his pinched little hand, and folks were edging away from him whenever his fist swung their way.

"Aren't you supposed to be looking after those babes?" Kathleen twisted in behind the counter.

"I got hungry."

She plunked an empty mug down on the newspaper in front of him. "You're always hungry." She waved an empty coffee carafe in front of him. "Need to make more. Bus is way late. They're getting nasty." She nodded to the crowd. "Did Sadie get off okay?"

Casey felt the heat in his face rising too quickly once more. "Look, Kate. It's not the way you think."

"Hey! Kathleen! More coffee over here!" A wizened man with no teeth and a gnarly index finger—Casey didn't recognize him—waved at her.

"Okay, Jerry," she yelled back. She leaned over and whispered to Casey. "Don't leave. I'm due for a break. As soon as the bus gets in." She was gone.

Casey's stomach had begun to growl the minute he'd come through the door, the minute he'd had a sniff of the baked goods. Now it was hurting. He checked his watch. Casey pictured the bus in a ditch on the side of the road or trapped in traffic in Boston but pushed it aside. Nope, the bus would get there. The day had been going so well already. He picked up his empty cup and stared inside, wondering if anyone would mind if he helped himself.

He didn't feel a thing, no tap, no word; maybe he smelled the scent of trouble, but Casey knew. He turned on his swivel stool, and there was Sam, frozen curls sticking out in every angle, grinning.

Casey's world grew even sunnier. They stared at each other for a second and then laughed at the same time. Casey leaned back against the counter and smiled up at his brother, as Sam's hand landed on his shoulder and tightened in a brotherly squeeze.

"Where the hell did you come from?" Casey rose and gave Sam an identical squeeze on Sam's shoulder. "Hey." He looked past his brother for the bus that wasn't there. "Did you walk from Boston?"

Sam's eyes danced. "The driver ditched 'er. Wait." He picked up Casey's empty cup and handed it to him, grabbed the newspaper, opened it on the counter, and then jumped up onto the stool and from there the counter. Firmly on the paper and towering above the crowd, he clapped his hands together twice, sharply, to get noticed. It worked. Casey heard Kathleen squeal out Sam's name from across the Hole. Then she was over, laughing, pulling on Sam's jeans, obviously having forgotten all about everyone else in the restaurant.

"How could you sneak in like this? Get down from there," she squealed.

Sam winked at her. "Could I have everyone's attention, please? Please, anyone, waiting for the bus! Hey! You guys!" Folks began to quiet down and stare up at Sam. "I just walked from Collins Corners. Everyone's fine"—he raised his hands higher to reassure—"but the driver lost her. Put her in the ditch, so you might want to drive on up. Everyone's okay—just stranded." Sam jumped off the counter, down on the other side, as the crowd began moving and the muttering doubled as those who had paid earlier left and the rest headed for the cash register. Sam scooped up Kathleen in his arms and twirled her around while Casey gathered up the dirty papers.

"I missed you!" Sam hung on to Kathleen, and Casey wondered where this new exuberance had come from. "Glad to have me back?" Sam pushed away from her as if to get a good look.

"You're freezing!" she cried, laughing with him.

"That's all I get? You're freezing." He mocked in a feminine, squeaky voice, rubbing his hands together for warmth.

"I'll have a cruller, please," Casey said, trying to move things along and acquire something to eat at the same time. "Kathleen? Anyone?" It appeared to be missed on Sam as he wrapped his arms around Kathleen once more. Casey wondered if maybe Sam had won the lottery.

Wanda came around the counter. "Thank goodness this is a pay-when-you-order place," she said.

"A cruller? Wanda?" Casey tried to catch the corn-fed server as she grabbed the pot from Kathleen and started out once more to the remaining few customers.

"Come on." Kathleen pushed Sam backward a little. "Let's get a table." She looked across the shop. "I'm taking a break, Wanda," she called out to the other server. "Can you handle the register?"

"Sure," Wanda said, turning to the customers who were lining up to pay.

Casey watched Kathleen drag Sam over to a booth and away from the doughnuts. "Ah hell!" Resigned to the fact that he was never going to get a cup of coffee if he didn't take the situation into his own hands, he jumped over the counter, grabbed a fresh pot of coffee, balanced the tray of crullers on it, and then, grabbing two more mugs, made for the booth.

Sam, when he'd finally let go of Kathleen, sat down on the seat next to Casey. "Still the best coffee around," Sam said, shrugging out of his jacket.

"Here." She handed a paper napkin to him. "You're melting. Maybe you should put your coat back on. You'll catch your death. Here." She took his hands. "Wrap your hands around that," she told him, pushing the first coffee Casey had poured over to Sam. "You can talk to Casey on the way home. So tell me everything now."

Kathleen looked over at Casey, sudden realization spreading across her face, and he grinned back at her like a smug cloak-and-dagger spy. She placed her hands on her hips. "You! You knew! And you didn't say a thing!"

Casey poured her a coffee, then one for himself, and shoved half a cruller into his mouth, still managing a grin.

"Does the Beast know you're coming?" Kathleen's eyes glistened as she stared at Sam, and Casey wondered once again why his brother could have been so blind for so many years.

Sam was shivering as he held the coffee. "No. Let's keep it that way until tonight, eh?" He looked out the steamy window. "What a drive. Weird out there. All the rain shrank the snow into dark grit. Then the ice covered it all. Black glass everywhere." He looked at Kathleen like a kitten looking up at a half-opened can of kibble. "Can you get off work?"

"I'll get off all right!" Kathleen leaned back on her chair. "Oh, Sam! Wait till you see the babes!" She blanched, her eyes darting over to Casey's and then back at Sam. "I mean … Casey was telling me …"

Casey sighed.

Sam's eyes focused hard on hers as he tilted his head. It was his turn to look over at his brother. "She was there last night, wasn't she?"

"Came in right after you hung up." Casey finished off the doughnut and reached for another.

Kathleen slid down a little into her seat. "I wasn't going to tell you." Her face brightened up just as fast. "But you're here now, so it doesn't matter."

Sam's whole body heaved with his sigh as if he hadn't relaxed in years. "For the weekend. So … twins." His smile lit his face like a match to naphtha. "How are they?"

"Right as rain and pretty as a picture," Casey said, mouth full again.

"Twins," Sam said as if he still didn't believe it.

With three doughnuts finally down and the coffee hitting the spot, Casey was more than inclined to fill Sam in on the details of what had transpired the night before. Neither he nor Kathleen mentioned the sleepover. Both knew, even without words, the timing wasn't perfect. They talked about Libby. They talked about Sadie and how it could have turned out so badly, had she not shown up. While they talked, Casey watched Kathleen become more and more maudlin. Sam was talking about the days to come, the dreams of the business and showing cattle, and Kathleen was talking about the past, when she became the first girl to win Best in Show for her pet goat, Gabby, at the Athens fair, how they'd spent so much time building the rickety chicken house, how her father would go out every night in the winter and flood her backyard so that the kids could play hockey. Casey warmed at the image of Kathleen in her hockey skates. She was a terrific hockey player. She couldn't skate in girls' skates worth a damn, but in boys' skates, she could whip around an ice rink with a stick in her hand just as fast as any guy could.

Casey couldn't watch as Kathleen did her best to change the subject when Sam asked how her folks were doing, but she had always been lousy at hiding her tears, and she offered no reasonable explanation for crying but fatigue or that perhaps it was time for her parents to come home. The fifteen minutes had turned to thirty before she announced that she had to get back to work. Kathleen stared at the remaining crullers and the empty pot.

"I'll be over as soon as I'm done." She stood up, but Sam was up just as quickly, his hand on her arm, pulling her close to him.

"Can't you come now? They don't need you here. Here, I'll take that." Sam suddenly grabbed the half-empty tray of doughnuts and started back over to the display.

Kathleen tugged on Casey's arm as he chewed on his fourth and final doughnut and stared at his brother. He got up, wondering if Sam planned on going back to school. Something was definitely up.

"He's carrying the tray over for me? Since when did Sam start helping me with work? Is it me?" Kathleen stood, pot of cold coffee in hand.

"Exams … maybe," Casey said, watching Sam slip the tray into its place on the display as if he'd always done it. "Got to be the stress."

Kathleen whirled on Casey, her eyes boring into his. "Did you tell him?" She poked him. "About the house?"

"No." Casey rubbed his chest where her finger had landed. "When would I have a chance to tell him? He just got here."

"Well. Don't!" She poked him again.

"He's going to see the sign, Kathleen."

"Maybe not. Just don't tell him, Casey. Please. Not right now. He'll just get all upset." Her eyes glistened, and Casey hated that he'd brought her to tears once more.

"Okay, okay. Relax." Casey watched his brother chatting to Wanda, almost as if he liked her. "The way he's acting he already knows."

"No." Kathleen watched Sam. "He's happy"—she bit her lip—"but scared. I don't know. Something's weird."

Casey laid a ten on the table. "Well, all I know is Becket's home now, and we can all relax, right?"

Kathleen giggled and the tears spilt over and down her cheeks. She frantically wiped them away.

"What?" Sam said, coming up to them. He grabbed his jacket and pulled it on.

Kathleen took his arm. "Time to mount up, Becket," she said. "Battles to fight."

Casey tried to look busy but couldn't help but notice Sam's reaction, the way Sam was looking at Kathleen's mouth. He did a double check, but, yes, it was Kathleen's lips that Sam's eyes seemed to be focused on. Sam went to give her what looked to be a quick peck on the cheek, which in itself was rare, but hesitated slightly before his lips touched her skin. When he kissed her, he lingered there for a second, as if he didn't want to move, a scene right out of one of those romance movies Kathleen said she hated but watched late at night when she thought the boys had fallen asleep. Someone laughed from the other side of the Hole, and Sam snapped back to reality. Casey shook his head and turned away.

"Let's get out of here," Sam said. "Later!" He waved at Kathleen and opened the door for Casey. Casey started out the door, staring back at Kathleen who was touching her face, obviously feeling Sam's kiss on her cheek.

"I'll be damned," he muttered as Sam bolted past him on the way to the truck. Maybe it was happening, finally.

CHAPTER 13

Sam peered into the eerie fog rising from the frozen land around him. The temperature had gone up quickly, but he knew it wouldn't last. It would be cold again as soon as the sun went down. But as they drove the pale gray ribbon of highway to Saint Jude, the ice was melting away from the feet of the fence lines.

Casey hadn't said much on the drive from the Hole to the farm, but Sam hadn't really given him the chance. His jaw was beginning to ache from his jabbering. He hadn't shut up—about school, about plans for the farms, about the various competitions in which they would enter Libby and family. He talked about anything except Kathleen. An uneasy ache formed in his belly as he watched a birch limb snap and tumble and then shatter on the ground in the fading afternoon light.

"God!" Sam looked across the truck and out the driver's side as the setting sun turned the shimmering branches into silver glitter. "Fantastic. Ice fire."

"Yeah," Casey said with a half-smile on his face. "Strange weather. Freezing one night, spring the next." He glanced over at the trees as if studying them. Then he focused back onto the road. "Those new generators kicked in okay. Kept the water moving."

"Good." There was another silence as their world whizzed by.

"MyKate seemed kind of quiet." Sam tried his hardest to sound nonchalant. "Misses her folks, I think."

Casey's brow was furrowed. Their mother never picked up on it, that Casey's brow wrinkled up in just that manner every time he tried to lie; but then his mother wasn't the brightest light in the night sky.

Casey turned off the highway onto Saint Jude Road, past the Peddler's Pub, a local watering hole and supper spot for Sunday evening diners.

"Know what an ingénue is, Sam?"

"Uh-yup." Sam sighed as they came over the hill and the Brennan farm shone in the sun.

"That's Kathleen, an ingénue, a melancholy ingénue." Casey sprayed windshield washer on the glass to clear some of the salt away. The wipers scraped.

"You reading the dictionary again?" Sam laughed sadly when Casey shrugged. Everything was changing, and Sam wasn't so sure he liked it. He looked down at the faded car blanket that had fallen on the boxes under the dash and, picking it up, placed it on the seat between them. He tried to smooth out the fringe he'd been playing with since they'd left the Hole. He'd need the blanket shortly. "The Beast know I'm coming?"

"Nope. Figured you'd want to see the herd first."

Sam sagged into the seat and relaxed a little, staring out at the tree-lined pastures. "How is the Beast?"

"Pissed off, as usual." There was a pause. Casey looked at him and then back to the road. "It's worse than ever. She's angry about Libby. She's angry that Libby had the twins. She's especially angry that I called the vet in." He snorted. "She's one very angry woman."

"And Gran?"

Casey paused, slowing down for a curve. "She's okay."

"That doesn't sound too convincing. Is she?"

"Yeah." Casey glanced over at him as they neared Kathleen's house. "It's been a long winter."

"What the hell!" Sam jumped forward in his seat, his belt snapping at his neck. "Pull over!" Sam reached across and tugged on Casey's jacket.

"Get off!" Casey, struggling, pulled the truck onto the shoulder and stopped it parallel to the For Sale sign. It seemed to be lit up as it swung on its hinges.

Sam's eyes focused on a new enemy. "When did that go up?"

"Today, I guess."

"No wonder she was crying." He slumped back into the seat. "Ah, shit!"

"Yeah."

"This complicates everything. She'll never believe me," Sam said, and his hand went into the pocket of his jacket, searching for the ring box. "She'll think I feel sorry for her. Christ!" His timing couldn't be worse.

"What are you talking about?"

"She's never going to believe me," Sam said, his voice rising as he tried to remain calm.

"I don't see how this has gone from Kathleen's possible move to your … what, self-pity?"

Sam slumped down into the seat. "You know, if I had any luck at all, it would be bad." He sat for a moment, worn out, his head resting on his right hand, which was resting on the door of the truck.

"That's it!" Sam lifted his head and turned to Casey, a small light shining in the back of his head. "You can be my witness." Sam pulled the ring box out and handed it to his brother.

He opened it with a snap, and as he always did when he looked at it, he smiled at the tiny diamond ring. He'd had it since the summer before, when he'd purchased it from Vandersmack's Jewelry Shop just down from the Hole. It had been in their window for over a year, the ring Kathleen had joked about, the ring she said she'd choose should she ever hook any guy stupid enough to have her.

Carefully, Sam pulled the ring out of its case. He knew why Kathleen liked it. It looked just like the one on his grandmother's finger, tiny, with lots of fancy curlicues in the gold around the diamond. It wasn't the most expensive ring in the window, but it was the prettiest. He could imagine it shining on Kathleen's hand in the sun above the quarry.

Casey stared down at the ring. He glanced over at Sam and raised one eyebrow. "Oh, Sam, this is so sudden."

Sam shoved him.

"Who's it for?" Casey asked looking down at it once more.

Sam rolled his eyes. "For you." He snorted. "For Kathleen, of course."

"From you? Since when did you two start dating?" Casey smiled a little. "Hey. This is it. This is the one she liked."

Sam could see that Casey was more than impressed.

"How long have you had this?"

"Got it last summer."

Casey stared at the ring for a while and then closed it up, handed it to his brother and lookled over at the For Sale sign. "When it disappeared. You bought it? What? It's an investment?"

Sam glowered at him. "I should have given it to her then." Hell! He should have told her he loved her then, instead of pretending he didn't.

"What makes you think she'll say yes? It's not like you've been dating. We talk, Kate and me. Christ. You've never even kissed her."

"I did!" Sam said, opening the box once more. "The night of the prom."

Casey grinned. "Hate to break it to you, Casanova, but that was three years ago." Casey's grin widened. "Hell! I've kissed her since then."

Sam's head jerked around. "What?"

Casey's jaw tightened. "That's not our priority. We have to find a way to keep her here, and you're right. Your timing stinks."

Sam's closed the ring box and slumped back into the seat.

"Lookit, let's just play it by ear." Casey turned the truck back on. "Let's go." He put the truck in drive and then started up the laneway.

Because Sam's time at home was limited and his mother demanded most of it, Casey and Sam had formulated a routine for getting past her vigilant eyes and into the barn. It ran like clockwork. As they drove over the top of the laneway, just before they came within view of the front rooms of the house, Sam ducked down and pulled the blanket that had lain between them up and over himself. Hidden from obvious view, blending into the shadows of the cab, he didn't move as Casey drove past the house to the barn. Parking, passenger side to the barn door, Casey was the first out. They knew the Beast, like always, would be there at the kitchen window. Casey waved to the face frozen in the pane and then walked around the front of the truck and opened the side door of the cab. With practiced precision, Casey pushed on the barn door.

"Billy," Casey bellowed. Sam, watching through the vague weave of the blanket, could hear the joy in Casey's voice as they fooled their mother once again.

"Right here, Casey. No need to shout." Billy was suddenly poking at Sam. Sam snorted but lay still under the blanket.

"You know the routine," Casey said as he removed the box that Sam had kicked, the medicines for the cattle Casey had picked up from the co-op, always good to have on hand and an excellent reason for going into town. The Beast would know the box and recognize it, even from the distance between the house and the barn. She would also know that the medicine had to be protected from the cold. That's where the blanket came in. Billy took the meds and moved back a bit, putting them on a web-coated ledge under the first window.

"Ready?" Casey waved at his mother again and smiled.

"Ready," Sam said, preparing to move.

Casey pulled the blanket up and out of the truck, spreading it wide, effectively blocking the barn door from the eyes in the window. Sam moved. He was out of the truck and into the barn before Casey had the blanket all the way out. While Sam was giving Billy a bear hug behind the door, Casey carefully folded the blanket in just the same fashion his mother had beaten into him for so many years. He placed the blanket back in the truck and closed the door.

"Hey! Billy!" Sam gave his uncle another slam on the back. "You look whipped."

"There's a reason for that. Would you like to see your herd, son?" Billy put his hand on Sam's shoulder and moved him around to face the rest of the barn. Sam didn't need to be led.

The barn was once again clean and empty of nearly all the cattle. There were a few cows with their calves looking up at him, and he counted three that seemed ready to drop a calf at any time, but he really wasn't looking at them. He was searching for Libby. Sam hadn't seen her. He'd been at school when they got her, but he'd seen photos. The photos in no way could capture a dream.

Libby was lying there, just as the sun cast a ray of light through the small, web-covered window behind the cow. Sam knew that it was the last sun of the day that had attracted Libby to that spot. Stronger warmth. The calves were both asleep close to Libby, and the ray turned their brown coats to gold. Dust sparkled and danced around them.

"Wow," Sam said as Billy ducked into his trailer. "She's a beauty. And would you look at those two."

"Great, aren't they?" Casey said.

"Better." He leaned over the stall rail as the bull calf opened his eyes and sniffed at them. "Look at the back ends on them. God, they're pretty."

Billy came out of the trailer with a plastic bag and a grin. Out of it, he produced a package of cups, the kind you get at the picnic section of the supermarket. He opened the package and handed one to each young man. The bottle he presented next came as a surprise to Sam.

"This is good stuff. Costs over a hundred bucks!" Sam said. He felt Casey's curiosity rise. "I saw it in the liquor store."

"I have an in with a wholesaler," Billy said and removed the cork, glancing over at Sam.

"Right," Sam said, trying to keep a straight face. "Next you'll be telling us the Beast is beautiful."

"She ain't beautiful." Billy snorted. "Never was. Not even good in the sack."

Sam's eyes shot up. Casey stopped and stared at him, as if waiting for an explanation.

"Your father told me," Billy said, quickly turning red in the face. He poured some champagne into each glass, looking rather relieved that the subject was closed, and Sam knew: it was closed. "I bought the booze. I toast first." Billy paused and puffed up his chest, as he did once in a while when bragging about his herd to the occasional jealous breeder.

"To the herd and the two brothers who started the venture, two lads any man would be proud to call sons. To Casey and Sam Brennan." He drank it down. They did the same, and more was poured. More toasts were given. More champagne was poured. Another bottle surfaced, and Sam wondered if he might show up at the front door pissed.

An hour had passed too quickly for Sam, and it was Casey's turn again. He had to holler over the bellowing of Libby, who was by now more than ready for a ration of grain. "To Dr. Sadie Parker, without whom we wouldn't have any of this." They raised their glasses.

"To Casey's lady vet," Sam said, and he and Billy joined in and drank.

"Libby did all the work," Sadie said as she stepped around the corner, bag in hand.

Sam remembered Casey's words, how the new vet wasn't Sam's type. If he weren't already in love with Kathleen, and if Casey weren't so taken with her, Sam might have had a go at this new lady vet with the bright, friendly eyes. He saw calm strength in her face. This one had *friend* written all over her.

"What are you doing here?" Casey mumbled.

"Bad opening line," Sam whispered from behind as he shoved his brother. "Smarten up."

Casey shoved him back, never taking his eyes off Sadie as she walked up to them.

"I was up at the Campbell's place, and since it was on my way, I grabbed my camera. I wanted to see how they were doing."

Sam looked over at Billy, who had a slight grin on his face. Sam looked back at the vet. Sadie shifted from one leg to the other, clearly uncomfortable. Sam groaned to himself and poked his brother. Casey almost jumped over to her. Taking her arm, he escorted her back to the others.

"Sam, this is Dr. Sadie Parker," Casey said.

"Sadie," she said, smiling as she put her hand out to him.

Sam accepted it, noticing its strength as Billy handed her a new cup of wine. "Here ya go, Doc."

"If I'd known there was champagne, I'd have shown up earlier." She paused and then raised her cup. "To new friends, old friends, and the herd!"

"You have a habit of showing up at the right time," Sam said, watching his brother stare at the woman like a lovestruck teenager.

"I have my moments," she replied with a small laugh, handing her glass to Casey, pulling her hat off, and batting at her hair as it flew out around her head. She looked at Casey.

"Wouldn't your mother want to be out here and share this with you?" Sadie asked.

"No," the men replied in unison.

She nodded. "Doesn't she come out here at all?"

"No," the men replied in unison.

For the next fifteen minutes, they celebrated, Billy smiling too much, an effect champagne had on him. Sam was extolling the bad side of university, as opposed to how good it was to be home, when Billy rose, put his plastic glass in the garbage, moved to the gate, and unlocked it. He looked at Sam and motioned him over. Casey grabbed his vet by one hand and opened the gate for Sam with the other. "After you."

Libby plodded over to him as if curious.

"She doesn't know me," Sam said quietly.

"You've never met?" Sadie scooted out of the way.

"I was at school when we got her." Sam studied Libby's straight back and square shape, the curve of her neck and her nice tight udder.

The calves were up, curious and alert, watching Sam as he entered their home, their noses sniffing at the air, their eyes, moist and innocent.

Casey walked over to Libby and stroked her forehead. Sam raised his arm to Libby's nose so that she could smell him. He gently pulled on her ears and scratched behind them. She mooed as if she liked that best.

"Eh … Libby, I'm Sam." He began to pet her, his hand smooth on the warmth of her bronzed fur. The calves frolicked around their mother, dancing in the fading sunbeams.

Casey looked over at Sadie. "What about tattoos and tags?"

"Next week," Sadie said, and Sam looked up at her. "It will set them back a bit, and I'd like to see them put on a bit more weight."

The barn door creaked open.

"Hi, Kathleen!" Sadie called out.

"MyKate!" He ran toward Kathleen. Grabbing her, he twirled her around. "You have to see them, MyKate! Unbelievable!"

Sam and Kathleen ran to reach them.

"Hi, Libby," she said. "You are really beautiful. They're beautiful."

The calves jumped, danced, and sniffed, bumping her and playing with her. Kathleen squealed as the heifer knocked her to the barn floor and began licking her face.

Sam groaned when a familiar scent assailed them.

"Oh no! Calf poop!" Kathleen cried, raising herself and then lifting her right elbow and looking at the yellow substance on her coat. "Now I've done it! It's laundry time." She got up, Sam giving her his hand.

"What do you think, MyKate?" Sam said, wrapping his arms around her, ignoring the noxious-scented mess.

"You know, I thought that you were okay, but those calves beat you by a mile," she said to him grinning. "I should be going."

Sadie put her hand on her chin. "Kathleen, I have an idea." She picked her bag up and reached for her jacket. "Why don't we go get cleaned up and come back later, after they have Sam safely snuck back into the house or whatever it is that they have to do." She looked at the men. “What do you say? Let’s give Mama something to really worry about.”

Kathleen’s smile became wider and a bit evil. “I’m for it.”

Sam was falling in love with Casey’s lady vet. “Right,” he grinned, picked up some clean straw, and began rubbing the crap off Kathleen’s coat.

* * *

Long after the women had gone, after the champagne was downed and trashed, after Casey had gone to the house for his wash-up and dinner, Sam snuck out the back door of the barn and started the long walk back. The cold was settling like a starched sheet around him, glistening frost on brittle soil. Every now and then, his feet would go through the crisp and dirtied snow, the remnants that winter had kept guarded under the pines. He knew the path through the underbrush better than Becket knew his way to Stone Mountain. He’d taken it more. Just as he’d done before, he emerged from the trees and stepped onto Saint Jude Road, not too far from Kathleen’s house.

The black windows of her home made him shiver. She should have been home. If she’d have been home, he would have gone in, told her there and then what he had wanted to say for so long. He would have found the courage somehow. But she wasn’t there. No one was. And the For Sale sign creaked as he walked past.

He took his hands out of his pockets and trudged across the lawn to it, the dead grass giving way under his boots. Pulling up the sign, Sam carried it as far as the tree line between the two properties and then, with a heave, flung it into the spruce and cedar. The walk up to the farm became much more enjoyable after that, as he psyched himself up for the next round, the battlefront between his mother and his brother.

CHAPTER 14

Sam's head hurt from the pandemonium that exploded in the house whenever he came home and this time was the same. His mother's hysterical cackle made his nerves scream as she slammed the door closed behind him, twisting the lock as tightly as it would go.

"Look at what the cat dragged in!" she yelled as she clutched Sam's arm and pulled him into the kitchen. "Have you eaten?" She tugged at his bag. "How's school? You're not supposed to be home for four weeks." She continued, pulling on him, maniacally clutching him, and trying to pull his jacket off. "Oh my, you're so cold."

"Slow down, Mum," Sam said quietly, wanting to get out of her clutches, already nauseous from the overpowering scent of her artificial, lavender perfume. He took her hands in his and nudged her away a bit, playing with her a little so as not to tick her off.

"Ugh! You smell like barn!" She stepped back, appalled.

He wondered how she could smell anything over that stuff she called perfume. "Yeah, I know. Sorry. I managed to get a ride from the Hole in the back of old man Campbell's truck," Sam said with his straightest face.

"Well, go get those clothes off, and I'll start supper. Gosh, it's good to have you home, son."

"Samuel." Gran chuckled softly and slumped back in relief.

He smiled with relief and stepped over to her as his mother headed into the pantry, muttering about how he should have called and how they were only having meatloaf.

"Give your Gran a big hug and kiss," Gran said.

Sam relaxed into her embrace. He could forget a lot of things about home, but late at night, when he couldn't sleep, he always heard his grandmother's nightingale voice, singing lullabies to him.

"We'll talk later," he whispered and then turned and grinned at Casey, playfully punching him in the arm as he started jumping around like a prizefighter. Fists in the air for victory, he bounded straight for the stairs, yelling back. "We'll probably have MyKate here tonight, Mum. I saw her at the Hole. She's bringing a friend of hers with her." He was grinning as he raced upstairs, two at a time, leaving his mother's head swiveling in confusion.

Rachel turned around and called after him. "What? Who?"

Sam didn't bother to answer, a shower seeming like just about the best thing in the world to him, his mind already racing with the different ways he would approach Kathleen with the ring that was burning a hole in his pocket.

* * *

Throughout the meal, Sam kept his mother regaled with university stories. He evaded questions about what he had planned for the weekend, why he had decided to come home, why he wasn't going to his own graduation ceremony. He did stress that he had missed everyone so much that he had to come home in order to concentrate better on the exams. That seemed to satisfy his mother, and he told them his plans for the summer, the plans his mother would like. Sam knew it was better not to cause a scene. Overall, supper had gone well; the meatloaf was tasty, and the mashed potatoes were plentiful. He had to give his mother credit for her mashed potatoes. No one could beat potatoes into shape like Rachel Brennan. Sam noticed that Casey didn't seem nearly as starved as usual. Rachel, humming off key, insisted on doing the dishes, another rare break for Casey. Then Rachel told Sam not to worry about his room, for she had cleaned it thoroughly.

Sam raised a questioning eyebrow as Casey grinned again and pushed himself away from the table.

"I'm going upstairs." Casey poked Sam and started slowly up the stairs, rubbing his chin. "Think I need a shave."

Sam snorted. "With that peach fuzz?" But Casey was already halfway up.

"Don't you go anywhere, Casey Brennan. What did you buy today? Where did the money come from?" Rachel yelled up at him, her hand hard on the banister. Sam's stomach tightened as he braced for the wrath about to fall upon his brother.

"Didn't buy a thing," Casey called down, his voice ebbing as he headed down the hallway to his room. "I threw the money away."

Sam drew in a sharp breath when he heard the remark. *What the hell!* His mother turned beet red at the jab by her eldest. Sam could see by her expression that there was finally going to be the blowup that came with every meal.

"You come back here, Casey Brennan. I've had just about ..." Her voice lingered in the kitchen as she followed Casey up the stairs. Sam rose as he saw her go, knowing she'd be on Casey's back about anything she could find, still shocked by Casey's brazen tone. Sam started for the stairs.

"No, darling."

"Gran?" He felt her hand on his arm as he passed her in her rocker. There were times when Sam was filled with such a panic at the thought of the chair being empty that he couldn't breathe. His chest was always crushed by nightmares of coming home from school to find the chair gone.

"You don't have to do that anymore, Sam."

What was she talking about? His mother would be all over Casey now, and the last thing Sam wanted was his mother in a rant when the girls got there. "She'll be all over him, Gran."

Gran shook her head. "He'll be fine, darling. Thomas is up there, and there have been a few changes around here since you were home last."

"Yeah." He scratched his head. "I gathered." Sam had tried to talk to his grandmother three times before the meal, and his mother had interrupted each time. He never got enough time with Gran. He was never allowed it. He had to be there always to pacify his mother. Why? He had no idea. He sank down on the floor next to her by the stove, and taking her hand in his, he examined it.

Casey was right. Against his, her hand was smaller than he remembered. It was more delicate. Her skin had become a simple piece of translucent silk, floating over marbles that used to be joints. Still, there she was, knitting.

"How are you doing?" Sam said.

She smiled slowly, her eyes just as bright as ever. "I'm doing fine, young man. I'm not so sure about you."

He sighed and looked away. "Exams."

"Exams, my rosy-red butt." Her hands trembled a little as she laughed. "There's something else going on. Thomas knows, but he won't tell me."

"Almost over, Gran. I can handle it."

"That's what Thomas always says too." Her hand was in his hair, her fingers running through his curls, as she'd done forever. "You're so much like your grandfather, always trying to keep everyone happy. It doesn't really get you anywhere, you know, Sam. It's wearing you down, all this moving in every direction at once."

Sam couldn't hide the snort. "You always say that—that I'm like Thomas."

Gran chuckled. "You know, Casey always worried that you'd never come home. That something, anything, might happen and you'd walk away from the farm." She squeezed his hand. "Look at what Thomas went through, to get home. He walked for two days after he crashed that plane. Two days." She gave his hand a squeeze. "Everyone told me he wouldn't be coming back, but I knew the truth." She raised his hand and kissed it. "I told them he'd be back, even if he had to walk, and sure enough, two days later, there he was, so handsome in his flight suit, those blue eyes shining. He was so proud of himself, Sam, bragging about the walk.

"I told you, Mae," Gran said, lowering her voice, apparently trying to sound like Thomas. She smiled. "This is my home." She shook her head, her eyes glistening. "You're so much like Thomas, Sam."

"I guess Dad isn't much like Thomas. He took off."

Gran leaned over and touched his face. "There's so much you don't know, Samuel. Your father is a lot like me, you know."

Sam couldn't help the harsh laugh. "That's not true. You never left. There's not a cowardly bone in your body."

Gran's eyes became a darker blue. "I've done enough damage, darling. Like your father, I didn't mean to. We were all just doing what we thought was best."

Sam hesitated, not knowing if he should say the words that needed to be said. Better to dive in and worry about the depth later.

"Gran, I just took a course in psychology. What Mum did to Casey is criminal. I mean *really* criminal. *Against the law*, criminal." Sam felt his teeth chatter as the pain and anger built inside him. He didn't add that what Gran had allowed to happen wasn't much better.

Gran shivered and pulled away her hand. She sat back into her chair and picked up her knitting. She shook her head again. "You're so tired, and now's not the time to talk about it."

When is the time? Sam thought. He laid his head on her knees and closed his eyes. He wanted the whole world to disappear or at least slow down enough for him to get back on. He took in a long, deep breath as he thought about it. "Gran, can I ask you something … about women?"

Gran chuckled. "You can ask, but I can't guarantee an answer."

Sam pushed himself up, raising his knees, wrapping his hands around them. "Could a woman love a man for years and not say anything? I mean, I know men can, but, hell, women rabbit on about everything. How would a guy know, I mean, if she was scared to tell him she loved him, you know … to say so?"

Gran sat there for some time as if considering her answer and then peered into his eyes with passion. "Well, Samuel Brennan. That is one of the most stupid questions I've ever heard from you!"

Sam felt his face go apple red as he turned away.

"This is 1988, Sam, not the dark ages. We've thrown our skirts in the fire and melted down our chastity belts."

"Gran!"

"Don't you 'Gran!' me, my boy. You of all people! You have more notches on your belt than Clint Eastwood. Even Thomas is appalled!"

Sam looked back at her, not able to hide the grin. "From what I've heard, Thomas would be proud. I heard he was a bit of a Casanova before he met you." His grin widened when he saw the mock outrage in her eyes.

Gran's face glowed. "Kathleen loves you, Samuel Brennan."

He bolted up. "I didn't say it was Kathleen."

"You didn't have to."

A log in the stove popped and fizzled out as Sam sank down on a chair. "Love kills sometimes, Gran. What if love destroys what we have?"

"Real love does not kill, darling. It grows. Have a little faith in Kathleen. She's been hanging around you like a pup on a beef bone." Gran chuckled. "As a woman, I'll tell you right now: if she didn't love you, she'd be long gone to Boston." She ran her hand over his forehead again.

"It's more than just friendship, and now you know it, and it's about time." Gran turned back to her knitting. "And furthermore, even if I'm wrong and she loves you only as she loves Casey, she loves the both of you enough to never let that change."

"But what about me, Gran?" Sam tried to push down the panic that was chocking him. "Once I say the words, if she doesn't, you know, love me that way ... I don't know if I can handle it."

"Ah." She cocked her head as if she'd been waiting for the admission. "Now we're getting somewhere. Wait until I tell this to Thomas. Male ego! That's what this is all about."

Sam's eyes widened. "No! It's not about that at all! This has nothing to do with ego, Gran. I'm scared!"

His grandmother sat back, smiling a little and tipped her head as if she'd just proved her point. "Kathleen loves you." Gran reached over and softly raised Sam's chin. "You know your problem?" She took his hand in hers and held tightly. "You have to start trusting."

Both of them looked up when doors upstairs began slamming and the sound of footsteps stopped the conversation. Casey stormed down the stairs.

"All I wanted was time to shave," Casey said.

Sam couldn't make out what his mother yelled at Casey, her voice shattered by the pounding of a fist on a wall.

"I don't care," Casey said. "Christ! Shut the fuck up, or I'll—!" Casey stopped, looking abashed at his grandmother in the kitchen. He immediately went over to her. "Oh, ah, sorry, Gran."

Sam felt the room spin as Rachel barged down after his brother.

"Did you hear that?" Rachel boomed. "Did you hear his tone of voice? Did you hear what just came out of his mouth? I tell you ...!" Rachel was almost screaming.

Sam had heard. He looked at Gran and then at Casey. His brother had never walked away from the Beast, let alone told her to shut the fuck up. Sam didn't remember hearing Casey ever tell anyone to shut the fuck up.

"I will not put up with this. I'll have no more of this ... this ..." Rachel was still going on, barreling her way into the kitchen as Sam choked back the laugh. She turned at the sound. "I've changed the sheets on your bed,

Sam," Rachel said in a snotty voice. "No telling what diseases that woman carried on her."

Sam leaned forward, not quite believing what he was hearing as Casey faced her.

"She didn't carry any diseases. She was here one night, and she wore a clean flannel shirt. The way you treated her, it's a wonder she's still our vet."

"She slept in my bed?"

"Relax, Junior." Casey looked over at him. "Ice storm, remember? Kathleen was here too."

"Both of them?" His voice quivered his eyes huge with the wonder of this new bit of information. "In my bed?"

Casey just about strutted. "I was there too."

"What?" Sam said, gaping as Rachel gasped.

"Oh, darling," Gran said and put her knitting down, taking Sam's hand. "You would have loved it. Such a wonderful breakfast the girls made. Kathleen cooked up her French toast, and Sadie's a marvelous cook too. She did the bacon in the oven, and it was crisp and not fatty at all."

Sam stared at Casey. "The vet slept in my bed, with MyKate?"

"I'll get the card table out," Casey said, not waiting for an objection as Sam watched his mother turn splotchy with rage. She charged past them and over to the sink.

"Well." Gran started to rise and took Sam's hand as he helped her. "I do believe I heard Thomas go into our bedroom, and we have to talk." She laid her hand on Sam's face. "That storm that blew by took out the last trace of winter, I think. My bones are feeling better." She winked at Sam, and he watched her almost waltz out of the room.

"How could you?" his mother spluttered from over the sink at Sam. "The way he spoke to me."

Sam choked back a laugh and turned toward her, not quite knowing how to handle this new situation. As his grandmother had said, for all the years Sam had been the champion, the intermediary, the peacemaker, the manipulator. He could play his mother better than a hockey puck, but Casey seemed to be handling things quite well.

"You just sat there and let him." She slammed pots around.

Sam sat back against the table and crossed his arms. "I had nothing to do with it."

"You let him threaten me."

I let you beat him, Sam thought, jaw pounding as he clamped his jaw together. "It's been a long winter. He's just a little stir crazy."

"Winter, my ass!"

Sam gave a sharp laugh at her language.

"It's that bitch he's taken up with!"

Whoa, he thought. "She's not a bitch, Mum." He rose and walked over to her.

Rachel froze, a suspicious scowl forming. "Just when did you meet her?"

Sam took a step back as he realized his mistake. "Casey told me what she did for us. We know her father for the love of God! He's a fine man." Suddenly angry, he slapped his hand down on the table. "If we'd lost those calves—"

"Oh! Oh! Back to *those calves*! Right! Oh! Don't get me going on those calves!" She ranted on and on and Sam's head pounded. "He's led you straight down the garden path with all this, he has! He's made you forget all about your dreams."

Sam stood patiently through her tirade, washing his hands, making sure his mother was finished. He placed his hands firmly on the side of the sink. So many times Sam had wanted to hit her, but she was his mother. One didn't go around hitting one's mother. But Sam was extremely tired of telling her over and over again his plans, his dreams. She'd never listened. She'd always believed what she'd wanted to believe, always knew exactly what Samuel Brennan would do, where he would go, and what he would think. What he wanted had never entered into it.

"Mum?" He stood up straight, wiped his hands off, and threw down the towel. "Why do you hate Casey?"

She didn't flinch. It was as if she'd expected it. Her eyes never left his. His eyes didn't leave hers either. Sam held his ground and waited for an answer.

"Granted … we don't see eye to eye," she said finally.

He snorted. "There's an understatement."

"Don't you start in on me!" Her eyes looked grief-stricken as her fists went up to them, and he looked away disgusted by her typical mock tears.

"You didn't just hurt Casey, Mum. You hurt me."

"Oh, Sam." Her voice turned to syrup. "Don't tell me you're believin' the lies he's saying?"

"Casey couldn't lie to save his soul."

"Oh no. No, no, no. Your brother's had it easy. It wasn't easy for me ..."

"Not easy for you?" Sam watched her bottom lip quiver and felt his supper might come back up. "Not easy for you?"

"All I ever did was for you boys!"

"For me, Mum," he said, trying his hardest to keep his voice even. He stepped back. "You never did a damned thing for Casey. You would have starved him to death if it weren't for Kathleen and me."

Memories flashed through him like lightning. Kathleen handing Casey the extra sandwich her mother made her each day for her school lunch. The apples or pears, or pieces of cheese that Sam insisted he wanted, only to sneak through the dank corridors of the house to Casey's door, so that Casey would have something when locked up for days on end. Candy bars, muffins, canning jars filled with milk or water, pieces of chicken or ham that was heaped on Sam's plate—his mother was always so impressed by Sam's appetite. She never knew how he'd bring a handkerchief to the table and secrete away the food.

Criminal, and if there was a hell, Sam knew his mother was first in line for the flames.

Sam heard Kathleen's voice from the front doorway, and his hands began to unclench. "Thank God. The ladies are here."

He left his mother staring after him, muttering to herself, her voice lower than he'd heard in a long while and his grandmother laughing down the hallway, talking to his dead grandfather, something about the wind changing. Gran had that right. The place was swirling with changes. Spring had indeed finally arrived.

CHAPTER 15

For twelve years, Kathleen had wrestled, romped, grabbed, pulled, and rolled over the Brennan brothers, and they'd done the same to her. But when she felt Sam run his arm around her back with greedy eagerness, when she felt his hand on her waist, barely touching her through the outer layer of spring jacket and thin blouse beneath, it was like she'd never felt him before. This was pure heat and pleasure and the promise of the unknown. She didn't want the feeling to leave for fear it would never come again.

"Stopped off and got a two-four," Kathleen said, moving away, taking a deep breath, referring to the flat of twenty-four beers she had hanging from her arms. She shivered and stamped her grit-covered feet around in the cloud of condensation that was rolling out into the nighttime air. She hoisted the carton over to Sam.

"I should have worn something warmer than a jean jacket. It ain't spring yet," she joked as she took the large grocery bag that Sadie had been carrying. Jabbing Sam, she rolled her eyes dramatically at a lovestruck Casey. Sam smiled slowly and kicked the door shut. Casey, hesitating, his head down, seemed ready to bolt.

"Casey?" Kathleen nudged him, signaling him with amused eyes. "Her coat?"

"Huh?" He woke up. "Oh. Sorry. Your coat," he said to Sadie, with a shy smile, his voice no more than a murmur. Reaching over, he helped Sadie slip out of her suede jacket. Kathleen watched him run his knuckles over it unconsciously before he hung it up.

"I chose it because it was so soft," Sadie said to him. "It's really nice, isn't it?"

Kathleen pointed to the lagers. "They're already cold. No need to put them all in the fridge."

When she looked up, Sam's eyes were on the blouse she'd borrowed from Sadie. She shivered again. This time it wasn't the cold. She told her heart to slow down, scared he might see it pounding through the thin fabric. Kathleen hadn't wanted to wear it at first. She would have worn a simple T-shirt, her usual attire, but the color had swayed her. It was a shade of foggy silver, and she remembered how Casey and Sam had gone all gaga at the color when they'd seen it on her before, the color of her gown for the high school graduation dance. Though the blouse was a little large at the shoulders and longer in sleeve length, Kathleen felt pretty in it.

That's what Sadie had called her—*pretty*—after she'd explained to Kathleen how the *smart* comment had been a compliment and how it was nice to go in to the Hole and listen to someone who had a bit of common sense. And now Sam was studying her, the way Kathleen studied a subject she wanted to paint, and that fact alone lifted her feet off the ground.

Kathleen hadn't wanted to go home at all, so they'd gone straight over to Sadie's house, where her soiled clothes had been confiscated for the wash and new clothes had been offered up for her perusal. Kathleen hadn't used makeup or perfume since the night of the prom. Oh, she had known she should have tried harder, but doing the girl thing had always made her hands sweat. With Sadie, though, it had seemed natural, even fun. There she had been—hayseed Kathleen—pretty clothes, light rose lipstick, and some sort of eye shadow and mascara that Sadie had carefully applied. When Kathleen had looked into the mirror, she'd been surprised that she didn't look all made up. She had simply looked better.

Shivering, Kathleen tried to bring herself back down to earth.

"There's chips in the bag. I'll get some glasses and a bowl," Kathleen said, pulling away from Sam, unable to keep from glancing at him as she headed for the kitchen. Sam was watching her go as he closed the closet door. It wasn't her imagination. He was acting strangely. She felt her cheek, hot to the touch. Yes! She was blushing. All because Sam had put his hand on her waist? Or kissed her at the Hole? Or was it only in her mind, because her house was up for sale? Time to get a grip. Time to get the game going.

"Hi, Mrs. Brennan." Kathleen said as cheerfully as she could muster, barreling into the kitchen, the curtains waving hello in the breeze. "How ya doing? Hope your head's feeling better. That was quite a storm, eh? Haven't seen the likes of it around here for a while. Must be that global warming they all keep talking about. Isn't it great that Sam's home?" Kathleen plopped the bag of chips on the counter and reaching up, got glasses and a plastic bowl down from the cupboard.

"Don't worry," she kept going, closing up the cupboard. "We'll clean up for you. Far out, eh, Sam getting home? I mean, I know he'll be home in a few weeks for good. This is kind of a bonus, isn't it?" She pulled the chips out of the grocery store bag. "I couldn't believe when I heard he was home."

Turning, she heard Gran pad into the kitchen. Kathleen immediately held her hand out to the woman and walked her to her chair. Everything slowed down for Kathleen as she noticed Gran's hand shaking a little.

"Oh, darling. You're so cold, and you look so lovely tonight," Gran tittered as she took Kathleen's hands in hers. "Put those artist's hands by the stove."

"There's no money in art," Rachel boomed over at them. Then the Beast zeroed in on Kathleen. "I see your parents finally put your house up for sale. That Schmiester's good, but don't get your hopes up. Don't think it will sell fast. Oh no. Nothin' sells fast out here."

Kathleen had known that Rachel would try to hurt her. She always did. It was always when Sam wasn't there to hear it. Mrs. Brennan tolerated Kathleen only because Sam insisted, but she had never made it easy on Kathleen. Most of the time, Kathleen ignored it, but since the house went up for sale, Kathleen was unable to stand much of anything, especially Mrs. Brennan's barbs. And of course, the Beast would know about the house and know how to use it to hurt Kathleen.

Probably all of Killkenny County knew. Sam must have heard about it. That's why he'd put his arm around her. Yeah. Now it made sense. Reaching for the chip bag, Kathleen resumed refreshment duty, making as much noise with the bag as possible while Rachel droned on.

"Your parents are right on the ball. Boston, that's where you'll meet a man with real potential."

Kathleen tried to keep her voice even. It was time to get rid of Mrs. Brennan for the night. It was time to pepper the Beast with chatter.

"I don't think finding a man with real potential is exactly the problem, Mrs. Brennan."

"Don't listen to her, darling," Gran said. "Thomas says Boston isn't all it's cracked up to be. Besides, there are more than enough young men with potential right here."

Great. Even Gran didn't get it.

"Saint Jude is my home," Kathleen tried to explain. She grabbed a chip and shoved it into her mouth. Salty. They'd go well with the beer.

Rachel put the final dish on the rack and wiped her hands. "A good secretarial job in Boston. That's what you need. Back to the city, where you came from."

Kathleen stared hard at her. She wasn't a city girl. She'd never been a city girl.

"Oh, well," Rachel continued, smirking, as if she knew her arrow had hit its mark. "The pots will have to wait. I've a bilious attack coming on. Keep the noise down."

"Not a problem, Mrs. Brennan. You must be exhausted, what with Sam home and company and all. Have you tried honey tea for that head of yours? My great-aunt Bertha on the Kennedy side had a terrible time with migraines. She called them bilious attacks too, though they aren't—bilious, meaning bile—and they are really migraines in the head. Must be the old-fashioned term. Not to say you're old fashioned … far from it, Mrs. Brennan."

Kathleen moved out of the way, pulling her stomach in and leaning back on the table to allow Rachel past. "My great-aunt Bertha died young, my mother said. But that's not the case with you. You must just be tired. Sam too. He must be exhausted, up early for the bus. Yup. A short game or two. We won't be late." Rachel put her hand over one eye as she mounted the stairs. "Have a good sleep. We'll keep the noise down. Maybe you should try that tea. I can bring some up to you if you like."

Gran had been rocking gently with her eyes closed as Rachel pounded away up the stairs. She stopped rocking.

"That was longer than usual, darling." Gran put her hand up to signal Kathleen hush until she heard Rachel's door close. She put her hand back down on her lap. "You mustn't let the sign bother you."

Kathleen's face relaxed a little when she felt Gran's gracious eyes on hers. Looking back over her shoulder to check that Sam wasn't hovering around the door, Kathleen pulled a chair over to Gran and sat down.

"You heard about the house, eh?"

Gran nodded. "First, Thomas told me. Then Casey told me. Then Billy. Then Rachel." She chuckled lightly. "The only one who didn't tell me was Sam. I believe he's a little overwhelmed at the moment."

Kathleen figured Gran was right. Sam was acting very weird.

"So many strange things, Gran: first, twins, then Sam coming home. You know, when Sadie and I drove by this evening, the For Sale sign was gone from in front of my house. What do you think? Maybe they decided not to sell." She gave a harsh laugh. "Wouldn't that take the cake?"

Gran raised one eyebrow. "Perhaps the snowplow took it."

"Perhaps Sam took it." Kathleen giggled, despite her overwhelming sense of loneliness. She sat up straight. She was determined to have a good night. Glancing over her shoulder again to see if it were safe to speak secretly, she lowered her voice in volume. "What do you think of Sadie?"

"Thomas loves her," Gran answered and leaned forward in her seat, her finger pointing at Kathleen. "She's the one for Casey."

"I think so too. Who's the one for Sam?" Kathleen bit her lip, feeling the red heat of mortification rush to her face as soon as she said it. Her mother would have been ashamed by her daughter's brash mouth, would have locked her in her room, or at least threatened. It didn't seem to bother Gran though; in fact, her smile had grown wider, and her eyes twinkled.

"That has never changed, Kathleen Egan." Gran nodded to the kitchen door. "He's been hovering outside that door this whole time." She touched Kathleen's cheek. "You go on in there with him." She shook her head, her tongue tsk-tsking as she picked up her knitting.

Kathleen put her hand back on the older woman. "You're trembling. Are you okay, Gran? Are you warm enough?"

"I'm fine, darling. Go on. Thomas and I want to talk."

Kathleen kissed her on the cheek. "Gran, when Thomas was courting you, did he look like Casey does tonight?"

Gran's nod was barely perceptible as she stared beyond Kathleen at the heat behind the stove. "He still does." She looked back at Kathleen. "Now go."

Sighing, Kathleen pushed her chair back and tried to focus on smiling, on putting on a good face.

"Katie, darling."

Kathleen reached for the chips as she looked back over at Gran. "Yes?"

"Don't worry about the house. Have some faith."

Kathleen's lip was getting really sore from biting down on it to stem the tears.

"I've already decided, Gran. No matter what happens with the house, Killkenny is home. I'll manage." The old woman nodded and Kathleen picked up the chips, walked through the hallway, and stepped into the living room.

CHAPTER 16

Over the next two hours, Sam couldn't get Casey's words out of his head. *Melancholy ingénue.* He even blurted it out as an answer to a trivia question, incorrectly, losing a turn when the question read, "What is a sad-faced silent clown?" After blurting out, "Ingénue," he'd jumped up and yelled out, "No! Harlequin!" then "Pierrot!" By that time, they were all staring at him, looking confused, wondering what in the hell he was talking about, and wondering why he hadn't just answered, "Mime." Casey had a strange satisfied grin on his face all the while.

"Break time," Sam called shortly after. Maybe they should have chosen "Monopoly," but it was trivia, and they were all good at it, men against the women, game three: boys—two wins; girls—one. Sam wasn't trying to hide his smile. "Thirsty work, this winning," he said, as Kathleen glowered at him.

"I still say that last question was bogus," she stated firmly. "It all depends on whether you're talking geographical north pole or magnetic."

"Ambiguous, maybe, and a bit slanted, but," Sam teased, "we got it."

Sadie laughed out loud. "I can't believe I missed that signet question." She pushed her chair back, shaking her head and took Casey's hand. "Gannet! How could I have said gannet?"

"Did you see the look on Casey's face?" Kathleen grinned as she continued shuffling the cards.

"He didn't have to yell out, 'Signet, signet, baby swan! Signet!'" Sadie grimaced. "So I said gannet. I meant signet. I wasn't seeing a goose. I was seeing a swan." Sadie walked over to Casey. "Come on. Show me where you hide the cold ones." She hooked her arm in his, and Casey almost strutted with her out of the room.

Sadie reached for the coffeepot. "You know what Gran needs?" Sadie poured some into mugs for herself and Casey. "She needs a kitten."

Kathleen couldn't help her bitter laugh as her hands curled into fists.

"I gave her a kitten … a long time ago. She was the cutest little gray thing, no bigger than my hand. Gran called her Hope."

Casey stared out the window into the night, and Sam looked over at her. Kathleen shivered. Either it was the blouse or the fire was dying down, as she had goose bumps now.

"The Beast killed it," Sam said, taking Kathleen's hand in his, working out the fist. "She wrung its neck."

Sadie gasped. "No! Surely a dog maybe. A coyote."

Sam slowly shook his head. "I can still see it, its tiny head falling away from its body." He shuddered. "It was a good quick snap, no bite marks, didn't even break the skin. Not a drop of blood. She flung it into the bushes behind the house. Didn't even have the decency to bury it or even hide it."

"Oh no! No! No! No! No! No!" Kathleen mimicked the Beast. "Filthy thing!" She looked over at Sadie. "That's what she said when we found it. She was gloating."

Kathleen remembered every word as the scene played out in slow motion again in her head.

"I was with Gran when Sam and Casey came in with Hope. Sam stepped between Mrs. Brennan and Casey for fear Casey might say something to make the situation worse. By the look on Casey's face, he seemed about ready to attack his mother. But that time, I was the one who lost it."

"Beast," Sam said quietly but fiercely. "Kathleen screamed, 'Beast!' at Mum, giving a name to the monster of our home, a christening of sorts." His voice dropped. The death of a kitten paled compared to the way she'd treated Casey.

Sadie reached for Casey's hand. "I know it happens all the time in the country, farmers putting kittens in bags and then running them over or throwing them in a river somewhere. If they don't want kittens, they should get their cats spayed. But snapping a neck like that takes a whole lot of hatred. It's not bad enough, what she did to the kitten; keeping a child home from school for slave labor, starving a child, is much worse." Sadie took Casey's hand. "Sorry. Want to tell me about your father?"

Kathleen saw that Casey and Sam were watching Sadie. She leaned forward and slashed her hand across her throat as a don't-go-there signal, but she couldn't get Sadie's attention.

"He took off," Sam said as Casey shrugged. "I was five, Casey seven. Our father was taking turns with Billy, working in the mines up north when we were born. One worked the farm while the other worked away."

"That's a rough life, working away half the time," Sadie said.

"Gran says times were tough for all the farmers then," Sam said, not making it in time as Casey pulled the chip bowl over between him and Sadie.

Kathleen remembered those years and looked down at her hands. She had missed both men so much when they had to go away—especially the boys' father. Oh, Billy was great, but Mr. Brennan had a laugh that made her laugh, and he tickled her and threw her in the air. Up and down, he'd swing her. Her father used to do it too, but it was always more fun when Sam and Casey's father did it, because he was so tall, and with him, she felt she was flying.

"Lester!" Mrs. Brennan had screamed down the hill at him while he tossed Kathleen around. "I told you to get Casey up here." Mrs. Brennan had been moving down the hill, wiping her hands on her apron. "That son of yours just broke another plate. Do you hear me?"

She remembered how Sam had stepped behind his father's leg. Kathleen remembered this because Sam's father swore to himself as he lowered Kathleen. Mr. Brennan never swore.

"Dad?" Sam had said with real fear, as it was when he was watching *Tales from the Crypt*.

They weren't supposed to be watching anything like that, according to Kathleen's mother, but when the boys stayed over down at her house, they always managed to sneak into the living room after her mother and father had gone off to bed. Frank always held her, but her other brothers startled the boys, turning off the living room lights, yelling out boo as they would grab either Sam or Casey. Oddly, it was Casey who withstood the fear the best. Sam always hid halfway behind a cushion. But Sam would later sneak up behind one of her brothers and yell boo at him—right back at him.

Billy was like that. He'd get scared first, and then he'd get mad—not at them ever, but at Mrs. Brennan. He got scared whenever Mrs. Brennan was around Gran. Then he'd whisper something in the Beast's ear. She'd always retreat. It wasn't like that with Mr. Brennan. The boy's father always seemed like a hero to Kathleen, the strong, silent type. Her mother called him "serene" or "that poor patient man."

That's why it was so confusing to the boys and Kathleen when he left for good.

Kathleen wasn't there the night everything went to hell. She didn't find out there was a problem until the next day when Sam showed up for the school bus, again with no Casey—that wasn't unusual—but he'd been crying. When Frank asked him what was wrong, he'd said that Casey was in the hospital, that he'd fallen down the stairs, and that his daddy had hurt Casey.

"Daddy pushed Casey," Sam had blurted out while they waited for the bus. "Pushed him. I saw it. Pushed him right down the stairs."

"No," Frank said with concern. "Your dad's away."

"He came home. He did. He pushed Casey."

"Your dad wouldn't do that," Frank had said.

But Sam had been adamant, and then Mr. Brennan moved away. By the time Frank had told the story to Kathleen's mom and dad and they had set out to the hospital to visit Casey, of course, the story had changed. No one had pushed anyone. It was all a misunderstanding. Casey was going to be fine. He fell. That was all. He just fell.

"You know how accident prone Casey is," Mrs. Brennan had told them.

Kathleen had missed Mr. Brennan for a long time, missed how he sang to her and how he threw her high up into the air so she could fly.

"How does Billy feel about her?" Sadie asked Kathleen, staring right at her as if wanting an objective opinion. Kathleen knew her opinions were no more objective than Casey or Sam's opinions.

"Billy doesn't really hate her," Casey said. "He just puts up with her."

Sadie looked over at Sam as he sat, chewing. A puzzled expression ran across her face. "But why?"

Casey shrugged.

"You don't know?" Sadie said. "Was it an accident? Was he a drinker? I mean … that would explain your mother's bitterness. But why would he run away before he found out you were all right?" She stared hard at Casey.

"Billy says Dad stayed until he found out that Casey was going to get better, and then he took off. Lookit," Sam said. "Mum doesn't have legal claim to the house or the farm. Gran signed that over to Casey and me. My guess is that Billy and Gran let her stay so that she couldn't whisk Casey and me away. The Kluggs had a lot of power back then."

"So why does your mother dislike Casey?"

"Best we can figure is," Sam said, "he looks like Dad."

Sadie turned to Casey. "No one hates a child because the child looks like their father."

Casey pushed himself away from the table. "We're not exactly a *normal* family, Doc."

Sam picked up the deck of cards. "So what is it this time, hearts or euchre?"

* * *

Kathleen tugged on his sleeve.

"Come on. Your head, my lap." She grabbed their beers, tugging him over to the sofa. She dropped to the floor and pulled him down. She pulled down a worn afghan and placed it over them as she leaned against the sofa's matching chair. "Tell me about school."

Closing his eyes, Sam laid his head on her lap. It felt firm and soft at the same time and better than any pillow.

"You're acting weird," Kathleen said softly.

He relaxed his shoulders. "I'm fine."

"You're not. What's wrong?"

"Nothing." Sam stopped caring whether his brother had the good sense to make a play for his lady vet and crossed his stretched out legs. This was all he wanted, her fingers playing with his hair as she'd always done. She used to pull it, tease him by playing with the curls, stretching them out one at a time, and then letting them spring back into their persistent coils. He'd wake up later, and she'd be drawing him, a wild picture, his hair sticking out everywhere, looking like a lunatic. What if he lost that! What if he lost the simple pleasure of his head on her lap? He shivered.

"You're coming down with a cold, aren't you? You were freezing today, and now you've gone and made yourself sick." She grabbed the afghan and pulled it down over him.

"I'm fine." He didn't fight the afghan either. He needed the cover to hide the growing problem in his jeans, something she wouldn't understand at all. He had to focus, find the right words, and he realized it was neither the time nor the place with Casey and his lady vet not two doors away.

Kathleen felt his forehead. "You're not running a fever."

"That's because I'm fine."

"You're fine," she said at the same time, mocking him.

He looked up into her eyes. "It's just school. Besides. You're a fine one to talk."

She pulled her hand away from his head.

He had to get her alone. "I guess I'm kind of distracted these days."

She laid her hand on his head again. "What's to get distracted by? You're there to study. You're not at school to look at the blondes, Sam. How are your marks?"

He closed his eyes again. Why were they talking about school? "Straight As."

"So it's not the marks. You're not sick. What's the problem?"

Apparently, Kathleen wasn't going to quit. He was about to say, *I love you.* Then he thought, *No maybe. I've always loved you*, or maybe, *I have a confession. No*, he thought. *Damn!* Why couldn't he find the words? He threw the afghan off him and got up.

"Come on!" He grabbed her hand.

"What?"

"We're going to the stable. Come on!" He pulled her, laughing, off the floor and over to the doorway. "We're going for a walk. Don't follow us!" Sam yelled through the living room to the kitchen as Kathleen squealed.

"Wouldn't dream of it," Sadie called out.

More than glad to have Casey to herself, Sam thought. He stood up straight, and reaching into his pocket, he felt for the ring box. It was there, right where it should be.

CHAPTER 17

Kathleen and Sam had already disappeared when Sadie led Casey back into the living room. One dim light on the pole lamp in the corner softened everything. Casey was looking for that now, for softness around him. Gran had informed them halfway through the second game that she needed her rest and that she and Thomas were going to bed. Casey realized that for the first time, he and Sadie were really alone.

"Thomas sleeps?" Sadie asked with a kind smile.

Casey grinned. "According to Gran." He looked down. "He stays with her most of the time. Every now and then, she'll say he's off doing something in the barn or in the back forty."

"Does he ever scare anyone? Has anyone ever said they've seen him?"

Casey's breath caught in his throat. "No one that's told me. It's like he's her make-believe friend, her own guardian angel, I guess."

Sadie's eyes glistened. "I wish …" She trailed off and then abruptly changed the subject. She started talking about the horses and discussed articles she'd read in the same magazines to which he subscribed.

He'd been looking at her all night, pretending not to, looking away when she caught him. Her lipstick color was amazing, or maybe it was just her lips. He wondered if they tasted as pretty as they looked. She'd dressed to come visiting, nice jeans, and a pretty blouse, ivory and lace. He'd caught himself more than once staring at her blouse, where the curve of her breasts caught the fabric. Then his eyes would shoot straight down. He knew she was waiting for him to do something, to say the first word, make the first move.

He reached over to snag the plate of cheese and crackers Gran had placed on the coffee table for them before she'd gone off to bed. He had to twist to get it, and he wasn't thinking. As always, when he leaned over and turned sideways at the same time, the pain in his lower back sliced through him like fire-hot metal. This time, the blinding pain only lasted a second, but he knew the pounding would last for hours. He grunted, barely able to breathe as his eyes found hers.

"Do you have any painkillers?" Sadie asked, her face tightening with concern.

Casey had to take a second to understand what she was getting at. He edged away from her.

"No. Don't, Casey. Kathleen was right. With the ice and the weather … I have some painkillers."

"No. Sadie, really. I'm used to it." He wanted to sink into the cushions of the sofa and disappear. "I'm not hurting."

"Are you in pain all the time, Casey? You know there are doctors out there that know all about pain, specialists."

"No. My back only hurts when I wrench it, like when I fell out on the ice or when the weather is bad."

She nodded. "Are you sure we should go riding tomorrow?"

"Yes. I'm fine!" he said with a laugh that he knew was too loud.

She nodded and pulled back then changed the subject. "I can't believe I missed signet. I'm a vet! Signet! A baby goose is a gannet!" She played with her beer. "I think I got that wrong on my finals too."

He grinned. "We didn't deserve to win."

She raised her beer to him. "Oh, I think you did." She took another sip. "You didn't miss one science question or history."

Wow. She'd noticed. "I like them best."

Once again, he caught her staring at him.

"Sorry." He jerked his head away. "Your eyes. I mean … the color. I don't know what color they are."

"I've never been able to tell." She ran her hand up the bridge of her nose. "They're blue on days I wear blue, green on days I wear green. Mostly, they're gray."

"They're like the water in the quarry on a misty summer morning."

Her face sparkled. "You talk about Sam being good with words. No one's ever described them that way. You make them sound beautiful."

"They are." He smiled, gave a halfhearted nod, and then cleared his throat. He sounded like an idiot.

Sadie leaned back and crossed her legs at the ankles, her socks, heavy double knit. She shifted and looked down at her beer. "That was a good game."

Casey smiled and offered her the remains of the crackers and cheese.

"What a beautiful plate," Sadie said, putting her beer down on the table and taking the plate from him.

"These are the plates Gran chose for her wedding set. There's only two left of the original set she had when she was married." Casey was so used to seeing the plates that he never really looked at them. This one used to be white, but age and washing had yellowed and cracked the glazes. It was just an ordinary farm scene on the plate, but the outside of the plate had an intricate basket weave, and it was as if you were looking through a garden fence in on the quaint country home.

"It's old. She probably chose this pattern for their wedding." Sadie studied the plate. Leaning closer, she turned it over, pointing out the markings on the back. "Its Irish porcelain called Country Heaven. There's the date it was made."

"You make it sound like it's worth a fortune." He flipped it back and ran his fingers over the crosshatch around the rim.

"In cash, as a piece or two, not a lot, but as heritage and love, it's priceless."

Where had it all gone? He could remember when they had a hutch full of the china. He could remember his mother throwing them at him, breaking them piece by piece, and now Gran was down to two plates. Casey placed it carefully back on the table.

She picked up her beer once more and leaned back into the oversize harvest-gold crushed-velvet sofa.

He listened to the mantel clock tick off the seconds.

"Why didn't you to university, Casey?"

He leaned forward, his elbows on his knees, his hands locked as if confessing a grievous sin. "I'm not the brightest bulb in the room."

"That's bull. You won a scholarship. Why would your mother not let you go?"

He felt the heat rising in his skin once more, but he shrugged, feigning apathy, hoping she'd drop it.

"I'm better in the field. Mostly I like tinkering, not studying."

"You like machinery?"

"Yeah." He tried a smile. "I like things that I can feel. Billy says I can put a square peg in a round hole."

"I bet. But Kathleen said you were good at the business side of the farm."

It wasn't going to work. She could see behind his sad attempts to bullshit his way out of it. He felt his stomach clench.

"Math makes sense. Don't know why, but business is all about sense too, practical and logical."

"Didn't you like school?"

"Don't know. Wasn't there that much."

"Because of your back?"

"Huh? Oh ... yeah. I suppose. That and farmwork." He tried to hide back in the sofa.

"How could you do all the farmwork with a bad back?" Her eyes widened. "Your mother kept you home to farm? That's criminal!"

He looked down at his hands again. He'd never seen it that way. The work had to be done, and he'd always managed to get his grades back up. His mother never told the schools that he was being kept home for farmwork. She'd always blamed his bad back.

"I only had to work at home a little, early fall, late spring. Just sometimes." He looked up at her and wasn't surprised to see she didn't believe him. He cleared his throat. "There was always too much to do, what with Billy being the only one, and Sam needed the high grades. He was the one who Mum pegged for college."

Sadie looked at him as if confused. "But why?"

Casey let out a long sigh and leaned back into the chair. "Beats the crap out of me. Sam and I used to plan university when we were kids. I'd go to school, and he'd farm, and then we'd change after graduation. It made sense." He looked away from her, lost in the memories of painful arguments. Sam and he could never understand why Billy and Gran had given in to their mother so completely.

Sadie leaned against him and, looking up into his eyes as if for permission, moved his arm around her shoulders. He didn't mind. She felt softer than the sun on the clover and twice as warm. His hand was so close to her breast that he could almost feel heat from it. She smelled of the hardy geraniums that came back year after year, that and a pantry full of candy, nutmeg, and ginger, and suddenly Casey wanted to share a toffee apple with her.

Sadie kind of sprang her next question on him. "How did you fall?"

Panic snaked around his heart. How much to say? What if she thought he was just after attention or weak? She might not even believe him. "I don't remember it all, kinda vague. My mother said my father pushed me."

"Oh God." She snuggled in closer to him. "Did he ever hurt you before?"

"Not that I remember. He was a coward though. Probably thought they were going to come and arrest him. He was gone before I got home from the hospital. Took off. Mum tells stories about him, you know, him leaving her black and blue. Once he broke her wrist. She says that Billy and Gran protected my father, but the police did begin to suspect, and after I fell ... well ..."

Sadie had a confused expression on her face, examining his eyes owlishly. "Where's he now?"

Casey had long since given up on wondering. "No idea."

"Strange. I mean, Billy and Gran are so ... normal. You haven't heard a word from him?"

"Nope."

Sadie shivered. "What makes your mother so angry then?"

He grunted. "There's always been something wrong upstairs with her. We just ignore it."

Casey, looking down at her hand, feeling her warmth, wanted to use the right language. "I was only really free when she took one of her spells. She'd sit in front of her bedroom window and cry for days. Then it would turn angry, and I'd have to hide again. We could hear her snarling all the way downstairs. It was scary. She'd spend weeks in her room, ranting, and then suddenly she'd be out buying every rose plant at Dingle's Nursery and working dawn to dusk in that garden of hers. I've even seen her out there in the middle of the night, with a flashlight, pulling weeds, cursing at them. Kind of funny in a twisted way."

Sadie shook her head. "You need a doctor for her, Casey. Sounds like she's bipolar."

"Bipolar?"

She smiled kindly. "It's a kind of depression. They're just really learning about it right now. People swing from serious depression into rages or manic spells where they don't sleep or sleep around too much or …"—she seemed to struggle to find examples—"they can spend way too much money or clean through the night when they can't sleep."

Casey wondered and then shook his head. "She's mean all the time."

"You're not afraid of her now, are you? You're afraid for Gran."

How did she know that? "Yeah." He realized he was squeezing Sadie's hand and released it. "But no matter what I say to Gran, she denies it, says it could never happen." He wondered if he should say the words out loud, but then he pushed his fears aside. "Sometimes I wonder, you know, about me. If I might end up …"

Her eyes glistened with understanding. "You don't have a violent bone in your body."

"And you know this." He wanted to believe her.

"I know this, Casey Brennan." He watched her eyes melt in concern and then just as quickly turn angry. "What I don't get is how Billy and Gran let her do what she's done. They adore you and Sam."

He and Sam had tried many times to figure it out. In the end, none of it made any sense. "It's weird. Mum isn't so bad when they're around."

She gave him a troubled look. "She's never hurt Gran; that you know?"

"Never laid a hand on her. Billy shows up every now and then. It throws the Beast right off. That's a weird relationship too." He grinned sheepishly. "Face it, Doc. We're all nuts here. There's nothing can help her. She's your worst nightmare."

Sadie looked suddenly stricken. "No, Casey. Your worst nightmare is watching a mother you love waste away before your eyes." She stopped as if struggling with tears.

"I'm sorry. I didn't mean to upset you." Casey wanted to go back and start the conversation over.

"I couldn't do anything but hold her hand. She suffered so much, Casey, and the worst was, in the end, I wanted her to die." Her voice broke in a sob. Then she laughed raggedly. "It helps to talk. I haven't been able to talk to anyone. I love Dad, but he's been so upset that I haven't been able to bring myself to …"

"I can go get Mr. Rumples."

Her laugh changed back to a happy one. "I don't need Mr. Rumples, Casey. I have you."

He tried to look away from her, but he couldn't, aware that her hand was on his thigh. Her lips were just inches from his.

"Casey?" Sadie leaned closer to him. He could feel her breast against his chest, and he pulled away a little, afraid she might feel his heart thudding out of control. "Is it because I'm older?"

"Sorry?"

"That you're uncomfortable with me?"

"What?" His eyes popped open. "What? No!" He jerked up, ramrod straight. "No! That's not it at all."

"Okay then." Her face, dark, smoldering, turned up to meet his. "Kiss me."

Casey's heart took off faster than a thoroughbred out of the Belmont racing gate. He dissolved into her touch, the feel of her fingers on his face and the soft heat of her lips on his.

He'd been right. Her lips tasted sweeter than they looked. He wanted to taste her forever, feel her lush lips on his always, and know she felt the same about him.

CHAPTER 18

Sam felt the crisp bite of the cold on his face, could see his breath as it passed behind them while they walked. The farm glistened with black beauty in the starlight, and as always, the essence of barnyard cleared his head.

"Burnt sugar." Sam took in a deep drag of the air as it lay around them in a gossamer blanket. "The maple wood smoke smells like burnt sugar."

Kathleen gave him a tiny half-smile and sniffed the air. "Sweet." She nodded. "And kinda acrid."

"It's nice."

"It's smoke." She glanced over at him.

He didn't say anything more for fear it would all disappear—the smoke, the moment. Everything would be gone, and he'd wake up in his dorm and find out it was all a dream. Kathleen was walking too fast. They'd get to the stable too soon, and he wanted to talk. He needed to tell her right there under the moon with the earth crystallized around them.

"Stop!" Kathleen said. She turned and grabbed his arm. "Listen!"

Sam could hear them too—coyotes, howling in the distance, the sound moving up and over the hills, slow and woebegone.

"They sound lonely," he said, looking out over the darkness, the lights from the handful of homes twinkling in the moonlit valley.

She shoved her hands into her pockets and stared up into the night sky. "How can they be lonely? There's a bunch of them."

As if on cue, the others stopped and one cried a single song, sad, almost desperate. Sam snorted and looked at her, one eyebrow raised. She was shimmering and he was reminded of how she looked that night at the prom.

"Okay." She gave in. "So one might be lonely in a crowd but—"

"No buts—listen."

The moon slid behind a cloud as she faked a frown, stuck out her lower lip, and listened.

"Okay. So he might be lonely." She laughed lightly. "He sounds more pissed off to me. The black coyote of the family."

"He's misunderstood."

Kathleen snorted and blinked up at the stars. "A satellite."

"Where?"

She pointed to the north, and he agreed. "There's another. They outnumber the stars now."

Kathleen stared at him as if he just didn't get it.

"You know, you're really starting to piss me off, Samuel Brennan." She resumed walking. "Frig! Look at all the colors in that sky! Whoever says the night sky is black must be blind. All you've done since you got back is complain. You have Libby and those perfect babes." Her arms were swaying as she pirouetted around in the night air. "You couldn't be doing better at school. Casey seems to have found someone special and then"—she cocked her head—"you have me." She laughed again.

You have me? Sam stopped again when she said you have me. The barnyard light post felt strong as he leaned on it. He needed strength. The time had come, and he wasn't ready. *You have me.* She'd opened the door for him, and he knew it would never happen again. What to say? The words were suddenly gone.

Kathleen walked over to him as he leaned against the light post, laying her hand on his cheek, her eyes filled with concern. "Tell me what's going on."

All the lines he'd planned, all the pretty phrases he'd practiced, they were all gone, and blood was thudding in the vein on the side of his head. What if it changed everything? What if he ruined it all?

"MyKate," he began. He closed his eyes. He leaned the back of his head against the frozen post. "On the drive home …" He opened one eye to see if she was paying attention. She was. She was staring back, her eyes huge and innocent in the lamplight. "Casey told me to look up *ingénue* in the dictionary. I didn't have a clue what he was talking about, but I did it."

"Ingénue?" She broke into a mischievous smile. "Has Casey been readying the dictionary again?"

"Are you going to listen?"

"Sorry." She giggled.

"He called you a 'melancholy ingénue.'" Sam waited for it to register. Kathleen looked down, pursing her lips together, trying to hide the smile. "It means a sad, naive, young woman. Are you?"

Her eyes lit up, first in pleased amusement, and then they narrowed in confusion. "Naive's a bit of a stretch. Naive. Casey thinks I'm naive? There's no way. Wait till I talk to him. Naive!"

He wasn't getting anywhere. He hadn't come out ready to spill his guts only to have her get fixated on one word. "Is it because of me, MyKate?"

"What?" Her head jerked up.

"I've been, you know, so scared that things would change, but the more I try to hide from it, the more frightened I get." He saw the confusion on her face, wanting to slow the thudding of his heart against his chest. "I know I'm not making any sense, and I don't want you to think that this just came up. It's been there for so long that I … that … I love you," he mumbled.

She gaped at him. "Pardon me?"

He grabbed her arm. "I love you, MyKate."

She shook his arm off and stepped back, paling. "If this is about the house …"

"No!" His head shook as he straightened up. "It has nothing to do with your place. I've loved you for years, since the formal, since … I don't know. Since forever. Even when I was too stupid to know. Everyone knew but me."

She put her hands out in the stop sign, as if protecting herself. "It's about the house!" Kathleen shrank back a little.

"Oh, for the love of God!" He wrapped one arm around her and pulled her against him, molding her to him from breast to knee. "I love you, MyKate." His lips were on hers, his kisses hard and deep, and she opened up to him. She tasted like fine whiskey. A desperate, needy heat coursed through him, a heat that brought a moan to his throat. He was drowning in her, and he didn't want to come up for air. Suddenly, she jerked away from him.

"Let go of me!" she hollered; her hands on her hips as she stomped on the ground. "How dare you do this to me? You go off for years, supposedly loving me, sleeping with every blonde you can get, bragging about it … to me … and now you come waltzing back here and tell me that you loved me the whole time?" Her voice pinged all over the hills of Killkenny like a ricocheting bullet. She stomped her feet like a five-year-old, tears pooling. "At least before, I knew where I stood. What am I supposed to think now?"

"I tried telling you. I kept planning to."

"Really!" She lowered her head and leered up at him with angry eyes, and Sam wondered if perhaps it wouldn't be the smartest move to take off. "Kept planning to! But it slipped your mind! Well, thanks! You had plenty of opportunities to *tell* me this, Samuel Brennan."

"I'd get scared, MyKate." His voice cracked. "The thought of losing you … of everything changing …"

Her mouth dropped as she emitted an almost silent *oh*. She shook her head and looked down the hill. "Oh." Her voice was just above a whisper. "It is the sign."

"What?"

"It's because of the house being up for sale." She stepped back from him, her eyes snapping in the night cold. "I don't need your pity, Samuel Brennan. Haven't I put up with enough from you?" She turned around and faced the valley, and he wanted to stick a knife in his chest and twist it as he saw her sag into sadness.

"That's not it."

"You never knew I was alive. You didn't even ask me to the prom. Was Betsy Windsor everything you wanted? Apparently, I wasn't, not even when I tried to get you to notice! Did you? No!" Her hands went to her hips.

He leaned away from her, closer to the post.

She twisted back at him. "My mother spent hours working on that dress and you had the gall to throw your jacket over me and tell me I wasn't dressed? In front of the whole school?" Furious tears sprang into her eyes. "I was beautiful that night."

"You don't need sequence to sparkle. You're beautiful every night, MyKate."

She gasped. Tears finally fell over her eyelids. She quickly wiped them away. "I needed you." Her voice broke. "You didn't need me."

He hated the hurt in her voice. "I was a jerk."

"You said it!" She crossed her arms and turned around again.

"You never told me," Sam said. "Maybe if you'd told me you were jealous ..."

"Jealous? Of Betsy Windsor!"

He looked down and began pounding his foot on the ragged ground around the post. He took a deep breath in and held it, knowing what he had to do.

"They told me ... I call out your name." Sam tried to look at her, but the shame was overwhelming, and he knew Kathleen. He knew he'd have to take it down to the most humiliating act he could find to make the confession work. And this was it. "The cheerleaders, some after the sex, some during the sex. A few got up and walked out."

She looked back at him incredulously. "What do you mean?"

He cleared his throat. "When I was, you know ... having sex with them, well ... I was thinking of ..."

She turned back to him and gaped. "Me?"

He nodded slowly, fearing he'd said far too much but knowing it had to be said.

"Get off it. You're lying."

He shook his head. "No."

Kathleen choked back a laugh. "I don't blame them for walking out." She shook her head, standing there, feet firmly on the ground, hands on her hips, as if she was the conqueror of a new world. The giggle became a laugh. "You were thinking of me?"

Sam looked at her, laughing, then his eyes closed in pain for a moment. He deserved it, but she didn't have to enjoy it so much.

"Oh, Sam." She wiped her tears away. "Let's go to the stable. Come on," she said, pulling him on. "Stop looking at me like that." Kathleen touched his face. "Do you trust me?"

"You know I do."

"Then trust me now, Sam." She pulled his hands to her lips.

"You believe me?" It was too easy. Maybe she was going to hurt him.

Kathleen ran her arm around his waist and pulled herself to him. "Do I believe you love me? You've always loved me. Do I believe you're in love with me?"

Terror! Stark white terror was all Sam could feel. "MyKate, I—"

She put her finger on his lips. "It doesn't matter, Sam. None of that matters to me. They're just words."

"You have to believe me. You've always believed. Hell, I don't know how else to—"

"This isn't about you anymore, Becket." She shoved him away. "You threw the torch to me. It's mine to carry for a while, so shut up and let's go. I'm getting cold."

Sam had no idea what had happened, how it had gone so quickly from anger to sadness to acceptance. But he was not about to argue with her. He let her drag her through the night to the stable.

* * *

When Sam flicked the switch, the light washed the stable in a welcoming glow. Kathleen took a deep breath of hay and horses. She was shivering, but she didn't know whether it was the cold or Sam. His kiss still lingered on her lips, a tender ache, one she'd dreamed of forever, but one that had come so suddenly. She knew they had to talk, but she wasn't so sure that's what she wanted to do. It was more than she'd planned on and everything she'd wanted, but she wasn't prepared. Her mother had always said, if you grab the bull by the horns, you'd better have a good recipe for pot roast.

"I think we woke them up." She dropped Sam's hand and walked over to Kahlall, waiting for him to close the door. Then she pressed her index finger to her lips. Her heart leaped at the look on his face. Sam looked more set to stampede than cattle in a lightning storm. "We'll have to be quiet." She once again grabbed his hand and pulled him toward the back, headed for the tack room, for the bales of sweet hay and scent of soft leather. A barn cat, calico orange and black, ran across the path in front of them, sprawling over and around another, a jet-black male. They tussled and grabbed the other's necks, their back legs pushing and fighting, tumbling, but Kathleen knew it was play. Then the male turned, bared his teeth and a low, hissing growl came from its throat. The game was over.

Sam stumbled on his own feet. "Maybe we should go back to the house, MyKate."

"Not a chance, Sam." She laughed and pulled him on, headed now for the tack room. Kathleen didn't know what had changed or why, but she wasn't about to let this slip through her fingers. His hand felt strong but hesitant as she led him across the barn.

"Hey, Charger." She wrapped her arms around the stallion's neck. "Oh, you are so beautiful." Her voice wasn't loud when she called over to Kahlall and the others, and the horses' curious heads lifted and followed her as she pulled him into the tack room. Kathleen went straight over to the dusty shelf that held a first aid box, a fire extinguisher, and worn barn blankets and towels. She knew these blankets almost as well as she knew her own on her bed. She and the boys had built so many blanket forts in the old stable—back wall, roof, front door, blanket by blanket, building a home strong and safe enough away from the Beast—that she nearly knew the blankets by name. She picked up a grassy green tartan and laid it on the square bales so that they could sit and watch the horses. She glanced over at him as he stared wide-eyed at her. She smoothed out the wrinkles. "Come on. We have to talk." She pulled her jacket off and took another blanket, this time a faded blue thermal, the color of the morning sky. "Come on. Take your coat off." She held up the blanket.

He did as she ordered and then sitting, leaned back against the wall. He fidgeted, all the while watching Kathleen. She took his hand as she hopped down next to him and pulled the blanket over them both.

"You have so much to be thankful for, Sam. Those calves are the beginning for you and Casey."

"For us, MyKate."

It had to be the static from the blankets, she thought, the reason every hair on her arms was standing up.

He groaned a little. "You're part of this too." He stared at her hand, studying it like a piece of fine china. "There's nothing to it, your hand. Just like Gran's." She savored his touch as he kneaded it, feeling the bones and the knuckles as if it were a suede glove. "How can something so fragile be so strong, all those drawings you do, handle horses the way you can? I always wondered."

She placed her other hand on his face. "Why now?" Her eyes searched his, needing to know what was real.

"Promise me," he said suddenly, fear in his eyes. "Promise me you'll be my friend always, that you'll always love me."

She looked at his sad eyes and suddenly her heart quivered. There was something else, something darker. "You know I love you. No matter what happens, that won't change."

"Not just as a friend. That's not enough anymore." He brought her hand up to his lips and kissed it, and she felt the charge zing through her from top to bottom. "Nothing ever goes right. It's worked for so long, us being friends, but—"

"Is that what this is all about? You're scared that I won't be your friend anymore." She touched his cheek. "Was I your friend last Christmas and the Christmas before? I was your friend after the prom. I loved you then." She shuddered. "What do you want, Sam?"

"You. I can't lose you." Sam moved her hair behind her ear, studying it as if he'd never seen it before. "I can't do it without you, MyKate. I can't ever see my life without you, right next to me."

She trembled at the tenderness in his touch, his words, and his haunted eyes. Everything she'd ever wanted was right there for her to grab, and still she hesitated. "Is it because of the house, because if it is—"

"Would you stop with the house? I knew you'd think that, but that had nothing to do with it."

She remembered his reaction when he first came back. "You did hug me a rather long time when you arrived at the Hole."

"I've never loved any one of those girls, MyKate. I didn't know why. I thought that's how it was supposed to be, you know, like guy stuff. I was just lonely and they were sort of—there. All the while, there you were, right in front of me, and I didn't see it. I ached for you when I was away. Not at the beginning. I was so blind." He scuffed his boot into the crystallized earth and then looked up at her. She pushed the fork in the road out of her head once more. He had never lied to her, and she hadn't waited all those years to turn him away. She'd deal with whether he loved her in the morning. She placed her hand on his cheek. "When?"

He was staring at her as if he didn't believe her. "It changed at the prom, when you looked so beautiful. I kind of woke up. For two years, you've been everywhere, in everything, every place I looked."

"Get to the answer. It's important." *Please, please,* she thought. *Persuade me it's not because of the house.*

"Then you fell off Charger." He stopped as if that would do.

"So I fell off your damned horse." Kathleen poked him.

He nodded. "I couldn't breathe when I saw you all crumpled up. I knew instantly. First, I told myself you didn't feel the same way. Then I figured I'd mess everything up. Then I'd feel sorry for—"

"For the love of God, Sam, will you shut up and kiss me?"

Again, he stopped. "Really?"

She nodded, wiping beads of perspiration from his forehead, and watched his eyes move from hers to her lips. His hand came up, and he touched her cheek and then drew her to him.

"I don't know how."

She didn't mean to laugh out loud. "You're the expert. All those girls can't be wrong."

He rolled his eyes. "It's different with you. I always wanted this to be special."

She played with one of his curls, twisting it, letting it spring back. "Yesterday, when I was walking here, I saw this porcupine." She grinned as his eyes grew confused. "He was huge, bigger than a breadbox." She ran her hand through the hair above his ear. "He was all by himself, but he was moving, headed for the fence line and I thought, *He's going home. He's on his way to the missus* … and then it hit me." She grinned as he looked at her, skeptically now. "How do porcupines make love? I mean, with all those quills, how do they find each other, love each other, and not hurt each other doing it?"

"Porcupines." He grinned. "Do they mate for life?"

She scowled at him. "That's not the point. The point is they manage, despite all the odds and problems. There's a never-ending number of porcupines around each year."

He didn't say a word, but a slow smile spread over his face. He bent his head and kissed her. His lips were tentative as he pressed closer. He was shaking in her arms and running his fingers through her hair. She didn't want the kiss to end. His scent was warm and musky, filling her up, seeping into her skin. She took his hand and placed it on her breast. With his touch, pleasure seared through her, and Kathleen knew that all those years of waiting were over.

* * *

Sam held Kathleen, afraid that, should he let go, she'd disappear.

"You got the name right this time." She rolled over on top of him, her hair hanging down around his face.

He grinned sheepishly at her gall and then grew somber. "Why didn't you tell me, MyKate?"

She ran her hand up over his chest, letting it stop at his nipple.

"You never ... you're a ..." He grabbed at her hand, amazed at how quickly he'd become aroused again.

"A virgin?" She giggled. "I was."

"Dammit, MyKate. You should tell a guy that. I could have, you know, been—"

"Shut up, Sam." She pulled her leg up and over him. "I waited a long time for tonight. It was glorious pain."

"I just never ... I mean ... you went out with guys. Hell! You went to the prom with Casey. I just figured—"

She bolted up. "You figured what? Samuel Brennan! Did Casey ever say once that we—"

"No." He pulled her down to him. "No! I thought he was just being noble. You know Casey."

She shrugged a bit and grinned. "No. He probably wouldn't, but I sure as hell would have told you!"

Happiness washed over him like river waves. "All that time." He paused letting the thought settle. "You were waiting."

"Don't flatter yourself. I didn't have the time or the inclination. I mean, take a look at what's around here. Not a lot of porcupines to choose from."

Sam's head cocked a little. "Gee. Thanks. Do you believe me?" he said.

"That you love me? That you've always loved me? That you always will or that you call out my name when in the throes of passion with other women?"

"That will never happen again, MyKate. I promise."

"Those other women were just practice?"

"Just practice." He knew he had to make plans, get it all right. "Lookit, MyKate. I only have weeks to go." He pulled her close to him and tried to reach over for his jacket without letting her know. Her arms encircled him, stopping any attempt at moving away from her.

"Not a problem," she said.

He loved that she was laughing, happy, wanting him.

"We have forever, Sam." She pulled herself away and sat up. Grabbing her blouse, she began slipping back into her clothing. "That's all I ever wanted. Forever. I dreamed about forever, with you. Dating, engagement, white wedding in the front field with a tent on a sunny July day. Normal stuff."

Sam looked over at his jacket and then back up into her eyes. "Dating?"

"Yup."

"Before the engagement? It's not like we have to get to know each other."

She peered down at him as if he just didn't get it. "We can't date?"

"Ah … like this?"

She grinned. "Just like this. You said yourself that we only have a few weeks to go." She threw herself down on top of him. "I waited a long time, Samuel Brennan. I want to enjoy this."

"Say it," she murmured, her eyes shining brighter than any moon he'd ever seen.

He'd never thought Kathleen's voice could be smoky with lust. "What?"

"My name. Right now, right here, say it to me again."

He began to laugh, and she shuddered as he whispered in her ear, time and time again, getting louder, and soon the horses were whinnying and looking for sugar cubes. It was time to go back.

CHAPTER 19

Missy knew she couldn't stay long as she jiggled the copy of his key in Sam's lock. It had been so easy. She'd grabbed his key that one morning she'd woken up in his bed. She'd slipped it away. She knew he'd be there all day. She'd made the copy and slipped his back into his jacket when she visited him later that afternoon, pleading with him to maybe go out with her again or rethink their relationship. He had never even missed the key—or her.

She glanced up and down the hallway. It wouldn't do if she were seen. Someone might know Sam was away for the weekend. She should not have waited until Sam was away; she should have searched his room, maybe when he was in a class. But she'd only just made sense of the charts she'd copied from Lester. The ceaseless pounding music of Iron Maiden from down the hall covered the squeaking of the door as she opened it. She closed the door behind her. Missy skirted directly over to the window and pulled the blind down, her eyes scanning, searching, like a cat on the nightly hunt. Stumbling into the side of his bed, she cursed then crossed to Sam's desk. Fumbling around, knocking her hand on the shade, she turned on the small lamp that sat on a stack of rather tattered old textbooks.

She searched the desktop, starting with the papers next to his calculus book. Carefully but deliberately, she pieced through the papers, making sure nothing was left out of place, nothing to alert Sam that she'd been there. One by one, she shoved them back into place, and then she yanked open the pen drawer. Where was the key to the filing cabinet? She picked up the photo of Casey and MyKate that sat on his desk.

She slowly scratched her finger over MyKate's face and then put the photo gently back.

Find the key.

Erasers, pencils, two calculators, and pages of tables, she saw nothing of interest. She jammed the drawer back in and sat back. I wonder. Leaning over, she pulled and opened the file drawer. Of course. He wouldn't lock it. A satisfied smile appeared as she pulled out his chair and sat down facing the drawer. One by one, she pulled the tan folders from Sam's desk. These were highly organized, marked clearly as business files, farm files, files Sam had been sorting out, going through, and bringing up to date according to the newest accounting standards he'd been studying so diligently. Missy's fingers worked through them quickly, discarding those that were nothing more than bills, lingering on the papers he'd turned in over the last few years. She shook her head as she placed the stack down in front of her. Poor Sam. He really had kept everything for his brother as he'd told her he was doing. *Poor Casey, not being allowed to go to school. Weird family*, she thought.

Sam had labeled his folders by class. Her forehead wrinkled up in interest as she pulled out a file marked "Mineral Rights, the Landowner, and the Government." There was a bright A-minus printed on the cover of his paper. *Not bad for a class he hated.* She opened it. One after the other, she read and reread the pages. She picked up the final page and studied it.

"Damn!"

It was everything she hadn't been able to get out of Lester.

Scratching her head, she ran her finger down the page, she stopped at the description of a closed down mine—the quarry, of course—and a breakdown of their mining rights.

The principal resources were sand, gravel, and crushed stone—aggregate. Granite and slate, irregular, rough fieldstone used for landscaping projects. Gemstones. That was a pleasant surprise. Tourmaline. Of course. That made sense, it being the state stone. *Useless*, she thought. She read on—amethyst, quartz, garnet. *Not bad*, she thought. But where were the diamonds? It didn't mention the gold.

Missy sniffed. "Diamonds are a girl's best friend," she sang quietly.

The records said the quarry site was a source of fluorescent mineral specimens.

Where was the gold? She reread the pages and then put her hand over her mouth. The report was missing a valuable piece of information. She ran her fingers through her hair as she looked up from the page and then leaned back in the chair, smiling in satisfaction. Sam's scribble in pencil on the side of the page stared up at her. "Mined out, closed. Good for pasture only. All mineral rights—privately owned," it read.

Sam didn't know about the gold. Lester sure enough did. Sam should have figured it out by the other minerals in the quarry, but then he never was good with "rock class," as he called it. *Rocks are what you pull out of the fields.* Missy leaned over the desk. "You're such an idiot, Sam."

Closing up the folder, she stared straight at nothing in particular, completely focused, knowing what she was going to do with the information. Placing it neatly back into the folder, she returned it to the drawer and closed it away. Now. Her next move.

Placing her hand over her lower belly, she patted it and smiled. There's always a way to get what one needs, and Sam is such a good man. "I think I can. I think I can," she sang. Standing, she turned off the light, walked over to the door, and quietly left.

CHAPTER 20

Casey had never known a morning so much like spring. Spring had never mattered to him. It was just another season, tilling time, seeding time, calving time. But the sun was the warmest it had been that year, the air smelled new and earthy fresh, the frozen ground was melting with each step he'd taken, and not even his mother's insistence on a sit-down breakfast had dampened his spirits. Her blueberry waffles hadn't been half-bad, and she hadn't bothered him, having Sam there at the table to keep her busy. He threw open the top half of the double Dutch doors in the front of the stable to let in the freshness. They were going to move most of the horses out the back to the paddock for a bit of a sunshine, and the horses seemed to know it.

"Which horse, do you think?" Casey asked Sam as Bob grabbed a small cube of sugar from the flat of his hand, the horse's large, fleshy lips playing around his palm for more.

Sam grinned without looking up as he worked the surface of the saddle with a chamois. "For Sadie?"

"No." Casey snorted. "For the Beast." He moved over to the gray gelding in the stall next to Bob with the plaque that read "Silver Cloud." "Of course for Sadie."

Sam reached around the saddle, lifted it back on the side of the rail, and grabbed the straps. "How well does she ride?"

"Her mother rode all the time." Casey ran his hand down the gray's neck. "Sadie said she had lessons, so I'd say she knows the basics." Cloud nodded his head in anticipation, his ears up and alert. "Brydie or Cloud?"

"Take off." Sam looked over at him as if insulted. "Brydie's not a ride, she's a walk. Gran rides Brydie. Tell you what." Sam walked over and slapped Casey on the back. "I'll let her have Charger." He grinned, his eyes teasing. "She'll be right back in the saddle again."

"No way." Casey grunted and looked down, thinking about the last time Sam had let someone else ride Charger and how many days Kathleen needed to recover. And Kathleen could ride.

"Okay, Cloud." Casey began moving his hand down the gelding's flank. Cloud wasn't one of the top-three quarter horses in looks, but he had a grace, a strong, heavy strength. "Looks like you're going for a jaunt." He reached for the brush and began working the horse.

They both turned as the doors opened and the ladies stepped in, dressed for riding. Kathleen was in her regular garb, black jeans, black boots, black jacket, and black helmet. Sadie was in jeans and soft colors, but her boots were riding boots, and she was wearing gloves. Casey felt his heart jump.

"Oh, Cloud! Don't you look pretty!" Kathleen walked right past Sam and straight over to the gelding. "What a pretty boy. He's such a nice ride, Sadie. I told you it would be Cloud." She grinned at Casey and then looked up into Sam's eyes. Sam wrapped his arm around her waist.

Casey wasn't paying attention, his focus on Sadie.

"Hi," she said.

He felt the heat rise in his face once more, hating it. "Hi."

"He is pretty. Does he cut?" Sadie asked as she rubbed Cloud's neck, and he huffed and snorted, excited by the attention. Sadie let the horse smell her while Cloud rubbed against her and nudged her.

"Like a rodeo horse. Do you cut?" Casey grabbed the blanket and placed it on Cloud's back.

"Won first prize at the Athens fair, grade ten."

Casey's eyes widened. Holy cow! She could cut cattle. "No kidding?"

"I'm not as good at roping, but I don't do too badly at the barrel racing," Sadie said.

Kathleen laughed in delight. "Well, we'll find out." She pulled Cloud's western saddle from the rail and slung it over to Sadie. "Let's get this show on the road."

CHAPTER 21

Casey watched Kathleen throw a stone into the quarry and listened for it to hit the water below. The rocks on which they sat were warm in the sun and, although hard, much more enjoyable than the damp ground. The lunch had been amazing. The women had made chicken salad, and Casey didn't mind the black olives and red grapes tossed into it. Who knew olives could taste good anywhere? Even the egg salad Kathleen had brought along was tasty, not at all bland.

The silver of the willow against the forest green of pine and maple, the splatter of crocus yellow over the fields below, plus the woman beside him made Casey want to stay longer.

He smiled a little as he realized Kathleen hadn't brought her sketchbook along. She'd have no place to put it, what with Sam's head on her lap. It was unnerving at times, when Casey caught a glimpse of Sam's hand on Kathleen's breast. Sure, he'd yanked it away as if embarrassed but not quickly enough.

Casey had been surprised when he saw no sign of the ring on Kathleen's finger, but he wasn't going to say anything, lest he say the wrong thing. Kathleen was happy at last, and that was what mattered.

Yup, Casey thought. Life at the farm was definitely looking up.

"Did you go to your university graduation, Doc?" Sam asked as he tilted his head over to Sadie.

Sadie pulled up a blade of grass that was defining life by growing up through a crevice in the stone. "I don't think I would have bothered, but my mother wanted to see me graduate."

Kathleen glanced over, obviously concerned by the sadness in Sadie's voice. "She was sick then?"

Sadie nodded, staring down at the blade.

Kathleen ran her fingers through Sam's hair. He emitted a tiny groan of pleasure, but she put her hand down and shook her head. "My mother always wanted me to be an independent woman and whoosh!" Her hand sailed off in a sliding salute to the horizon. "Then after four years of art classes and competitions, she tells me to give up art and take business." She picked up a pebble from beside her, studied it like a prize, and then pulled out an elastic band from her pocket.

"How can I give up my art? It's who I am. Kathleen Egan." She placed the stone in the elastic band and let it fly out over the water.

Sam closed his eyes. "She knows you're part of the Brennan farm. You have the brains to run this place better than any of us."

Kathleen pulled her hand away. "Pardon me?"

"Your mother is a sensible woman." He smiled up innocently.

Her eyes grew wide. "My mother gave up a career in dancing because she fell in love with my father. If anyone should know how I feel, she should."

Sam opened a concerned eye and squinted up at her. "All I mean is—"

"That my mother wants me to give up everything to do your bookkeeping? Make it good or I'll slug ya," she teased.

"Now that's not what I said." He looked away. "Casey—"

Kathleen's eyes shot over to him. "Stay out of this, Casey."

Casey snorted. "Hey. I'm not stupid."

"I know why," Sadie interjected before Kathleen could slug Sam. "Mrs. Egan regrets having given up her career but not being a mother. She doesn't regret any of her family, but she wants to see Kathleen self-reliant. If the art allows Kathleen to be comfortable and happy, then her mother will be happy. Being an artist makes it a lot harder. You have to know that."

Yup, Casey thought. Dr. Sadie Parker was everything he'd ever wanted, and for a reason he didn't get, she wanted him too. She was a natural on a horse. Just the thought of how she'd look cutting calves, her golden hair flying around her as she rode Cloud, dodging and darting back and forth, happy to let the horse do the work, ready to take over and guide when necessary. Maybe it was her ability to sit back and see things objectively. That was a quality that he, Sam, and Kathleen lacked. Casey grinned as he leaned against a large quarry stone. "You should have been a psychologist."

Sadie wrapped her arms around her legs and raised her face to catch the sun. "No way. Can't deal with the secrets."

"We ain't got no secrets!" Kathleen said, kidding.

"Everyone has them." Sadie stared out over the quarry, and Casey got a sudden knot in his throat watching her. She had secrets too, and he knew she wasn't ready to share hers with them.

Sam rolled his head off Kathleen's lap, and he picked a dogged dandelion that had sprung up early, despite the ice, in the sunny crevice of the rock. He rolled the stem between his fingers.

"Did Casey tell you what we did up there, Doc?" Sam said, pointing the flower up the sheer face of the rock quarry wall, some fifty feet straight up, to where it met the top of the forested hill. Fifty feet below, the water reflected the sky back to them.

"You must have seen the rifle on the wall in Billy's trailer?" Sam said.

Sadie shook her head. "I guess there was just too much going on. You guys hunters?"

Casey nodded. "Your Dad hunt?"

"He did years ago. Prefers to watch hockey these days."

Sam nodded. "I do a little target shooting too. Pistol."

"We both have, since we were able to lift a weapon," Casey said. "Billy trained us. Trained Kathleen too."

"That was a long time ago," Kathleen said. "When I think of what we did back then, I shudder."

"We came up here for target practice." He straightened up and pointed over to the right. "You see that big old maple over there?"

The desperate fingers of the maple roots clung to the very edge of the sheer drop off.

"I would climb out and wrap a clothesline around it. We'd slide a dummy down the rope, and then I'd climb back over to the other side and tie the rope to that gnarly pine up there."

Casey watched Sadie look over to the pine, this tree leaning precariously over the precipice.

"We ran a new rope every year, sometimes two or three a summer." Sam said.

Sadie shook her head, her eyes revealing her alarm. "My God! You could have fallen. How old were you?"

Sam hesitated. "He was nine. I was seven when we started." His voice faltered, and then he nodded slightly. "While I ran the rope, Casey loaded the guns. Kathleen was lookout," he said.

Sadie shuddered, looking a bit concerned at Casey.

"Yup." Sam laughed and grabbed the grass from Kathleen's hand. "Casey used the shotgun and I used an old pistol Billy kept in the back of his truck." He snorted. Sam looked up at the trees and pointed. "Kathleen used to stand between us and call it—you know, ready, aim, fire. Then we'd shoot the shit out of the bag."

"Hey! I got to shoot sometimes!" Kathleen mocked outrage. "I never missed."

"My God!" Sadie stared, shocked. "Nobody knew you were up here?"

"Probably figured the neighbors were shooting groundhogs."

"Didn't anyone hear you?"

"There's no secrets like our secrets." Sam took Kathleen's hand and pulled her to her feet.

Casey felt Sadie shudder. Who wouldn't be shocked? Looking back at it, he wondered why they hadn't fallen or even shot each other instead of the effigy. They'd been very lucky, and all the while, they thought it was perfectly all right, normal, that everyone did it. Even though they made sure not to tell anyone who might stop them—Kathleen's brothers or Billy. They'd kept it well hidden.

"That was a long time ago," Casey said, having to stop it. "The horses are getting restless." He saw tears in Sadie's eyes, and her tears shouldn't be wasted on them. "Come on. I'll give you a hands-up."

She blinked and looked back at him as if trying to swallow bad medicine.

Kathleen put the elastic band back into her pocket. Taking her reins in hand, she put her foot in the stirrup and jumped into her saddle. "Frig! Look at those clouds! Don't I wish I could capture those?"

Casey helped Sadie up into her saddle. "That's the thing about clouds. You never run out of them. There's always more on the horizon."

CHAPTER 22

The bus ride back to school on Sunday was harder than Sam had expected. It was the late bus, it was crowded, and he dreaded his hard bed. *Early night*, he thought. He was going to be ready for that exam. He was going to nail it and each one he had to take, and then he was going back home.

Saying good-bye to MyKate had been harder than ever. Her tears broke his heart.

"Three weeks," she kept saying as if she needed to believe it.

"Three weeks," he'd replied, trying to kiss her tears away. As the bus pulled away, he felt he was in an old movie of soldiers going off to war, waving to their darlings, not knowing they'd never come home again.

The trip seemed to last forever, a blur of highway signs and car lights. He felt every bump in the road. It all seemed worse, as he still hadn't given Kathleen her ring. He could have given it to her any number of times, but they'd get sidetracked, plus they never had any time alone. He wanted it to be special. He wanted to take her out for a romantic dinner and ask her there, or go for a ride, just the two of them, back to the quarry. He'd bring champagne and strawberries, and he'd ask her there. He wanted her to feel spoiled. And if he was being honest, he wanted to be there with her to enjoy their engagement.

His bones ached by the time he got off the bus, and a sense of foreboding crept over him as he walked across the campus in the dark. *Exams*, he thought over and over. *Get them done and go home.*

The hallway was unusually quiet. There was no heavy bass pounding from the room farther down. He pulled out his key and then froze. There was light shining under his door. Someone was in his room. He opened the door. Finding Missy there made his stomach turn.

Just what he needed. He wondered if he should go find a motel room.

Missy was wearing silk pajamas, not too risqué but soft and seductive. She had lit a few candles; the air was thick with waxy fragrance. He picked up the scent of rose. It smelled more like rotten rose petals. She was juggling her balls, but then she got up from the bed and moved over to him.

"Hello, darlin'," she sang.

He rolled his bag off his shoulder and looked at his watch.

"Oh, Sammy. Don't be angry." She closed the door behind him and stepped back.

"How did you get in Missy?" He moved past her into the dorm room and over to his desk.

She held out a key. "I came to give it back to you."

"Back to me. I don't remember giving one to you."

Her smile changed into a sad pout. He took the key from her.

"Thanks." He stared at her clothes. "You going to a pajama party?"

She sat down on his bed. "Sammy, we need to talk," she warbled.

Sam looked at his watch again. "No, Missy. I have calculus in less than seven hours. I don't mean to be rude but—"

"We have to talk. Now!" She ran her hand down his arm as she tried to pull him to her.

He turned away and shrugged off his jacket. She took it from him. "No, we don't. It can wait."

She sniffed his jacket. "This stinks." She dropped the jacket and looked back at him. "I tried calling you."

"My mother doesn't answer the phone."

"Seems no one does."

He picked up his jacket from the floor and threw it on his chair. "How did you get my home phone number?" He picked up his bag and began removing its contents—book, book, briefs, jeans, toothbrush, photo of Kathleen. She was staring at the photo as he propped it up next to the previous one. She walked over to the bed and sat down.

"Lookit, Missy"—he turned and finally faced her—"we agreed."

"I'm pregnant."

He staggered as if he'd been struck. She didn't sing it. Maybe there's song for I'm pregnant.

The room became a vacuum. "What?"

She nodded. "I was hoping to drop this on you in a better way, but …"

Sam stared over at Kathleen's picture on his desk.

"I have calculus first thing tomorrow morning." He looked at his watch yet again and laughed, a little too high and sharp. "Seven hours from now."

"What about us, Sammy? What about the baby?"

"I have to sleep," he said.

"I don't know what I'll do, Sammy. I can't bring a love child into this world." She, of course, sang the "love child." She tried tears and a little quiver in her voice. "Maybe an abortion."

She reached for him, but he moved away, revulsion growing like bile in him. Rising from the bed, he grabbed his calculus book. She watched him put on his jacket again and then stop and pick up Kathleen's photo. He said nothing as he walked out and left her in his room.

CHAPTER 23

Casey watched the three weeks move along faster than geese toward summer lakes. The barnyard was melting, and although all the other cattle were out on the sacrifice field—the one designated field that could be torn up by heavy hooves and left alone for pasture, not cropping—Libby and the babes were not. He knew that the first days of spring were the worst for cattle, the mud able to do more damage and spread disease faster than any other time. Casey had put Libby and her calves in a special wood shavings–covered paddock with a concrete pad underfoot, free from all the muck and damp. It was the same for the horses. No muddy paddock for them.

Life at the farm had returned to normal, but Billy had shown up with two more Limousin heifers, two more beauties, and Casey was leaning against the paddock rail, enjoying the morning air and studying them as they munched on corn.

He pointed. "That one on the left, she's a Lydia. And Lulu. Yup. I like those names," he said to his uncle as Billy walked over to him. "They're almost as pretty as Libby."

Billy scuffed his boot under the bottom rail. "Got them for meat prices."

"Right," said Casey. "You'll have to introduce me to some of those friends of yours." He laughed at the innocent expression his uncle was trying to pull off. "I've got to go to the Hole, drop in on Kathleen. Sadie and I thought we'd take her to a movie tonight."

Billy's head went up. "Perfect. Wait for me. I have business in town. I'll only be five minutes."

"Right." Casey watched Billy head back to the trailer, wondering what was up with his uncle. Casey had caught Billy three times during the last two weeks in the kitchen of the house, talking to Gran. Granted, each time his mother had been nowhere near the place, off at one of her garden center sales, but Casey wondered why the conversation had always come to a grinding halt when he appeared. Another mystery. Casey checked his back pocket to see if he had his wallet and started over to the truck.

Billy took a while. Having changed out of his coveralls, removed his stinky boots, and put on his best shirt, he was walking back outside with a briefcase in his hand. Casey stared at him through the rearview mirror, wondering if someone had died. Billy hadn't looked that good since he went to the funeral of Bad-Luck Brian. Billy wasn't a good friend of the guy, but you have to feel sorry for someone who gets run over by his own tractor five times.

Casey blinked, trying to clear his eyes. A briefcase? He didn't know Billy owned a briefcase. But there he was, next to Casey, official-looking briefcase on the floor between his legs. They bumped over the newest ruts and gullies that the winter had gouged out of the roadway. Something was definitely up with Billy. Weird. Out of place. Then the movement on Kathleen's front lawn caught his eye.

"Ah, no!" Casey plowed the brake pedal into the floor of the pickup as the truck slid on the mud, stopping a bare three inches from the Egan's mailbox. "Is that Schmiester?" He stared at the woman who was hammering away on the sign in Kathleen's front yard. "What the hell?"

"Take it easy, Casey."

"Shit! It's sold!" Casey stared through the windscreen at the new sign. His hands locked around the steering wheel, knuckles white. "Christ!"

"Now relax, son."

"Sold! Not sale pending! Sold. Does Kate know?"

Billy pinched the bridge of his nose. "Why don't we go and find out?"

"Ugly old bat," Casey said, staring at Schmiester as he pressed the gas pedal and headed down the road. Trying to erase Leena Schmiester's nosy wave from his head, he focused on Kathleen. What if she didn't know yet? She'd been at the barn the day before and hadn't said anything about it, hadn't acted as if anything was wrong. No. Casey knew she hadn't known the day before. She'd been at work all morning. She might not know at all. He knew he'd have to calm down or he'd make it worse. He also knew he'd have to come up with a plan. He hadn't heard from Sam—nothing—in three weeks, and that was ticking him off, but even that didn't matter right then. He'd have to be there for Kathleen with ideas, answers.

For miles, he tried. The drive seemed endless and then, when the Hole came into view, Casey realized he wasn't ready. He didn't have a plan, and his hands felt slick on the wheel.

"We'll have to move some grain to the stable soon … running low," Billy said, picking up the briefcase.

"Yeah. Right." Casey stared over at Billy, his mind on more important things. "Where do you want to be left off?"

"I want a doughnut."

Casey shot another glance at his uncle. "You don't eat doughnuts."

"Sometimes I feel like a doughnut. Besides, Kathleen might be upset. We have to talk to her."

Thank God, thought Casey. He could use the help.

Billy was out of the truck before it had come to a full stop, and Casey felt his shoulders relax. Billy was going to take care of it. The thought of someone else living in Kathleen's house was more repugnant than thoughts of his mother. Casey switched off the engine and got out of the truck. He braced himself as he opened the door of the Donut Hole and the smell of baked goods and coffee, usually a welcoming aroma, made his stomach lurch.

* * *

Kathleen spotted them immediately. "Get a booth. I'll take a break." She looked over her shoulder at the new girl. "Natalie, can you handle it?"

"Sure, Kathleen!" the curvy redhead said, stuffing a dozen doughnuts into a box.

Kathleen poured some coffee and grimaced. "If you need me just holler." Collecting the mugs and doughnuts, Kathleen pushed her way over to the men. "Wanda should be here in about ten minutes," she called back over her shoulder to the server. "Billy, what brings you out here? Oh …" She stood coffee in hand, her heart pounding. "Sam's home?"

Billy grinned. "Not yet. We came to see you and that smile of yours, Katie."

She sat down next to Casey. "One and a half weeks to go. I guess I can wait that long. So! What's happening?" Kathleen studied them both closely. She felt her face flush with embarrassment at the sight of Casey staring at the blank spot on the wall next to the washrooms.

"Your painting's gone." Casey raised one eyebrow and put his arm around her. "You sold it."

She batted her eyes at him. "Folks from Black Rock dropped in yesterday and decided it would look good in their dining room. Definitely into ducks."

"See! Told you. Put them on the walls and stick a For Sale tag in the frame, and they'll fly out of here." Casey grabbed her hand and squeezed.

She couldn't help but giggle. "Uncle Dick said I should bring another in. He likes his commission." She sat down, wondering what was going on. "You find a briefcase, Billy?"

Billy ignored her and looked at Casey. "You go first!"

He cleared his throat. "Sadie and I are going into town for a movie tonight, and you're coming."

"Love to," Kathleen said. "Did Sam sound strange when you were talking to him? He called me about a week ago, and he sounded, well, strange."

Casey nodded. "Just tired, I think." He looked at Billy.

Billy shrugged. "Sounded fine to me." He looked at them. "That's it? My turn, I guess." He took in a deep breath as if nervous, squared his shoulders, and placed the briefcase on the table with a thump. Pressing the buttons with both thumbs, he opened the ebony case.

"Casey's gran seems to feel that we're in need of more property," Billy said.

Casey was staring at his uncle with the same kind of bemused expression Kathleen was trying to hide. So. Gran was getting into real estate? Kathleen waited for the punch line.

"She's always had her eyes on the McGregor's lot," Casey said, one eyebrow rising as he tried to look inside the case. "Don't know where else we can expand."

Billy shifted a bit in his seat. "I don't want you to get all excited like you do Kathleen."

She stared at him, suddenly concerned. Why should she be excited? This had nothing to do with her.

"I haven't told Casey or Sam yet, but their Gran and me, we talked it over. We've always wanted that parcel. The orchard and all. Gran and Thomas used to sneak off to it to … well … it belonged to the Brennan's anyway, lost it years ago and when we found out it was for sale, well …"

Kathleen's felt her mouth drop. Casey stared, eyes wide, a small smile beginning to form on his face.

"I've been talking to your parents, and we sort of reached an agreement, no thanks to that Schmiester woman," Billy grumbled. "We'll still get dinged with the realty fee."

"You bought it?" Casey's voice cracked.

Billy smiled at their surprise. "On condition."

"What?" Casey and Kathleen said in unison.

"On condition Kathleen uses it as a studio."

"Pardon me?" Kathleen sort of swayed, and Casey wrapped his arm around her.

"You get the house as your studio and go for art classes. You keep up the property at the same time, and we get the orchard and a few of the paintings of our herd. I got here the pamphlets and such about the courses …" He looked down and pulled out various leaflets and application forms. "And I have copies of the agreement with your folks … it's not a studio in Boston"—he stared over at her—"but it's a start."

Kathleen felt her world begin a slow spin. "No. Billy! What are you doing?"

"We're not doing this outta the kindness of our hearts. Your folks struck a mean deal, but Casey's Gran has always wanted that parcel back."

"Billy." She felt giddy as the room swam around her.

Billy took a deep breath and grinned wider than she could remember. "Lookit! There's no sense arguing. It's a done deal. Besides, if Mum and I hadn't done it, Sam would've. He came to me about a loan." Billy grinned. "Can't wait to see the look on his face when he finds he's been outbid."

Casey turned to Kathleen and grabbed her hand. "If Sam was right there, he'd be telling you to stop denying and start enjoying it."

"I have to talk to Mum and Dad," Kathleen said a bit bewildered, not daring to believe him.

"Good. Get your things, and we'll drive you home."

She stood and wobbled a bit. "You bought my house?"

Casey moved up and over to her. "Hey, beautiful." He put his arm around her. "I saw Schmiester hammering in the Sold sign."

"And I'm really going to school?" It began to sink in. "My house?"

"Your studio," Billy said.

"Does Sam know?"

Billy grinned. "Nope."

"Maybe we'll let him throw another sign into the scrub," Casey said with a grin.

CHAPTER 24

In the sultry night, overlooking the sparkle of Rio lights, Lester Brennan jumped at the warble of his phone. Leaning over to grab it, he wondered who'd be calling this late, this line, the third little light blinking on and off. He picked up the receiver and stared out into the night.

"Yes." He said it cautiously and then slumped as he heard music, strained, plunky music. The music made his head ache as he listened to a faint guitar and recognized the familiar voice.

"A-hunting we will go," she sang. "A-hunting we will go, heigh-ho, the derry-oh ..." The guitar continued on as she spoke. "Hello, Les."

His face, always controlled, always rock hard, crumbled as he sat in the dark, staring into the horizon. How he hated it when she did the clown thing. "The farmer takes a wife ..." she sang on.

"What do you want, Missy?"

"About not coming back to work." Her voice was bitter and cold. "We left on such bad terms."

"How much, Melissa?"

There was a pause, as she began playing her guitar again. "You hurt my feelings, Les. Don't you want to know why I won't be back?" Another pause. Only the music could be heard on the line.

"Why not skip the games and tell me."

"It's not about money, Lester. You know that, darling. It never was about money. I love you." Her laugh was hostile, dangerous. "But I just got married, Dad. You're going to be a grandpa."

Les felt his world collapse in around him. "What are you talking about?"

"Sam."

His head began to spin. "What? How long?"

"Have I been pregnant, have I been married, or how long have I known him?" She stressed the word *known*, and he knew she loved every minute of it. "Since September, darling. You know when you told me to—what was the phrase you used? Oh yes, use my claws to snag a smaller bird. I took your advice. Sam just stepped out, or I'd put him on the phone. You could congratulate him yourself."

"You fucking bitch," he growled, as his eyes darted around the room as he tried to think of a way out.

"It was so easy, darling, plucked right from the nest."

"How much?" He wondered if she could hear his heart pounding. "How much?" It had to be money—money in exchange for his son.

"You know, I haven't really figured that out yet, but as soon as I do, I'll let you know." She laughed. "You have to be happy for me, darling. Happy for yourself even."

His grip on the phone tightened and he wished it were her neck. How much had she told Sam? Not much, he figured. She'd lose her edge.

"He's such a wonderful man, Les; must take after his mother. You wouldn't believe it. He bought me such a beautiful ring. Wouldn't consider an abortion and insisted he'd take care of me." Her laughter rolled over the line. "He really is a nice man."

It was as if he'd been kicked in the stomach. No. It couldn't be happening. "You won't get away with this."

"Oh, Lester. That is so cliché."

"You have no idea what you've done."

"Oh yes, I do, Les. It's checkmate." Her voice was rock-steady.

Checkmate? Far from that. His laugh started out slowly. "Missy, Missy, Missy ..."

"You're not scaring me, Grandpa."

"That's too bad, Melissa. You should be very scared."

She snickered. "Sam will never let you hurt me. He hates you." She stopped playing the guitar. "You don't want him to know all about you, do you?"

Yes. He was right. She hadn't told Sam anything yet. He had time.

"We're leaving for home tomorrow, Les. Why don't you simply wish us all the best?"

He had time to fix it. "Watch your back, Melissa."

"Like I said before, you don't—"

"Scare you?" Lester sat back, already formulating what needed to be done. No. She wouldn't do anything for a while, which gave him a bit of time. "Scare you? You haven't met the family yet, my dear." He shook his head in the dark and growled out a mean laugh. "This hornet's nest you've stepped on is way beyond your control." He hung up, but he didn't put the phone down. He phoned his brother.

Lester thought the phone would ring longer as Billy was generally off doing some odd job at that time of day. He knew he could catch him most nights between nine and eleven. The man had no life, was Lester's opinion. Lester knew that that was partly his fault.

From the time Lester had left home, Billy had suffered at least as much. His once footloose brother had given up his dreams of seeing the world, a girl in every port, and the fast life of the city, everything Billy had always talked about. Instead, Billy was doing the farming, going to the sales barns for cattle, and watching over his nephews, something Lester did not begrudge the man but instead envied. For over seventeen years, Les had gone without his boys, lived a lie, so that the Beast wouldn't keep her oath and kill Casey. All that was crumbling now, and he had to find out if it was time to let it do just that.

Lester Brennan wanted to go home. Brazil was never his home, just the city where he lived until he could find a way back. Finding a way back was trickier than leaving, and far more dangerous. He'd planned on waiting a few more years but hadn't planned on Melissa Anne King.

He had to give her credit. She was a lot sharper than he'd thought. He couldn't count the "I should have knowns" after her phone call. He should have known when a small girl from his hometown called up wanting a job. He should have known when she wiggled her bottom into his office staff, so quickly for a part-timer. He should have known when she made her pass at him and he'd so greedily surrendered. He should have known when she'd kept coming back, when she'd made him feel special, when she asked all those questions about his past life, when she'd disappeared the September before with the photo of his sons.

Les heard Billy pick up the phone and the sound of the kettle screeching in the background. Billy sounded cheerful, but then, Les knew, it was spring and the real work was about to begin.

"Thought you'd be out spreading muck," Les said, surprised by his own smile.

"Done." There was a chuckle. "Seeding the chicory now."

Les wondered how to go about it without raising suspicions or getting Billy all worked up. "So … how's business?"

There was a pause on the line, and Les grimaced. How's business? What was he thinking? Billy was laughing softly.

"Business is fine … here. How's business with you?"

That meant, Get on with it. I haven't got time to waste.

Les began again. "Do you know the Kings from up Parkland way?"

"Last I heard they were in France."

Les sank back into his chair and stared at the photo of his sons on his desk. "That's the guy. Did you ever meet him or his family?"

"Nope."

Lester paused. "Didn't they make the papers a few years back when he got the job?"

"What you after, Les?"

"Financial stats. His net worth. His daughters." Lester wanted anything he could get on the man, and he knew Billy was just the guy to get it.

"Planning on marrying the lads off to money?" Billy chuckled. "He doesn't have much in the way of good land. A bit of riverbank's all."

Les wished it were that simple. He didn't want to say too much, as Melissa could be lying.

"We might have a problem." He heard the silence from the other end of the line as Billy waited. "His daughter. She called me from Sam's phone. Sam's room."

Billy didn't say anything.

"She knows me, been working for me the last few summers. Suddenly she knows Sam."

"Could be nothing."

"Could be blackmail, Bill." It was the first time Lester had said the word aloud. It was the first time he dared think it. "I don't know what she'd capable of, but she's no innocent. She's got to know about the gold."

"He'll be home tomorrow. Don't see how she can do anything much between now and then."

"Don't underestimate her. I'm going to start a check." His voice dropped as if hiding a secret. "You know, Bill, maybe it's time we began letting things drop about the past … to the lads." He picked up the photo. "Rachel has to have softened somewhat."

He snorted. "I'll talk to Mum."

"Tell Mum I'm staying put if Rachel's as bad as she was. She could still kill Casey and get away with it." Lester placed the photo back in its spot. "Anyway, this one's name's Melissa … *A* for Anne, with an *E* … King. She has a sister, deceased. See if Sam mentions her."

Billy told him to stop worrying and have faith in his sons. So Les finished with the business and launched into the seeding plans, the fence lines, the weather, and then they both knew it was time to go. When Lester had hung up, he was feeling no better than before he called. He had to wait a little longer. Lester Brennan had waited for over fifteen years, and now he wasn't going to wait anymore.

CHAPTER 25

Casey scowled at the damp gloves he was taking from his hands. They were covered in the grime of wet and grease, reeking from backed-up pipes as he walked across the barn. He couldn't think of one redeeming thing about pipe work, or plumbing for that matter. A barn cat scurried away as if it too were disgusted by the grime. Tossing his gloves on the ledge beside the barn phone, he heard the pipes groan as Billy turned the water back on and it banged and gurgled through the lines. All was well. Sunlight streamed into the barn, and he knew it should be a good day. Should be. Could be. He reached for the phone, feeling the chill from a slight breeze blowing dust devils around the stalls. He should have felt terrific because of Kathleen's future, but Kathleen had been right. Sam had been acting weird. It was if he couldn't get him off the phone fast enough.

He's hard at work, she'd told Casey. Leave him alone. He doesn't want to be disturbed, she'd said, but Kathleen was always ready with excuses or explanations as she called them. Most times Casey was willing to give Sam the benefit of the doubt. Maybe life was too good. It was Casey's belief that if life seemed too good to be true, it wouldn't last.

He checked once more. The calendar was smudged with grease and muck, pencil and pen, but April 21 was circled bright and red. One day away, and Sam was supposed to be arriving by bus, but there had been no phone call.

Casey placed the receiver to his ear and pushed out Sam's number. As Casey ran over the jobs and appointments for the month while waiting, he noticed that the ring had an odd chirp to it, tinny, as if the connection had a kink in it somewhere. He picked up the red pen on the ledge next to the calendar and drew two stars next to the upcoming weekend. They were starting their pasture rotation and had to do some major fence work—electric fencing, state of the art—and Casey felt exhilarated every time he thought of how much grass per cow they could get with this new system, rotating the cattle from one smaller field to another. The phone warbled three times, and Casey was about to put it down.

"Hello?" The voice was female. Casey wondered if he'd called the wrong number. The voice said hello once more.

"Ah … hi. I'm looking for Sam Brennan."

"He just went out for a few minutes, but I expect him home soon."

Casey forgot all about pasture rotation. It was the way she'd said, "I expect him home soon," as if she lived there. A hole began to form in the pit of his stomach as he stared at the phone.

"Who shall I say is calling?" The voice had a lilt to it, and Casey thought of old Celtic harpists and soft, plaintive maidens.

"His brother." He almost laughed at her formal address. "His brother is calling."

"Casey! Sammy's told me all about you!"

Sammy? Casey stared at the receiver and blinked, feeling the floor begin to move under him. *Sammy? No one called him Sammy. Sam hated Sammy.*

"And you are?" Casey was more than curious.

"Well, I'm Mrs.—"

"Casey!" Sam's voice was strained, almost desperate, as he obviously grabbed the phone. Casey pushed the potential interesting story to one side. He could hear muffled noises in the background and then the slamming of a door.

"Where the hell you been?" So it sounded a little rough. Casey wanted to ask who the woman was. He didn't like the knot in his gut.

"The exams have been murder."

Casey waited for more. There was only silence. "You coming home anytime soon?"

There was a long pause from Sam's end. "Yeah. But there's a change of plans." Sam's voice dropped. Sam didn't do it deliberately, but he lowered his voice every time he wanted to talk secretly. It was a dead giveaway to Casey and Kathleen. Their ears picked it up immediately, and they zeroed in on what he was trying to hide. They'd told Sam he did it, told him he should do something to change it, that it was more obvious than the Beast at a flower show, and though Sam knew it and had tried, he was never able to shake it. His voice had dropped to such a low murmur that Casey had to strain to listen. Something was definitely up.

"We're coming up tomorrow. Driving." Casey heard a muffled crackle, as Sam put his hand over the receiver and began talking to the woman, Casey figured, unless there was a party going on.

"Who's we?" Casey knew he was getting loud.

"Yeah. Coming by car this time."

At least he was coming. "So should I get Kathleen and Sadie?"

"No! It might be late! We'll just wing it, okay, Casey?"

What the hell was going on? "You gonna call Katie and tell her?" Casey asked.

Once again, there was a hollow silence on the line. "Casey, I need a face-to-face."

Casey pulled the phone away and stared at it, his hand too hard on the receiver. A face-to-face was serious. Too serious for the phone. Face- to-face was a code the boys used to communicate when their mother was nearby. So whomever Sam's visitor was, she was not someone Sam confided in. Casey felt that was good to know.

"Lookit, Casey. It's been a long couple of weeks. I'll explain everything tomorrow."

Casey didn't like the sound of that either. "It had better be good."

There was another pause on Sam's end. Then he said his good-bye, leaving Casey staring at the date, circled in red on the bottom of the calendar, trying to stop the burn in his stomach.

CHAPTER 26

The laneway was dry, the April breezes having dried up the muddy ruts. The sky was jay blue, and the sun was turning the pasty ecru fields a golden green in the valley below. Casey could feel the heat warm his bones as he strolled down the hill to Kathleen's house. It always looked so pretty going down the lane, what with the checkered hills and the lazy houses. He'd half expected to see Kathleen out sketching the view. The orchard behind her home was thickening with the new growth on the tips of the fruit trees, and he knew that given the same sun, the leaves would be flush with pear-green and apple-blossom pink before the next four weeks had passed.

He left the lane and cut through the orchard, ducking beneath the bows of plum wood. He knew the trees by heart, every curl, every knot. The sparrows scattered from the feeder as he jumped the few steps to the back door, the screen exposed and the inside curtain waving a yellow hello. His heart warmed at the sight of the new curtain. Kathleen was redecorating already. Her parents had only just that morning driven their rental moving van out of Saint Jude, and already Kathleen had happy-sunshine curtains on the door. Sadie's influence was spreading. Casey opened the door and walked in.

"Hello," he called out.

"In the studio," she warbled from the living room.

Casey couldn't help the grin. So it was a studio already. He braced himself for what he might see in her *studio.*

Everything faintly resembling her living room was gone, having made the trip to Boston with her parents. Even the lacy curtains had been replaced with blackout drapes for perfect lighting, he suspected. She'd set up what looked like old bridge tables and littered them with bottles and bottles of brushes and fluids and paint thinners. He didn't know where she'd procured the lights—her father he figured—but she had light standards pushed to the sides and reams of fabric for draping under still-life settings. He stepped out of the hallway and into her studio and raised his eyebrows while she put down her paintbrush. Wiping her hands, she stepped away from the canvas on her easel.

"You're working on something."

"Extremely abstract stuff. No paint, no subject. I just think about it."

He grinned and then walked to the front of the painting. "Wow." He studied it in critical fashion. "This is … big." It was a large, square canvas, pulled taut on a wooden frame, five-by-five feet, and it stank of oil, linseed, and turpentine, but it was covered in pastoral elegance, cows and calves and gentle countryside. "Nice."

She put her arm around him. "I can always count on you for a good critique."

"I know what I like." He looked around the room at the canvases, the paints, some in buckets, the brushes, and tarps. He snorted. "Didn't take you long."

"I do what I hafta."

He finished the statement with her. "Yeah. You can work here? With all this stuff?"

"I'm an artist. I work best in clutter." She giggled, and then a frown darkened her face as she stared up at him. "What the hell's going on, Casey? He's due back tomorrow."

"He's coming in tomorrow. He's getting a ride."

She thought about that for a moment, and then her face blossomed into a more brilliant smile than the plum trees in her painting. "Tomorrow? Frig! I have so much to do. Tomorrow! Look at this place! It's a mess. Oh Casey," she said with sudden urgency. "We really should take the sold sign down."

Casey looked around and knew nothing would be changed, whether Sam was coming home or not. "No. Let him see it. And you don't have to clean this. This is you."

"No!" she said from the corner where she'd rushed to pick up a bucket of rags and was standing there, looking like she didn't know where to deposit them. "Finally. Tomorrow."

He walked over to her and took the box away. Putting it on the floor, he took her hand and nodded to the painting, hoping to bring her back to down to earth. "That one for the show?"

"Do you believe it!" Kathleen wheeled around and faced him, almost springing from the floor in her excitement. "A showing, Casey! Wait till I tell Sam! What do you think? Maybe I'll get a write up." She sat down on the armrest of the old spring-sprung couch they'd had in the rec room/basement and picked up a paintbrush, a small fan-shaped instrument that Casey was sure was made to tickle someone instead of applying paint to a white board.

"It can't last, Casey." Her eyes filled with tears as she shook her head and blinked them back. "Something terrible has to happen. It does in all the movies." Her eyes widened in fear. "Why's he driving? There's going to be an accident. Why isn't he taking the bus?"

Casey put his arm around her. "Would you stop?"

He looked around the room for any sign of food. "Have you eaten today?" She could only shake her head. "Come on. Put that down, grab your purse, and I'll take you into town for a burger." He grinned as she scowled. "Fine. A salad then. I think I can afford a salad." She didn't hesitate, and he had her back to her bubbly self before they tore out the back door.

CHAPTER 27

The long drive home was even longer for Sam, as Missy, secure in her red 1987 Mazda RX-7, sped along the highway, top down, carrying Sam to his doom. She owned a car, something else she'd neglected to mention. He watched her reflection in the side window. When had it become strange? When did it go from "she's a funny clown" to "something's very weird here, folks?" The wind stung his eyes and blasted out any kind of tenderness he might have had as Sam tried to control his windblown curls and worried that the bags might blow right off the small ledge she called a backseat. He ran his hand along the leather. There had to be a lot of money invested in the expensive car. It appeared that Daddy had given her everything she wanted, especially since the death of her sister. Her father couldn't be all bad. Sam was beginning to ask questions about her sister too—Sarah Emily King. Had she been a clown too? Was her mother a clown? The only thing Sam knew for sure was that he never wanted to see another clown again.

He hadn't said a word from his room on up past all the little towns that dotted the highway to home. He'd just stared out the window, holding on tightly to the ring he wanted to give to MyKate in his pocket. He could catch Missy singing every now and then when the wind whooshing past them slowed. "The More We Get Together" appeared to be one song stuck in her head. He wondered if she had a calliope stashed away somewhere. She was the Pied Piper of clowns. She could probably play the circus theme song that lured so many men to her tents. Baby or not, he had to find a way out of the circus. He'd made a jumbo mistake. Sam snorted.

He had to get to Kathleen first, alone. He had to explain why he'd done it. That was the problem. He didn't know. Marrying Missy had seemed the only solution at the time, and now he could think of so many others.

"Go this way and that way and that way and this way ... the more we get together, the happier we'll be ..." she sang. At least he thought so. The wind warped her voice so much she was almost howling at him.

"Shit! I have no room to move here." His boot tip stuck into the lip of the case before he was able to untangle it and cross his legs the other way.

After a while, she looked over at him and yelled. "You don't talk about your father very much."

"Nothing to talk about."

She removed her left hand from the wheel and rested it on the door. "It's been my experience that fathers are usually expendable. Mine was around all the time, but that doesn't mean he was there for me."

Sam looked off into the hazy horizon. "I'd never do what my father did. I'd never leave."

Missy leaned over and placed her hand on his thigh. "That's why I love you, Sammy. You'll be a good father."

It was pointless. He rubbed his eyes and focused on the scenery once more. "People use that word too much—love. I mean look at us. Is it love or responsibility? You say you love me, but you don't know me."

"I do."

"No!" He immediately regretted snapping at her. "No one knows me. They think they do, but they're wrong, all of them."

He turned and looked back out the window. They were going to find out who Sam Brennan really was.

Missy tapped her fingers on the wheel as if counting, as his mother did when she was ordering rose bushes from her catalogues, trying to decide which ones she wanted most. "If I can't get a job with the government right away, I could always be a clown. I wouldn't mind volunteering at the schools. It's best to get in good with the teachers. It helps move a child along." She turned and looked innocently at him. "Really."

Sam shook his head, trying to clear it.

"Sheesh." She must have confused it with a no. She looked away, her faced puckered up a little in annoyance, staring at the countryside around her, at the little houses and crumbling older ones scattered about as they bounced along in the car. The three o'clock sun was beginning to cool. "We'll need another car. The gravel will play havoc with my paint job."

"There's the old Ford I use—"

"I'm not using some old truck!" She shot an angry glance at him.

No. He hadn't supposed she would. Sam was strangely curious how his new wife would react when she set eyes on the farmhouse, when she realized it wasn't the country manor she'd described to her parents over the phone. The connection to France had been a bad one, and she'd had to yell. Sam had leaned back in his chair, listening to her as she explained how she'd married into the family of a cattle baron. The farm had suddenly become a ranch, the stable, a riding center. She'd seemed surprised and hurt when her father told her to not expect much.

"And the house, Mama, it's an ancient old stone, Mama. All redone inside, high on the highest hill overlooking the whole valley," she'd said, going on and on when she called to tell them that she and Sam were married.

He'd wondered if he should grab the phone and say to his new mama-in-law, "Non! Non! N'est pas vrai! Votre fille! Elle est nuts!"

She had managed to break the news to them deftly, first the estate, such as it was, then how much like Papa her new husband, Sammy, was, though Papa was fifty years old, six feet tall and blond, in his opinion, completely opposite to her Sammy. Sam wondered why he didn't realize right then—she was a liar. It was only after that when she exploded into the good news that if the baby was a girl they were naming it after her long-suffering dead sister Sarah, or Emily or Mathurine, and if it was a boy, Pierrot.

That was what she'd said. *Pierrot*! Sam and she had had a long discussion after he realized she wanted to name a son of his after a centuries-old groundbreaking clown. No son of his would go through school named Pierrot, no matter how high up on the ladder the clown had been.

Over the previous three weeks, Missy had been able to juggle her way through, cautiously and methodically. He wondered how well she'd be able to juggle his mother.

"Missy, about my mother."

"Don't *you* try to scare me!"

"What?" Sam turned to her, surprised. "Who else have you been talking to!"

She laughed quickly and a little hysterically. "My mother." She looked in her rearview mirror, to check as she pulled out to pass a maroon-colored K-car that seemed to be being driven by a tweed hat and eight gnarly, country knuckles. "Why don't the old geezers stay on the slower routes?" She seemed to Sam, unusually flustered. "She warned me to watch out for all men and their mothers." She cackled, a little too hard, he thought.

"Yeah. Well, mine can be a little ..." He paused, pursing his lips, trying to find the one single, appropriate nonthreatening word. "Eccentric."

"Who wouldn't be—squirreled up in that farmhouse all those years? I'm sure that once I get there—"

"No. You don't understand. She's not just lonely. She's kind of warped, a little, by her childhood." Sam wanted to throw up, the pressure almost unbearable as they shot down Saint Jude Road, so close to home. He leaned back against the door and stared at her as she drove. How to describe the Beast? Humor, perhaps.

"She was an only child, no friends. Her father gave her a puppy when she was five. She named it Stay. But the puppy left her too. It got confused when she tried to teach it to stay. After all, Fetch, Stay! Come here, Stay!"

He waited for the laugh. Nothing. She looked over at him as if expecting the rest of the story. It had to be his timing. His timing was all off. "It's a joke," he said.

She gave a soft *oh* that was lost to the wind and looked at Sam as if she felt sorry for him. "Don't worry about your mother and me, Sammy. We'll be fine."

You think so, he thought as he sighed and turned back to the road. Once again, he could hear Kathleen's voice inside his head. A couple has to laugh at the same things or it just won't work. She'd been talking about Frank and his wife and how well they suited each other. Kathleen had heard that puppy joke a million times. She always laughed.

Sam couldn't have sunk lower into the seat if he tried as they passed Kathleen's house. *Hide*, he thought. Hopefully, she wasn't sitting out on the deck as he'd feared. He needed time to explain. He peeked up again as they took the crest of the hill, well past Kathleen's eyesight.

Missy's eyes opened. Then her mouth opened, and she emitted a small gasp. She didn't try to hide the look of dismay when she pulled up in front of the house. The manor home she'd so enthusiastically described to her mother looked nothing like the run-down Georgian farmhouse. Her eyes focused on the house, the red-chipped brick, the rotted vine–covered eaves that his mother refused to replace. Pulling over in front of the picket-fenced rose garden, she turned off the car and sat there. She stared. He listened to the cattle in the front field. The cardinals were singing. She didn't seem to hear them. The lilac hedge was blooming, but she wasn't looking at it or drinking in the luxurious aroma. She was still staring at his home as if it were a scab on the hill.

His legs felt like rubber as he stumbled around the car and opened her door for her. He tried desperately to find another joke, maybe about the garden or the cattle, anything to replace the ashen cloud of fear descending on him.

He grabbed the one bag from the backseat. How she'd managed to get so much luggage in one little car was beyond Sam. Hers took up the entire trunk and most of the seat behind her. His one bag was buried somewhere beneath her guitar and clown fixings that had cramped his legs on the hours long drive back to his home.

"I'll get the bags later," Sam said. "Let's get you inside to meet the family." Sam's eyes, not leaving Missy's face, soaked it all in, the shock, the revulsion, her realization that the Brennan farm was just another farm, like any other farm despite its pretty name, the fact that it wasn't a mansion. He scowled, seeing the disappointment in her face, and that hurt him more than anything else did; she didn't see it as a mansion. Because to Samuel Dominic Brennan, despite everything, it was.

She cleared her throat and searched the yard as he opened her door. "Does anyone know we're coming?"

He pursed his lips and helped her out. "You should walk over to the center of the garden later with me. You can see the whole valley from there. There's a walkway down through the—"

She grabbed her purse and leaned further in. "Didn't you tell them anything? I told you to tell them."

He closed the car door and tried once more to joke the situation away. "Nope. Wanted to give you the chance to make a dash for it." Again, the kidding didn't work. She grabbed up her clown bag. "Maybe you should start the introductions then." With a fervor that Sam hadn't expected, Missy unlatched the gate and started up to the front door.

The boards creaked underfoot. The porch needed its spring coat of white, shabby from the long winter. Grabbing hold of his courage as well as the doorknob, he squared his shoulders, took a deep breath, opened the door, and escorted her into the vestibule. He had expected to hear the soaps blaring away on the television, but the only sound was a muffled, heartbeat countdown of the mantel clock on the fireplace in the living room. Pushing open the door to the living room, he ushered her inside and heard her gasp again.

Sam had never studied the living room before, not through someone else's eyes, never really caring what his mother did or didn't do with the house. He'd seen it through his grandmother's eyes, Casey's, and Kathleen's, but never once had he ever felt shamed by it. Sure, the curtains were a joke, but never had it seemed shabby. Missy's expression made it shabby.

"Have a seat," he said, trying to remain calm. "I'll get you some water and track someone down."

"Don't leave me!" She grabbed his arm, staring at the curtains as they swayed from the breeze of the door. He thought he saw genuine fear on her face.

He was a little taken aback by her nervousness, realizing it was genuine.

"Missy. Nothing's going to jump out and grab you." He thought of Thomas and hid the smile that threatened to spread over his face. He hoped Thomas wouldn't jump out and scare her, maybe jump out and save him, knock some sense into him. Leaving Missy staring at the Hummel figurines that cluttered the doily-covered corner table, beside the photos of roses and awards and endless jars of rooting stems in murky water vials, he slipped through the hall and into the kitchen.

Gran's blouse was covered in a netlike abundance of pink roses and silver kittens, and her slacks were faded gray. She sat as if waiting for him, her eyes misty-lake blue, and her cheeks, warm red. The air behind her shimmered from the heat of the woodstove. She smiled sadly.

"Samuel."

He put his fingers to his lips, as the door to the living room closed behind him, and he came over. Sinking to his knees, he hugged her. She glanced over her shoulder and put her hand up in a stop sign. “Be quiet, Thomas, darling. Let me talk to him first.”

Sam felt his stomach contract. What could he say? He didn’t want to hurt Gran, but he knew he would. Worse than that, he was going to disappoint her.

“I’m okay, Gran, but I need your help.” He paused, glancing back at the door. His grandmother looked up behind him again. Then shaking her head and clucking a little like a chicken, she reached out and ran her fingers through his hair.

She reached for his chin and lifted it. “We love you, no matter what.”

He tried to remain calm, finding it hard to breathe. “I don’t know if you still will, not after I …”

Her eyes glistened with all the strength she’d had over the years, strength she’d never lost. “Thomas said there were problems coming. He’s been very worried about you.”

Sam stopped suddenly, feeling a strong touch, a sudden warmth on his shoulder. He looked down at it, forgetting everything else, remembering the feeling, and he smiled. “Thomas. I haven’t felt that in a long time.”

“He has his hand on your shoulder, right now.”

Sam nodded, seeing nothing but still feeling the warmth. He wasn’t frightened, not freaked out, as he’d often joked. He felt safe again.

Gran almost whispered. “Introduce me to her.”

Sam looked at his grandmother. She knew. “Wait here. I’ll get her.”

“No.” Her voice shook him. “I’ll meet this one on my feet!” Gran was already struggling as Sam helped her up out of the chair. She felt larger on his arm than before.

“Don’t go having a stroke or heart attack or anything like that,” Sam said, tightening his grip on her.

“I’m not half as fragile as you and your brother think.” She opened the kitchen door wide and, crossing the hallway, proceeded to the living room.

Missy wasn’t seated. She was inspecting the meager room, picking up the photos, the chipped china figures of Victorian ladies, and the gauche porcelain figurines of carriage horses and glancing up at the curtains. She turned as they entered.

"Gran, this is Melissa Anne King. Missy, this is Gran."

"Melissa." Gran faced the young woman like the teacher she'd been for so many years, as if appraising a wayward student. "Are you a King from Parkland?"

"I'm a Brennan now. Sam and I were married three weeks ago."

Sam felt a stabbing pain, right between his eyes, when Melissa said it.

Gran stepped up to the taller woman and stared at her with cobalt eyes. "You are certain you're pregnant. How far along would you be, dear?"

Sam strangled a snort. Bluntness was not a tone he'd heard often in his grandmother's voice.

"Yes, I am." Missy said, trying to regroup from the insulting assumption. "Sam and I love each other very much."

Gran swayed and turned her head slightly. "You may love him, my dear, but Samuel, I promise you, does not feel the same." She looked over at her grandson. "How is Kathleen taking all of this? You have told her, Samuel?"

Sam's heart constricted. "No."

"Your mother and father, dear." Gran turned back to Missy. "Do they know?"

"Yes. They're in France, or they would have been there for the wedding. I should phone them and let them know I arrived safely."

"I know your mother, dear. We did charity work together for the Women's Institute years ago. Charming lady."

Sam knew by the way she said it that Gran couldn't stand the woman. He was surprised by the smirk on Missy's face. Missy understood the insult and was in complete agreement. Missy didn't like her mother much either.

"Your mother told me you were studying environmental something or other." Gran picked up a framed photo of Sam, Casey, and Kathleen and placed it back on its original spot.

"Yes. I'm studying law."

"So will you return to Brazil?" Gran said. "I heard you worked there in the summer."

Sam watched his new wife turn the color of sour milk. Gran lifted her head regally and turned her back on his new wife.

"There is much to talk about, Thomas. It's not every day that Sam brings home a bride."

Missy stared, her mouth open, as Gran talked to someone who wasn't there. Then she seemed to rally once more. Sam had to respect that trait of Missy's. She could bounce back. "The bottom line here is, Gran … may I call you Gran?" She didn't wait for a reply. "Sammy and I are married whether we have your blessing or not."

The light in the room dimmed suddenly. Sam smelled his mother's perfume and felt her presence before he saw her. His mother, shaking with rage, reminded Sam of the badger he'd cornered two summers before.

"What? You did what Sam?" Rachel's face began its usual rush to purple, her voice as mean as that badger's he'd cornered. For the first time, Sam saw Missy visibly shrink.

Sam's mind moved like a roller coaster. *Here we go. She'll break something in fury. Her head will explode into migraine.* She'll pull him close and squeeze the life out of him. *Or,* he thought hopefully, *she might very well kill me.* He didn't care anymore.

"You slut!" Rachel seemed to double in size as her fury focused on Missy.

It was like the clouds lifted and angels shone down on Sam. All those years, all the strength it took to learn the craft of manipulation, the time spent learning to placate his mother, to win her over for everyone else, all those years of practice had been for this. He didn't have to manipulate his mother at all this time. For the first time in three weeks, Sam felt a bit of relief. He knew just what to do. He turned and walked over to his mother, looking like the kid who got caught with his hand in the cookie jar, his eyes wet and droopy like a puppy caught peeing on a rug.

"Mum, I'd like you to meet, Missy King. This is my mother, Rachel."

"You slut!"

"Mum," Sam said softly. "We're married. It's legal. She's going to have your grandchild. That's the end of it."

It should have been so simple. His mother should have exploded, erupted in insane fury at Missy. Missy should have been struggling to get out the door and away from the Brennans as quickly as her little red sports car could take her. But she wasn't moving. She was staring at the doorway to the hall. Sam watched in horror as all eyes around him focused on the shadow in the doorway, a small flickering light, dimming. He knew even before he looked over.

"MyKate."

He could feel her heart break. He could hear it shatter on the floor. He could already taste her tears. She swayed in front of him.

Kathleen didn't say a word as all color drained from her, her mouth opening a little, her hand reaching for the door frame as if to steady herself. She took one step backward, her eyes still on Sam's face. Then, as he called out to her again, she turned her back on him and fled.

CHAPTER 28

Casey had some one hundred and one chores he had to do that day, but he didn't care. He was taking the perfectly good day off, had the boss on the radio, a two-four of beer in the back to celebrate Sam's return. Best of all, Sadie was chattering on next to him. The drive had been pretty, the kind of scenery Kathleen would paint behind a cow. The sun peekabooed through charcoal clouds, turning the field into patchwork quilts, and the lilacs were tantalizing. His mother had been totally preoccupied in her thorny roses, pulling the burlap from them, and planning the gardens. He couldn't beat that.

And their herd was doing great. The twins had almost doubled in size and weren't at all skittish. They'd show well, and Sam and he needed those ribbons on the wall to show breeders that they were prizewinning quality.

He and Sadie had gone off to look at western saddles inlaid with silver and turquoise, and as he drove, he'd been daydreaming of how she'd look on Storm, cutting and roping. She'd been talking about maybe signing up for the competitions at the local fairs in the summer. And Sam would be home. Yes. Casey was happy. He didn't see Kathleen run through the juniper and out onto the road until he heard Sadie scream.

"Kathleen?" Sadie was already undoing her belt.

Casey slammed on the brakes as Kathleen stumbled and went down in front of them, blind to everything, running away from the farm. Casey rammed the gear into park and jumped out.

"Katie?" He didn't bother slamming his door. "Katie." She wasn't crying, just kneeling, her hands flat on the ground, staring at nothing but the gravel and stones.

"Oh, Katie." Sadie leaned over her and picked up her hands. Sadie turned them over and grimaced at her bloodied palms as Casey reached down and lifted Kathleen's chin.

"Hey, beautiful." He took her elbows and lifted her to her feet, feeling sick at the sight of her, at the panic growing inside him. "Katie? Is it Gran?"

She muttered something, shaking her head, and he leaned closer, knowing it wasn't Gran.

"Come on, beautiful." He put his arm around her and glanced at Sadie. "Let's get you home."

Kathleen stared up at him with horrified eyes.

"He's married!"

The force of her words almost knocked him down. Casey stared in disbelief at her. It couldn't be Sam she was talking about, but he knew it already. No one else would affect her that way. It was a mistake, but there was no other explanation. He struggled to catch her as she collapsed.

"He got married. Oh God, Casey!"

Casey gripped her harder than he should have, but Kathleen didn't seem to notice. Sadie did. She put her arm around Kathleen. "I'll take care of her. You go find out what the hell is happening."

Casey couldn't take his eyes off Kathleen. It couldn't be true. Sam had done some stupid things before. "But he loves you," he said to Kathleen, more perplexed than shocked.

"Casey!" Sadie grabbed Kathleen away from him. "You aren't helping."

"Right." He stepped back until he saw Kathleen stumble. His head swayed as he took hold of her again. "Come on. We'll get you cleaned up."

His eyes shot over Kathleen's head to Sadie's face. "It's a mistake."

"Casey!" Sadie gave him a curt knock-it-off look, and Casey realized that Kathleen—brave, strong, able-to-conquer-anything Kathleen, now stumbling back through the orchard to her home—was broken and his brother was responsible.

Anger rose in him like slew water from the lock dams on an angry Killkenny River. Casey stayed long enough for Sadie to get Kathleen inside, and he was out again and on his way up the hill.

The woman on the phone. He could hear her voice as if she was right there beside him. The one Sam didn't want Casey talking to. He didn't bother with his truck but left it, keys on the seat, for Sadie if she needed it.

There was no wind. Not a leaf moved and even the birds were silent as if waiting to see what would happen next. Sam couldn't have married anyone. He had a ring all ready for Kathleen's finger. Casey reached the top of the hill and jogged around the curve. When he saw the sports car parked in the driveway, any doubt disappeared. He didn't even try to stem the bile that rose in his gut. There would be no back door for him this time. He vaulted over the picket fence and took the front porch in two strides. Then, banging open the front door, he barreled through the foyer and into the living room.

Sam's face drained of all color.

"Where's Kathleen," Sam said. "I have to tell—"

"Casey?" Missy stood up and stepped forward. "So nice to finally meet you." She put her hand out.

Casey looked down at the wedding band and looked back at his brother. He couldn't find the words that showed how pissed off he was. Gran moved toward him.

"Now, Casey. Let's all just calm down."

"It's true." Casey stepped closer, his jaw aching.

"I have to talk to MyKate," Sam said. "I have to—"

Casey hit him, one good blow to the chin. Sam went sailing. The flimsy coffee table didn't stand any more chance than Sam did as it broke into pieces over the floor. Rachel screamed, Missy jumped, and Gran began asking Thomas to take charge. Sam, sprawled across the rug, shook the shock from his head, and stretched his jaw as Casey flexed his fist for another strike. Gran put her hand on Casey's arm.

"You stay out of my way!" Casey leered at Sam, turned around, and headed for the door.

"Stop, Casey! Please!" Sam turned to grab Casey, but Casey ignored him.

"Sam?" Missy grabbed Sam by the arm, but he was stopped by his mother as she pushed her way in front of the door.

"This is not the time to explain anything to your brother," his mother said. "Not that you should. I don't know what is wrong with that young man. Hitting you. Disgraceful."

Sam stared out the window as Casey headed back down the hill to Kathleen's house. Jumping over to the window, he pulled it up and screamed Casey's name. Casey didn't turn back.

"Is that Kathleen?" Missy said with a bit of concern. "Sammy? I would have thought she'd be happy for you." She cocked her head. "Just what kind of *friend* is Kathleen, anyway?"

"Maybe you should go get your bags, dear," Gran said, putting her hand on Sam's shoulder. "We all need to calm down a little."

Sam felt smaller than the Hummel figurine shattered on the floor in front of him. He'd broken Kathleen's heart and didn't know how he was going to mend it, but he had to try. That's all he thought about as he made his way out to the car for the bags, craning his neck to see down the lane to Kathleen's home. He was thinking of nothing else as he carried the bags upstairs and followed behind Missy down the hallway to the first door on the left, his room, the room he'd intended to share with Kathleen until they could build their own home.

He was thinking of that as he heard his mother ranting in the kitchen.

"Oh no. No. No. No. This isn't happening!" He heard her slam her hand on the table. The cups jingled in the saucers.

When Missy turned and faced him, her face was the picture of concern. "She seems a little upset. She'll come around, Sammy, won't she?"

Sam had no idea how to tell Missy that his mother was not going to come around. His mother was not particularly fond of babies. Maybe he should have explained more, introduced her to his family before he'd married her. She might have called the whole thing off, but then, what about the baby? His baby.

"My mother can be a little, well, overwhelming at times," he said, carefully choosing his words. "You can't let her upset you."

She nodded an okay. "Do they like music?" Tears sprang into her eyes as she listened to what had to be crockery being thrown and broken in the kitchen. She looked like a trapped animal, and Sam felt guilt descend on him once more.

"I'd wait." He suppressed a hysterical laugh. The woman was worried about clown songs. "Lookit, Missy," he said as he took her hands and sat down on the side of the bed. "We're going to have to give them a little time for all this to sink in." He knew he'd have to calm down, get everyone to calm down. "I'm going to go get you some milk and maybe a cookie or two. Mum bakes good cookies."

Missy nodded, the tears tipping over her eyelids and down her face. "I'm so sorry, Sammy."

He was beginning to wonder and looked around his room. She hadn't seemed so sorry when Kathleen had walked in. The tears had only appeared as they'd come upstairs. She was staring at his ceiling. Taking a big breath, he stared at his posters.

"I'll take them down later." He moved past her into the room and threw the bags on the bed.

"No." Missy reached out for him, her hand wavering a little. "I just didn't think … I mean, I thought the ones at school were all you had." She turned slowly around studying the posters.

He unzipped a bag and began unpacking her things with a frantic zeal. "No. They have to come down." He stopped and looked up at Kathleen's Becket. "Well, most of them. At least from the ceiling, I mean."

She nodded and smiled uncertainly as he began moving socks and underwear from his top dresser drawer and started shoving them into his bag.

"You can put your things in here." He opened the second drawer and began removing T-shirts, depositing them into his bag. He turned to run out of the room. "Just until we figure out the accommodations."

"Sammy?"

"I'll put my stuff in …" He went for the third drawer. "In Casey's room. He has an extra dresser. Maybe trade my desk for the dresser." He zipped up the bag and pulled it to the floor.

"You don't have to do this, Sammy. I …"

He ignored her. Then he stopped and struggled to hold back the scream building inside. She reached out for him.

"Where are you sleeping tonight?" she asked.

It was an honest question on her part, as they hadn't slept together for over two months. Their marriage was not even truly valid, as the union had not been consummated, a fact that was noted more than once by the bride. Sam had no desire to bed Missy anymore. He was never openly mean about it, very good at coming up with reasons why he no longer felt aroused when near her. She didn't push it, and he was grateful for that. He wished he could love her more, at least try, but he felt nothing for the woman except the duty she was owed as the mother of his child.

"Well?" she said, her eyebrows rising in almost humor as if she found something terribly sad but funny at the same time. "I understand." She walked over to her bag. "Will you be staying in the house?"

"It's my home." He looked around the sterile room. It wasn't his anymore, and he knew it never would be again.

She nodded with abject compliance, a faint, amused smile on her face.

He swallowed hard. "I may have to go out for a little while."

Kathleen. Somehow, he'd get to Kathleen. He had no idea where she was or if she'd even talk to him, but there was nothing, not even his unborn child, that was more important to him at that moment.

CHAPTER 29

Casey tried his best to draw oxygen into his lungs as he stormed over from Kathleen's house to his truck, but it seemed as if the afternoon had sucked all the air from the sky. She hadn't said a word. Casey had felt ill, watching her sit there, mute, staring at nothing. His Kathleen should be screaming, raving, and overreacting. That's what she'd always done when she'd been hurt or insulted. She never sat zombielike while life went on around her. Sadie had told him she'd take Kathleen's car and drive them both over to her father's place, get her away from the farm. Casey had nodded in agreement, feeling the knot in his gut loosen a little. By the time he got to the barn, it was strangling him once more.

Casey slammed through the door, banging it against the cinder block, his leg shooting hot pain through his back as he marched over to Billy. Billy's relaxed smile disappeared at the sight of his nephew.

"Sam went and knocked up some blonde. He married her!"

Billy's stared at his nephew, his mouth open, his eyes almost as round as the full moon the night before.

"Kathleen found out when she walked into the parlor."

Billy lowered the wrench from the pipe he'd opened and then grinned as if it suddenly made sense. "That's rich. Did Katie put you up to this?" He chuckled.

"Sam got married, Billy."

"Quit takin' the piss outta me!"

"It's true," Sam said from behind Casey.

"You son of a bitch!" Casey swung, catching Sam in the jaw with his left and his right landed squarely in Sam's gut as he spun. Somehow, Sam managed to stay on his feet as if needing the third blow. Casey obliged with another left, and this time Sam fell. "Get up! Come on!"

Billy pulled Casey back as Sam slid around on the muck of the barn floor. "There's nothing to come from violence," Billy said. He leaned over and grabbed Sam by the back of the shirt. Sam moaned as Billy pulled him up and looked Sam square in the face. "You're going to tell me what's going on."

It took Sam a few moments to finally start talking, and he kept stopping and looking up at Casey as if expecting another onslaught of fists. Casey stared out the window at the rain now falling. He couldn't stand to look at Sam. Billy sat on the concrete ledge between the stanchions, listening, his concentration focused solely on Sam.

"Did you have a preg check done, son?"

"She showed me the test," Sam said holding his gut, rocking.

"But did you go to a doctor to have her checked?"

"It was positive." Sam began to pace.

"That's the oldest trick in the book," Billy murmured as Casey snorted.

"I made her take the test in front of me," Sam yelled at them, hands rising up in frustration.

"Right in front?" Casey asked, disgusted. The more he heard, the more Casey wanted to hurt his brother again, the more he wanted to tell him the state Kathleen had been in when he'd picked her up from the gravel. "Your wife took the test in front of you."

"Don't call her that." Sam looked relieved that Casey was talking to him again.

Casey tightened his fist. "What? Your wife!"

"Don't say it that way. It's not that way!"

"Yeah? What way should I say it?"

"Knock it off," Billy shouted over both of them. "That test ain't certain." Billy rose and laid his hands on Sam's shoulders. "Now you're going to listen to me, son."

Casey shook his head in disgust and looked away again.

"We, you and me"—Billy pushed his finger into Sam's chest, and Sam couldn't hide the groan of pain—"will go with her to Doc Innis and get her checked out." Billy turned away, rubbing his forehead, mumbling. "You don't know her from a hole in the ground." He looked back, raising his voice. "That don't mean she don't know you. There are lots of reasons she might want to marry into this family."

Casey snorted, finding that kind of funny and highly unlikely.

"If she does happen to be pregnant, which I highly doubt, you get a paternity test done. I know a lawyer who'll be more than happy to set it up for you. He'll make sure it's done legit. If it is yours, it's a Brennan and always will be. We'll go for custody." He sighed. "Keep the calf, cull the cow."

Sam's expression seemed to tighten a bit, and Casey wondered just what kind of feelings Sam might have for the woman.

Billy was still talking. "Divorce. Annulment. What needs to be done?" He looked up. "If that's what you want."

"But she could get the baby." Sam turned away from his uncle.

"If—and that's a real big if, son—if there's a baby." Billy was pacing now, thinking. "Who is she? What does she do?"

"A clown. A lawyer." Sam rubbed his eyes. "Probably both. I don't know anymore." He laughed. "Sorry. I haven't slept for a while. I've been staying at a motel near the school. I swear I haven't slept with her. Well, not since MyKate. I swear."

Casey figured his brother was just short of hysteria. Good, he thought, feeling his knuckles pound with pain.

Billy stepped in front of Sam, his shoulders squared. "As of right now, you and your wife are officially separated. Don't talk to her, except to be civil. Don't discuss any of what you're up to. I presume she's staying in your room." He waited for the nod. "Stay out of the house. I'll get the legal crap going. Casey will get your things."

Sam nodded.

"Where's Kathleen?" Billy said, heading back to his trailer.

"Sadie took her over to her place." Casey could taste blood. He held up his hand and saw the red stain of Sam's blood on his shaking fingers, from a rather nasty looking tear in Sam's upper lip.

"Tell her the truth this time." Billy looked back at Sam, his eyes colder than Casey had ever seen them. Billy disappeared into his trailer.

Casey's eyes never wavered as he walked over to his younger brother. "You're a goddamned liar."

Sam braced and stuck his jaw out. "I love Kathleen."

"Funny way to show it!" Casey stepped closer and shoved him. "No more chances, Junior. You get it right, for once! Go get in my truck!"

* * *

Sam couldn't remember a time Casey had punched him before. Casey had never struck anyone before, not even in play. But there he was, driving down the laneway, using one hand, flexing his left hand over and over.

"Stop!" Sam cried when he saw it.

Casey ignored him and drove right by Kathleen's place, the Sold sign shining harshly in the front yard.

"When did it sell?" Sam couldn't take his eyes off it.

"Roll down the goddamned window," Casey said as he rolled down his. "You stink."

"Why didn't you tell me?" Sam said, feeling anger rise in him, finally.

"Seems to me to be none of your concern," Casey said. "Roll your window down. You stink."

Sam looked over at him and back to his door and then rolled the window down, breathing in a bit of fresh air. The wind whipping by him felt soothing on his face, soothing on what he knew would be a whopper of a bruise.

"Sorry. Guess I fell in some shit." *When you hit me*, he thought, once more astonished.

"Shut up."

"Right."

The drive over had been one of Sam's longest, the silence unnerving. Every time he tried to bring up the Sold sign, Casey told him to shut up.

"Why?" Casey didn't look at him but stared hard ahead as they passed the Hole.

"It's my child. I can't walk away." He waited for Casey to say something. "And Missy has no one."

"Shut up."

"Right."

"Did you ever, just once, think first?" Casey jammed on the brakes too hard as he turned onto the dirt road to the Parker farm and pulled over to the side. He shut off the engine and sat staring straight ahead at nothing, the sound of the windshield washers, scraping at the light rain. "All you had to do was ask for help. Katie was so happy. You did that to her. Then you shot her down." Casey's hands turned knuckle-white on the wheel. "If I didn't have Sadie, I'd marry Kate tomorrow! You know that? I'd do it! I'd make you watch. Day after day. I'd love her better than you ever could for the rest of your stinking life!" He rubbed his hands around the wheel. "I'd make you watch! I'd make you crawl!"

"I'm going to make it right."

"Right!"

Sam looked out the window. "I did what I thought was …" Sam's stomach seized, and suddenly he wanted to throw up.

"Look. Just shut up."

"It's my job. Remember? Keep everyone happy."

"I said shut up!" Casey sighed and pried his hands off the wheel. "Keep everyone happy." Casey rebuffed him. "The only one you kept happy was Melissa."

"What about my child? What would you have done?"

Casey looked over and sneered at him. "I'd have trusted Katie."

"I do! But I had to think of Missy and my child too."

"Yeah!" Casey slammed his hands on the wheel. "That Melissa doesn't need any saving, Sam. She seems to have everything under control."

Sam couldn't stop the sob that tore through him. "I did what I had to. I have to. Make everyone happy. For years, you needed me."

"I can stand up for myself. I don't need you …"

"Yeah! Well! When did that change?" Sam reached for the doorknob, his heart pounding so hard it hurt. "I'll walk."

"No," Casey said, turning the truck back on. They sat there while the engine idled.

Sam lowered his hand from the knob and looked over at Casey. "What in the hell is going on with Kathleen's home? Is it all over … I mean … you know? Everything? Our plans? For the farm?"

Casey took a deep breath. "That was always your problem. People can change their own plotlines." He spit out the window. "I did."

Sam grimaced and felt a stab of excruciating pain.

"Lookit! You ain't no hero." Casey looked over at him and grunted. "Billy and Gran bought Kathleen's. It was supposed to be a surprise, but you blew that away."

"They bought it?"

Casey proceeded to explain the situation to Sam.

"Give Kate some time to scream at you and then tell her the truth." Casey started the truck up the road toward Sadie's as Sam stared out over the April fields.

Sam nodded. "I'll make it right."

"Shut up."

CHAPTER 30

Kathleen had washed and reapplied her eye makeup. She'd spent too much of her final paycheck on the fancy face masking, so she decided to really apply it, too heavy, too much. Now she looked the part—floozy, bitch, whore. She studied herself impassively waiting. For what exactly, she had no idea; Sam, she supposed. He could see her for what she now was. Her eyes, caked with green powder, stung and her red-stained lips were too puffy. All they were good for was breathing, as her nose was no longer working. That wasn't the worst, though, nor was the pain in her gut, the feeling that she'd be sick at any time, or the dizziness she felt every time she moved; it was the shaking. Sadie had mumbled something about it being shock. She had offered hot tea and brownies that, under usual circumstances would have worked miracles for Kathleen. Sadie had offered conversation and even suggested sleep. Kathleen had simply sat there at the kitchen table, rudely clutching her purse, trying her best to stop the tremor that spread up from her fingertips to her wrists and even up farther.

Fifteen minutes before, Sadie had led her to the garden room attached to the south side of the house that looked out over the fields behind their farmhouse. The room was filled to overflowing with chintz and parlor plants. Down the three steps, surrounded by walls of evergreen plants, she stepped out into the main room, framed in glass, long, a sitting area on one end, the Jacuzzi on the other. Kathleen could smell a faint floral scent, lavender or lilac, that Sadie told her was just an artificial fragrance, nothing real. It was to Kathleen far more real than anything else in her world was. The hum of the Jacuzzi motor was almost lulling.

Sadie had glanced over. "I can turn the hot tub off if you like."

"It's lovely," Kathleen said. "I like the sound of the water. It's soothing."

"You can barely hear it, what with the motor." Sadie sounded like she didn't quite know what to say. "Mom loved plants. Dad and I try, but we're gradually going fake silk and artificial fragrance. I don't know if she'd like it. I don't really have a green thumb. Mom would be appalled."

Kathleen had smiled politely and turned away. "Your mother would love anything you do."

"Will you be okay if I go and get the tea?"

Kathleen nodded. "Thank you, Sadie."

"Sam loves you. Remember that, Kathleen," Sadie said. "Listen to what he has to say when he gets here."

"Shouldn't he be with his wife?" Kathleen was very tired of the niceties; nevertheless, she tried a smile. "Go."

Sadie had nodded and then walked back up the steps, and Kathleen had heard the brittle snap of the door behind her.

It hurt when Kathleen took in a long, sad breath. Her purse was very heavy with the new makeup she'd purchased.

She pulled it up on her lap, but she didn't put it down. Instead, she hugged it closer to her and took another look around. It wasn't such a bad place to be, a paradise in Killkenny, complete with blossoms, fragrances, floral cushions, and the sound of running water. Kathleen knew he was somewhere close. She'd heard Casey's truck outside. Sam would be with her soon, she'd have to listen, and she didn't know if she was up to it. She wondered if he'd like the shade of her lipstick. It was new. Pearl Harbor Pink. Sure, the name sucked, but it was a pretty color. What kind of moron would name it Pearl Harbor Pink? She'd bought it just for today. She wondered if he'd laugh at her or lie and tell her it looked lovely.

Sam really hadn't lied to her. He just hadn't told her the whole truth. No "Oh, by the way, I'm married" or "Hey! Did I tell you she's having my baby?" Kathleen pulled her feet up onto the cushions, and curling up, she turned and faced the back of the chair.

Was it worth it? One weekend of absolute love for a lifetime of regret, angst? Angst made an artist great. Bring on the suffering. That's what they'd say years from now. Oh my, how she suffered. Can't you just see it in the color, the misery in the hearts of those beautiful beasts? She really caught the look of cows being led to slaughter. She closed her eyes and drank in the scent of artificial flower, mixed with something new, something she couldn't place—musky, smoky. The voice seemed so far away.

"Kathleen?"

Kathleen thought Casey sounded weirdly sad and soft as if he was outside the glass of the windows. But how could he? Allergies. Or a cold. He was coming down with something. Poor Casey. Kathleen wasn't up to talking.

"Go away," she told him without looking up. What was he doing there? They all wanted to see, eh? Everyone wanted to do their bit to console poor little Kathleen. She wondered if the Beast was worried for her too. Probably not, and now Casey was going to defend Sam, as usual.

"I'm okay, Casey, really." She felt him touch her cheek. Then he brushed a lock of hair from her face. Feeling like a baby, she turned farther away from him, trying to hide her face in the back cushions, but she felt his touch on her cheek once more. She opened her eyes and turned around.

"Casey! Would you—" She stared at him, her eyes swimming with tears and stinging from the eye shadow. Something was different.

"You got a haircut?" His hair was short. How had he found time for a haircut?

Maybe she'd completely lost her sense of time. She reached up to wipe the salty film from her eyes. Her hand came away covered in green. He moved his hand from his coveralls and brought out a pipe. Kathleen's mouth dropped as she stared at the pipe. She had smelled that delicious scent so many times over the years; she wondered how she'd missed it. She watched the room fade away, and suddenly he was perfectly clear. Shouldn't she feel goose bumps? Shouldn't she be afraid? Instead, she felt an easy calm.

"Thomas." She reached out, but her hand could have been touching mist. She tried again as he smiled softly at her. It was his eyes. For a moment, she saw Sam. "It is you?" He gently tamped down tobacco in the bowl of the pipe. "Thomas?" He hovered like a pleasant distortion, a funny mirror reflection at the crazy house. "Gran was right." He had Sam's eyes. She pulled herself around and faced him, somehow knowing he wasn't going to vanish as quickly as he'd come. "You are right here." She realized why he was there. "Oh. Because of Sam." She pulled the purse hard against her heart. Fine time for Thomas to show up. Closing the barn door after the horses got out. Anger sparked through her as she stared down a specter. "What's your grandson's problem, Thomas? How could he be so stupid?"

She wondered how Thomas had somehow managed to light the pipe. She hadn't seen a match, but there he was, puffing away, the smoke encircling his head. Kathleen wasn't sure where the smoke ended and he began.

"He loves you, Kathleen."

The words drifted out of sync with his kind smile.

"He loves me? Don't say that to me! I'm so damned tired of hearing how much he loves me."

Right! She was arguing with a ghost. He was talking to her, somehow, taking Sam's side. "His sin wasn't loving me, Thomas. His sin was not talking to me. You're talking to me! Hell! I'm talking to a ghost! Why couldn't he just talk to me?"

She didn't know why she was so furious with Thomas. It wasn't his fault, not really. *But showing up now! Now!* After the damage was done. Weren't ghosts supposed to forewarn? The cushion was hard beneath her, the smell of his tobacco and the flowers now cloying. She stared as the solarium dimmed and rain dotted the outside of the glass.

"Where were you all these years? Where was Sam's father?"

"Billy was right there the whole time, Kathleen."

"Not good enough."

He reached out for her and Kathleen felt her hair move. "Sam is coming."

"I don't want to talk to Sam! Let's talk about you, eh? How could you have let the Beast loose on Casey? Where were you, eh? What she did to him was a crime. Sam was right. You really did desert us."

"He needs you."

She shivered. "He always needs me. That's the problem." Kathleen was getting uncomfortable with the way Thomas drifted in and around her. "Is this how Gran sees you, kind of wishy-washy?"

He smiled at her, puffing smoke around his head, as if he had a secret he'd never tell. He took the pipe from his mouth, and his face darkened. "Kathleen, it isn't as it se—"

"I don't want to hear it. I don't!" She was looking through him now. "Go away!" She felt the tears she didn't want to cry. She wouldn't cry. She'd been through worse than this. She blinked as hard as she could to stop them. Her mother's request, she would go to Boston. "What do you think, Thomas? Boston's not that bad. I could rent a garret." She snorted. "What about that? All the greats do their best work in garrets."

There was no answer, and when she turned back, she was alone. Apparently, he had no answers either.

Then she heard Casey and Sam upstairs in the kitchen and it was time to make some decisions. She'd been talking to a ghost. Kathleen curled up into a ball around her purse and bitterly laughed at what was left of her life.

CHAPTER 31

Sam stepped silently down the stairs, seeing nothing except the leaves of plants around him, hearing nothing but a remote hum from a pump and the muted lapping of water. The plants were nice, but it was like walking through a forest. He'd grabbed a pair of workpants from the box in the bed of Casey's truck. They were too long, and though they didn't get rid of the stink, they were better than nothing. His jaw was pounding, and he knew his gut was going to be sore for the next few days. Sam couldn't see Kathleen, but he heard her laughing.

He stepped into the middle of the room, turned, and spotted her. His heart constricted as pure pain grabbed it and squeezed. She was on the couch, curled up in the fetal position, staring at her hands. It was a hysterical laugh, and it made his heart break. He strangled back a cry and took a step toward her. *Not too fast,* he thought.

"Kathleen?"

She looked over at him and stopped laughing. He took another step forward.

"Katie, please." He moved closer.

"I've thought about it. I don't really want to talk to you. Go away."

"Not without you, MyKate." His voice broke as he moved slowly forward. "I lose everything if I lose you." He reached out for her, but she turned away.

"You just missed Thomas." Her laugh was harsh. "You're too late. You're always too late." She looked around her. "I don't want to be here either, Thomas. I don't belong anywhere. It's over, gone."

Sam searched the solarium as she yelled into the air, talking to someone else.

"Go away!" She covered her face with her arms. He sighed. He knew she was talking to him again.

"Please, MyKate." Sam, reaching, took her hand. She shrank back.

He sank on rubber legs to the floor in front of her, his back against the chair. The wicker stuck into his skin like thorns, but he didn't care. All he cared about was the sound of her breathing. *Odd*, he thought, that he could hear it above the hum of the whirlpool, the birds outside the open windows, the rain. Time stood still as he sat there, trying to come up with any words that might work, his heart thudding in his chest. *Honesty*, he thought. *No games or exaggerations, tell her everything.*

"I'm going to talk, and you're going to listen. Are you listening?" He got no response. Sam reached around, pulled her off the couch, and down into his arms. He groaned in pain as her elbow hit his chest. "Dammit! Look at me, MyKate!"

She twisted and her face ended up somewhere between his arm and his chest.

"Thomas told me you were coming." Her muffled voice, coming out of his armpit, was that of a child.

Sam wondered if he was hearing her properly.

"I thought he was Casey, was jabbering away, and then I realized—flight suit." Her laugh was insanely muted by his chest. "How could I have been so confused? Oh well. I figured it out in the end." She pulled her head out and looked at Sam. "I guess that beats you out, eh? I saw him. Talked to him. Bet you've never talked to him face-to-face or, no … wait … face to—what would you call it … ectoplasm? Imagine. Now that's something I can tell Frank's kids." She sighed and her body sank into him. "He was right here. He was so nice. Imagine. We have a chivalrous ghost."

"MyKate …"

She pushed herself away and shot him a furious glance. "Don't call me that anymore."

"Kathleen." His eyes stung. His vision blurred.

"I'm tired, Sam. You should go."

"I'm not going anywhere. You promised." He raised her chin, searching for her eyes, needing her to stop hiding and really look at him. "You said you'd always be my friend."

"So now we're talking promises?" Grunting, she pulled her legs up closer, wrapping her arms around them as if protecting her heart as best she could. She rocked, back and forth, over and over again. This is what he'd done to her.

"I never lied to you." He took her hand.

"Omission of truth." She sniffed and jerked her hand away. "This is pointless, Sam. Go back to your wife."

"I'm not going anywhere until we talk."

"Oh!" Her laugh was harsh, a cackle. "Now we're going to talk!"

He saw it all in her eyes, nothing but pain, pain he'd caused. He took a deep breath.

"I screwed up, big time. I know. But my dreams came true four weeks ago, when you told me you felt the same way, that you loved me. I left here, walking on the moon, full of plans to finish exams and come home. That's when she told me she was pregnant. I never loved her, MyKate. I never once told her I loved her. She said she understood, but we had to think of the baby." He scratched his head, suddenly unable to look at Kathleen. "Maybe I shouldn't have married her, but it's my child." He touched Kathleen's face. It sounded so lame, the truth. "She said she knew a doctor, that she'd end it. What was I supposed to do?"

She stared at him incredulously. "All you had to do was talk to me, Sam. You should have told me about her right there that night, right under the lamp in front of the barn, before we went into the stable."

"I didn't know she was pregnant. I'd ended it with Missy. Don't you understand, MyKate? I wasn't thinking of her." The rain was falling harder outside, hitting on the glass and crying little rivulets down the pane.

She closed her eyes. "It doesn't matter. You could have phoned me. You didn't trust me." She began rocking once more.

"She has no one, Kathleen." He needed her to understand when he really didn't know why he'd married Missy.

She opened her eyes and stopped rocking. She stared at him, incredulously, and then took a long, deep breath, as if bracing herself. "Do you love her?"

He recognized the terror in her voice. His Kathleen would take on the devil in hell, but she was shaking with fear now.

"No." He pulled her tighter to him. "She said she'd get an abortion."

Kathleen's head shook slightly. She took a few seconds before she asked her next question. "Who is she?"

Sam felt the grip on his heart loosen just a little. "She's a law student from up Parkland way."

"And you felt sorry for her. Why?"

"Her sister died from cancer a while ago, and her folks don't give a shit about Missy. It was Casey and me all over again." He rolled his head trying to find a way to explain Melissa Anne King. "She's not your average lawyer type. I mean, I can't see her litigating anything, but she has this plan to work for a cleaner environment. And … and … and …" he stammered as he tried to find the right words, "then she has this career dream of being a singer."

"A singing lawyer?" Kathleen chewed on her lip as she took it all in.

"Pierrot is her hero."

"Who?"

"A clown. I guess a famous one."

She gaped at him, waiting, and he thought he might throw up. Rather than think about it, he blurted it out. "She's a clown. Okay?"

Kathleen blinked, stared at him, and then blinked again.

He nodded. "She works kiddie shows and sings. She plays the guitar."

"Oh no." Kathleen stared at him, expressionless. "This is too good."

Sam wondered if there was enough space for him under the couch. He closed his eyes. "She's complex."

Kathleen's snort sounded strangely sad. "You're screwing a clown?"

He cringed. "Was. I was. This is why I didn't say anything about her. She seemed like a good person, Kathleen. She donated marrow for her sister, and no one cared. She didn't have anyone and—"

"You just had to go and save her." She was nodding her head. "Wait a minute. She said she'd get an abortion?" She stopped nodding and studied him. "That doesn't make sense." She shook her head. "None of it makes any sense. A clown who loves children … all alone in the world … would kill her own child?"

"Well, she has parents, but they're in France or Brazil. We're not really sure." Sam was really beginning to feel the pain in his jaw.

"This does not make sense at all." She sat up and twisted to face him. "No. It doesn't matter." She began to rock again. "You should have told me about her."

His head fell back, and he sighed. "I didn't see it coming. It was just one night. Hell! There was never a *we* to begin with. She was just another girl." He watched her head droop. "I haven't touched her again. Not since we … me and you … please, MyKate."

"It doesn't matter. You did what you had to do. Now it's my turn." She stopped rocking and straightened up. "I talked to Mum yesterday, and she thinks I should be there in Boston to really push my work." Kathleen picked at her thumbnail with her fingernail as if she wanted to remove either one or the other. She choked out a short laugh. "Did you really have to marry her, Sam?" She put her hands up in front of her face, in the stop position. "No. It doesn't matter."

"Will you stop saying that? Everything matters. Billy and Casey are taking care of it all. I would"—he wanted to disappear—"but they told me I'd already done enough damage and to make it right with you."

"You're damage control?" Kathleen smiled, and he wanted to cry as he realized that, thankfully, she still had her sense of humor.

"I don't know what she'll do. She's already gone through so much, and the stress of having a baby is hard enough, but to be hated by the whole—"

"Will you just listen to yourself?" Kathleen's eyes burned fire at him. "She's old enough to get pregnant; she's old enough to bear the consequences." She choked back a cry and broke free of his grasp. Kathleen put her hands over her face, shaking with what Sam couldn't decide was grief or rage. She pushed him away, and pain once again ripped through his chest. "You've never felt sorry for me have you, Samuel Brennan. Good old reliable Kathleen. She-Can-Handle-Everything Kathleen. I didn't need saving, did I?"

Sam reached under the sweater he wore and pulled out the tiny box he'd been carrying around for almost a year.

"You are the strongest person I know, MyKate, but I know even you need saving once in a while." He took a deep breath. "You can ask Casey, if you want. I showed him. I told him when I came home last time." He dropped the box into her hand. "I bought it here before I left last September. I have the papers to prove it."

Kathleen looked down at the maroon box. Shaking, she opened it and stared into the velvet. Even without the sun, the ring sparkled. Tears sprang to her eyes at the sight of the ring. "This is the ring."

He nodded.

"You bought it?" She stared up into his eyes and then dropped her hands on her lap and her smile turned into an angry pout. "For frig's sake, Sam, why didn't you ask me or tell me in the stable or anytime when you were home? You had every opportunity."

"You said you wanted a proper courtship."

"What?"

"You and I didn't have very much time alone, did we? There was always someone there, and … well … I was going to do something really romantic when I got home."

"Are you nuts?" She yelled at him, her eyes wild. "You should have asked me. Even in front of everybody. You had this ring for me and went and married a … a … clown?" She shimmied away from him. "No. I'm not ready for this right now. You've ruined everything."

Panic rose like lava in him. "MyKate."

"No. You listen to me." She handed the ring and the box back to him. "I need more time."

His heart began to pound. "Don't you love me?"

"Yes. No. Of course, I love you, I think. I don't know what love is anymore, but this is nuts." She sat up and faced him. "I can't do this right now." She shoved him. "You're married! You can't be married to one woman and engaged to another!"

"What am I supposed to do?"

Kathleen sat, looking at the ring box for some time, her face showing no expression as she stared at it.

"Keep the ring. You have obligations. God! I can't believe I just said that!" She took his hand and pulled him to her. "You have to do this right, Sam. You have to find out for sure if she's pregnant. I'll bet she's not even pregnant. You have to figure out what you're going to do."

Sam sagged against her. "Billy said I have to stay away from her."

"That's all well and good, but you aren't taking up with me in the meantime, not where we left off." She shook off his hand.

He looked up at her, her eyes shining as brightly as he'd ever seen. "I can't live at home. Can I stay at your place?"

"You saw the sign." She smiled just a little. "Did it work? Did you get crazy?"

He nodded. "Would have had more impact if I hadn't been so worried about you."

Kathleen leaned over to him and ran her hand along his jaw. "You stink. What happened?" She touched his jaw. "Did Casey do this?"

"I need a shower. And a couple of painkillers."

Kathleen touched his lips. "Then we'll get you fixed up."

Sam felt himself crumble. Four weeks of hell appeared as tears, and as much as he tried, he couldn't keep them back any longer. Kathleen's arms around him, he let go and surrendered to the pain.

CHAPTER 32

Beyond the hills, the hungry clouds were growing, graying, waiting to swallow up the sun as Casey pulled up in back of Kathleen's house, turned off his truck, and closed the door behind him. Kathleen's cat needed feeding, and her rabbits too, he supposed. It took only minutes in the house to pamper Penelope Puss with canned food, and then he went out to the garage and was staring at the rabbits. The kits had really grown. They were of equal size now, the runt having caught up to his older brother. The mother rabbit tried to bite him twice when he was feeding her. Casey still didn't like the dam and wondered why Kathleen kept her. But then Kathleen had the patience and optimism needed to deal with most problems. He hoped she had the patience to deal with his stupid brother.

It caught his eye when he turned to leave. It sparkled in the dust of the garage, up on the shelf above the rabbits. The butt stuck out from behind a can of car oil. *Cripes.* He'd forgotten all about it.

He closed his eyes and heaved a sigh of relief—Kathleen's pistol, right where she kept it. He bit into his lip, thinking of all the possible nightmare scenarios that could unfold if she'd remembered it. Or maybe she had and just chose not to take it. But Casey knew it couldn't stay there, not with things as volatile as they were right now. Leaning up, he grabbed the gun and stuffed it into his jacket. *One less problem,* he thought as he left the garage.

Parking the truck, he looked around the yard, hoping for a diversion—maybe a calf caught outside a fence line or a chicken not cooped up and safe for the night—just so he didn't have to go into the house. There was nothing there but the house, just as cold and unwelcoming as ever, if not more. He fought the urge to turn and run when he entered the mudroom and heard his mother's voice, complaining and angry. He was too tired for this crap. She was cursing the heavens, obviously furious, using cuss words he'd never heard from her before. So she could use them, and he couldn't? Well, fuck her! He felt a new rage simmering inside him. It didn't help that his hand was now aching more than his back. All the cowboys and cops on TV never complained about the pain in their hands after they'd punched the crap out of someone. It hurt. Casey swore he'd never do it again.

He couldn't have Sadie to hold him; she was babysitting his brother and Kathleen. He'd been quite used to the feel of her hand on his forehead at night, of her head on his heart, of the sound of her father puttering around a noisy house and an open invitation to all the pie and cookies he could eat. Four weeks was all it had taken Casey to become a happy man. He'd been able to ignore the Beast, able to stand up to her without flinching, and even study how she hunted. She'd become less a nightmare and more a bad dream. Bad dreams eventually fade away.

He hung up his coat, and his eyes widened in alarm as he felt its weight hit the wall. The pistol. Standing in the dim light, checking through the opaque glass to see if anyone was watching from the kitchen, Casey reached into his coat pocket and removed the small revolver. It felt strangely cold in his hands as he studied it. Snapping the gun open, he removed the bullets and slipped the pistol into the belt in the back of his jeans where it would be hidden by his flannel shirt. He tucked the bullets deep into his pocket, and taking a deep breath, he opened the door.

"Rachel," Gran snapped at his mother. Casey's eyebrows rose a little at the sound of Gran's voice, stronger than it had been in months. There was no answer from behind his mother as she set the table for supper. "Rachel!"

"What?"

"Could you sit down please?"

The cutlery clattered as Rachel threw it on the table. "I don't believe this, that damnable bitch."

Casey studied his mother. She had diminished in size considerably since breakfast. Her eyes were red, as if she'd been crying—genuinely crying.

Gran, though, was stoic, more like the Gran who'd raised him and his brother. "You're going to break something," Gran said to his mother. She smiled at Casey as if everything was under control. "You have to control yourself, Rachel."

Rachel shot a glance at Casey. "Where have you been? Is Sam with you?" Her voice quavered as she turned back to Gran and began sliding the cutlery into place. "I don't believe for one minute that cockamamie story about her going to be a lawyer. Lawyer, my ass! She's no lawyer." Her voice was a roller coaster, up and down as she sailed from shock to anger to pain to disbelief. "That ridiculous story about her sister? I've never heard such malarkey! A baby. No." She shook her head. "That's what we'll have. No baby."

Casey felt his heart lurch at what he knew was a threat. He studied his mother.

Gran gave a startled gasp. "What did you say?" Gran said. There was no reply. "Rachel!" Gran's mouth was set in anger.

"No child!" Rachel shot him a monstrous glare. "Don't you look at me like this is my fault! Oh no! My fault? No. This one's a real gold digger. Not me! This isn't my fault! Hell! I would have taken Kathleen over that whore upstairs any day." She wagged her finger at him. "At least I can control Kathleen!"

Casey snorted and sat down at the table. Like that was the truth. This was getting better by the minute. Gran was more alive than he'd seen her in a while, and his mother was talking as if she knew Sam and Kathleen were meant to be together.

"She could be carrying your grandchild," Gran said.

"There's no baby. Sam's been hoodwinked. Those Kings were always good for nothing, no more than snobs." She looked over at Casey.

"Don't you believe he was hoodwinked?" his mother said to him.

Casey stared, amazed at the fear in her voice, amazed that she was asking his opinion. That the Beast was crying did not cause Casey's heart to break. The Beast was good at crying when she needed tears. It might work on others, but he'd had a lifetime of his mother's crocodile tears, and they weren't going to soften him now.

Rachel slowly turned away, her head shaking a little. She bristled and stared at Casey. "I would have expected it from you."

Ah. Nope. Casey snorted and looked away.

Casey looked over at the rather stylish luggage bag at the foot of the stairs. The bag would have looked like quality, except it was covered in clowns.

"I'll take her bag up," Casey said, knowing his mother's wrath was about to fall on him. He rose, leaning on the chair a little before he pushed it in. "I have to get her car keys from her. We have to move the tractor out for seeding tomorrow, and her car's parked right in the roadway."

"They're in the car," Rachel said.

Casey stared over at his mother as he picked up the bag, not wanting to hear how she knew.

"She told me." His mother growled and headed for the pantry. "Like I'm the hired help and I was supposed to move it. It'll be a cold day in hell when I move her car for her. You can tell Billy to just plow it away with the tractor. No. She can't leave if she has no car." She leered at Casey. "You move her car." She looked away again. "Supper's in an hour. Down here. You can tell her that!"

"Right." To Casey, the day was getting a little more interesting, now that the shock was over and lines were being drawn. Missy's bag was heavier than it appeared as he carried it up the stairs. It was obvious the clown planned on staying.

Gran stood up and placed her knitting on the chair. "I was going to get some fresh towels upstairs for her before she took a bath, but from the sound of the pump, she's already in there."

Missy was indeed in the bath, singing something about a ducky, a song Casey didn't recognize. He placed the bag just inside Sam's door and made a dash for his own room. He didn't bother to close his door all the way, wanting to hear if the bath began to drain and the bathroom door open.

The wooden slats of the old flooring were wide and worn, and they came up easily in fingers that knew where to lift. He'd had the secret hiding place for as long as he could remember. His treasures—bags of chips, candy bars, wrapped cakes, anything that would keep—he kept under the floorboard, there for when his mother refused to feed him. Slipping the pistol into the hole, he dropped the bullets next to it and then replaced the board.

"Casey?"

He jumped. His head jerked up and panic flooded over him at the sight of Gran standing at the doorway, laundry in her hands.

"I think these are yours?" She nodded at the navy towels on the top of her bundle. "I'm giving the pink ones to Melissa." Her eyes never left him.

He hopped over and took his laundry from her, knowing Gran had seen him place the gun in the flooring. "She's sure making herself at home."

Gran smiled, warily. "We'll all have to take a few steps backward and figure out what we're going to do. Anyway … that's it for the laundry. The rest can wait for tomorrow. These old bones need some sleep."

"Okay, Gran." Casey put the jeans on the bed. "Gran?"

She stopped and turned back to him.

"Gran?" He pulled her in and closed the door behind her, lowering his voice. "You don't trust Missy, do you?"

She eyed him with a frown. "You do?"

"I don't know. One minute she seems so helpless … the next …"

"Don't, Casey Brennan," Gran put her hand around the doorknob. "I watched her after you left. She walked out to the barn. She was sneaking, looking around to see if anyone saw her. She just arrived. What would she want in the barn?" Gran tsk-tsked as she shook her head. She smiled then and looked back at him. "Where did you get that gun?"

"I found it in Kathleen's garage when I was feeding her rabbits."

She nodded. "Make sure you cover that treasure hole well." She sighed. "It could have been much worse, you know, Casey. Kathleen did the right thing leaving it behind." She nodded. "You see what I mean about common sense? Kathleen could have made it so much worse, but even in her darkest hour, she left the pistol behind. You did the right thing."

She stepped out and closed the door behind her. Casey looked down at his treasure hole, wondering if he should move the gun somewhere else, and then he realized it was Gran. The gun would be safe. Billy. He had to talk to Billy. Billy would know what to do. Right now, he had to move Missy's car.

Rather than risk confrontation from his mother, Casey once more did the unthinkable and used the front door.

Her car was pretty. Casey walked around it and ran his hand along the hood. They could buy a lot of cattle for the price of an auto like that. He glanced over at the old truck Sam used and tilted his head a bit. Quite the change. What a mess.

He opened the door and sank his butt down on the leather bucket seat. It even smelled good. Then he tried to lift his legs in. No matter which way he twisted, he could not get them between the steering wheel and the seat.

Moving the seat back a little helped, but even Sam would have a rough time driving this. He looked on the dash for the keys. Nothing. They weren't on the passenger seat either. Leaning over, he pulled open the glove compartment. Everything tumbled out, the keys landing on the floor.

"Christ!" He reached over and gathered up the books and registration cards.

The photo was oddly shining in the hazy yard light, throwing the glare right back into Casey eyes, blinding him. He picked up the picture. Suddenly, a spark burned through him. Missy and a man were staring out into the jungle. They appeared to be on a balcony overlooking a rainforest. The man had his arm around her. He was in safari clothes, as Kathleen would say, a tall man, slim, and he had a cigar in his hand. He hadn't looked back at whoever was taking the picture. Missy had, though, and she was radiant, her blonde hair blowing in the wind, wearing an ivory, gauzy dress, the kind that Kathleen always said belonged on Caribbean beaches.

But it was the man in the photo who bothered Casey. He felt an odd dread as he studied him. Who the hell was he? They seemed so cozy, and the man's back seemed familiar. For a reason he didn't quite understand, he stuffed it into his pocket. He shoved everything back into the glove compartment and put the keys in the ignition. Casey was getting really tired of feeling sick, again. Maybe a quick drive would help. Putting the car into gear, he turned it around and gunned it, leaving a trail of dust behind him.

Chapter 33

By six in the evening, with no word from Sam as to when she could expect him back, Rachel had had enough. She'd be goddamned if she missed an opportunity to pounce on Sam's new little kitten. She tried to steady her hands, but the more she tried, the more the tray rattled. Perhaps she'd entice her down for supper. Tea-and-cookies time, clown face. Balancing the tray on her left hand, she knocked on Sam's bedroom door.

"Oh." Missy frowned when she opened the door and saw Rachel standing there. She seemed refreshed, clad in tight jeans and a light peach sweater, the expensive kind, pampered wool, angora. Men loved the feel of angora. Rachel had never been able to afford angora.

"Out of the way and I'll bring this in." Rachel didn't have to be nice. She brushed past Missy, checking to see that nothing had changed in the short time she'd taken over Sam's room but for her bags and a guitar that rested on a stand by the window, and there was a yellow curly wig on a stand on the dresser.

Rachel turned and faced Missy, forcing herself to be pleasant. "I come from out your way. Farther down, though, closer to South Berlin," Rachel said.

"One of those dilapidated shacks in the woods?" Missy gave her an uppity smile and then studied the china cup, her nose in the air. "Where's my husband?" Missy sat down on the side of the bed.

Rachel examined the room for signs of abuse. The guitar lay across the bed with what looked to be some sort of costume. "Don't look like stuff a lawyer would be carting around."

Missy's eyes narrowed. "Do you know where he is?"

Rachel wanted to slap her.

Missy hesitated as if not sure how to approach Rachel, as if she knew Rachel wasn't going to make it easy.

"Look, Mrs. Brennan—"

"No. You look, Missy. You just watch yourself around me. I've dealt with much worse than you."

Missy laughed. "Don't waste your breath, Mother Brennan." Missy rose and walked over to the desk, brushing past Rachel. She grabbed a cookie. "Mmm. Oatmeal raisin. Did you make these?"

Rachel felt her blood percolate. "How much do you want?"

"Oh God! Not that again. You people just don't get it. I love your son." Missy bit into the cookie and poured herself a cup of tea. "You can bake." She waved the cookie in front of Rachel. "I'll have to avoid you. Don't need the extra calories."

"Everyone has a price," Rachel said.

"Sam loves me."

Her eyes flew open like umbrellas in a downpour. "Loves you!" Rachel stuck her tongue between her lips and blew raspberries at the young woman, spit flying everywhere.

Missy stepped back in revulsion, wrinkling up her nose.

"What do you think you're going to gain, old woman? They want blood tests done. Doesn't that scare you, Rachel, blood work? There's all kinds of nasty secrets that can come out of blood work these days, aren't there!"

Rachel's felt the floor drop away from her.

Missy twirled and took a bow. "You should be worried about any blood tests, Mother Brennan. You might just get results you weren't bargaining for." She dropped her arms and slowly turned looking out of the window and over the valley before her. "It is pretty here. We could tear this decrepit house down and put up a proper home."

Rachel shook her head. "Oh no. This isn't about being pregnant and loving my boy, is it? This is much more. You're after a bigger prize."

Missy laughed again, hard and certain. She walked over to Rachel and opened the door wide. "A bigger prize? What kind of big prize could there possibly be in this dump? You asked what I want. I want your son, lady. That's what I want. Now ... if you'll leave me, I'll get some rest. The baby ..." She patted her stomach.

Rachel felt the blood return to her head. "Baby? Really? I'm sure by tomorrow at this time, there won't be a baby." She picked up the music book that was lying on Sam's desk and then glanced over at the young woman. "A lot can happen to a pregnancy in the early stages."

"Is that a threat?" Missy cocked her head, batted her eyelashes, and then grinned slowly. "I'm a lot smarter than Sam is. There are things he'd love to know, tidbits of truth that you never told him, and if I were you, Mother Brennan, I'd be very nice to me."

"And just what do you know?" Rachel hesitated and then sank down onto the bed, her voice breaking a little. "What?"

Missy stared at the cookie as if it were suspect, then smiled and bit into it. "Do you know where Lester's been all these years?"

Rachel felt the room begin to spin.

"Ah … now we're getting somewhere." Missy took another bite of the cookie, munching as she spoke. "I knew you'd be glad to hear about Lester. He thinks about you all the time, the little wifey back home." She laughed. "He's so lonely. He talks about the boys. I found out about Sam and Casey, three years ago, Rachel. Cute kids. I saw the photos, while I was sleeping with your Lester."

Rachel gripped the bedclothes, pulling them into her fists. "He's gone, won't be back. He wouldn't dare."

"It doesn't really matter, does it, whether I'm pregnant or not. Now that you understand how complicated life really is, how hard it is when a woman loses a baby, you'll be there for me, to support me. Won't you? Sam would be heartbroken if he lost this baby." Her laughter rolled through the walls as she crossed her arms. "He really is a nice man." Missy sat down next to Rachel. "Look, Mom. I can call you Mom, right? I know a hell of a lot more than you think. Lester told me things, things I never believed … until I met you. It didn't come out of him easily. I had to get him really drunk to talk. Birthdays were the hardest, those and Father's Day, Mother's Day. It was a birthday, I think, of one of the boys, when he broke."

Rachel's stomach lurched as she jumped to her feet. "You won't get away with this, bitch. Oh no! I've given up too much."

Missy snorted again. "You? Les was the one who lost everything." She picked up her guitar.

"This doesn't make any sense." Rachel stared at her out of the corner of her eye. "Why Sam? Why did you go after him?"

"Les is loaded." Missy positioned her guitar and began to sing. "Lavender blue, dilly, dilly," she stopped and twirled the other way. "Lavender green. When you are king, dilly, dilly, I shall be queen." She smiled.

Lester was loaded? Surely, she wasn't talking about money. There was no way. He'd had nothing when she sent him packing.

"You had no idea?" Missy said, laughing at her. "He's stinking rich. Where do you think all these farm animals came from?" She was shaking her head, mocking Rachel. "I can't believe you're really that dense. Lester Brennan made himself a fortune in a gold mine in Brazil. He got into emeralds too."

The bottom of Rachel's world dropped away from her and she was left floating, stunned by what she was hearing. Not her Lester.

"I spent years working on that man," Missy continued, nonplussed by Rachel's amazement, "and he spurned me. So Sam will have to do. Besides, Sam was a lot easier." She tittered as she picked up a ball from the bed. "He thinks he knows so much about women." She rolled her eyes. "Sam's problem is that underneath all that womanizing, he has a heart. But you wouldn't know that, would you? You don't know him at all." She tossed the ball into the air. "Did you know he hates university, Mother Brennan? Did you know he's in love with Kathleen? Do you know how much he hates you?

"No. You didn't know any of it. Did you know that Sam calls out Kathleen's name when he makes love to me?" She sneered. "Les didn't call out your name. Why would he when you tried to kill him? Wouldn't Sammy love to hear that one?"

Rachel couldn't listen. This was worse than the noises behind the walls. She headed toward the door.

"So. You're finally getting it, aren't you?" Missy sat on the bed again and smoothed down the wrinkled cover. "That's good. Take some time. Think it all over. You have nothing to lose by playing along, Rachel."

Rachel groaned. She covered her eye to stem the shooting pain, and then she fumbled with the doorknob in her panic to get out. Missy's laughter cut through her as she stumbled down the hallway. She had to think, figure out her next step. No baby. There could be no baby. Lester was loaded. That was a game changer.

Chapter 34

"I moved the tractor out. That car of hers is pretty slick." Casey pulled over the stable office chair and sat down. The horses were still calling him because he hadn't stopped to pet them as he usually did. Billy was at his desk, farm paper open to the local sales and a notepad with numbers scribbled across it. He closed it up when Casey looked over to see what he'd circled.

"How'd it go with Sam?"

"Better than before." Casey grinned. "He'll be staying at Sadie's tonight, coming over tomorrow."

"So … tell me about Sam's wife," Billy said, leaning back. "I saw her out poking around the barn a little before you got home."

"I haven't really met her yet, but I heard her singing." Casey nodded. "You aren't going to believe this one."

"Try me."

"She's a clown."

Billy stared wide-eyed at him.

"Yup. She's studying to be a lawyer, something to do with the environment, and her hobby is being a clown. She gets all painted up and sings at children's parties. At first, I thought Sam had flipped out, but then I saw her bag. It's covered in clowns." Casey proceeded to tell his uncle about Missy's familial woes, everything Sam had told them about his new wife. He leaned closer. "She juggles." He looked up. "I didn't ask if she rides a unicycle."

"Well, can't say as I ever had much respect for that father of hers. Too slick. Nope. Fruit don't fall too far from the tree." Billy took a sip of the coffee. "Ah. That's good. So. Is she all settled in?"

"Like she's lived here all her life. Mum is upset, of course, but Gran is great, completely in charge."

Billy leaned back into the chair, his head falling back with relief. "Things are going to happen pretty fast tomorrow, Casey. I'll need you to stay close."

Casey nodded. "What about the seeding?"

"That'll have to wait. We want to be here. We have some processing to do, anyways. If we leave those bull calves any longer, they'll be breedin'. Do you trust Sam to be here? I think he should stay at Sadie's. He's too close to her here."

Casey smiled. "We can't keep Sam away from here. He's been waiting to be here for so long. Kathleen's got a good hold on him. I doubt he'll get away from her too easy, and I wouldn't go putting any bets on the new wife against Katie."

Billy laughed. "No. I don't expect there'd be much of a fight."

"Oh. Forgot." Casey put his hand in his pocket and brought out the small photo. "Found this in her car when I moved it." He handed the photo over to Billy.

Billy looked down, brought the picture closer, then held it farther away, swore, and reached for his glasses. He didn't say anything when he finally saw what he was looking at, but Casey watched his uncle's interested expression turn into concern. Just as quickly, Billy tried to cover it up.

"That don't tell you nothing," Billy said, shrugged and handed him back the photo. "Put it back."

"But that's another man." Casey felt a knot in his gut. Now Billy wasn't telling him everything. "She's with another man." He shoved the photo over once more, pointing at it with his finger. "That's not her father, Billy. Look at him. Look at the way she's holding onto him."

"It could be anyone."

"It could be the father of her baby."

"If … she's pregnant. Here. Give it to me." Billy stuck his hand out, and Casey handed it over. Billy put it in his pocket.

Both men looked up at the sound of the stable door hinge as it creaked open, little by little. Billy slowly raised his finger to his mouth. Casey nodded and leaned back into his chair as Billy focused on the tack room door, his head tilting just a little at the sound of the horses snorting and whinnying on the other side of the wall. A sharp crack of Charger's hoof as it hit at the stall reverberated throughout the stable. Missy stepped in.

"Sammy?"

"Afraid not." Casey didn't extend his hand. "Just us."

She curtsied. "Casey. Nice to meet you again. Everything was such a mess in the house. Whatever have you done with my Sammy?"

"You know, Missy, I wouldn't call him that anymore if I were you. He hates Sammy, always has," Casey said.

"Oh. You must be Billy," Missy said, turning her attention to Billy, not missing a beat. "I heard so many good things about you from Sam, and when I saw Casey come in here, I just had to come over."

Casey cleared his throat. Billy's mouth formed a phony smile. "You're a curious little kitten, aren't you?" Billy muttered.

She glanced at Casey. "Have a nice drive?"

Casey nodded slightly. "Nice car. Wouldn't waste good cattle money on it though."

Her smile grew stiff, and she shifted her gaze back to Billy. "Is this your office?"

"I'm sitting here, so it must be one. What exactly do you want, young lady?"

"Gosh. I was hoping you'd be different from the rest of them." She sighed. "I'm already bored. I have to keep busy, Billy, until Sam realizes where he belongs and comes home." She looked around the tack room, fingering the bridles on the wall next to her. "I've had a long chat with Mother Brennan, and we seem to have reached an understanding." She studied the silver on the leather. "This is really nice, the whole place, at least the stable. It's nicer than the house. The barn too."

"Uh-huh. Did you enjoy rooting around the barn earlier?" Billy leaned back, his elbow on the desk, as Casey looked up, surprised. "Did you find what you were looking for?"

"I was just checking out the place."

Billy smiled a little. "So. I couldn't get a full picture from Sam. You're what? A clown, a singer or—what did he say?—right—a new-fangled en-vi-ron-mentalist."

"That's the way of the future," she said demurely.

He nodded, a little amused, and scratched the back of his ear. "I've been reading about them. The theory's good, but you're going run into a whole lot of trouble from the old school farmers."

"I suppose environmentalists need good lawyers." Casey grinned.

She stiffened. "Where's Sam?" Missy sounded genuinely worried.

"Sam didn't tell you much about us, did he?" Casey said, watching her sniff and stick her pug nose in the air. He leaned over to her. "Within a few days, I guarantee, you're going to want to be gone, as fast as that pretty little car of yours can take you." Casey knew all about wanting to be away from the house, and it felt strange to him how he wasn't the bottom rung of the ladder anymore.

"You can't keep Sam from me." Missy's voice broke.

"Lookit," Billy cut in as he stood, put the book he'd been working on in the filing cabinet, then closed it abruptly, and stuck the key in the top lock. "This ain't Romeo and Juliet. We aren't the ones keeping you apart. Sam needs time to figure things out. Surely he must have mentioned Kathleen."

She shivered. "I know he had feelings for her." She looked up at him with innocent eyes. "We didn't mean for her to find out that way."

"Yeah. Well." Billy leaned back. "That don't really count, young lady."

"Casey." She switched her focus on him as if she knew he was the weakest thread. "You have to believe me. No one else here believes me." Tears rolled over her lids.

"It's gonna take time, Melissa," he said.

"Then you believe me? That I love Sammy … ah … Sam?" Tears ran rivulets down over her painted on blush. "I don't know what I'd do if I didn't have him. Losing my sister was bad, but if I—"

"Ah … don't cry." He put his hand out to her and then drew it back again. What in the hell was he doing? He handed her his handkerchief. She refused it, giving him a small, appreciative smile.

"You never answered my question." Billy came around the desk. "What were you doing rooting around in my things?"

She cocked her head as a surprised expression crossed her face. "Whatever would I be looking for in your barn?" She walked over to Casey and reached past him to the awards and ribbons that were hanging on the walls. She took a first place red down and studied it, and Casey felt he was going to be ill from the perfume she was wearing. "Who won this?"

"I did." Casey pushed his chair away from her, overwhelmed by her scent.

"Cutting?" She looked up at him. "Do you do the whole rodeo thing? The history of the rodeo clown is really a fascinating one."

He took the ribbon from her offering fingers and stuck it back on the wall. "Just kid stuff."

"Are any of these Sam's?"

"This is not a social visit. Is it, Missy?" Billy sat on the edge of the desk.

She shot him a sharp look, and Casey was amazed at how quickly her expression had gone from sadly innocent to aggressive control. "Oh, Billy. I don't know if tonight's the right time to talk business." She smiled at Casey. "I do have some questions about farming here and how it differs from where I spent most of my summer vacations." She glanced over at Billy.

"As opposed to Brazil?" Billy said.

Casey watched Missy take a step back.

Billy slowly smiled. Walking to the door, he pushed it fully open. "It's going to be a busy day tomorrow, and I'm tired, so if you two don't mind, get out."

Casey laughed out loud. "Sure." He took Missy by the elbow. "Come on. When the boss says it's time, it's time. Supper's probably on the table."

She hesitated, staring at Billy over her shoulder as Casey escorted her out. His uncle was staring at her with hard anger, his eyes cold. Something else was up, but Casey knew he wasn't going to get any answers. What the hell was going on? Maybe he'd take a look at some of the files in the barn. He thought of the photo he'd taken from her car. Maybe he'd show the photo to Gran, even if he could see her reaction. He wondered if Sam might know. Tomorrow.

CHAPTER 35

A cool mist enveloped the valley below as a pair of hawks screeched at him, muffling the cries of the Canada geese as they moved in a *V*-shape, higher across the sky. The morning sunshine had not yet begun to bend through the barn windows; but it had all the markings of another promising day. Casey had wanted to stay in the barn, had wanted to be as far away from the fireworks as possible, but Billy had told Casey to go back to the house, that Billy would do the chores. He'd even shoved his nephew out the door.

"This place is going to blow shortly, Casey, and you gotta be in that kitchen at ten a.m. on the dot. Be on her like a wasp on garbage; you got that?" At first, he'd thought Billy had been talking about the Beast, but he hadn't been. He had been talking about Missy. "She has to take the divorce papers."

"What? Divorce papers?" Casey had stared at his uncle, his stomach gnawing once more. "How'd that happen? I thought these things took longer to get processed."

"Connections," Billy had said, and Casey had nodded, rolling his eyes. Of course, connections.

"And don't worry about the horses. I'll brush them down too." With that, Billy had shut the door on Casey so fast that Casey had wondered if his uncle had been hiding from this new beast too.

He'd already brought in enough wood to fill the stacks on the walls across from the stove. *Like a wasp on garbage*, thought Casey as he tried to look hungry or busy, anything to justify his being in the kitchen with his mother and grandmother at nearly ten in the morning. He turned at the sound of Missy descending upon them, and he almost laughed out loud. She was singing. He shook his head to make sure he wasn't mistaken, but, yes, she was singing.

"The more we get together … together … together …"

"This might be good," Casey muttered as Missy came through the doorway.

"Good morning, Gran, Mother Brennan." Missy smiled brilliantly for him. "Casey." Walking over to the fridge, she opened the door, her robe draping over her curves, very sexy until he saw the fluffy bunny slippers on her feet. Casey rubbed his face, his eyes peeking out from beneath his fingers as he tried to keep from laughing.

"Is Sam home yet?" she said with no apparent discomfort.

His mother, the image of a war mask on her face, her fists clenched together in a tight knot on the middle of her apron, stared at the girl, and Casey worried that Sam's wife might push her luck too far by the way Missy stared back.

"Good morning," Gran said politely, like Casey, staring at Missy's flimsy, canary-yellow negligee that was peeking out from under the robe. Gran glanced down at the slippers as Missy walked over and sat at the table, pulling a basket of oatmeal muffins toward her. "In my house breakfast is at six, and you come to the table dressed," Gran said. "Sit down and have some tea. How did you sleep, dear?"

"I slept very well, thank you. My, these look tasty. Did you make them Mother Brennan?" Missy, her lips a shade of shivery crimson that didn't match the warmth of the yellow robe, smiled coolly up at Rachel and then looked around the kitchen as if inspecting a scab. "The sun woke me. It was shining directly onto my pillow." She leaned closer to Rachel, Casey suspected, to emphasize her unhappiness. "I'm not a sun person. I have migraines, you know."

Casey choked. *Christ.* She was just like the Beast.

"Blinds." Missy's eyebrow rose as she inspected the curtains over the stove and knocked the top off her muffin. "You cornered the market on curtains, but we could use a few blackout blinds."

Casey looked out the window over the sink and turned the water on, hoping they couldn't hear his laugh. He grabbed a glass and poured himself some water. How he wished Sam and Kathleen were here to witness this. *No. They'd be more trouble than they were worth. Sadie. Sadie would love this.*

Missy prattled on. "I need my sleep. You ladies understand all about that I'm sure." She patted her stomach. "At least I still have my maidenly figure. Some women get so big so fast. I have enough cousins and friends who've all gone through the whole pregnancy thing. They glowed."

She glowed all right! Like radioactive waste! Casey watched his mother stiffen up and turn into something caged, rocking, muttering. It was more than obvious that his mother hadn't had such a wonderfully relaxing, glowing kind of sleep.

"Married. Oh no, no, no," Rachel said as she poured the tea with unsteady hands. "This isn't happening. Forever? No. This is a nightmare."

Missy stared at Rachel, bewildered. She looked over at Casey as if asking to whom Rachel was talking. He smiled and took a sip of his water. Raising her hand, Missy pointed her finger at her temple and rotated it. Casey laughed out loud. Missy was finally getting it.

Gran shot a glance over at him. "Open the window, Casey. Let's get some fresh air in here. Tell us about yourself, dear. You met Sam when?" Gran said.

Pushing on the window, he opened the kitchen to the dewy spring breeze. This was more entertaining than anything he'd ever watched on TV. He listened as Missy talked all about how gallant and tender his brother was. She spoke with her hands, not in the bubbling, exuberant way Kathleen did but with precise and deliberate gestures. *Performing*, Casey thought, *like she was constantly in the spotlight.* He could almost smell popcorn and hear the roar of the lion. Casey wondered if she was going to whip out a top hat or burning ring. He grunted, clearing his throat, once again holding his hand over his mouth to stifle the laugh. Maybe she could teach them a few tricks.

"You just can't forget eyes like Sam's." She stared over at Rachel maliciously. "Must have gotten them from his father."

A shadow passed over Rachel's face, and Casey thought that if his mother were a cartoon character, he would see steam coming from her ears.

Gran uncrossed her arms and reached for her teacup, her movements taut and nervous. "He has the same eyes as his uncle, doesn't he, Rachel?" she said.

"Ah, yes." Missy's face lit up. "Now that you mention it, he does rather resemble Billy, doesn't he, Mother Brennan?"

"How would you know?" The words burst from Rachel's lips with such force that Missy jumped as if something tiny and black had flown up her nose.

"I met Billy last night, didn't I, Casey?" She didn't bother to look over at him for confirmation. "Lovely man. Gets right to the point."

Casey grew interested at the look of warning his mother gave his grandmother, and what really bothered him was the look of understanding written all over Gran's face. More secrets, he assumed, and for some reason Gran seemed to be right in the middle of them.

Rachel's eyes turned cold. "Sam looks like me."

Missy dismissed her with a wave of her hand and a lawyer's laugh. "I know it was short notice, but I'm a great believer in love at first sight, fate, that kind of karma thing."

"And then there's the baby," Gran said with a polite smile. "You didn't say yesterday. How far along are you?"

Missy's smile seemed to disappear when she spoke to Gran. "Long enough for the tests to be positive. I keep good records."

A grunt came from Rachel who sat down in her chair, not drinking her tea, a twitch jerking her upper lip. "The doctor will know." She began rubbing the table with her middle finger, dragging her nail against the wood grain as if dredging for splinters.

"Did you call your parents, Melissa?" Gran said.

"Yes, I'm afraid I did. I'll have to reimburse you. It's pricey, calling Brazil."

Casey watched with surprise as Gran's eyes shot up. "I thought they were in France."

"They're on holiday right now." She looked back at Rachel. "In Brazil."

"Long way from Killkenny County, Missy," Casey said, and all three women looked at him as if they'd forgotten he was there.

"My parents travel a lot."

"You have to admit that's quite the story," Casey said as he put the empty glass down on the counter and opened the fridge. He peered into the cold. "I mean, you're a local girl whose parents live in France but vacation in Brazil. You're a science major who wants to be a lawyer, who plays with clown balls and sings kiddie songs. Did I get it all?"

She peered over at him with an expression of pure contempt.

He closed the fridge back up, not really hungry, getting what he wanted in her cold response. He pulled the cookie jar over to him once more.

"Okay." Missy crossed her legs and her arms. "It's been long enough. Will someone tell me where Sam is?" she said, almost demanding. "Can I at least get a phone number?"

Gran smoothed down her tan slacks and did up the top button on her cardigan. She craned to peek out the window. "I hear a truck. Early in the morning for company. You see what I mean, Melissa? You never know when someone might drop by."

Casey leaned closer to the window above the sink and then checked the clock. He had to admire his uncle. When Billy said ten, he meant ten, and Casey knew the delivery van wouldn't be there for any other purpose than to help push out the newest Mrs. Brennan.

"You know, Gran, I think it's going to be a nice day," Casey said as the van pulled up and stopped behind the house. "I've got a lot to do today, but first things first. I have to get up to Sam's room and take his posters down."

"They don't bother me." Melissa smiled demurely.

"That's not the point," Casey said, watching her carefully. "Sam wants them down." He stared at the truck outside.

"Flowers." He looked up in false surprise and feigned confusion. "Did I miss a birthday?"

The van was as ordinary as any white van, with the dust of the county covering the rust from the winter's salt. "Petals Aplenty" was plastered on the side, and within minutes, someone Casey had never before seen got out and walked around to the van's side door.

"Flowers?" Gran said, looking back behind her. "Really, Thomas, you shouldn't have."

Missy stared at Gran from the corner of her eye and pulled her negligee closer to her. "It's obvious they're for me." A huge smile formed on her face as she stared at Rachel, her head cocked to one side. "I told you Sam loves me."

Casey watched as the man outside lifted a vase of what Casey guessed must have been two dozen white roses from the back of the van and started toward the house. Rachel was the first to move as they all jumped at the sound of the knock on the door.

"No, Mum. I'll get it." Casey spoke up and placed his hand on her shoulder, pushing her gently down as he moved past her to the door. "Morning. Come on in."

The deliveryman stepped under Casey's arm, balancing the vase like a seasoned pro, an envelope, probably his delivery papers, neatly tucked under his arm.

"Good morning, ladies. *Be-a-u-teeful* day out there, isn't it?" the man asked, peeking from behind the flowers. "Would I be able to find a Melissa Anne King Brennan here by any chance?"

Missy bounced, clasping her hands together. "I am she." She stood up, her nightgown drifting in wisps around her, her robe open now, revealing more than Casey really wanted to see of her diminutive breasts.

The man walked over to Melissa, pulled the large manila envelope from under his arm behind the bouquet, and with little difficulty put in her hand. "You're served," he said and winked at her. "Now, as for the roses, which one of you lovely ladies is Mae Brennan?"

"Oh, Thomas." Gran's hands went up to cover the flush on her face. "Really. How sweet."

"They're rather heavy, ma'am." The driver looked at Casey.

"I'll take them." Casey reached out for the flowers, watching Missy gawk at the envelope in her hand. They were heavier than he'd thought, and he remembered why he didn't care for roses as he snagged the top of his hand on a thorn. He placed them on the buffet, close to Gran's chair so that she could admire them and then reached into his pocket for a twenty.

"No need," the deliveryman said. "It's already been taken care of." He swung back to the door. "Have a nice day." The man was in, out, and gone as efficiently as he'd arrived. Casey was sure the pride and love he had for his uncle could be seen all the way into town.

"Gran, there's a card. Do you want me to read it?" Casey reached into the roses and removed the card.

"What is this?" Missy demanded. Anger burned her face as she stared at the envelope.

Casey looked back at her. "You've been served. Legal talk. I thought you were studying law." He heard his mother hoot and slap her knee. The Beast had laughed at something he'd said. Another first.

"You've got to be kidding!" Missy's eyes tore right into his.

"Nope. It's a done deal." He told himself not to gloat, that it was only check, not checkmate.

"Sam wouldn't … not this soon. No one has …" Missy's voice petered out as a flash of sudden insight crossed her face.

Casey didn't like the look. Once again, he was missing something. Had Billy been behind this? Missy's face hid more secrets. She shook the envelope at him. "You won't get away with this!" She brushed passed him and into the living room, her lingerie billowing around her, sobbing softly. Casey wondered which song she'd break into when she put her sorrow to music. Perhaps "D.I.V.O.R.C.E." or maybe "Yesterday." No. She'd probably go with a kiddies "London Bridge is Falling Down?" That would be appropriate. He wondered if he shouldn't go get her guitar for her, and then a stab of guilt rose in his gut like heartburn from one too many hot dogs.

Well, Christ, he thought. No one else was going to see if she was okay. Someone had to tell her to pull herself together, if only for the baby. Did someone have to make sure she opened the envelope? He grumbled and followed her into the living room.

Missy was on the couch, a wash of buttercup-yellow fading over the harvest-gold upholstery. The envelope rested on the coffee table in front of her, the documents already out and in her hands. Casey noticed the slight tremble, tears running down her cheeks as she ran through the pages.

She glanced up at Casey.

"He's served me with a restraining order." She held up a legal-sized sheet of paper. "Separation papers." She picked up another. "Divorce papers. Even an annulment." She looked back down at the papers. "He's even filing suit on rights to the child … should there be any." Missy threw the papers on the coffee table. "I've lost him." Her whole face melted down into this red contortion as she wailed and sobbed into the arm of the couch.

Casey rolled his eyes as he walked over to her. "Missy."

She appeared not to hear. Casey sat down next to her. "Missy?"

"I thought he loved me." Her voice was muffled and petulant. Her head come up from her arms, surprisingly pretty for someone sobbing the way she'd been. "What am I going to do, Casey?" With that, she threw herself onto his lap and commenced crying once more.

Casey froze, overcome with disgust and pity, his hands in the air above him, wishing he'd stayed in the kitchen. Her shoulders shuddered, and her head rested heavily on certain parts of his anatomy, parts that were very rarely shared with anyone. Sadie's head had been the only one, and he did not like the position Sam's new wife had put him in. He squirmed a little. But Missy did not appear to be moving. Casey tried to edge himself away.

Her hair slid down over her face. "Why does Sam hate me so?"

Was this woman completely brain-dead? He could think of a least one reason. Pregnancy to trap a guy into marriage wasn't a good start.

But this was a new Missy. She seemed genuinely upset and very vulnerable. So Missy was a little complicated. Most artists were, except for Kathleen. Kathleen didn't seem that complicated. Missy's sobs were almost meows now, and Casey was hoping that maybe she would get off his lap before anyone came in and got the wrong idea.

Casey's head shot up at the shadow in the doorway. His back jerked ramrod stiff. He turned to the doorway and stared. Sadie's expression said it all. She seemed about to throttle the woman or him. He felt the bottom of his world drop away.

"Sadie." He knew it sounded lame. "Sadie." He tried once more.

Missy's head shot up. "Oh no! I've done it again. Why does this kind of thing always happen to me?"

"Oh, please!" Sadie said as she looked at Missy with disgust. Then her eyes shifted to Casey.

Sadie studied him, her eyes boring holes into his. Her face changed from outrage, to disappointment. He knew she couldn't have been more shocked if her mother had walked into the room. Her eyes left Casey and focused back on Melissa Anne King, at the flimsy robe, the hair, the smudged lipstick. Sadie glanced abruptly down to Casey's lap, to the smear of brilliant whore red on his jeans and then back to Casey. Her lip trembled slightly as she spoke. "Billy wants you at the barn. We're castrating today."

Melissa had begun to move, but Casey was faster in his attempt to extricate himself from his shaky situation. As he jumped up, Melissa fell on the floor with a thud. Sadie seemed almost satisfied by that. Casey picked up the scattered papers and handed them Missy as he helped her to her feet.

"Oh God! I'm sorry!" Missy said.

He looked up at Sadie as if for help and then turned back to Missy.

"You'll be all right. I think you'd better read the papers over," Casey said.

"I'm sorry. It's not what it seems." He didn't look at Sadie but hightailed it past her, with what little dignity he could muster, wondering which of the many ways he would approach explaining what had occurred.

Sadie was right behind him through the kitchen and out the back door. "What in the hell was that all about?"

"She was upset! That's all!" He wasn't stopping to face her. He couldn't. He could hardly keep up to her.

"She was all over you!" She forged ahead.

"I was … comforting her," he waved his hand in the air. "She was upset and alone, and I just sat down and then … and … then …"

"Casey! Please!" She turned and grabbed him.

"It wasn't how it looked."

Her head tilted slightly. "I know."

"Oh." He stopped to think about that. She took his hand and pursed her lips, as if trying to figure out what to say. "You have to watch out for women like her, Casey. She uses men."

He blinked several times and looked away. "What would she want with me?"

"Casey!" She touched his face. "There are all kinds of women out there who would want you."

He closed his eyes and looked away. She had that wrong. He'd just been really lucky when Sadie had breezed into his life.

"It's not just you, Casey. I don't know what she wants, money maybe, the land, security …" She shook her head. "She doesn't really want Sam, or she wouldn't have been on the couch with you. She'd have been dressed and out of here last night and over at my place, banging the door down to get to Sam. That new bride let him walk out yesterday straight into the arms of another woman. That doesn't make sense, does it? She's happy just to be carrying his child and lying in his bed. Does that sound like love to you?"

Casey's face slowly soothed into a half smile. "I felt sorry for her, getting the papers, crying on the couch."

Sadie stopped, suddenly confused. "Getting what papers?"

"Divorce papers."

Sadie took a step back and then grinned. "Good." She smiled as she shook her head. "Come on." She grabbed his arm. "They're in the barn with Libby. Kathleen brought … damn!" She stopped dead. "I forgot the ice pack."

Casey pulled her forward. "We're not going back in there."

"But that's the reason I came to the house."

"If he wants an ice pack, Katie can go in and get it." Sadie stopped as if she was thinking it through.

"On second thought, that might not be such a good idea." He put his arm around her and moved her toward the barn. "You wouldn't believe what happened in there earlier." Sadie's face relaxed as he gripped her hand with enthusiasm. He stopped and listened to the horses. They were whinnying at the sound of voices outside.

"Quite the ruckus. Charger's hyper today. Hope Sam can handle him," Sadie said, her voice filled with concern.

Casey smiled. "If he can't, no one can."

She grabbed Casey's arm, pulled it tighter around her, and they continued the walk to the barn.

Casey pulled the barn door open. "Hey! We're here."

Casey was glad to see Sam finally occupied. Sadie hadn't been kidding when she'd blurted out about castrations. That's exactly what they'd planned on doing. According to Sadie, Sam had been hard to manage that morning, bored, wanting to get to work. Only Kathleen had kept him from going stir crazy; and that was because she wasn't talking to him.

Kathleen hadn't really recovered from the day before. Her arms crossed in front of her defensively, she seemed to be watching everyone with a new, cold suspicion. She wasn't saying much, but Casey knew Kathleen was doing her best to keep her anger under control.

"This is nuts," Sam muttered, slipping his arm around Kathleen's waist. "You look really good. Then you always do when you wear black." Kathleen removed his arm and stared at him angrily.

"Like that will work," she said.

He backed away a little. "There's seeding to be done, and Billy says the fence lines are a mess."

Kathleen's face softened as she turned to Sam and took his hand in hers.

"You're not seeding, Sam," Kathleen said. "You're not fit to do anything, let alone go out on a bumpy tractor. We shouldn't even let you go riding this afternoon. You'll slow us down."

His head popped up, his relief at Kathleen's hand holding him. It turned into a look of pure pleading. "I'm going riding," he said.

Kathleen's eyes studied his jaw. "The ice will help." She looked over at Sadie, raising her eyebrows.

"Sorry," Sadie said. "It's a zoo in there. I forgot all about it."

"I'll go." Kathleen turned toward the door.

Sam shot her a cautious no. "Casey should go." He looked over to his brother as if beseeching, don't let her anywhere around Missy the Clown.

"Oh no," Casey said. "I'm not going back."

"I'm perfectly able to go into the kitchen for ice without killing the woman." Kathleen put her hands on her hips.

Sam laughed harshly. "No. You're not. Kathleen stays here."

Casey shook his head, agreeing with Kathleen. *Hell! More fireworks!* "Katie will be fine, won't you, Kate?"

"In and out," Kathleen said. "Won't even see her. Besides, I have to get my sketch pad." She started out of the barn with a shake of her determined head and waved back at them.

Billy came out of his trailer and passed by the boys, directing his gaze at Casey. "I'm going into town. Keep Melissa away from him."

Casey stepped out of his way. "I don't think that will be a problem." He grinned and nodded as Sadie and Sam talked to Libby. "Kathleen's in rare form. I think she's scaring Sam. Hell! She's scaring me." Casey studied his uncle. "That was pretty slick this morning."

Billy slowly grinned and gave a quick nod. "We do have our ways. Did it go off okay?"

Casey nodded. "What's with the *we*? You did it all. All I did was escort the guy inside."

"Always helps to have friends. Remember that." Billy patted Casey on the back. "Your father would be proud of you, son."

"Yeah ... well ... his opinion doesn't count for much," Casey replied.

Billy looked down and quickly away, and then he stopped, his shoulders sagging as he turned back to them. "It's not all black and white, Casey."

"Right." Casey turned away and wandered over to join Sadie and Sam in front of Libby's stall.

Billy grunted, nodding toward the stable. "Have fun." He patted his work pants for his wallet, and he swung out the door. "I won't be long."

"That's fine. We'll hold down the fort." Casey waved.

"Maybe we should move them out to the grass too." Sam turned away from Libby and her calves and waved to Billy. "We can't keep them isolated forever."

"We can't let Libby out with the rest of the herd," Casey said.

"Why not?"

"What if she comes into heat?"

"This afternoon? She just had the twins." Sam stared at his brother and laughed. He winced and grabbed his jaw. "They aren't house pets. Help me here, Sadie."

Sadie put her hands up. "Oh no. This isn't my fight."

Casey wrapped his arm around her. "I didn't say they were pets. It's just …"

Sam shook his head. "They should be on the grass."

"A few more days. Maybe we could put them on the front field," Casey said.

Sam looked down at his feet and kicked at the boards. Then he nodded. "Right. The front field then. Today. Not only is the grass ready, but it would be good business-wise for the locals to see what they're worth." It was a regular habit for fellow breeders passing by to stop and study each other's livestock.

"I don't know if today's good." Casey rubbed his chin. "We don't want to put them out too early."

Sam groaned. "If you had your way, you'd have them bunking in the house." Sam stretched his jaw. Then Sadie glanced out the barn door.

Sam peeked out the door of the barn too and across the yard to the house. Casey raised one eye. "Would you stop worrying about Kate, Junior?"

Sam's jaw locked. "You know, Casey, I hate that almost as much as *Sammy*."

Sadie stood, her arms crossed, watching for Kathleen as Casey turned to him, his face, a mask of disbelief. "I thought you liked it."

Sam snorted and turned back to the grain. "I didn't want to hurt your feelings. You seemed to get braver when you said it. Kind of ..." He rubbed his chin. "Never mind."

"No." Casey's head turned. "You started it."

"So I'm ending it."

"No. I've always called you Junior." Casey bent down to remove sneakers and put on his barn boots. Then he looked over to Sadie with an embarrassed grimace. "You never said anything."

"That's because when you said it, you seemed older, kind of like the older brother I nev—" Sam stopped talking, looking as though he'd rather change the subject, but Casey wanted an answer.

"The older brother you never had?" Casey said.

Sam closed his eyes for a moment. "It's not that bad. There have been times, a lot of them. When ... well ... you know."

"Sorry. I don't." Casey said, and Sadie reached over to take his hand.

"You know ... when you acted like a big brother," Sam said.

"Right. Like?"

"The prom." Sam closed up the iodine and placed the box of castration elastic bands on a wall brace.

Casey smiled slightly and slipped into his shoes. "You were a knob."

Sadie tried to hide the smile. "Casey told me. You were, Sam."

"I know. I know. And then yesterday ... when you hit me." Sam smiled sadly.

"I said I was sorry," Casey said.

"Don't be." Sam rubbed his face. "I've never been prouder of you." He looked away, rolling his eyes. He looked at Libby. "I deserved it."

"You ain't near absolved, Junio—Sam. You're on your way though." Suddenly Casey's eyes shot over to Sadie. "Great." He rubbed his hands together in anticipation. "Let's get this castrating done so we can enjoy the horses."

Sam looked up at him then back. "Do you think MyKate will keep it cool?"

"That's it," Sadie said. "You guys hold down the fort." She headed to the door. "Don't worry. We'll be right back."

Before they could say either a yea or nay, she was out of the barn, trying to catch up to Kathleen.

CHAPTER 36

The day was hanging on to the sapphire blue above but was fading to a white haze of cloud on the horizon. Kathleen rolled up the sleeves of her blouse. It was going to get hotter in the afternoon before it rained.

"Hey!"

Kathleen turned at the doorway of the stable and grinned as Sadie ran to catch up. "Are you the cavalry?"

"The guys got concerned. I'm here as a 'just in case.'"

"They probably thought I'd go in and shoot her." Kathleen giggled. "I was worried about the horses. They're really worked up today."

"I should have gone back for the ice." Sadie had a rather guarded expression as she looked over at Kathleen, as if she were nervous. "I don't know if it's a good idea, you going in." She pursed her lips together. "But if it makes you feel any better, I found Missy on Casey's lap, crying about the divorce papers."

Kathleen stopped dead. "No."

Sadie nodded and took a long, deep breath. "Thing is that technically I have no right to react like I did, but—"

"You have every right, Sadie."

Sadie's expression changed from concern to introspection. "The trick with women like Melissa Anne King is to let her do the talking. It's harder than it looks. If you just pull back a bit and let her talk, you'll find out all kinds of things. But you have to listen. She's a pro at listening. She takes it all in, without you knowing she's studying you, and then when the time is right, she strikes. The thing is she doesn't know anyone else can do it." Sadie stopped and faced Kathleen. "You can listen, can't you?"

Kathleen's smile grew wide and a devilish tingle ran up her spine.

Sadie laughed.

"Sadie?" Kathleen chewed on her lip. "I've never seen Casey so happy. He really loves you. I always knew that when it happened it would be fast and sure."

Sadie turned the color of the hummingbird feeder.

Kathleen needed to know. "You do love him, don't you?"

Sadie laughed aloud, tears springing to her eyes. "He doesn't know it yet, but I'm going to marry him."

Kathleen whooped. "Knew it. Just like I said."

Sadie started walking again. "How about you and Sam?"

Kathleen's head wobbled. "I waited a long time for Sam to wake up, and now it's all gone to hell." She looked down at the ground. "I don't know if I can get over what Sam did. How can I marry someone who has such little trust in me?" Her head jerked up, and she stared at the stable. "Wow! They want out. You hear that?" Kathleen said as she heard the horses calling them and a loud thumping coming from the opened stable door. "Charger's ready to go. He knows Sam's home."

"They were like that when Casey and I came by."

Kathleen nodded as they reached the house. "All they need is a bit of fun." She closed the house door after them and, moving ahead of Sadie, opened the mudroom door to the kitchen.

It was more quiet than usual without the sound of Rachel's television, but the steady beat of the mantel clock in the hallway was soft and comforting. Gran wasn't at her chair, but it was rocking anyway, a sight Kathleen had seen time again and again. The room smelled of the roses. Kathleen exclaimed, "Wow!" when she studied them.

"Hello," Kathleen warbled out. "Come on in," she said and pulled Sadie into the kitchen. "Would you look at those?" She walked over and cupped a rose under her nose. She studied the card. "They're for Gran."

"The ice, Kathleen. A baggie works best," Sadie said and headed for the drawer next to the fridge as Kathleen opened the fridge door. Kathleen stopped. There were voices coming from upstairs.

"Do you hear that?" Sadie whispered behind her. "That's Missy. Who's she talking to?"

Kathleen walked over to the bottom of the stairs and then tilted her head to hear. "What is that?"

Sadie stepped over and listened too. "I think that's music. Is that music?"

Kathleen nodded and turned to Sadie. "Sam says she doesn't talk. She sings children's songs. Listen."

Adrenaline coursed through Kathleen's veins as the plan unfolded before her eyes. She grabbed Sadie. "Leave the ice." She pulled her into the hallway and started down toward Gran's room.

"Where are you going?" Sadie said, following along. "Kathleen."

"Shhh." Kathleen opened Gran's door. She put her hand up in front of her mouth to silence Sadie. "Get in here." Pulling Sadie into the tiny room, she closed the door behind them.

Gran's room used to be the sewing room years before. It was no bigger than a large closet, but it had a window that faced east, and it was painted a pretty periwinkle blue. The dresser was antique but still held its shine, without mar. The oval mirror above the dresser was framed in carved mahogany that matched the dresser. On the top of the dresser was a linen cloth that Kathleen had embroidered for Gran years before, tiny little daisies and kittens. Kathleen didn't know how Gran had managed to keep it so clean and crisp all the time. It had hardly faded and was always on the dresser when Kathleen entered the room. The bed had an old iron head and foot and was covered in Gran's matrimonial quilt, ivory and eggshell lace on top of cotton. The mattress was only a three quarters, but Gran said there was more than enough room because Thomas never took up too much of the space. Kathleen took a deep whiff of sweet tobacco. "Do you smell that?"

Sadie's eyes registered amazement as she studied the room. She sniffed. Kathleen didn't have time to stop and luxuriate in ghostly vapors. She headed straight for the closet and opened the door.

"Kathleen!" Sadie whispered, sounding obviously concerned.

"Shh. Come with me." Kathleen pushed on the back wall. It gave way and moved back.

Sadie gasped but put her hand next to Kathleen's to move the door back.

"This is the old stairway. It was used for the servants in the original house." Kathleen poked her head in, and shimmying through a bit, she used her back to push the door all the way. "We generally never use this during the day, too risky, but it's great at night." She moved through, grabbing two out of three flashlights they kept hidden on the second step for just such occasions. Flicking it on, she handed one to Sadie, turned on her own, and motioned her to follow.

Kathleen moved cautiously, pulling cobwebs down. "We can hear everything from up there." Sadie moved in and closed the closet door but left the wall door open, taking the chance that Gran wouldn't notice the draft or noise.

"No. Wait. Kathleen. We should turn around."

The stairs creaked a little, but not too much, surprising for their age, but they weren't the problem. It was the dust and spiders, wires, and crackling plaster between the lathes that seemed to unnerve Sadie.

There was an almost inaudible crackle. Sadie gasped as she stared down at the floorboards.

"Are there rats in here?" she asked, the light shining straight ahead and all around them.

Kathleen put her index finger in front of her lips, trying to keep it as quiet as she could. "Don't tell me you're afraid of mice," she said softly.

"Mice, no. Rats?" Sadie said as quietly as she could, but it came out forced and frightened. "Tell me there are no rats in here."

"There's no rats in here."

Kathleen grinned when she heard Sadie give a skeptical laugh. They stopped at the top step, just a wall away from the conversation going on in the hallway.

"That's Gran's voice." Sadie leaned over and whispered. "You can hear everything from here."

"They're in Sam's room." Kathleen shone the light on a dusty exit. "If you go farther on, you can get into Casey's room and the Beast's lair." Kathleen fell sharply back on the top of the stairs, and wedging her arm up, she wiped the dust off. "Have a seat," she whispered. "You have a spiderweb in your hair. Here." Kathleen reached over and batted at Sadie's hair, hitting her hand on the beams above. She shook her head, laughing quietly. "Did I say there wasn't much room in here?"

Singing. Missy was definitely singing. Kathleen tried to place the song. Then she remembered her nephews Mick and Mac clapping along to their mother's voice, their tiny little fists reaching for her hair as she sang it, "All the Pretty Little Horses."

"Do you know this one, Gran? It's an old lullaby," Missy said to Gran, her voice haughty. "It's Lester's favorite."

Kathleen gasped. *Lester?* How in the hell did Missy know Sam's father? And she knew him well. Mr. Brennan had always sung that to them, minus the stanza about the bees picking out eyes of the pretty little horses. That part always made Kathleen sad.

Missy was singing again. "Way down yonder in the meadow lies a sleepy little lambie, bees and butterflies, pickin' out his eyes. Poor little thingie's callin' mammie."

Kathleen's head lowered, and her jaw stuck out a little as she hummed. *Frig!* She hated that song! Missy was now talking.

Sadie signaled Kathleen. "Where's the Beast?"

Kathleen shook her head and raised her shoulders.

"Would you stop, please?" Gran said. She did not sound happy. "Rachel"—Gran raised her voice—"is a very dangerous person, my dear, and you could make the situation worse."

Kathleen had hardly ever heard Gran angry.

"I can take care of Rachel. All you have to do is accept me as Sam's wife. I love your Lester." Missy replied emotionless. "Think about it. He could come home. We could be a happy little family. After all, Casey is an adult now. You don't have to protect him anymore."

"What did she say about Casey?" Sadie said.

Kathleen turned her ear closer to the wall. "Shh."

"If you love Lester, why did you marry my grandson?" Kathleen heard Gran ask.

"I get what I want, Gran. Besides … I love Sam."

"I hate to tell you this, dear, but we had all agreed it was time for Lester to come home. You've just taken a bad situation and made it worse. You don't know what Rachel is capable of, and if anything happens to either of those boys, it will be on your head, and you will get nothing."

"Why don't we go ask her?" Missy said.

"What are you doing in here, Gran?" Rachel said, abruptly, obviously angry.

When had she entered the room?

"I'm getting some clothes for Sam," Gran said, too quickly.

Missy's voice weakened as if she were leaving the room. "If you ladies will leave and let me change, I'm going for a ride."

Missy's words sent such a chill through her that it numbed Kathleen. She must have heard it wrong. There was no way. That woman was not going to ride her horses, not any one of them! The Brennan men had always talked about the horses as hers as well as theirs. She'd always been a part of the farm because Sam and Casey made her feel this way, and now, here was this wife acting like she could just waltz in and take over the stable.

"Come on." Sadie pulled Kathleen down the stairs. "Damn!" She'd banged her head on a rather old beam. "We need to get out of here." She pushed open Gran's door, and Kathleen followed her through into the kitchen. "We can't look like we overheard."

Kathleen blinked at the light. "Right." She took a deep breath and then coughed out dust. "Right."

"Hopefully they didn't hear us. Hell! We're covered in grime." She patted down Kathleen's flyaway hair and then began wiping the cobwebs off her arms. "You had to wear black. Let me see your back."

Kathleen didn't care if they knew she'd overheard. She looked into Sadie's eyes. "What am I going to tell Sam?"

"The truth." Sadie moved past her and grabbed the box of baggies. She pulled one out and headed for the freezer. "We'll fill a few of these with ice. You get a towel. Maybe Billy. You could run it by Billy, but I think both of them need to know, Casey as well as Sam." She began shoving ice cubes into baggies as she talked. The ice cubes cracked and scraped against each other. "Right now we have to get out—"

"There you are." Both girls froze as Gran stepped into the kitchen.

CHAPTER 37

Billy always felt the need to pound in fence posts whenever he passed the No-tell Motel. That wasn't its real name, but that's how everyone knew it. The sign had toppled over five years before. With its post snapped in the middle, the sign now rested in a flowerbed in front of the office. It read sideways, Nortell Motel, but the *r* had been rubbed off thanks to local delinquents in aid of a good joke. The black shutters on the white paint and bent sign made it appear seedier lately, and now Billy was about to enter room number eight.

Why did it have to be room number eight? This is where it all ended for him, years before. Now he was back again, to the same room, to fix the mess he'd made. Squaring his shoulders, he grabbed his keys and opened the truck door, pulled his cap down over his eyes, and stepped out. He hardly glanced at the rusted-out truck parked there in front. Keeping his head down, he walked up to the door and knocked, feeling as dirty as the paint shavings that flaked off and stuck to his knuckles.

"It's open." The voice inside was low and strong.

Billy paused, only for a moment, and then he turned the knob and entered. His eyes weren't as fast at adjusting to light and dark as they used to be. The door closed behind him.

"Been a long time, Billy."

Billy turned and looked at his brother's face. There weren't many times when Billy had seen his brother scared. All of them involved the lads. Same this time. Billy was surprised by the lines, the graying hair, and the little-boy-lost expression on Lester's face.

"Should never have been this long," Billy said and held out his hand. Les took it, and what started out as a shake became a bridge between the brothers. All the pain, all the loss, and all the anger seemed to fade a little, and the room became a bit brighter.

Billy grabbed Lester's hands with both of his and began to pump away. "Jesus Christ, Lester! Did you ever get old! Those circles under your eyes. And skinny!" He stepped back for a better look. "Don't you eat anymore?" Billy grinned.

Les shoulders slumped in relief as he smiled. "Taken a look at yourself in the mirror, lately? You look just like Uncle Joe. Remember Joe? Bald, short, I think he had a mole, didn't he? On the right side of his nose. There was a hair, one single hair, growing out of it."

"I don't look nuthin' like Uncle Joe."

"Hope you don't smell like him." Lester chuckled. "Have a seat, Billy. Want a brew? They're cold." Lester went over to the small fridge that had been gurgling and spluttering like an old locomotive.

"Sure." Billy braced for what was coming. "It's five somewhere." Billy was ready as the beer flew toward his head. With reflexes as good as his nephew's reflexes, he caught it, opened it, and managed to get most of the volcanic brew down his throat instead of all over his shirt. Triumphantly, he drained the last of it and held the beer can over his head. He let out a long belch, looked at his brother, and smiled. "Still better at it than you."

Lester leaned back in his chair. "At belching maybe." He pushed another over to his brother along with a towel. "She get the papers?"

"Casey said it went off like clockwork."

"Where's Sam?" Lester took a swig of the beer.

"Back at the barn with Casey and the ladies."

"The ladies?" Lester leaned back into his chair and sighed, shaking his head. "They have ladies."

"Fine ladies. You going to stay long enough to meet them?" Billy didn't look at his brother, scared he might get the wrong answer to this one.

"That depends on the lads. They may not want me anywhere near home."

Billy looked up. "I don't expect that, Lester. They've lived with Rachel a long time and grown up some. They're asking questions now. Want answers."

"What about Mum?"

Billy smiled slightly. "You know, before this whole mess started, I'd have given her maybe a year at the most, but when Sam walked in with that clown, it's like it gave her another twenty years. I swear she'd stare down the devil himself if he tried to hurt those kids."

"Good. So it's down to business." Lester opened a file on his desk. "First things first. Let's go over the plan. Then"—his eyes darted over to Billy—"I have to talk to them."

CHAPTER 38

Kathleen froze at the sight of Gran standing in the doorway. "Ah … ice pack … for Sam." Kathleen knew she sounded lame. All she had to do was look into Gran's eyes to have it affirmed.

Gran didn't smile. "Thomas told me you were listening. So how much did you hear?"

Kathleen didn't hesitate. "Most of it."

Gran nodded. "You'll want some answers I expect."

Kathleen nodded. "When you're ready."

"Sam is where? The barn?" Gran didn't have her usual charming naiveté as she stepped over to her rocker and sat down. In fact, Kathleen hadn't seen Gran looking this upset since Hope disappeared.

"Yes." Kathleen walked over to her. "With Casey."

Gran nodded. "I need to talk to Sam. Where's Billy?"

Kathleen could hear them coming, recognizing the heavy pound of Rachel's step. She felt trapped, wanting to run, but strangely curious as to what would happen next. Nor did she like the stress in Gran's voice. "Billy went off to town and Sam plans on coming in with Casey later, to see you." Kathleen took Gran's hand. "You've known about their father for years, haven't you?" she whispered.

"Hush. One problem at a time, darling." Gran leaned closer and whispered in Kathleen's ear. "I have to talk to the boys but not here. In the stable, later, perhaps."

The thumping grew louder as Rachel barreled down the stairs, her fist hitting the wall with every second step she took as if she couldn't navigate without pounding something. "I want you out, out, out!" A brittle laugh, coming from upstairs, followed behind.

Rachel stopped in the doorway and studied Kathleen and Sadie top to bottom. "Where did you come from?"

"Ah … the barn." Kathleen stepped backward a little, and a chill ran up her spine as she stared at the Beast. Rachel Brennan was no longer a prowling, hungry animal, needing to feed off the pain of others. No, this was worse. She now looked wounded, ready to kill anyone or anything that got in her way.

"Where is he?" She leered at Kathleen.

"Who?" Kathleen tried to smile.

"Samuel?"

"Gone off to work the east acres. We came back to get some drinks for them," Kathleen said, knowing that she had to come up with something good, a story Rachel would buy quickly. "Those fields are growing rocks. You know that. I hope the old tractor is up to it."

"I want to talk to him. I need to, I tell you!" Rachel slammed her fist on the table, and once again, the items on the top, the silk arrangement, the candles, all shimmied about.

Sadie seemed mesmerized, her hand in midair between the baggie and the container of ice cubes. Kathleen moved over closer to her and reached for a tea towel, hoping to somehow get Gran out of the kitchen and away from Rachel or, even better, talk Rachel into a 'bilious' attack.

"Sit down, Rachel." Gran took over. "You'll just hurt your hand or break something. I'll make tea." She rose and started over to the stove.

Kathleen's shoulders loosened a little. Rachel nodded and it looked like the worst was over. Kathleen saw Sadie stiffen, and a tight smile formed on her face. Kathleen felt the room get colder. She'd been waiting for her, from the time she heard Missy's voice. Looking past Rachel, Kathleen took a good long look at Melissa Anne King.

Missy stared right back, her arms folded in front of her, a riding crop in her hand. She was dressed like a toy doll, in a complete equestrian outfit, ivory jodhpurs, leather English riding boots, and a tweed jacket. Her hair was pulled up into a chignon, and her foot was tapping to one of her songs, Kathleen thought, possibly, "A-Hunting We Will Go."

Kathleen felt Sadie step up behind her and place a bag of ice in her hand, probably as a reminder. It was hard and cold. She heard Sadie's voice in her ear: "Let her talk." Kathleen remembered. Sadie hadn't let her down so far, so she'd try.

For a second, there was nothing but the sound of Rachel's finger scratching on the kitchen table as the Beast glowered at the houseguest.

"Where is Sammy?" Missy's voice was staid, almost pleasant.

Where's Sammy? Like she owned him. Kathleen handed the ice back to Sadie and faced Sam's wife.

Kathleen knew Sadie was wrong. There was no way they could all sit down with a cup of tea and talk it out. Duke it out perhaps. Noting Missy's scrawny frame, Kathleen knew she'd have a good shot of removing the nose from the clown's face.

"I'm Kathleen Egan." She stuck her hand out, still wet and cold from the ice. Missy didn't bother to take it, so Kathleen pulled it back and placed her hands squarely on her hips. "Don't call him Sammy. It's Sam. He must have mentioned me. I'm best friends with both Sam and Casey. We do everything together. Sam, Casey, me, and this is Dr. Sadie Parker."

Missy gave Sadie a curt once over. "We met." She smirked and turned back to Kathleen. "Where is Sam? I know you have him here."

"Locked in a cage out back?" Kathleen smiled, wanting to laugh out loud. "He has told me about you." She tilted her head a little. "Funny, you don't look like a clown, but then I've never met a clown before. Fascinating. I'd love for you to tell me all about it, you know, the tricks of the trade." She watched Missy's mouth droop a little. "And a probable lawyer too. Wow! I bet that's a big help, you know, in case someone dies laughing, you know, at a party. I mean, that would be horrible, and they might sue. Well, their family would do the suing." She giggled. "I mean, they'd be dead, having died laughing."

"You're Kathleen?" Missy stared through suspicious eyes. As if she didn't believe it. As if Kathleen was a joke. "You're MyKate?"

Kathleen's face tightened, and she leered at Missy. "I'm Sam's MyKate. No one else's!"

Missy smirked sweetly and turned to Sadie. "I hope you didn't get the wrong impression earlier."

"I got exactly the right impression earlier," Sadie said, demurely smiling, and Kathleen snickered.

"Enough. Where is he?" Missy looked back to Kathleen.

Kathleen stuck her chin out. "Who?"

Missy's jaw clenched. "My husband!"

Kathleen gave Missy her best I'm-confused look, her eyebrows knit up in supposition.

"Where's Sam?" Missy hissed.

"Oh. Sam. My Sam." Kathleen turned to Sadie. "It's just so strange thinking of him as married. He isn't the type." Her eyes widened. "God!" Her right hand went flying out in exaggeration to emphasize her point "The times he's had in high school and university. A regular Casanova." Her eyes were gleaming as she turned to Rachel. "No offense, Mrs. Brennan. I do tend to go on. I shouldn't go on. My mother says I go on."

"Enough!" Rachel slammed her hand down on the table, so hard that Missy jumped, and the napkin holder bounced, spewing paper all over the wood. "I'm not well. Bilious attack!"

"She just calls it that," Kathleen said to Sadie, her hand up to her mouth as if it were a clandestine remark to Missy. "It's really a migraine."

"No. No. No. It's a bilious attack …" She pushed her chair back. It scraped against the floor. "I have weeds to hoe."

Kathleen could picture Rachel, out in her garden, decapitating dandelions with one swing of her sickle-like hoe. Rachel bridled as she passed Missy. Her eyes narrowed as she leered at the new bride, her face frozen in a fury Kathleen had never seen before.

"Don't go near those horses," Rachel said. "They don't belong to you and never will." She pushed past Missy and started up to her bedroom.

"Riding?" Kathleen's heart stopped. She had forgotten about it, having been too busy in the simple act of confronting the new beast. The riding outfit had been no more than a clown's costume. It had never occurred to her that Missy would actually go riding. She tried to remember Sadie's words, to listen instead of lose control, but the thought of this jezebel anywhere near what she considered to be her horses, as much as Sam and Casey's horses, as much as Billy's horses, left her gasping for air.

Once again, Gran stepped in front of Missy. She turned to Kathleen and put her hand on her arm.

"Melissa has decided to go riding," Gran said.

"Well, whoop-de-doo," Kathleen said.

"With Sam," Missy said most emphatically as she looked at Kathleen over Gran's shoulder. "But I'll go on my own if I have to."

"And you ride?" Kathleen said, ignoring the riding jodhpurs.

"I ride all the time. Every chance I get." Missy spread her arms as if presenting the riding outfit as if saying, why do you think I'm wearing this, stupid? "Six years of English at Dartmouth equestrian." Missy cocked her head. "There isn't a stallion I can't handle."

"You haven't met ours." Kathleen wondered where the meek little clown that Sam had described had gone. "You don't know our animals though. They aren't your ordinary trail horses. If you must go, you should stick to the quarter horses but not Bob. He belongs to Casey, and only Casey rides him. In fact, if I were you, I'd wait until Casey is out there, or Billy, before you go choosing which one to take out."

"You aren't me."

Kathleen's hand went out, and Sadie grabbed it.

"I would listen to Kathleen," Sadie said in a calming voice. "She's been riding the Brennan horses since kindergarten, and she knows their temperaments. Take it from me. Those Arabians are rather high-strung."

"And you're the hired help?" Missy's nose rose a little higher, her eyes sparking as if she'd found a new rival. "Doctor?"

Now Kathleen could now feel the pure heat of anger off Sadie.

"Why, you—" Sadie said.

Kathleen grabbed Sadie. "You really should wait, Melissa, until—"

"I'm perfectly capable—" Missy moved toward them.

"You're pregnant. What if you fell?" As soon as Kathleen said the words, she suddenly realized that was Missy's plan. She was planning on falling. She wanted to lose the baby. If there was a baby and even if there wasn't, a fall could make it look as if she lost the baby. Kathleen tried to get her breath back as she retreated a bit. "Melissa, I know things are rough right now." Kathleen tried to remain calm. "But until we get this mess all settled—"

"There's nothing to settle. I'm Mrs. Samuel Brennan, carrying baby Brennan, heir."

"Heir?" Kathleen snorted. "Heir? Boy! Are you barking up the wrong tree! Missy, this is a nice farm, comfortable and all, but look around you. Why don't you go hang out at a marina in Boston and net a rich yachter?"

"Because I'm married to Sam." She smiled slowly. "MyKate."

Kathleen's elastic band of tolerance snapped. She reached out for Melissa Anne King's throat, crying out for Sadie to let go of her as she felt Sadie's arm encircle her and lock into place.

"I'm going riding," Missy said and scooted around the wildcat.

"Leave the Arabians alone," Sadie warned her. "I'm quite sure Sam and Casey would never let you ride them."

"Don't you touch my horse! You got that?" Kathleen wanted so much to break free of Sadie's grip and tackle the new Mrs. Brennan. "So help me God! I'll kill you!"

"The guys won't let you ride the Arabians. For your own good, Missy," Sadie said over Kathleen as Kathleen twisted and kicked trying to break free. "The black belongs to Kathleen." Sadie groaned as Kathleen struggled to get loose. "And the white is downright dangerous."

"Dangerous?" Kathleen stared up at Sadie, shaking with rage. "He's not! You stay away from Charger. You hear me. And Kahlall!"

Missy laughed and let the door slam behind her, almost drowning out her whoop-de-doo.

Sadie was struggling against Kathleen, harder than Kathleen had expected. "But she can't—oof!"

Sadie strengthened her hold. "Are you going to stop?"

Kathleen caved in, and Sadie loosened her arms as Kathleen stood up straight, blinking back furious tears. "How dare she!" She whirled, wanting to break something or, more to the point, someone. "Those horses—"

"Will you calm down? She won't go near them. She's not that stupid. Just breathe a bit." Sadie bit her lip and took the ice pack from Gran, who had a satisfied smile on her face as if she'd just seen a terrific theatrical performance. "You were terrific, Kathleen." A smile began to form on Sadie's face.

Kathleen felt humiliation burn her face. She'd let everyone down.

Sadie nodded, wrapping the ice in the towel. "You were great … in case someone dies laughing?" Sadie grinned. "Priceless."

Gran took Kathleen's hand. "You were wonderful, darling." She took a long deep breath, and Kathleen realized how stressed the woman was. "I know you have a lot of questions," Gran said, her hands shaking a little, "but if you could wait, for just a while, I'll have the answers for you."

"You want me to wait?" Kathleen tried to get her heart to slow down.

"I'm asking for time. That's all. For everyone."

"But you knew all along." Kathleen could never remember a time when Gran disappointed her before.

Tears welled up in Gran's eyes. "Please, Katie. Don't make any judgments until I have a chance to talk to the boys."

Kathleen leaned over and kissed her on the cheek. "Don't cry. I won't say a word." She turned back and nodded to Sadie. "We have to get that ice out to Sam. He'll be wondering ..." Her voice petered out. "I still have to get my charcoal from home."

"I'll take the ice out to the barn." Sadie took hold of Kathleen's elbow. "You go get your supplies. Straight there and back! Right? Leave the clown alone."

Kathleen nodded. "I've had enough of that one today."

"Good. You two go ahead then. I have to talk to Thomas, and then I have a few phone calls I have to make," Gran said and headed to her bedroom.

Kathleen didn't wait around but let Sadie lead her outside. Once again, she listened to Sadie. She had to calm down, so she promised Sadie she'd just go straight home and straight back to the barn. She watched Sadie head for the barn. Finally, someone with common sense.

Kathleen tried her best to look the other way when she walked down to her home. How could she keep quiet about this new information? Sam's wife knew Sam's father and Kathleen knew she'd have to tell Sam the truth. What would he do when he realized that Gran knew all the time? After all, Gran always told him the truth. Kathleen's eyes stung as she realized that she hadn't been completely honest with Sam on many occasions. Maybe if she had told Sam that she loved him, none of this might have happened. Omission of truth. She was just as guilty as Sam was.

Chapter 39

With thunderheads forming on the horizon, the promise of a stormy night was almost as sweet to Kathleen as the scent of new grass. She'd thrown together a lunch of sandwiches and cookies in her kitchen and stuck it into her bag along with her art supplies. On her way back to the barn, she forgot about everything else as she studied the billowing anvils on the horizon, how they boiled up and churned, how the colors changed as they moved. Usually stopping where she was, she would have dropped her bag from her shoulder and, rifling around it as it lay in a heap on the grass, whipped out her sketchbook and a piece of charcoal and brought the sky to life on the page in front of her. Intermingling with the boiling shapes, she would have dotted down tiny notes, printed instructions on the time of day, various colors to be used, and the mood of the afternoon. She would even note the sound of the grackles in the trees. Clouds were subjects Kathleen had always found difficult, but these seemed just about perfect. It would be raining by supper, but for now, not a breeze could be felt, and the air was heavy. As she continued on her way, hundreds of blackbirds rose from the field and headed out over the tree line, a huge black specter undulating and dancing above her. Even the birds were acting strangely.

The shortest distance between her home and the barn, as the crow (or blackbird) flies, was directly across, up the slope of the orchard, and over an uneven field of winter wheat. That line took her past the stable, the left back corner of the paddock just touching on the route. No matter how often the field was turned over by the plow or seeded down, or how many rows of corn had been planted, there was always a path worn through from Kathleen's home to the barn. She could feel her ankles getting wet from the dew at ground level, and she jumped as a killdeer screeched and flew at her. Must be too close to the nest. It limped and staggered about in front of her, screeching, spreading one wing like a fan dance before it took off, flew at her, and feigned injury again. Kathleen scanned the grass around her so she could move away from the nest. Let the poor thing relax. Kathleen marveled at their ingenuity, being able to draw the enemy away from their nests by acting injured. Such clever birds.

She almost tumbled on a rut and shivered. The sun had gone behind a quicksilver cloud, and the day seemed suddenly heavier. There was an eerie silence around her, and for some reason she didn't understand, she suddenly felt the need to move more quickly.

The sudden movement in the garden in front of the Brennan house caught Kathleen's eye first. Rachel must have been feeling better, because she was prowling through her thorny roses, fast, as if she might have cut herself, going from the front beds, through the garden gate, headed to the stable. She was a perfect picture of lurking as she headed for the stable. The Beast was up to something.

Faster. Kathleen knew she'd been gone too long. Casey and Sadie couldn't hold Sam back, not if he really wanted to go. And he'd be worried by now. Sadie was right. The time for secrets was past. Sins of omission were sins just the same, and Sam would be the first one to admit it, at least now. Kathleen remembered Gran's face.

Gran had secrets. Possibly Billy too. And her heart bled that they'd never said anything. Kathleen didn't know how much time to give Gran, but she knew it wouldn't be long. Sam and Casey deserved to be told the truth.

Kathleen scanned the horizon, wanting but not wanting to see Missy out somewhere on a horse. She looked at her watch. Maybe Missy had gone back inside, after all, having decided not to ride. It didn't matter, Kathleen thought as she climbed over the rail fence behind the stable paddock.

"Casey. No!" a woman's voice cried.

It was just a small movement inside the stable, no more than a flash. Kathleen stopped dead, panic rising up her spine as she turned toward the building. She wanted to be anywhere else. Her heart began to pound. Then a screech tore apart the afternoon. Kathleen stopped dead.

"Oh God! Sam!" Then another scream.

Her heart went to her mouth. Her head jerked toward the stable.

Through the open doors of the barn, Kathleen saw Gran, standing alone outside the stable entrance, one hand on her throat, one pointing. But Gran wasn't screaming. She was calling Thomas's name.

The screaming tore through the open back door of the stable. The horses were mad. The earsplitting whinnies were almost unbearable. Her ears hurt from the piercing mayhem. Her foot slid out from under her in the muck of the paddock. Her art bag flew out of her hand and landed in the sod as she went down. She scrambled to rise, yelling at Gran to go back to the house, but the din from the horses blocked it out. The Dutch door was closed at the bottom but opened at the top. The sounds of terror came from the horses inside. Kathleen struggled to rise. She grabbed at the door, but the latch refused to give. She fought with it as she watched the shadow of an animal rear. She tugged and fought with the latch. She had to open the door. Another strangled scream ended abruptly. There were only the terrified screeches of horses now and the racket of wood breaking in the onslaught of panicked fury.

"No!" Kathleen screamed. "Charger! Steady!" She knew she shouldn't be yelling. She should be calm and reassuring. She heard boards shatter and break. It wasn't the Beast. The Beast's voice was distinct. Was it Sadie?

Kathleen vaulted the lower door and fell hard on the stable floor.

"Charger!" Kathleen screamed out as she scrambled back to her feet and her eyes tried to adjust to the change in light finally focusing on what was left of Charger's stall.

"What the hell is …?" The screaming was horrific. The sound of cold fury, pain, the shriek of fear. Another scream. "Charger!" Kathleen ducked away from a flying barn board and then charged toward the frantic horse. She tried to grab the stallion as he reared and lunged, wanting past her to freedom. Her hand slid over his neck as he jumped and bolted out the door into the paddock. Kathleen looked down at her hand and recognized the red sticky mess. Blood.

In the midst of the frenzy, unaware now of the furious panic around her, the hooves all trying desperately to get out, the cries of fear from the rest of the horses, Kathleen looked from her hand over to Charger's stall. Turning her head away, she moved closer, unable to look away from the pulverized mass of human form on the straw in the back of the stall—English riding boots, covered in blood. Someone began to scream.

CHAPTER 40

Casey raised his head and turned, listening.

"Do you hear that?" he said. Neither Sam nor Sadie answered. *I'm imagining things*, he thought.

"Kathleen's been gone too long." Sam looked over at Sadie as Casey took the halter off Libby. He'd said it every five minutes since Sadie's return.

"She's fine." Sadie looped her arm in Sam's arm. "You shouldn't worry so much about her, you know. She's stronger than you think."

He smiled and looked at her meekly. "I depend on that."

"Hey." She hugged his arm. "She'll come around." She let go of his arm and headed for the door as Sam turned the water off. "If it makes you feel better, I'll go get her." She pulled open the barn door. "You should let some fresh air in here, maybe open ..." Sadie stopped talking, and Casey again looked up to see what the problem was.

"Son of a bitch! Charger's out!" Sam cried as he stared out the front barn window next to the door. Casey ducked down to look out the window. Sure enough, he saw the horse flash across the paddock. "Goddammit! Missy! I'll bet she tried to ride him." Sam moved, heading for the door.

"Whoa!" Casey yelled at him, grabbing him by the arm. "You're not going anywhere alone."

"Take off, Casey." Sam pulled away.

Casey knew the horse wasn't just loose. He knew Charger was incensed. More than that, the shadow on Charger's front didn't seem right. "Why don't we all just go to the stable and get the rope and his halter," Casey said. "Sadie and I will hold down the fort in the stable while you get Charger." He looked at Sam. "Charger's fine. Let's not bump into the little wifey." Casey had to grab at Sam, trying to slow him down.

Then Sadie called out. Sam and Casey both jerked around as she took off, running, yelling back for them to hurry. Then Casey heard it too, as he got closer to the door, the bloodcurdling racket coming from the stable.

"The horses!" Sam yelled and took off running. "Charger!" Sam whistled as he lunged out, Casey right behind him. Both men ran, bolting from the barn at the sound of the terror in the horses. Then Casey's heart went cold with dread when he heard Kathleen's scream.

"No." Sam voice cracked. "She's in there."

Nerves in Casey's back and up his neck flamed into electric sparks. He couldn't run fast enough, and Sam was moving faster.

Gran stood in front of the door, ghostlike, her hand out as if pointing, staring into the stable.

"Gran? Get to the house!" Sadie yelled at Gran. Howls screeched from inside the stable. Gran was simply frozen, staring. Sadie grabbed her, whirled her around. "Gran?"

"Kathleen." Gran pointed inside. Then Sadie turned her and headed her to the house. "Call 911," Sadie kept repeating. "Call 911, Gran." She let Gran go and headed to the barn.

Sam reached the stable door, Casey right behind him. All the horses were screaming and rearing, trying their best to get out of the stable. The barn was too dark to see. There was clutter everywhere, broken rails and boards and nails. Kathleen was just standing there in the middle of it, staring down at the back of Charger's stall.

"Look out, Kathleen," Sadie cried as Kahlall's hooves came down and down, pummeling the boards, trying to escape.

"Kathleen!" Sadie pulled Kathleen to her. "Kathleen!"

"Not like this." Kathleen muttered in such a hushed voice, drowned out by the cries of the horses. Sam grabbed her and wrapped his arms around her, his head slumping in relief, gasping in relief.

Casey smelled the blood as Kathleen collapsed, sobbing in Sam's arms. *Blood. Christ!* There was blood everywhere, shattered barn board, nails, and splinters. The horses were deafening, still screeching, bucking at their stalls, trying to get away. Kahlall wild, rearing, and screaming, was half in and half out of her broken stall.

"Not like this," Kathleen moaned.

Casey grabbed Kahlall and took a deep breath, trying to get the horse calmed down a little. Pulling boards out of the way, he yanked open the horse's door and let her run past them, outside, where she could be with Charger and not able to hurt anyone inside the stable.

"MyKate?" Sam kept murmuring as Casey pulled boards away from what was left of Charger's stall, to where Sadie was staring.

Kathleen swayed. "Oh God! Sam." She half nodded to Charger's stall. "Not like this."

Sadie whirled around and pointed out the front door. "Get her out of here. Now!"

Sam didn't argue, didn't stop to look. He just moved. He scooped up Kathleen and carried her out into the sunshine, away from the horror.

Moving Sadie out of the way, Casey stepped into Charger's stall toward the mass that was left in the back, the bloodied form on the floor. Moving boards and a pitchfork, he stiffened at the sight. Sadie groaned as she studied the bloodied heap, and he grabbed her and pulled her back. Sadie quickly regrouped, and pushing herself away from Casey, she stepped into the remains of the stall. She bent down over Missy and reached for a hand, trying to find a pulse. She shook her head.

"What the hell happened?" Casey couldn't move, his hands shaking. "Jesus." He went over to her.

She looked around the stable. "Get me a blanket."

He didn't want to, but he left her long enough to go to the tack room and grab a blanket. She was still kneeling at Missy's side when he came back. "Sadie. Don't do this to yourself. There's an ambulance coming."

"Do you think they're any more prepared for this than I am?"

"Here." Casey handed her the blanket. "What do you want me to do?"

Sadie leaned over to Missy's head. He watched her, stunned, unable to move as she tried to assist, as if there was something she could do. She wasn't a doctor. She wasn't a miracle worker. Casey wanted her out of there.

"I think I have a … no pulse." Sadie's voice began to break.

He leaned over her, took Missy's hand in his hand, and felt for a pulse. Shaking his head, he laid her hand down and pulled the blanket up over what was left of Missy's face. "Come on, Sadie. You can't help her."

"I can't leave her, Casey. I have to do something." Her voice broke as he placed his arm around her waist and lifted her. "Oh God!" Sadie fell against him, and he wrapped his arms around her to try to stop her shaking, at least Casey thought it was her shaking. Maybe he was the one shaking. Casey didn't look back at what remained of his sister-in-law or stop to calm the horses.

"Come on, Sadie." He pulled Sadie closer as they walked around the mess and out of the stable, trying to blot the bloodred image from his head. What in the hell had Missy done?

Sam was at the side of the stable, over Kathleen, holding her up with one hand, holding her hair back with the other as Kathleen threw up into the dirt in front of the side paddock.

"I'm sorry," Sam kept repeating until Kathleen pushed away from him.

"Enough! Enough," Kathleen said, trying to stand up, wiping her mouth on the bottom of her shirt, her hands on her face as if trying to hide, but she couldn't help but look at the sight before her.

The screaming from the horses had subsided a little, probably because Casey had been in there, but he wasn't in there any longer. He was right next to them.

"Oh, Katie." Casey took Kathleen's hand and then looked at Sam. "We should get her inside."

"Missy?" Sam was struggling to ask, terror in his eyes as he tried to comfort Kathleen and learn about his wife.

Sadie took his hand. "I'll take her inside. You should go be with your wife."

He nodded, expressionless.

"Don't touch anything, Sam." Sadie wrapped her arms around both Sam and Kathleen. "The police … they're going to have—"

"What the hell happened in there?" Sam didn't budge. "Is she …"

Sadie stared at nothing, looking out over the fields. "I thought I had a pulse." She looked up at Casey. "You felt a pulse, right?"

Casey shook his head.

Sam sobbed once, hard, and then buried his face in Kathleen's hair. He didn't look up. Kathleen's hold on Sam tightened.

"Oh God!" Kathleen's shaking became worse, and Casey thought she might throw up again. Kathleen jerked around and threw herself at Casey. "What were you doing there?" She pinned his arms to his waist in a fury Casey hadn't seen in years, a fury never brought down on him.

Casey staggered back a step, confused and concerned, as his eyes widened. "I was helping Sadie, Katie."

"Not now, before." She flung her hand back, pointing at the stable. "What were you doing in there with Missy?"

"What?" Casey looked past her to Sam. "I wasn't in there, before."

"Yes, you were. I heard her screaming. She was screaming. At you."

Sam stepped between them. "He was with me in the barn the whole time, MyKate."

"No." She blinked wide-eyed. Her hair, tousled and matted, gave her the look of a wild woman. "That can't be true. You were with Missy. She was terrified. You found out, didn't you? You found out, and you went after her. You weren't supposed to leave Sam and now … now … you're playing dumb?"

"What are you talking about?" Casey took her by the shoulders. "Kate, I was with Sam."

Sadie tried to interject, but Sam turned Kathleen around.

"He was with me, MyKate. Come on," Sam pulled her into him once more, not understanding any more than Casey did what Kathleen was going on about. "Come on. You're upset."

"She called you too," Kathleen pushed away from him. "You both could have been …"

"They were with me in the barn, Kathleen," Sadie said.

Kathleen moaned and looked over at Sadie, holding Gran up, leading her back toward the house. "Oh God. Gran." Kathleen looked at Sam. "I have to check on Gran."

Sam looked toward the barn doorway and shivered. "Casey, are you certain? She can't be dead." Casey was shaking his head. "I have to do something."

"She's gone, Sam. You can't do anything for her."

"The hell I can't." He looked down into Kathleen's upturned eyes and knew she gazed back with understanding eyes. "Let's get you inside. Someone has to call what, an ambulance, the police?"

"I'm okay." She smiled weakly back and began to cry softly. "You have to look after her. I'm okay. Look after her."

"I'm looking after you," Sam said as Casey turned to go back to the stable.

She pushed away from him. "I'm fine. You should be with your wife. Charger's hurt." She pointed over at the horse. "Someone will have to get him." She looked over at Casey. "I'm sorry. It's just I heard Missy calling you. Missy was calling your name and Sam." Kathleen looked like she didn't know what to think any longer. "What happened in there?"

Casey stopped then and turned around. His mother should have been the first out the door of the house to witness the commotion. She never missed a trick, and yet she was nowhere to be found. "Find the Beast, Kate."

Sam's eyebrows rose for a second.

"Okay." Kathleen touched a wayward curl on Sam's forehead and slipped it back to where it should have been. "Go on."

Sadie put her arm around Kathleen. "Do you want me to …?"

Kathleen shook her head. "No. I'll be okay." Tears rolled down Kathleen's cheeks. "You go help her. I'll call 911. Gran … she'll be so upset."

Sadie nodded and, without even glancing back at them, headed back inside the stable.

Sam held her away from him a little and groaned at the amount of blood on her clothing. "I should be with Missy when the police get here. They'll want to talk to me. Casey, you go and try to coax Charger into a halter. The police will want to look at him too, I guess." There would be questions, questions for which they had no answers. "Let's get at it then," Casey said. "I'll get his harness. Don't want to get him more upset than he already is."

CHAPTER 41

Sam's head was dizzy as he watched Kathleen stumble into the house. She was looking back at him, her final protestation that she should be out there with them. He didn't agree. She'd seen enough. It was his turn. It was his wife in there, broken into pieces in the back Charger's stall, his responsibility. It wasn't up to Sadie either; it was up to him, his responsibility. Bracing himself for what he was about to do, he started back into the stable.

The horses were still screaming, and Sam didn't know whether to let them out or keep them locked inside the stable. Would the police want to see them, or would they simply make matters worse with their wild panic? Sadie moved past him and over to Melissa. He didn't know how Sadie could be so controlled. She probably wanted to bring Missy back to life, probably trying to fit the pieces all back together.

Sam picked his way through broken boards, trying not to disturb anything, trying not to slip in the blood, Missy's blood. It covered everything, the walls, the bedding, splattered in places, streaked in others.

What good was it? Even breathing seemed futile to Sam as he slipped stepping over a broken rail and grabbed the nearest thing he could to keep from going down, the pitchfork that was straddling Kahlall's stall in a preposterous angle. Kahlall screeched and reared, wanting freedom, wanting away from the blood, wanting him to release her. He took a deep breath and looked down at his wife.

The sirens were somewhere too far away, but they were coming. The world began to twirl like sticky oil in a dirty drain as he sank down next to Sadie and stared at what was left of Missy, the coppery smell of blood suffocating, cloying, and nauseating. What he saw in no way resembled his Missy Mouse. She'd had such definite facial features, so pale, and her head had been oddly round and big, perfect for wigs he'd always thought. That was all gone.

"She's in no pain, Sam." Sadie laid her hand on his shoulder and rose on shaky legs. She took another blanket from Casey.

Sam forced himself to look down again as Sadie stepped by him and laid the other blanket over Missy once more as if trying to keep her warm. Reaching, he picked up Missy's hand, her fingertips callused from the guitar strings, still warm, the ring he'd bought her covered in blood and slime.

"What in the hell happened?" Sam said.

"She probably died with the second direct blow," Sadie said.

He knew she was just trying to make him feel better. "Jesus!" He gagged and tore his face away.

"Her right arm is broken midway. She must have put it up in front of her face to protect herself."

Sam looked slowly back and listened to the sounds of the sirens, knowing they were already too late.

Sadie's hand touched his. "We tried to tell her, Sam. She was determined to go riding."

Sam blinked tears from his eyes. "You were talking to her?"

Sadie crouched down next to him. "For a moment. She was dressed to go riding. I warned her. Kathleen warned her."

"MyKate was there?"

"Yes. And Gran and your mother." Sadie couldn't look at him, and Sam felt apprehension grow like thorn vine in his gut. "We shouldn't have let her go, but Missy seemed to know what she was doing, and she was adamant."

Sam knew that was the truth. No one could tell Missy what to do once she made up her mind.

"How did she get back here?" He studied the remnants of the stall, the shattered wood, and closing his eyes, tried to block from his mind the images of what must have happened. It didn't make any sense. "She knew horses. Why would she go in behind Charger?" Sam looked up as Casey picked his way through the mess to get to them. Sadie stood up.

Casey put his arm around Sadie and helped her to her feet. His brother was trying his best not to look at the form on the floor, and Sam couldn't blame him.

"They'll be here any minute, sweetheart," Casey said, taking her hand. "I have Charger tied up outside. He's okay. Nothing broken ... but he's covered in ... Sadie, why don't you go inside with Kathleen and Gran? The cops are going to want to ask them questions too."

Sadie glanced down at Sam as if unsure what to do. "Do you think ... I might be able to ...?"

Sam shook his head. "Go. We'll be fine out here. You said yourself there was nothing we could do."

Sadie didn't argue anymore. She gave Sam a kiss on his cheek and then started out of the stable for the house. Casey watched her go and then turned finally and stared at Missy's body.

"We should get the horses out of here, into the paddock maybe," Casey said, leaning over to Kahlall. "We'll have to move them around until we get Charger's stall fixed up." He looked into Kahlall's stall.

The sirens were closing in. By the sound of the sirens, Sam figured they had to be on Saint Jude Road. "Not until the police get here."

Across from Charger's stall, Casey murmured to Bob and ran his hand down her nose. "Christ! What a mess." He picked up the pitchfork and looked down at it. "How did this get here?"

They never left the fork out next to a stall where it could fall over and possibly hurt an animal. The fork was always over with the hay. Casey turned the fork upside down and stared at the tines. "Is this Missy's blood or Charger's blood?"

Sam stared at it. Why would there be blood on the fork? "Could Missy have been feeding Charger?"

Casey gave him an incredulous look. He stared at the fork tines for a moment, and then picking up a handful of straw, he quickly wiped the blood off the ends. "Forget it for now. The last thing we need is the cops asking a lot of questions. It was an accident. It's gonna stay an accident." He drove the fork into a pile of horse manure in front of the stall.

"What in the hell are you doing?"

Casey stared at him. "Forget it for now."

"Do you think someone did this deliberately?" Sam's heart stopped.

The sirens hurt Sam's ears as Casey turned back to him. "Until we know for sure."

"What? We cover up?"

"Think!" Casey crouched down to Sam once more, and Sam felt Casey's hands tighten on his shoulders. "Lookit. We don't know what happened, whether Missy tried to defend herself or someone speared her or someone speared Charger. Sam, we just don't know and if the cops … well … they're going to start in on whoever was out here and—" He grabbed Sam's arm and squeezed. "Think. Who was out here, Sam?"

Kathleen. Kathleen hated Missy. Kathleen knew her way around the stable. She had disappeared before the accident, and she had discovered the body. Of course, the cops would think that. Kathleen had a temper, but she would never hurt an animal, let alone another human being. And Gran? Gran couldn't raise the pitchfork, let alone stab a woman or a horse with one.

The police were pulling up outside—two cars. The flashing lights and sirens scared the horses once more into shrieking and whinnying.

Sam felt Casey's hand let go.

"Let me do the talking," Casey said as the uniformed cop got out of cruiser number one. "You got it?"

Sam wanted Casey to stay, but his brother was already moving to the stable doors.

"In here," Casey said to the first cop out of the cruiser as the ambulance pulled up.

Sam watched the red and blue lights flicker across the stable like a crazed carnival attraction.

"We didn't know whether to move the horses out," Casey said as they walked in. "You'd better brace yourselves."

"I've seen about everything, son," the plainclothes officer said, sucking his gut in. "There's nothing that will bother me."

Want to bet, Sam thought as he slumped against the bloodied stall, still holding Missy's hand, wanting to wake from the nightmare.

The younger cop moved past him and, raising the blanket, looked down. He jerked away and gagged. "Jesus."

A medic was there next, medical box in hand, crouching, trying to get to Missy.

"Son." Someone else touched Sam's shoulder. "Son?"

Casey leaned down. "You have to get out of the way, Sam." He put his hand under Sam's arm. "Come on. Let them do their jobs."

Sam didn't argue. He looked at the younger cop, the first one in, the one who'd almost thrown up. He seemed vaguely familiar. "She shouldn't have been in here."

"A female?" the medic said, opening his bag. He pulled the blanket back. "Christ! Her face. You her husband?"

"Yes," Sam said.

The medic looked up at Casey, nodding at Sam. "Get him out of here."

"Come on." Casey pushed. "Outside."

The sunshine hit Sam so hard his eyes hurt. He put his hand up to shield them as he followed Casey's lead. People moved in slow motion around him, just blurs in the surreal world, strangely warped and fractured. The grass was too green, the sky too blue, the clouds too white. Someone turned the remaining siren off as Sam stumbled past him or her, ignoring the lights. He found himself looking for any sign of Kathleen and then remembered he'd sent her inside. Charger! He had to get to his horse. Moving straight over to the paddock, he focused on not throwing up. The cops were conferring together with Casey, Casey explaining what had happened, Casey, taking charge. When had Casey started taking charge?

Tied to the paddock rail, Charger pawed at the ground, his head bucking and tugging on the line as he cried out to Sam. Holding out his hand to the horse, Sam walked over and began examining the animal from top to bottom.

Blood covered the horse's head, as well as his front quarter and neck. Charger's muzzle was filthy, his nostrils were flaring, and his eyes were terrified. Sam put his arm around Charger's neck, despite the blood, and murmured to his horse.

"This isn't your fault," he told Charger, lulling him softly. "This isn't your fault, boy. This is mine."

He couldn't examine Charger, not with the cops there, and it was beginning to sink in, what kind of mess they really had on their hands. Sam recognized the junior constable then, the one who'd gagged, Kevin Cochran. He and Kevin had gone to school together. Kathleen always said Kevin looked like a Play-Doh boy, soft and puttylike. Kevin had never struck Sam as police material, but there he was in navy blue, gun strapped to his side, badge shining like a target on his chest. Sam didn't know the plainclothes cop, the one at the cruiser, but he appeared close to retirement, beet-red from the simple act of walking from the cruiser into the stable and back. Sam felt his stomach tighten as he saw Kevin leave Casey and walk toward him. Kevin looked pale, Sam thought, but then who wouldn't?

"Sorry 'bout your wife, Sam," Kevin said as he reached him. "Rough way to go."

Sam said nothing but stared at the stable door as if expecting Missy to get up and walk out, pronouncing it was all just a bad joke, that she was only clowning around.

"I never heard ya got married." Kevin moved to touch Charger, and the horse screamed out again and kicked out his back legs. Kevin jumped back as Sam struggled to control the animal. "Hell. He's a wild one." He looked at all the blood and then looked away, grimacing.

"She's pregnant," Sam said, not really talking to anyone but himself.

The cop started to say something and then stopped and stared at the bruise on Sam's face. "Wow! That must hurt. D'ya get in the way?"

"What?" Sam's hand flew up to his jaw. "No. Casey and me, we were in the barn until I saw Charger running."

Kevin was studying Sam's bruised face. "So who gave you that?"

"Casey. We had a bit of a boxing match yesterday."

Kevin's lower lip pouted as if he was suddenly a little interested. "Looks like he won." Kevin whipped out a notebook and took a pen from his pocket. "Just a few questions, Sam." He looked up innocently. "You don't mind, do you?"

Sam shook his head and turned his attention to Charger.

"Yeah. That sure looks like it hurts. I don't remember ever seeing you twos fightin'."

"We're brothers. We fight." Sam watched as the plainclothes officer talked to Casey.

Kevin waved it off. "What I can't understand, ya know, is what was she doin' in the back of the stall, ya know? In front of the horse?"

Sam's head began to ache, and he rubbed his forehead.

"I mean, I just don't get why a woman who wears expensive riding boots would be in the back of a stall." Kevin pointed at the horse. "Jesus

H. Christ! He scares me just lookin' at him. Yeah, with that kind of gear, you'd think she'd know enough ..."

Sam bit deeply into his lip. "I don't know why she did it," Sam said, not listening anymore, talking to himself more than anyone else. "She told me there wasn't a horse she couldn't ride. We told her to stay away from them, especially Charger ... at least until one of us went with her. Charger can be high-strung at times, especially with someone he doesn't know."

Kevin was nodding, not really listening, just studying the horse. "We might have to call the vet in, to get him put down."

Sam snapped. "You want the vet?" He flung his hand out, pointing toward the house. "The vet's right there, right over in the kitchen there! She was the first one in to Missy, the first one to get there after it happened!"

"Constable Cochran." The plainclothes officer walked out of the barn with Casey and over to them, frowning. Sam recognized him now too. Sergeant George Klugg. Great.

"You're Sam?" He put his hand out and then retracted it when he saw all the blood. "I'm Detective Inspector George Klugg." He flashed his badge.

"My mother's a Klugg," Sam said. "Rachel."

Klugg snorted. "That so?" He gave a tight arrogant smile. "Rachel? Right. Rachel." He pointed back to the stable. "I hear the deceased is your wife."

Kevin closed his notebook up and stuffed it back into his pocket. "I used to go to school with Sam. His Gran, you'll meet her inside, the librarian a way back." His eyes rose as if he expected the detective to know. "Good person." Kevin rocked up on the balls of his feet and back down again.

Klugg wasn't listening. He was fiddling with a camera, well into the mundane of a routine job. He looked almost bored, as if it was all over and just as plain as the bulbous nose on his face.

"This guy's quite a beauty," Klugg said, raising his camera for a shot of the horse. "That's the trouble with women. They all want to ride, but none of them is very good at it."

Sam wondered if he'd get away with pounding some sense into the cop as he thought of Kathleen, flying as she did in the saddle. Shame seared right through him when he realized he didn't know if Missy could ride that well.

"Just because she said she rode and had the clothes didn't make her a rider," the detective said. "Fancy gear. The boots might be expensive, but she was way out of her league with this fellow." The older cop was putting away his camera, obviously finished with Sam. "I'm going into the house, talk to the women. Just a formality, Sam. It's pretty clear that one misjudged a good stallion." He looked abruptly at Sam and cleared his throat. "Sorry for your loss, son."

"Shall I take any samples, Detective? Put up some yellow tape?" Kevin was talking too fast, as if wanting to slow the old cop down, enthusiastic about his work—more than he'd ever been about school. "We haven't really examined the horse."

Klugg looked at Kevin like a dog at an annoying pup. "Paperwork. The coroner will want his say-so. That's all there is to this job. You can run a bit of tape around the stall for the coroner." He placed his camera in his back pocket as though he wouldn't need it when he went into the house. Then he looked back at Sam. "Son, we'll only have your wife for a while. I'm afraid there'll be an autopsy." He scratched at his chin. "There shouldn't be a problem."

"She's … was pregnant." Sam's eyes stung with tears.

Kevin, looking like he was confused, put his hand hesitantly on Sam's shoulder. "I sure am sorry, Sam."

Sam nodded. "Can I wash down the horse now and get the others calmed down?" He knew it sounded cold, but he didn't care.

"Yeah. I told your brother to go ahead and move the other horses outside. We only have a few more things to ask the women. The coroner won't be long. There'll be paperwork and the funeral arrangements. You got someone to help?"

"We can take care of it, but the women are really upset." Casey interjected, coming up from behind, "Gran's been under the weather. She's getting a bit dotty, Kevin."

The older cop cut in. "Only a few questions. Get the poor beast cleaned up." McIntyre turned and shoved his rookie. "Well, come on," he snarled. "There's nothing more to be done here." With that, he marched across the yard. Kevin gave Sam a cautious look, turned, and followed behind.

"Shouldn't we shoot the horse, Sarge?" Kevin called forward while he hurried after the sergeant.

Casey stepped between the cop and the horse and watched as the coroner pulled up.

"Don't be ridiculous," the older man said without looking back. "It wasn't the horse's fault she didn't know what she was doing." With that, the cops moved to the house, seemingly more than eager to be there than anywhere near the stable.

Casey grabbed Sam's hand as it reached for the rein. "Check him over well," Casey said. "But don't wash him down until after the coroner leaves. I'll get the others outside. You go get the stuff to clean him up." Casey turned and started off to the inside of the stable once again, and Sam watched him go, realizing how great it was to finally have an older brother.

CHAPTER 42

Kathleen hardly noticed the police as they entered the kitchen. All she wanted was the shaking to stop and perhaps go back in time. She wanted a do-over. Missy didn't need to die. Kathleen never wanted her to die. As the police officers introduced themselves, Sadie tried her best yet again to entice her away from the window. How could she, what with Sam so broken, holding on to Charger as if the horse was the only solid light in his world?

Stinging and itching, Kathleen knew her eyes were all bloated up from the crying. She was surprised at how hoarse and raspy her voice was when she answered their questions. Must have been all the screaming, screaming they'd told her she'd done. She'd scrubbed her arms, hands, and face raw, trying to remove the blood. She knew that only a shower would remove the blood from her hair. That wouldn't happen until after the police left. She was drowning in an undertow of questions and regrets. Looking back out the window, she watched a stretcher being carried into the stable. She shuddered. There was a coroner out there. *A coroner!*

Why couldn't she shake Missy's voice screaming out Casey's name? Why was Gran standing outside the stable? Had Gran gone out to show Missy the horses? Kathleen had tried to ask Gran, but Rachel was always there, or Gran found a way of disappearing. Kathleen stopped trying. Gran was shaking as much as she. That wasn't good. The two medics opened the ambulance door, preparing to put Missy's body inside. The medics should have been inside the house, looking after Gran.

Somewhere far away, Kathleen heard Gran talking to Thomas, muttering as she paced in the hallway, asking him why. Somehow, through the muted chatter, Kathleen heard Sadie talking medical jargon to the cops, Sadie's take on what she had witnessed when she bent down over

Missy's body, how upset Sam was, how Casey had told them there was nothing that could be done.

Kathleen felt her pulse explode as Rachel offered the policeman cherry pie and tea, prattling on ... poor Missy this and poor Missy that ... I want to be with my son ... the stifled sob before she clutched her heart and cried out dramatically, my grandchild. Rachel Brennan had missed her calling. She should have been an actor.

Kathleen felt her stomach heave again, reliving Missy's final words. She glanced over at Gran, who was finally coming into the kitchen. The older woman shot a pleading glance at Kathleen, beseeching her with her eyes.

"Where was Thomas?" Kathleen said to Gran.

"What's that, Miss?" Kevin said. He pulled on his collar as a trickle of sweat ran down his cheek. Why wouldn't he? It had to be a hundred-degrees Fahrenheit in the kitchen.

Kathleen jerked around to him when she realized she'd spoken too loud. "I'm sorry," she added quickly. "I'm sorry, just upset. I was just praying to Saint Thomas." She didn't know where the idea had come from. She had no idea how Saint Thomas could help, but any saint at the moment would be good if he or she would make these men go away.

He pulled on his collar. "Does Sam's mother always keep it so hot in here?" He grinned slightly. "I think the detective is melting."

When she didn't laugh, he cleared his throat. "So you found the body, eh, Kathleen?"

Kathleen smiled a little, remembering how, despite the uniform, Kevin was just the same kid he'd ever been. Her eyes filled with tears when she thought of how innocent they had all been back in high school. Four years seemed like ages ago. He stammered apologies when he saw her start to cry. But that didn't stop him from asking her questions.

Get it over with, Kathleen thought, feeling Gran's cautious eyes focused on her from her rocker. They remained on Kathleen throughout the gentle interrogation.

"Where exactly are Melissa's parents?" Kevin said, his pencil ready.

Kathleen wondered. "We're not quite sure."

"France," Rachel said. "Or Brazil."

"Someone has to tell them," Klugg said.

Gran spoke up, saying that wouldn't be a problem.

Rachel rabbited on to Detective Klugg about the family, his lovely wife, and how his career had gone so well. Then she told to the police how she had warned Missy not to go near Sam's stallion, and you can't tell some young people anything, how the girl was from bad money, and most of the other women, the respectable women in the Women's Institute, had never really like Melissa's mother. Rachel told them again that the girl had ignored her warnings and went off on her own.

Gran got up and walked out of the room.

"Accident," Klugg said to the younger constable, as he handed over his empty pie plate to Sadie. He looked out the window and nodded at the ambulance. "We should be leaving shortly."

Kathleen felt a weight lifted from her shoulders when the police officers declined more pie. The officers left a phone number with Rachel and marched back to their cruiser, grumbling about paperwork, but instead of leaving, they sat there, filling out whatever it was they had to report. Kathleen knew it was far from over.

Five minutes. That's all it would have taken. If she'd only been five minutes faster, maybe. She might have been able to do something. Maybe if she'd been five minutes faster, they wouldn't have had to scrape Missy into a body bag. Maybe if she'd trusted Sam more, stood up to Missy the day before, maybe. Sure, she'd wanted Missy gone and the baby gone, out of their lives, but not like that. No one deserved to be pulverized under the fury of hooves. Not even Missy. *No*, Kathleen thought. *Not even the Beast.*

Sadie had been sitting at the table, saying very little, holding onto the blanket Gran had been using until it became too hot. Kathleen had almost forgotten she was there until Sadie handed Kathleen a glass of ice water and sat down beside her.

"We should be out there helping." Sadie put her own water to her head and looked over as Rachel emptied a bag of white flour into a large bowl. "You're not baking bread?" Sadie stared over at Rachel. "Why are you baking bread on a day like today?"

"Don't you have bulls to steer?" Rachel reached for a pound of lard and dumped it into the flour.

Kathleen jumped up, and it was only Sadie's laugh that kept her from leaping on the Beast.

"You go into the living room. I'll be in shortly," Sadie said to Kathleen. "I'll make a pot of tea for Gran."

Kathleen didn't argue. She couldn't get far enough away from Rachel Brennan. She wanted everything to go away. She wanted Sam. She wanted to lay next to him, have him run his fingers through her hair, have his voice next to her, rumbling as he talked about showing Libby or why they were planting corn on the back forty this year, normal chitchat. Then she wondered if there was such a thing. She wondered if it would ever be the same.

The living room was sunset dim, Gran having pulled the drapes closed as was her custom when a family member died. Like it or not, Missy had been family. Kathleen walked over to the end table next to the sofa and, flicking on the lamp, she gazed around the living room.

"Where are you, Thomas?" She sat down, still staring about but trying her best not to lean too close to anything she could stain with the blood from her clothing. Maybe the living room was a mistake. Recognizing the faint whiff of pipe smoke eased the tension in her shoulders a little. "I could really use a bit of conversation right now." She laughed a little hysterically. "An explanation would help too."

As if in answer, Kathleen became aware of a soft melody. Then it stopped. Maybe she'd imagined it. She looked over at the corner table and noticed something that hadn't been there before, a tiny music box, Gran's. The music box had been in Gran's room for as long as Kathleen could remember. Kathleen had longed to touch it as a child, to wind it up and hold it as it played, but Gran very rarely allowed that. It was one of her few treasures—three tiny porcelain ponies, in pastel pink, blue, and yellow, dancing with the butterflies on meadow grass. The details were gaily decorated in childish whimsy. *Strange,* she thought, *that it's out here.* Gran never moved it from its spot in front of her framed photo of Thomas holding Lester when he was a baby. Kathleen wondered if she should dare to pick it up and crank up the disc. She reached for it.

Without warning, it began to turn on its own, as if someone had wound it up and set it down to listen. It rotated, plinking out its melody by itself as if possessed. Kathleen gasped, watching the ponies dance, remembering the tune, "All the Pretty Little Horses," the same song Missy had been singing.

Kathleen couldn't breathe. The hair rose on her arms, and the room seemed to disappear into the shadows. Why would it be playing? She hadn't touched it. She hadn't even come close. But there it was, rotating, playing its music, letting the ponies twirl. She watched it, fascinated, as the horses danced until it slowed and slowed and then stopped once more. The silence suffocated, stole the air. Kathleen felt a strange stirring. She'd been given a message, an urgent message, meant just for her. Damned if she knew what it was though.

"Here we go," Gran said. The light seemed to grow as Gran came into the room, followed by Sadie, who was carrying a tray with all the makings for tea. Kathleen didn't want tea. Kathleen wanted some answers. She rose, glancing over Gran's shoulder, to the hallway. The last thing she needed was the Beast to be listening in on their conversation.

"Ah. That's where I put my music box." Gran went straight over to it and picked it up.

Kathleen watched Gran grip it as if it might disappear if she were to let it go, protecting it as if frightened it might suddenly break into a million tiny pieces.

"Do you feel okay, Gran? Can I get you a blanket?" Kathleen said. Then she shook her head. "I must be nuts. It's friggin' ninety in here."

"Hush, Kathleen." Gran's eyes misted over, her fingers shaking. "What have we all done to you? Whatever were we thinking, Thomas?"

Kathleen touched Gran and pointed to the overstuffed armchair. "Sit down, please." Kathleen's heart hurt, having to question Gran, but Sam and Casey were out there mopping up blood, and it wasn't exactly making Kathleen feel better knowing that Gran and Billy had been lying all those years.

"Where is Lester, Gran?" Kathleen said.

Gran looked down, wringing her hands on her lap. "Right now? I don't know."

"Missy was having an affair with Sam's father?" Kathleen took Gran's hand.

Gran paused. "I'm not certain."

Kathleen slumped down onto the seat by the window. "You have to tell Sam."

Gran clasped her hands to her heart, and Sadie walked over to comfort the old woman. "He's going through so much right now, darling," Gran said quietly. "Perhaps if we wait."

"We have to tell him, Gran." Kathleen wanted Sam to know his father was still alive. He had to know that's why Melissa had trapped him. "Right now, he's out there thinking this is his entire fault!" She glanced over at Sadie, knowing how much it would hurt Sam and Casey to know that their grandmother and uncle had known all along about their father.

Gran studied Kathleen's face, seeming uncertain of what to say. "We had our reasons."

"Your reasons?" Kathleen's voice broke, and she shook as she tried to keep it quiet enough so that Rachel didn't overhear it in the kitchen. "Your secrets. No more, Gran."

"Kathleen," Sadie warned her with a reproachful look, and immediately Kathleen felt the heat of regret rush through her.

"I'm sorry. But all those years, Gran. You and Billy knew, didn't you, where Lester was?" Kathleen waited for a denial, desperately wanting a denial but knowing there wasn't one coming.

Gran rose, walked over to her, and placed her cool hand on Kathleen's cheek. "There's always another story, darling. The time wasn't right before. I don't know if the time's right now. But circumstances being as they are, well …" Gran shook her head. "Katie, you have to be a little more patient. We did the wrong thing perhaps, but we thought we were doing what was best, and for very good reasons, I might add. We had to deal with Rachel and my dear, she's …" Gran searched for the word.

"Crazy? Mentally ill?" Sadie looked over at Gran while handing a cup to Kathleen.

Kathleen's teacup shook in her hands as she thought about the Beast. "Crazy is talking to ghosts and marrying someone just because she's pregnant and baking bread in the middle of a hot day when she can get a loaf in town. Sadie's the only sane one, and she's a nervous wreck now. Welcome to the Brennan farm! This whole place is crazy, Gran." Kathleen paused. "Do you think the Beast is crazy enough to kill?"

"I'm not so certain any longer," Gran said, picking up her teacup. "Stay close to Sam, darling. I know he hurt you, but he really thought he was doing the right thing." She took a deep breath, and when she saw her cup rattle in the saucer, she put the tea down again. "You know, usually about this time of night, I've got a bit of spirit, but tonight ..."

"Do you want me to stay?" Sadie asked, and Kathleen recognized exhaustion on Gran's face, the lines dark and heavy again.

Gran shook her head. "I don't need anyone babysitting me. Besides, I need to talk to Thomas."

The men's voices in the yard grew louder, and when Kathleen pulled the drapes back a bit, the police were pulling away. Kathleen darted a look back to Gran.

"Just give me a little time." Gran's eyes never wavered from Kathleen's eyes. "Why don't you two go out with the boys?" She didn't have to suggest it twice.

Chapter 43

Casey almost fell from the shot of pain that coursed through his back when he leaned over to rinse off Charger's neck once more. The blood had stained the coat, and he was having the devil's own time trying to bring it back up to white. He wanted to get every trace of blood, every spot.

Neither he nor Sam was talking. They were simply scrubbing, coaxing, and calming down the horse. Both looked up when they heard the screen door slam.

Not reacting nearly so calmly as his brother, Sam dropped Charger's rein and moved. Jumping the fence, he caught Kathleen as she flew into his arms, Sam mumbling apologies to her.

Casey opened his arms for Sadie, feeling her press against him. Then Casey realized he was soaking wet.

"Oh Christ!" He pushed away from her. "Sorry."

She took Casey's face in her hands. "How are you doing?"

The feel of her hand on his face eased his pain. "I'm fine. How'd it go in there?"

Sadie grimaced, her head nodding from side to side. "Considering? Ducky!"

He smiled sadly at Kathleen. He'd seen Kathleen upset before, but he'd never seen her face so frantic.

"This wasn't supposed to happen. Oh God! Sam … I never …" Kathleen looked over his shoulder at the horse and past him to the paddock behind the barn. "Kahlall. Are they all out? Oh God! How's Charger?" She was gone from Sam, headed for his horse. "Poor baby." She lifted her hand to his muzzle. "Is he hurt? There's so much blood. Frig." She looked from Sam to Casey, her eyes filling with fresh tears. "What did she do to him?" Although her hand was rubbing fast enough on his neck to work up a burn, Charger didn't seem to mind. "Oh God! Why did she do it?"

Sam walked over to her. "Who MyKate?"

Kathleen shifted and looked away, and Casey wondered what she was hiding.

"Is Charger hurt?" Sadie said, touching Sam's shoulder.

"There's a lot of blood, but I think you should take a look at this, Doc." Sam pointed to Charger's flank.

"He's hurt?" Sadie's eyes shot over to the horse.

"Under his belly." Casey took her by the hand and guided her fingers down. "Just be careful. He's still edgy."

"*He's* edgy," Sadie said sarcastically. She stopped suddenly and then leaned down to take a closer look at where her fingers were touching. Then she looked back up at Casey. "Punctures. I figured splinters maybe, but those are holes."

Kathleen shot over to them and peered underneath. "Puncture holes?"

Casey's head dropped, and his eyes peered up and over at Kathleen. "Someone forked him from behind. Look at the direction of those, Kathleen. Someone knew Missy was in there and shoved the pitchfork into Charger from the back to the front." Casey looked into her eyes as she stared at him in shock. "I found the fork. It had blood on it."

Sadie stood up. "Did you tell the police?"

Casey hoped she'd understand. "I wiped the fork off and threw it in the muck."

"What exactly did you hear, MyKate?" Sam said. Kathleen shuddered and stepped back. Sam moved behind her, wrapping her in his arms once more. "We need to know," he said. "What happened?"

"I was coming up behind the paddock." Kathleen closed her eyes and swallowed. "I was cutting across the field. The clouds were pretty, so I stopped … I wanted to get back, to stay out of trouble, to keep you"—she looked up at Sam—"out of her way. So as I was going by, I heard the horses, all upset and then … then …" Kathleen began shaking once more.

Casey had never seen that look on her face.

"I heard her scream," Kathleen said.

"Who?" Casey said.

"Missy, at least I think it was Missy. Someone screamed. At first I thought it might be Sadie or … or Gran, because I'd seen Gran at the front door, but Gran could never scream like that, so I thought it might be Sadie. It was a terrified scream." She faced Casey down. "Then she screamed out your name … then Sam's."

Casey leaned over and gave her a kiss. "You've got to calm down, Katie. There was no way Missy saw me. I was in the barn with Sam."

"You don't get it, Casey." Kathleen reached for him and took his hand. "She screamed your name! She screamed *Casey*! I thought you were in there. I thought you were under the hooves."

Kathleen straightened. "I saw it in Gran's eyes. She knows. That's why she was there. Thomas must have been in the stable too."

Sam wrapped his arms around her. "Don't, MyKate. All these years and Thomas finally decides to help us by killing my child?" He laughed out in pain.

Kathleen slumped. "No. I suppose not. Some ghosts do though."

Sam held her closer and smiled kindly. "Thomas could no more do it than you could." She straightened ramrod straight as she stared at Sam. "You think I did it, don't you!"

Both men jabbered nos.

"You do." She sank a little, and Sam pulled her into him once more.

"No, we don't." Casey grabbed her arm. "Smarten up, Kate! You love those animals more than anyone I know. Besides … you'd have used the fork on Missy." Casey said with a slight grimace, and she moaned a little and then shook her head as he muttered an apology. "I'm sorry. This isn't funny."

"I never wanted this," Kathleen said as the tears spilled over and rolled down her face. She looked at Sam. "I never could want …"

"I know." He ran his hand through her hair. "We know that. We never once thought it was you, MyKate. It wasn't Gran either or Thomas."

She said what they were all thinking. "The Beast."

CHAPTER 44

Sam stared while Billy's truck came around the corner of the lane a little faster than normal. He drove hell bent up to the stable and skidded to a stop. Billy emerged from the truck with fear in his eyes.

"Where the hell have you been?" Sam said.

"Take it easy, Sam." Casey stepped back out through the front door, shaking his head.

Kathleen stared wide-eyed at the inside of the barn, and Sam stepped in between her and the damage. "Sadie, why don't you and Kathleen go check the other horses?"

Sadie moved fast and wrapped her arms around Kathleen. "Good idea. They could have splinters."

Kathleen nodded mutely, going with Sadie, her hand still reaching out for Sam's hand as they walked around to the other side of the stable.

"What's wrong?" Billy asked, his face awash with concern, looking at the horses, the bloodied soap, the state of Charger.

"Inside, Billy." Casey watched for his uncle's reaction as they entered the barn.

"Holy jumpin' Jesus! What happened?" Billy stared into the stable at the broken wood and blooded walls. He paled. "Mum?"

Casey put his hand out and grabbed his uncle's arm, knowing then, right at that moment, that Billy didn't know a thing about what had happened there that day.

"Gran's fine. Missy's dead, Billy," Sam said. "She got too close to Charger and ended up in the back of the stall. The cops are calling it an accident. But we found things."

Casey cut in. "Someone got Missy in Charger's stall in the back of the stall. Someone speared Charger in the underbelly. He went berserk.

I found blood on the pitchfork before the cops got here. I put it into the manure pile."

Billy raised his eyebrow. "And you suspected … who?" Billy grinned.

Casey looked away.

Billy's head tilted a little, and he coughed out a laugh. "If I wanted to kill the girl, I'd never allow you anywhere near here. Besides, I got an alibi." They stared at his abrupt change. He turned away, muttering to himself, and then picked up a big chunk of railing. "Shit! Was Charger hurt?"

Casey and Sam both shook their heads. "Aside from the punctures … no. Someone has to notify Melissa's folks," Casey said.

"I'm her husband. They have to hear it from me." Sam took his hand and rode it down Charger's neck.

"Did she ever talk about them?" Billy said, looking back at him.

Sam looked away. "Not much."

"Do you have the phone number?"

"No. But I'll look through her things for it."

Billy bent down and picked up another board. "If you don't find it, tell me. Maybe I can get it. Where's your mother?"

"Don't know," Casey said. "She's the only one unaccounted for."

Billy snorted and pointed his finger at them. "Do not underestimate your mother."

Casey saw the look of concern wash over his uncle.

"My God, Billy," Sam said. "What is it with this woman? Why do we all think she could do …?"

"That's enough, Sam," Billy said sternly.

"No, it isn't. What don't we know? She's got to have something on you!"

They got no reply, just the sound of starlings cackling insanely outside the barn. "Billy! Don't you think it's about time you told us the truth?" Casey said.

Billy was looking at the hideous scene around him. "Look around you, lads." His hand moved slowly over the vista of carnage. "Someone is responsible for this. Whether we liked Missy or not, if what you're saying is true, someone killed her. Your mother is capable of anything, trust me." He stared down at the bloodied bedding. "I have phone calls to make, things to take care of." Billy turned back toward his truck. "Keep tomorrow morning open; we have business in town. Tell the girls they'll have to entertain themselves. Now … let's get this place cleaned up."

CHAPTER 45

It was approaching five when they finished clearing the stable and getting all the horses settled in for the night. Casey wanted a beer and a shower. It felt like he'd been up for days, and it wasn't even five when he followed Sam into the kitchen.

Casey wondered what to do first—if he should phone the morgue, if the cops would call them, or if maybe, one of them should go to the station, be there with her body.

"Shit! It's hot in here," Sam said at the same time as Casey felt the heat hit his face.

"I'm making you some bread, Sam. That's exactly what you need. A little comfort food. Bread. Bread. Bread. Roly-poly baker's bread." Rachel placed two perfectly formed loaves of unbaked white bread on top of the oven. She looked as fresh and clean as the smoothly kneaded bread in front of her.

"Where's Gran?" Sam said, staring at the flour on the counter.

"In the living room." Rachel sniffed, wiping her hands on her apron. "Gran sure as hell isn't wasting any sympathy on me." Rachel laid a tea towel over the bread and placed it on the stove mantel to rise. "Your favorite."

"My favorite?" Sam looked back over to her, dazed.

Casey had to do a double take. She was talking about the bread. The bread?

"Your favorite."

Sam gaped at his mother. "My child …"

"Your child?" She laughed as she checked the heat of the oven and closed the door. "She was no more pregnant that I am."

Sam stared at her incredulously and then pulled a chair out from the table. He turned it around and sat down, facing her. "About tonight. We have several options, Mum." He stared hard at her. "Casey and I can go to Sadie's, we can go to Kathleen's, or we could stay here. I would prefer to be here in case Missy's parents call or the cops or the funeral home. It would be difficult from another house, but I'll do it if you make me."

Casey braced for the eruption as Rachel placed her hands on the table and lowered herself slowly into her chair. Then she whirled around to Casey. "This is your fault, you—"

"Enough!" Sam jumped up. The chair fell beneath him, rattling on the floor. "I'm so damn tired of you blaming him! Casey has never done anything wrong. I was the one, Mum. All those times, I was the one playing the tricks, breaking your things—"

"Sam." Casey put his hand out before Sam could make it worse, but Sam pushed it away.

"I think we'll be spending the night here. The girls should go home," Casey said with authority.

"No." Sam's eyes widened, adamant now. "There's no one down there for MyKate, and I won't leave her."

Their mother's eyes grew wild. "There's another one! She's just after the farm, you know. She doesn't love you." She turned her mouth into an animallike growl. "I saw her hugging that brother of yours just—"

Casey jumped to hold back Sam, who had gone white with rage. "I'll kill you, you old bat!" Sam leered at her. "You go anywhere near MyKate, and I'll—"

"Enough," Casey said calmly. "You'll just get the girls upset."

Rachel had backed away, diminished somewhat, Casey thought, shocked by Sam's words.

"Why are you acting like this, Sam?" Rachel turned her head slightly. "Are you blaming me? I had nothing to do with it. I just heard the noise and ran to get help."

Casey pushed Sam to the chair closest to the door and pushed him down. "I'll get you a beer." He moved over to the fridge and turned at the quiet voice in the doorway.

"Is Thomas in trouble?" Gran walked over to Casey, her hand out, reaching for him. "Surely no one will be blamed. It was after all an accident. The poor horse was just startled. That's all it was." She took Casey's hand.

Gran thought Thomas had spooked the horse. *This is a madhouse*, Casey thought as Sam looked from Gran to him. Casey took two bottles of beer from the fridge and made his way back to the table. He handed one to Sam.

"Supper is what we need," Rachel turned and went into the pantry.

"Rachel." Gran sat down on her rocker and sighed, shaking her head. "I don't know if anyone is terribly hungry. After all, that poor girl ..."

"It's a blessing from the Lord; that's what it is," Rachel called from inside the darkened pantry. "Divine retribution."

"How are the girls?" Sam said, his eyes incredulous, staring at his mother's back.

Gran took his arm. "They're fine, darling. Sadie hasn't left Kathleen's side." She rubbed sweat from her forehead. "Lord, I can't stay in here. It's much too hot."

"Baking bread, Gran," Rachel said, bustling back into the kitchen with potatoes and a package of stew beef. "I thought Sam might like a bit of fresh-baked bread." She looked when Casey groaned and eyed Sam suspiciously.

Sam moved before Casey could stop him, but he wasn't headed toward Rachel. As fast as he'd ever moved, Sam grabbed the loaves of bread and tossed them out onto the mudroom floor.

"I don't want bread. I don't want anything to eat. No one does, you crazy old bat!"

Sadie and Kathleen came into the kitchen and stared at Sam as if seeing someone they'd never seen before.

"What is going on?" Sadie said.

Sam immediately went to Kathleen's side. "I don't care whether it's your place or Sadie's, but we're getting out of here."

Kathleen backed away a little. "Sam?"

Sam took Gran's hand. "You're coming with us."

Gran sat straight up in her chair. "Listen to yourself, Samuel. I'm not going anywhere. This is my home. Thomas is here."

"Thomas will come too," Sam said as Casey shook his head and sat down next to the fridge.

"What the hell is going on?" Kathleen said. "Sam, please. Calm down."

"Gran doesn't have to go anywhere," Casey said. "I'll stay here and Billy's coming in."

Rachel's eyes focused in rage on Kathleen. She went for the ties of her apron. "I spent this whole time making bread, and he just tosses it away."

"Mum!" Sam snapped at her. Rachel backed away from him. Sam closed his eyes, his head falling back. "Shit."

"This is all my fault, Thomas," Gran said, her voice shaking more than her fingers. Casey didn't like the fatigue on Gran's face.

"Some water, Gran," Sadie said, heading for the fridge. "Everyone has to calm down, or we'll never get through this day." She pulled a jug of water out and rooted through the freezer for the ice. "You reached Missy's folks?" Sadie asked.

Casey got up and reached in the fridge for a couple of beers. "Sam did, out in the stable."

Sam grunted. "They aren't coming home. Too busy in France. They're having a service there, *en Francais*. They're going to mix her ashes with her sister's." He opened the beer and drank down half the bottle.

Casey squeezed Sadie's hand and leaned into her ear. "There was a sister. She wasn't lying about that." Pulling a chair out from the table, he sat and leaned over closer to Gran. "What the hell happened out there, Gran?"

Gran picked up her needles and began furiously knitting.

"Gran?" He leaned farther down and handed her the glass of water. "You were right outside the door. And Kathleen said Missy was screaming out my name. I was nowhere near inside." She paused knitting.

"Thomas didn't mean to scare Charger. He was trying to warn the poor thing, to get Missy out of there." The ice was clinking from her shaking. She looked up at Casey and tears welled up in her eyes.

Rachel laughed. "Hah! Thomas done the dirty deed? That's priceless. Priceless, I say."

Casey put his hands on his grandmother's hands. "I know Thomas didn't cause this, Gran. Thomas couldn't pick up a pitchfork and ram it into an animal. Someone"—he stressed the word—"someone deliberately hurt Charger. That person knew exactly what they were doing. Someone else was in there."

"Well!" Gran straightened up and stared him down. "It wasn't me!"

Casey heard Sadie try to stifle a laugh.

"I know." He pursed his lips to keep from laughing and pulled his chair closer, watching closely to see her reaction to his next question, whether she might automatically glance over at his mother. "Who else was there, Gran?"

"Casey, I didn't see anyone," Gran said stoically. "I was focused on Thomas."

He wiped tears from her cheek. "Don't cry." He looked over at Sadie and took a deep breath, downed the rest of his beer and felt the old ache grow worse. He shifted his weight on the chair and then felt Sadie's hands kneading deep into his shoulders. Closing his eyes, he gave in to the luxury of her touch and tried to forget for a moment.

Sam wasn't satisfied. "Where were you when Missy died, Mum?"

"What?"

"You heard him." Casey opened his eyes and stretched his legs out, his pants cracking with dried blood.

Rachel's eyes closed to slits. "I don't have to answer to you."

"Yes, you do," Sam interrupted, his anger showing once more on his face.

"I was in the house … here." Rachel's voice was unusually high.

Kathleen jerked up, obviously upset by what she had heard. "That's not true. I saw you. You were running through the front garden, toward the stable, just before it happened. You didn't tell that to the police though. You lied."

Rachel shrank under the onslaught of eyes. She turned to Sam. "Are you going to allow her to talk to me that way? Your wife isn't even cold, and this one is—"

"Enough!" Sam's fist came up, stopped by Casey.

"No!" Kathleen stepped in front of Sam. Casey watched as Sam lowered his hand while their mother paled. "What are you doing, Sam?" Kathleen reached over and took his hand. "It doesn't matter anymore. None of it matters. Let's go down to my place." She walked over and put her arms around Casey. "Why don't you and Sadie come on down too. Gran will be okay. Billy told me he's moving into Sam's room."

Rachel put her hand over her heart. "What? No."

Sam wrapped his arm around Kathleen. "You come anywhere near us, and you'll never see me again. Do you understand that?"

Rachel nodded, backing up once more.

"What is going on, Sam?" Kathleen said.

"Get a shower, Casey. You look like crap." Sam nodded toward Sadie. "I wouldn't let her get away tonight."

Rachel was spluttering with fury, apoplectic, her left eye twitching as she glared at Casey.

"Your fault," she bellowed. "This is—"

"It really does … always come back to you, doesn't it?" Sadie said and took Casey's hand. She swung it back and forth.

"Shower," Kathleen said, pulling Sam out the door.

"Relax, Casey," Sam said called from outside.

"I'll take good care of him," Sadie called after Sam. Her hand was strongly wrapped around his as they made their way upstairs.

CHAPTER 46

Les had opened and closed the heavy curtains over his greasy window so many times he wondered if the man he'd seen in the house across the dirt road might think he was signaling for help.

Where in the hell were they? Billy had said they'd be there by seven, and Les had been waiting since five. He looked at his watch. It was after eight, and they still hadn't shown. What if his mother had had a stroke? What if Rachel had somehow found out?

Les took a deep breath and walked over to the old TV set. He turned it on. Through the snow, he could just pick up the news program from the city. He groaned, not in the mood to hear the local news. He turned if off again and wished he had coffee.

Lester had never been sure this day would come, and the dream he'd had the night before had shaken him. He'd woken in tears, having dreamed his mother had died. She and Thomas were waving good-bye just as he bounced up the laneway in his '64 Ford, tailgate missing, underinflated tires sluggish, going not nearly fast enough. He was locked in the truck, unable to get out, and Rachel was sitting next to him, laughing, telling him it was too late—for him, for Gran, for Casey. Les shuddered and made himself remember that he had indeed made it to Killkenny County and would make certain his sons would no longer be in harm's way.

Lester's head shot up when he heard the rap on the door. That couldn't be them. He hadn't heard Billy's truck. In two steps, he was at the door, pulling the chain back, twisting the lock. Turning the knob, he opened the door to the evening's glow.

The scent of lilacs in rain hit him hard and swallowed him whole as he saw her standing in the shadow of Billy's safe form. She was smaller than he remembered, one hand, the one with her purse, over her heart, her other hand suppressing a cry from her mouth.

"Mum." He stepped into the darkness and wrapped himself around her as she leaned into him, shaking and weeping with laughter. Billy, the starry night, the man across the street, all disappeared as he closed his eyes and rocked his mother's love and strength back into him. He'd made it, done his time, exile complete. Lester Brennan was home. He knew he was never going back. He didn't know how he was going to explain it all to his sons or what he'd have to do to make it all right again, but he knew that with his mother's strength, there was no going back.

Gran pulled away from him, with eyes just as blue as the day he left, just as clear and determined, without a hint of the foggy clouds age can sometimes bring. Tears streaked her flushed cheeks, but she was looking at him with such tenderness it brought tears to his eyes.

"I told myself I wouldn't be an old woman, blubbering all over the place. Don't you boys go telling your father." She ran her hand through his beard. "Billy has an extra razor or two at home. Are you all packed?"

It surprised a laugh out of him. "Didn't bring much of anything. Why don't we go inside, Mum?" Lester tried to edge her into the room.

"We're not staying here, Lester," she said, refusing to release his hands. "We're going home, Billy. Thomas wants Lester back home."

Lester put his arm around her and whisked her inside. "Let's talk first, in here, where we're alone."

"But Thomas—"

"Dad would want you to calm down," Les said, herding her over to the lone chair, faded but cozy, in the room. "You're shaking like a linden leaf."

"Don't fuss, Lester. It's just a bit overwhelming." She sat. "There's no need to stay in this place any longer than needs be." As he turned on the small bedside light, she looked down at the corners of the floor as if expecting something to crawl out from the darkness.

"Mum, we need to talk," Billy said and handed her a glass of water he'd collected from the bathroom. "Here. Have some of this."

She took the water from him and set it on the bedside table next to the bed. Billy picked it up and tried once more to have her take some, but she waved it aside.

Lester sat down on the side of the bed next to her. "Does anyone else know I'm back?"

"No." Billy rolled his eyes and put the water down on the table once more.

"Where are the boys?" He looked up at Billy.

"At Kathleen's, I think. I told them to be at the Hole come eleven tomorrow." Billy pulled a chair over, and turning it around, sat down, his arms resting on the back, and took a deep breath. "Lookit, Les. About Melissa. She's dead." He paused to let it sink in.

Les' eyes narrowed for a moment. His brother wasn't kidding. He looked at his mother for confirmation.

"Well, hell!" Les tried to focus. Billy answered the unspoken question.

"Happened when I was here with you." Billy shook his head. "Not that that would stand up in a court of law."

Les' gut hurt. It wasn't the first time Rachel had hurt someone. He had the scars to prove it. "Where's Casey?"

Gran put her hand out and took his. "Great armies never won by defending, Lester. The time has come for action. It's time to strike first."

Les nodded.

CHAPTER 47

The sun was reaching through the kitchen window early the next morning as Casey came in to check on Gran. As usual, he found his mother there in the kitchen with his grandmother, and he lost his appetite. Staring ahead at nothing, Rachel was at the table, rubbing her fingernail on the wood, looking like she hadn't caught as many beauty winks as she'd needed. Her hair was sticking out, wild and wiry, like the crinkled mesh from some discarded window screen. Her eyes were heavily shadowed, the unnatural kind of darkness reserved for the near-death ghouls that came out on Halloween. She was in her bathrobe, which in itself was unusual, the buttons done up incorrectly, giving her the overall impression of someone who'd stepped out for a visit from an asylum.

"Good morning, Casey," Gran said, opening the window to let the spring breeze flow through. Casey's eyes rose, surprised by his grandmother's peppiness. He gave her the biggest gentle hug he could without breaking her.

"Mornin'. Did you sleep?"

"I slept very well, thank you, Casey. And you?"

"Not a lot," he said with satisfaction and pride. "But what I got was enough." Casey pulled the kettle to the sink and poured water for tea. He placed it on the stove. "Sadie had to go the clinic early, but she should be off later on." He stood watching, waiting for the water to boil as his mother rocked, muttering to herself. Gran was talking to Thomas, telling him he'd have to behave himself today, how much he'd be needed, and how maybe he should go out and give Billy a hand with the stable.

"What are you doing in here? Not enough work outside?" Rachel swiveled her bulk toward him.

"Ah … oh …" He half expected to feel the knot of apprehension tighten in his stomach, but it didn't. "Billy says I should stay in here with you ladies for a while … till he works things out."

His mother smiled from the side of her mouth and swiveled on her chair to Gran. "You know, no matter how much he says he doesn't care, Billy's always there when I need him," Rachel said.

Casey choked. Since when did his mother depend on Billy?

"Don't you have chores?" Rachel slammed her hand down. The teacup rattled as she hit the table.

Casey watched his mother lick her wounds, and he almost felt sorry for her. "Your robe's buttoned up wrong," he said, trying to be polite.

Instead of grabbing her robe and undoing the buttons, she shrugged. The lid of the teapot shook as she poured herself a cup.

Shaking his head, he looked out the window. It was a crazy house. It had always been a crazy house. He'd never realized it until he'd been to Sadie's house. Oh sure, Kathleen's home had been normal, but Sam and he had grown up hearing their mother telling everyone how the Egans were nuts. The Egans weren't nuts. The Brennans were nuts.

He tried to relax by rolling his shoulders as he watched his mother scratch at the tabletop, digging her finger slowly across the wood, lifting it, and then repeating. Her hand crossed and hovered over the worn and bloodied tabletop as if the gouge were invisible. It hurt Casey just to look at it.

Gran was watching her, shaking her head. "You should put some salve on your fingers, Rachel."

His mother pushed back her chair, leaving her breakfast untouched, and without saying a word, rose, turned, and walked away. It could have been a normal moment, except she was in her housecoat, with bleeding fingers, as she walked out the front door and into her garden. Casey watched as she began pulling the buds off the plants.

"Okay …" His eyebrows rose. "Gran, I have a lot to do today, so I'll have to leave you with her." He put the lid on the teapot and started back to her.

"Don't worry, darling." She smiled at him. "I'm very good with a gun."

His head jerked up at the remark, and then he laughed. Casey couldn't imagine his grandmother with a gun. "When did you learn to …?"

He stopped and stared down at the table. "Holy shit!" He put the teapot down without another look at it, examining instead the wood near the edge of the old maple table. Christ! That wasn't blood from the day before was it? There was a blatant red stain of dried ugly blood in a deep gouge in front of his mother's chair. Two inches in length and ragged, it was caked with bloodied splinters.

"Jesus Christ!" he muttered, running his hand over it. Gran sighed at his language. "Sorry, Gran, did you see this?"

"I'm afraid so. Rachel was pretty bad last night," Gran said, devoid of all surprise. "She's in a state."

He stood, stunned, his eyes rounder than the tea cozy and turned to his grandmother. "One of her moods? This is blood." Casey felt the floor below him open up. "Has she ever hurt you?" he muttered. His eyes, locked on his grandmother's eyes, were now terrified. "Has she?" He recoiled at the realization. "Has she ever hurt you?" His finger ran over the mark, feeling the ragged splinter touch the tips of his hand.

Gran took hold of his arm. "She's sick, Casey. Sometimes, it's worse than others. She hasn't had one of her spells in such a long time. Billy and I will just have to watch her more." Gran's face had a resigned matter-of-fact look that terrified him.

"But has she ever hurt you, Gran?" Casey immediately regretted his voice barking the way he did. "I have to talk to Sadie. She'll know." Then maybe not. She was a vet, not a shrink, and she had already asked him if his mother had ever had help for depression. But this wasn't depression was it? This was just plain dangerous.

"Casey." He felt his grandmother's hand on his hand, cool and fragile, and heard her voice, authoritative but quivering slightly. "I told you before that there are reasons for everything. I will explain it all to you and Sam, but not right now."

Casey got angry at his grandmother for the first time in his life. "I've had enough of the secrets, Gran. We're running out of time," he shouted. "Ya know? This place used to be a hellhole; now it's a crazy house!" He paused, shaking, appalled at the way he'd spoken to her. There was no way she could stay alone with his mother. His grandmother might think she was spry and up to a fight, but she wasn't. Not against this. "Gran, we have to get you out of here."

"She won't hurt me. She may not respect me much, Casey, but she fears me."

"Fears you?"

"I can be dangerous," she smiled at him, a little too assuredly. "She's rather like a gorilla, darling. She beats her chest a lot to scare enemies off but doesn't attack until cornered."

"Right."

"With my boys here, she won't touch me."

Casey wasn't so sure. "I'm going to get Billy. I'll be right back. Maybe you should go talk to Thomas, maybe in your room." He knew he was talking like a lunatic, but he knew she wasn't going to budge. "I love you, Gran."

She touched his cheek. "I know, darling."

He ran out the door. Billy had to do some explaining. "Christ. I just get one thing sorted out …" Casey stopped, suddenly unable to breathe. Would he become like her? He'd rather be dead.

"Billy!" Casey threw open the barn door.

"Where I always am," Billy yelled from the back of the barn. He didn't look up as Casey walked over to him. "No Sam yet?" He looked up when Casey didn't reply. "Where's Sadie?" Casey didn't answer him and heard his uncle walk over to him.

"All these years," Casey leaned on the railing and looked out the small window at the light outside, "why did you hang around here?"

Billy rubbed the stubble on his chin and leaned on the top rail, putting his foot up on the bottom. "Something happen I don't know about?"

"It's a simple question." Cased faced his uncle. "The Beast's nuts, isn't she? I mean, really, totally fucking bonkers! She can't be left alone, can she? That's why you stayed all these years."

Billy turned away for a moment as if to steady himself, and Casey realized he'd never seen his uncle quite so shaken. It was true. All those years he'd suffered—all the torment, torture, hiding, crying, pain, and for what! Casey tried to stop shaking.

"I thought it was my fault, Billy. But you must have known it wasn't." He turned away from his uncle. "Billy, why wasn't she put away?"

"How?" Billy threw his hands in the air. "How could we? Son, she isn't sick all the time. They'd have just come and taken …" He stopped and put his hand Casey's shoulder. "This isn't the time. We could make it all worse."

"Worse!" Casey shoved his uncle's hand off his shoulder. "How could it be any worse, Billy? I thought it was all my fault!"

Billy laid his hand once more on his nephew's shoulder. He stared hard at Casey, squeezing his shoulder. "I promise. By the end of the day, you'll have all your answers."

"Fine." He looked over at Libby and her calves. Billy had never gone back on his word. Maybe he was overreacting. "Sam and Kathleen probably haven't even crawled out of bed yet. What say we get Libby and family out on the grass?"

Billy smiled slowly, shaking his head. "Something positive. I like that. Let's do it."

CHAPTER 48

Sam couldn't find Kathleen. Nothing made sense in the fog, and it was getting worse by the second. Walking was a struggle, the ground covered by a ghostly mist. Sam could hear a rustle, the snap of a twig somewhere near, but the noise was diffused, muffled, and heavy. The Beast was prowling somewhere out there; Sam knew it. He flailed about and tried to catch hold of the wisps that danced around him. He wasn't alone. He heard male voices that didn't belong to Casey. He heard Billy, but then another. Sam knew the second voice, his father. Sam moved toward it, but the wind blew it away. He lifted his hands but couldn't see them in front of him. Sam searched for Kathleen, tried to call her, but his voice made no sound. He'd never find his father. Why did he want to? He didn't need that voice anyway. But he didn't want it left there, either, drifting in the fog. It was his father who had caused this mess, this mist, wasn't it?

"You're wrong, Sam."

Sam turned, finally facing a new voice. "Casey?" Sam took a good look through the mist. "Shit Casey! You scared the crap out of me. What are you doing out here? Hey! Where'd you get that flight suit?"

Sam watched him turn away and float to an opening in the clouds. All that fog and Casey had no sign of a limp. Then Sam knew. "Thomas."

Thomas didn't look back at him but down through the mist into the kitchen, to the stairwell, with the door open, to the child quaking at the top of the stairs. "Look harder, Sam."

Sam's eyes opened with a jolt. Sunshine was melting into the morning window, painting auburn highlights on Kathleen's coffee hair. Her hair, like silk, lay like a blanket on his chest, and he hardly breathed for fear of changing anything. Her arm lay languidly across him as if she were unconsciously holding him there forever. Her heart's beat lullabied him, the gentle rise and fall of her breathing, like the tide, carrying him, saving him. He knew he wouldn't go anywhere without her ever again.

She moved in his arms, her breathing soft and even, her hand resting right on his bruised belly. Sam wondered how he could move it without waking her. Any other position would be preferable, except maybe his jaw. She seemed so happy, her eyes darting under the lids and a slight smile on her face. He wondered what she was dreaming. It certainly had nothing to do with him. Maybe Libby's calves or Kahlall. Maybe Thomas was talking to her.

He didn't know anyone who could go from happy to sad and then back to happy as fast as Kathleen could. He didn't know that anyone would cry so hard and so long for him, or look so beautiful despite the puffy eyes and lips. He didn't know women might cry after orgasm, for so long, because of him. She'd told him it was okay. She'd told him she needed it and him, and it was beautiful. He'd held her tighter and made love to her again.

She shifted her position, her arm over the cotton sheet, and the sharp pain made him cry out. Her fingers found his right nipple, and this time flitted around it, sending power surging, shivering through him. He gasped and grabbed her hand, bringing it up to his lips and kissing it. She turned her head up to his and looked at him, trying her hardest not to giggle. She turned and her breasts gently brushed against him.

"Have pity. I feel like hell!" Sam groaned.

She touched his jaw softly. "Oooh. That really does look like it hurts. I can't believe Casey did that."

"Sucker punch."

She snorted. "We'll get you fixed up with some pain killers." She shot him a seductive smile. "Maybe you should stay in bed."

"You staying with me?"

She snorted again. "You're fine."

"Is that all I am, just fine?"

She giggled and moved up and over him, her breasts barely touching his chest.

He pulled her closer. "You were dreaming."

"Was I?"

"You looked happy." Sadness and shame ate at him once more. "When I thought I lost you, MyKate—" Tears sprang into his eyes surprising him. He blinked them away.

Kathleen sat up. "You didn't lose me. Not for lack of trying." She grinned a tiny bit. "I can't believe this is finally happening. I never really felt I had a chance. The girls you picked were always so beautiful."

He shook his head. Then turning, he lifted her face toward him. "You. Those eyes of yours, this ..." He ran his fingers through her hair. "I don't have words, MyKate." This woman was bringing tears to his eyes and for a reason Sam couldn't understand, he didn't feel at all embarrassed. "Thomas told me I had to look harder."

She broke into a smile. "You talked to him?" She sat up in the bed. Through the window, the sun played on her breasts, and she looked like a Greek goddess carved in marble.

"A dream. Haven't had one in so long." He ran one finger down her arm, enjoying the simple pleasure of touching her, of seeing all of her, something he'd seen before, but never like this.

"He appeared to me, Sam, at Sadie's. He was there. I thought he was Casey at first until I noticed what he was wearing and ..."

"What?" She sounded like Thomas walked right through the door. "He never leaves Gran."

Kathleen giggled. "How do we know that? We're talking about a ghost. Besides, I think he's been to my place a few times. I told you and Casey, but you—"

"He spoke to you?"

"Uh-huh." Her voice dropped. "Told me you loved me. Sam, he touched me." She grinned like she had a brand-new, wonderful secret. "Moved my hair and then, well ... I kind of told him off."

Sam grinned at the thought of his Kathleen, tearing into a ghost.

"I asked him why he hadn't done anything to help you and Casey when you were growing up." She moved over to the side of the bed and reached down, snatching something before he could pull her back to him. "He said the strangest thing, Sam. I didn't know ghosts could be indirect."

He laughed a little. "He wouldn't answer your question?"

"No. He was making excuses for your father. I suppose that's natural. After all, when he's a father, he's supposed to stand up for his son."

"But?"

"Well, when I asked him why Lester was never there for you guys, he sloughed it off, said Billy had been, as if that made up for it."

"He's right."

She shook her head. "No, Sam." She looked up at him with such intensity that he wondered what was really bothering her. She'd only ever had that look on her face when she was hiding something like the time she'd promised Sam she wouldn't give Charger free rein and like the time she'd let Casey take her to the prom.

"What is it?" The time for games was past, he thought.

She looked away. "I just think it's time we sat down with Billy and Gran and talked about what happened back then."

"That's it?"

She nodded.

"Fine." He closed his eyes, thinking of the scene the day before, the horror. "You know how you always said Picasso painted pain, and I said it was all bull, all that square stuff and too many eyes and figures moving over and over."

"Your words, if I remember, were, 'Money in the meat grinder.'"

He pursed his lips and nodded. "I was wrong. I saw it just like Picasso yesterday … after Missy was killed … when everyone was moving around, doing something useful and all I could do was watch. It was like being in one of his paintings."

Her face softened as her smile spread.

CHAPTER 49

Casey was hanging up the phone when Sam poked his head into the kitchen.

"Is it safe?" Sam tried kidding. Their mother didn't seem to be around. "Where is she?"

Casey looked at the clock. "Don't know. She was around here earlier."

"Where's Gran?"

"She went off with Billy somewhere." His head swayed as he remembered his mother in her robe and the scratches she'd gouged into the table. "It's a good thing. Mum's gone off the deep end." He paused and rubbed the back of his neck. Sam knew Casey didn't know how to say what it was he wanted to say.

"Just tell me."

"We heard from the coroner." Casey took a deep breath.

Sam smiled sadly, already knowing. "She wasn't pregnant, was she?"

"No, she wasn't. I'm sorry, Sam."

Sam looked away and kicked the door. She had lied. She would have been—what—at least eight weeks along. How could he have been so completely stupid? He was experienced. He'd been so careful, so smart. He knew women inside out and backward, and still, she'd made him think she was pregnant.

"Thank God," Casey said.

Sam turned and stared at him. "I wanted that child."

Casey looked away. "I know. But it was a lie, Sam." He leaned over and took Sam's hand. "Kathleen's real. Everything about her is real."

"What do I do?"

"Bury Missy," Casey said. He pulled his wallet out and checked his cash. "Be thankful. Only one life lost. We don't have long. Billy said we have to be at the Hole at eleven. Sadie's going to try to take off early." He walked over to the basement door and then looked at Sam, nodding to the steps in the hallway to upstairs. "Watch for the Beast, will ya?"

Sam's gut tightened as Casey approached and then opened the cellar door as if he'd done it all his life.

"When did you start using the stairs?"

"We all have to grow up sooner or later," Casey said, his voice shaking just a little. "I've been working on it."

Sam watched Casey reach over the abyss of warped boards that zigzagged sharply to the dirt floor twelve feet below. Their mother called them the basement stairs. They weren't. They were a treacherous obstacle course of unprotected boards that passed by heavy plumbing pipes and ended on concrete and compressed earth. Any normal person would have torn them down and put in a safe stairway. But his mother was in no more hurry to make them safe than to fix the knob on the back door.

Sam stared, amazed. He wanted to slap Casey on the back and say good job. Casey wouldn't have been able to open the door a few months before, let alone reach over to get at the pistol they'd always hidden in the rafters, but there he was, taking it from their web-covered hidey-hole.

Sam felt panic crawl up his back at the sight of Casey and the gun. "What's with the gun?"

"Just wanted to make sure it's still here."

"Are we overreacting, Casey?"

Casey snorted. "This from the king of overreacting." He glanced over at Sam with a look that made Sam shudder. "You should ask Kathleen where Frank keeps his gun."

Where had that come from? Mr. Egan had all his guns locked in the gun safe. "What are you talking about?"

"I found Frank's old revolver in her garage. It's a piece of crap. I put it in my box."

Sam rubbed his chin as he thought about the last few days. "Did she have it?"

Casey shook his head. "I don't think she even remembered it, but—"

"I'll ask her about it. She should know it isn't where she put it."

Again, Casey shook his head. "The last thing we need is Kathleen with a gun." He grinned.

Sam didn't laugh. It was his fault she was in the state she was, and she sure as hell should not be anywhere near a loaded weapon. "I don't know. After what Mum said yesterday—"

"No one is going to hurt Kathleen," Casey said directly to Sam.

Casey cleaned the dust from the Glock. Releasing the safety, he opened up the chamber of the semiautomatic and let the magazine drop free. The bullets were all there. He looked over at Sam. "It should be cleaned, but we don't have time." He pushed the clip back in. "Do we leave it here?"

Sam sat down on a chair. "Why wouldn't we? It's safe enough there. She hasn't found it yet, or she'd have taken it."

Casey's eyes drifted a bit as he seemed to weigh each side. "She's acting weird, and with what happened yesterday, I've never seen her like this."

"Do you think Mum's that dangerous?"

"Do you want to take the risk?"

Sam shook his head. "She doesn't know it's there, and besides, I doubt if she would know how to use it." He got up and pushed his chair in. "Leave it."

Casey nodded and placed it back in its hiding place.

"Don't close the door." Sam wandered over and looked down the stairs, rubbing his chin. "Casey, do you remember anything about when you fell?"

Casey stared down the stairs and took a step back. "Nope."

"You must remember something." Sam stepped back, trying to picture it in his head.

"I don't remember much." Casey was trying to edge his way past Sam.

"No. Don't close the door." Sam knew Casey didn't want to think about it, but the dream he'd had was bothering him. There was something wrong with the story. "Mum was standing here." He stepped behind Casey, closer to the outside of the doorway. "You were at the top of the stairs, right here?"

"Where's this going?"

"Wait." Sam stepped away from the door. "Say I'm Dad. Which way was I coming from?"

Casey sighed. "How the hell should I know? I was too busy crying to be paying attention to him."

"Exactly my point," Sam said, going through the sequence of events that had played out in his dream. "Dad wasn't coming from the table. He was coming in the door." Sam stepped forward again. "That means Mum was between him and you."

"Fine." Casey moved and closed the door. "Come on." He waved Sam on. "Let's go."

"Yeah, yeah." Sam grabbed his jacket and followed him out the door. Casey didn't get it. Their mother pushed him down the stairs. Not their father.

* * *

Rachel leaned back against the hallway wall so that neither son would know she was there. So much to take in. Casey thought he was so smart. Hiding a gun up there. She wondered how long it had been there.

She leaned back against the doorjamb and digested what she'd just taken in. Sam knew the truth, that she was the one who'd pushed Casey down the cellar stairs. It seemed that Sam had turned against her, but given time, she could win him back. She was not going to give up without a fight.

CHAPTER 50

"The place is quiet," Kathleen said, holding the door of the Hole for them, sniffing in the familiar baking smells. "Mmm. Smells like there's fritters in the oven."

"This is unreal." Casey glanced over at Kathleen, opened his jacket, and took out his wallet. "What are we doing here? We just had breakfast." He pulled a twenty out and stuffed the wallet back into his pocket.

"When Billy says we meet him here, we meet him here," Sam said.

"You get a table. I'll get the coffees." Kathleen waved at Natalie, who was bent over the case, with a bottle of cleaner and a chamois, rubbing vigorously.

Sam shrugged out of his jacket. "Did you get a load of that truck outside?" He kept his voice low and looked over at the one other customer, nicely tucked behind a wide-open newspaper in the back corner. "Piece of crap but those tires are brand new."

Kathleen had noticed it too. It was rusted out on the wheel wells, dented and caked with mud on the hood, but the tires were spotless. She shushed him with a finger to her lips and called over to the counter. "Three coffees, Natalie, please; cream, no sugar for two and a double-double, and a dozen mixed, maybe a couple of the—"

Sam groaned. "I don't think we need a dozen. No one's hungry." He pulled out a chair, turned it around, and sat down facing the back.

"Speak for yourself," Casey said, sitting down. "I'm hungry."

"Whatever, Kathleen, just help yourself, will yaz?" Natalie said, not really paying attention to the lads. She reached over and poked Kathleen. "We miss you around here, kiddo."

Kathleen shuffled around the counter to pick up a pot of fresh coffee, glancing at the only other patron, a stranger, half-hidden behind a copy of the local newspaper.

Natalie lowered her voice and studied Kathleen's face for a reaction. "Kind of busy out your way yesterday."

Kathleen looked quickly away. "Doesn't take long for news to get out around, does it?" She took three mugs from beneath the counter, anchoring each, one finger per cup. "Don't believe everything you hear."

Natalie looked over at the stranger. "You wanna give that guy a top up before you waltz off with the pot?" She half grinned, and Kathleen felt her own back ache. She knew how glad Natalie was just to have a chance to straighten up and stretch.

Kathleen nodded from Natalie to the stranger. "Is he the guy with the old truck out there?" she quietly asked.

Smiling to the ends of her horsy face, Natalie leaned down, relishing the chance to talk about the unusual. "Yeah. Came in yesterday too, but …" She paused for dramatic effect, her voice just above a whisper. "You saw that old wreck of a truck he drove up in? It don't make sense, Kathleen. Get a load of those boots he's wearing. They must have cost him hundreds. I'd be calling the police. Why's a man drivin' an old piece of crap like that but wearin' those boots … unless he stole them."

Kathleen laughed out loud. "Thanks, Natalie," she said and continued over to the man and to ask him if he'd like another.

"Like old times." Kathleen grinned and lifted the pot up so that Sam and Casey could see, nodding over to the man on the other side of the Hole. She grinned as Sam shook his head. Casey turned back to the window, watching as if at any moment Sadie might ride in on a chariot through the clouds to whisk him away.

It wasn't the boots that stopped Kathleen or the way that the man sat, half-hidden. It could have been the hands, well-manicured fingernails, veins high, large knuckles, on sensitive looking fingers. Though they seemed familiar, that wasn't what stopped her. The stranger was singing softly. And it wasn't just any song.

"Black and bay, dapple and gray, coach and six little horses …"

He was singing "All the Pretty Little Horses."

Flagpole thin, the man, she remembered that was what her father had said about Lester Brennan. She remembered how it hurt her neck to look all the way up to his eyes. Kathleen had never forgotten his wise, old owl eyes that twinkled when he played with Casey and Sam and her and a gentle way of reprimanding Sam when Sam was too rough with the ponies.

The paper slowly came down, and the man from somewhere in the long ago looked at her, his eyes, almost frightened, just as blue as Casey's, the color of Thomas's eyes but ringed with age and sadness.

"Hush a bye, don't you cry, go to sleepy, little baby …" she sang in a whispered hush.

"Hello, Kitty Kate."

* * *

Billy didn't know what to expect when he walked through the back door into Rachel's kitchen. Holding the door open for Gran, he let it slam behind him, the slam making Rachel jump.

"Don't fall, Mom." Billy walked through the kitchen toward the hallway, his hand on her elbow.

"Stop fussing, Billy. Maybe a cup of tea. Rachel? What do you think?" Gran looked over at her. "You feeling a little better, dear?" She slipped out of her coat, and Billy took it from her and hung it on the peg by the door. "My. It's a glorious day." She squeezed Billy's hand. "I think I'll go and change into my slacks. It's far too nice to be inside." She shuffled past Rachel, humming, as she made off to her bedroom.

Rachel stared at Billy. "She's in a good mood."

"Like she said. Nice day."

"You had business in town?" Rachel tied the apron behind her, angrily, jerking at the ties, pulling the knot so tight, Billy thought she'd hurt herself. "No one tells me anything. But then that's normal, isn't it? Is she hiding something, Billy?"

Billy smiled slowly and, turning, leaned his rump against the counter. He caught himself chewing on his lip as he studied his next move.

Rachel let the steamy water run. Reaching over, she picked up the soap and squirted some into the sink, smirking at him. "What's on your mind, Billy?"

"You killed that girl, Rachel. We both know that."

She snorted. "It was a terrible accident. We're all upset. I'm going to make something special for supper, for Sam." She walked around him and reached into the cupboard.

"Aren't you interested in the police report?"

"Oh, is that where you hightailed off for? No, not really. Like I said, it was a tragic accident." She turned the water off in the sink. "What do you think—steak or chicken?"

Billy had wanted to throttle her before, but oddly, it had gone beyond that. Now, he simply wanted her gone.

"I know you killed that girl. You tried it with Lester, and I know that you'll try it with me, but by God, I'm telling those boys the truth. They can make up their own. I want you out of here now."

She laughed as she walked to the fridge and pulled out a plate on which sat a raw chicken. She placed it on the counter and looking up from the meat, grabbed the cleaver. "You know, it really hurts that you think so badly of me, Billy. I did us all a big favor. Missy knew all about the gold. Didn't she tell you?"

"Are you telling me you did do it?" His stomach clenched so hard it hurt. "You killed her? My God, Rachel!"

"Chicken!" She slammed a white, pocked carcass on the counter. "A nice chicken, perfect for the occasion and"—Rachel slammed the cleaver down between the leg and the breast—"you're not going to tell anyone anything." She snapped the bones and tore the fleshy leg from the body. "You see, I'm not going anywhere. You'll have to kill me." She paused and stared at him. "And we both know you don't have that kind of backbone."

"Don't be so sure, Rachel."

She gave a harsh snort. "I want that quarry opened up, Billy. We both know what's out there. And leaving it all to the boys? Now that hurts."

Billy leaned forward to study her eyes. How the hell did she know that? How long had she known?

"Oh, don't look so surprised. I've known for years. Someone called from the mining group." She shook her head. "Can't remember the name, but he wanted Lester, and when I told him my loving husband was out, he told me to reconsider mining the gold. I told him to send the details, and I'd try to make Lester understand." She cackled. "It was going to be nice," she said, lost in the past. "You, me, and Sam. You always wanted to travel the world." She faced him. "We could have had it all. But no!" Her lip curled into a snarl. "You just had to hide it from me."

"Has it always been about the gold?" Billy ran the whole history through his head—the way she'd gone after Lester with the rifle when he'd laid the law down, the way she kept Sam close to her all those years.

He leaned closer to her, so close he could feel her breath on his face. "I've already been in this prison so long it don't matter—hey, weekly visits, three square meals a day—just knowing the lads are safe. Mum would understand, Rachel. She's given up everything too." He was talking brave, but he didn't feel so brave. "You've played all your cards. You're not holding anything now. I'm going to the police. I'm going to tell them everything."

She cocked an eyebrow. "Oh really? Remember room number eight?" She pulled the cleaver out of the meat and raised it again. "Come on, Billy, you weren't that drunk. I remember room number eight, No-tell Motel."

The cleaver came down again, and Billy recoiled. He hadn't forgotten. He'd never forget.

"I hadn't slept with Lester for a whole year. Then I slept with you. That one night, that's all it took. You did have stamina." She brought the cleaver down, and it crunched as it separated socket from bone.

Billy leaned against the counter, the room spinning around him.

"When I knew I was pregnant, I slept with Lester again. After all, he was my husband, and you didn't want anything to do with me."

Billy's world turned black as he backed up, closer to the door.

"Sam was such a small baby, so perfect for a preemie. Everyone thought so. So many times, he's been told how much he looks like you. Everyone says so." She looked over at Billy. "Oh no. No, you won't say anything to anybody about this. Could you do that to the boys—sons, that's what you call them—after all this time? All they've ever had is each other. You know how close they are. No. You won't do that to them."

Billy stood there for a moment, struggling to remain on his feet. Could Sam really be his son? He'd always wondered, but Rachel had never said anything. She'd waited twenty-two years for the perfect opportunity to let it drop, and her timing was perfect.

No more, Billy thought. He should have told Lester years ago. He should never have let Rachel stay, and he should never let her hurt the boys the way she'd done, and he swore he would never let her kill Casey, no matter what had happened in the past. Billy turned and walked out of the house.

* * *

Kitty Kate. She remembered. Her heart broke in two when he used his teasing name for her. How could she have forgotten? She heard a chair crash back onto the floor and turned to see Sam standing, Casey staring. Bolt. They were going to bolt. She knew the look. She'd seen that same look on the horses on occasions when the head vet came through the stable door. She'd had to stop it then too. Without another thought, she put the coffeepot on the table in front of Lester Brennan, and Kathleen rushed over to Sam, standing firmly between him and the door. Having risen too, Casey was white, except for a red burn of fury in his cheeks.

"Sit down, Sam." Kathleen prayed for help. Thomas. She could use Thomas right now. She grabbed Sam's hand.

Lester's eyes moved from Casey to Sam. "We need to talk. Now. Before anyone else gets hurt." Lester rose, put the newspaper down, and walked over to his sons.

Casey stared at his father as if he couldn't believe the old man had just dropped by for a casual chat. He pushed back his chair, his other hand clenched in a tight fist. "No. Don't bother."

"Casey. No!" Kathleen put out her hand to physically stop him. Lester ignored Casey and picked up Sam's chair. Placing it in front of the table, he pulled out another and sat down.

"What makes you think we want to hear anything from you?" Casey asked, stepping back a little, sounding to Kathleen a little weaker.

"The hell we don't." Sam snapped at Casey. "We want answers. What the fuck are you doing here … now?"

Lester gazed at him steadily, waiting for any sign that either might listen.

Kathleen couldn't believe she was seeing the same man, the man they'd all blamed, the coward, sitting in front of them, like an archangel with tarnished sword and broken halo.

Lester's eyes hadn't moved from Casey. "You have to hear me out."

"You miserable old piece of shit! That's it," Casey said as he started for the door.

Kathleen grabbed him. "Sit down! Casey! Sit down for Gran's sake, for Billy. Billy obviously set this little scene up. Do it for Gran."

Casey stared down at her. "I'm not going to sit here and chat with a man who—"

"Sit. Or by God, I'll slug ya harder than you hit Sam!" Kathleen realized her fingers were digging deep into Sam's arm. Sam hadn't moved. "What would Sadie want you to do, Casey?"

Casey rolled his eyes and then stared at Kathleen. "What in the hell is wrong with you, suddenly so sympathetic? He—"

"No. Kathleen's right." Sam put his arm out too. "Sadie would never let you walk away, would she?"

Casey's face twisted in fury as he gulped in air and stared at his father. Kathleen felt her heart race in her chest as she prayed for Casey to relax.

"Does Gran know you're here?" Casey reluctantly sank back into his chair.

Lester nodded and stopped to give his sons time to take it all in.

"They've known where you were all along," Casey muttered.

Sam took his chair from Kathleen and sitting down, pulled her onto his knee, as if for protection. "Where have you been?"

Lester turned to him. "Brazil, working the gold mines."

Sam's hand tightened on Kathleen's hand. "Brazil."

Well, Kathleen thought. *No wonder Gran reacted the way she did.* "When did you get here?" Kathleen asked.

Lester's eyes moved to Sam. "The day after you showed up married to Melissa King!"

Kathleen felt her stomach clench. She tried to stay calm if only to keep Sam and Casey focused on what was really important.

"Did you kill Missy?" Sam asked.

Lester's face tightened, and a desolate chill entered his eyes. "No."

"But you knew her." Sam leaned forward.

"You're Billy's connection?" Kathleen looked from Lester to Casey and then back to their father. "You arranged for the horses, Libby, everything? You bought my house."

"It was all I could give you," Lester said, and Kathleen knew he wasn't reaching Casey. "You're not kids anymore. The time has come to make things right."

"Bullshit!" Casey said, leaning forward, his fists hard on the table. "You could have done this a long time ago. Why now?"

"Hey, Kathleen." Natalie loomed over them, eyes snapping, more than curious as to what was going on with the stranger. "Are you finished with that pot over there, or do you want some coffee?"

"Not now, Natalie." Kathleen stood up and shooed Natalie away. "I'll get it." *Why always restaurants for these scenes,* she wondered.

Sam's eyes shot back to his father. "What he said, why now?"

Lester's face twitched just a little. "It's a big world out there, Sam, with a lot of very ugly people. I've met them. Yours? I met her in Brazil."

"Would someone please ...?" Casey jerked forward.

Sam turned to Casey. "Missy spent the last summer doing research work at a gold mine in Brazil."

"Three summers." Lester leaned closer to Casey, his eyes desperate, as if knowing he'd never have another chance to make it right. "The Kings were down on vacation. I recognized her father and gave her a part-time job. Missy was all over the office. She found out something about the farm, something that made it very attractive to her. I had a picture that Billy sent me of you three. The picture disappeared the day Missy left. My guess was she recognized you, Sam, and she moved in for the kill."

Sam slumped back, and Kathleen ran her hand through the curls that licked his neck. Kathleen squeezed his hand. It all made so much sense.

"Melissa called me the night she married you to tell me the news. I didn't believe her." Lester stopped, his voice breaking. He took a deep breath. "When I found out from Billy and Mum about your new bride, I knew the time had come. But I didn't kill her. I was with Billy the whole time."

Casey slumped back into his chair. "Great, just great. You're Billy's alibi," Casey said, clenching and unclenching his fists, as he sat. He sighed. "Why don't you start at the beginning?"

Lester cleared his throat nervously, clearly uneasy, but he began, and his sons listened.

Like Sam, Lester had been taken in by a woman. Kathleen stopped herself from cutting in, interrupting with questions that were popping up faster than Lester Brennan could address.

"Years ago, Rachel set her sights on Billy, but when Billy spurned her, she went after me to get even. She filled my head with lies about Billy, and I believed her." He looked down at his hands. "I fell for it, hook, line, and sinker. Within months, she was pregnant, and I was more than willing to marry her."

"I have a hard time thinking anyone would want her," Casey said.

His father laughed softly. "She never loved me. I know that now. She stopped sleeping with me as soon as I married her. I kept finding her out at the barn lookin' for Billy. Finally, Billy couldn't take it. He got a job out west on the oil fields and took off. Then you were born." He looked at Casey. "The only thing that mattered to me was you, Casey."

Lester leaned back into his chair. He took out his wallet and pulled out a frayed photo, staring at it for a moment before handing it to Casey. Kathleen leaned over as Casey looked down at a photo he'd never seen, a photo of a young man cradling a newborn. Kathleen's eyes misted up. Lester had such a look of complete joy.

Lester's hand was shaking on the table in front of them. "You were such a beautiful baby. So happy. Perfect. But the marriage wasn't working. Mum was worried; the farm was losing money, and Rachel was plain nuts. She spent her time hiding in her room. She never went near you, never played with you." He shook his head.

He kept talking, seemingly lost in the memories of how Billy's job had dried up, how Lester had to work in the mines up north, and how, finally, and for a reason he couldn't figure out then or now, Rachel had suddenly warmed up to him again.

"She welcomed me into our bedroom again. Eight months later, Sam was born."

Casey looked like he wanted to throw up.

"You were so small, Sam. We were lucky you lived." His eyes were on Sam. "Then it all started over again. Your mother locked the door on me. I wasn't allowed to ever take you anywhere. I guess she was afraid I'd take off with you. I should have known then, but I had such hopes for you boys."

He placed another photo onto the table. In this one, Lester was standing in front of the barn, Billy at his side, holding Casey. Lester was holding a newborn as if offering him to a jubilant god. Sam studied it and then passed it to Casey.

"I had a good job, you know? The mining paid for the farm, but I was away all the time. I blamed myself back then for the whole mess, but I've had over fifteen years to think about it, and it wasn't all my fault." He stopped as if trying to regain control. Then he placed his hands together on the table in front of him.

"Rachel, she started it all over again. She was yelling at me like a banshee. Nothing I could do pleased her. She treated you, Casey, like shit from the very beginning, but you couldn't get her away from Sam. We all knew—me, Mum, and Billy—that she was mean but not how crazy she was. Sure, she came from rough beginnings. That father of hers was nothing more than a drunk, but she never seemed that bad.

"I worked my tail off, kept the money coming in while Billy worked the farm. I hid some of the money and gave it to Billy to build up the herd. She got the rest for the housekeeping and family budget. It was never enough. She wanted the land in her name, and we weren't about to do that." He snorted. "She had me insured. Took out a policy. I was already insured with the company, but she insisted on more in case she was left alone to bring up you boys." Les stared at Casey. "You were six, almost seven. The company offered a better death benefits package." Lester shuddered. "She'd seen the policy and her eyes went straight to the payout. The look in her eyes was like a cornered badger. You must have seen it. It scares the shit right out of you."

Again, he looked at both of them. They couldn't argue, but Kathleen knew. She'd seen it, that look. She and Sam had learned to protect Casey whenever they saw that look.

"I guess right after that she figured she'd had enough. She told me we had groundhogs in the back fields, so on my next day off, I got my shotgun and headed out to get rid of them. Billy was dehorning the calves in the barn and saw me go off. A few minutes later, he says he saw Rachel follow me out with a rifle in her hands." He stopped and took a deep breath.

"It was weird. Rachel didn't like to hunt. Too many bugs and ticks. I was just on the other side of the knoll. You know the one the cows gather on under the elms? I felt the bullet hit me before I heard it."

Kathleen felt a fluttering in her belly as the truth of what he was saying registered.

"I mean, I felt the pain and the shock, but I just couldn't believe the blood. Didn't know what hit me, but I knew I was in trouble when I fell. Then I saw Billy. He was standing right behind her, his pistol right at her head. He was talking to her, and she was moving. Her rifle was on the ground. Billy told her to pick me up. Somehow, he managed to keep the gun on her as they carried me to the truck. I don't remember any more then, shock and all, but I remember waking up in the hospital with Billy there." Lester's voice shook. "If it weren't for your uncle, I wouldn't be here now."

The boys stared as Lester slowly opened his shirt to reveal a rather nasty-looking scar in his chest. "A hunting accident was what we said."

Kathleen gaped as Casey's mouth dropped.

Sam gave a strangled laugh. "Are you saying she shot you?"

Lester began to pull the shirt out of his pants. "You wanna see my back."

"No!" Sam cried out, his hand up in a stop position. "Billy's gonna say all this is true?"

Lester nodded.

"We were at sort of a deadlock." He smiled slightly. "I'm not all that stupid. Those insurance policies, I made them out to you two, in care of Billy and Mum. Billy tells me he's never seen a face like that before or since, when she found out the truth, when she was told the insurance papers weren't made out to her. For a woman so scheming and vicious, she's pretty stupid." Lester almost grinned. "She was furious." He shrugged as if it wasn't even worth stating, and then he froze as he remembered. Lester's hand moved slightly toward Casey.

"I had to leave. Billy promised he'd stay and look after your Gran and you. It wasn't my own skin we were worried about."

"You didn't have to leave," Casey said. His voice was almost a growl.

"I did, Casey. She changed her target. Billy found her one day in the barn." Lester, blinking back tears, looked away from Casey.

"Go on." Casey sat back.

Kathleen watched the hair on his arms begin to rise. "The barn?"

"She had you locked in the mow, and she was standing below you, lighting matches and dropping them into the straw while you peered down at her." He stopped as if his voice had failed him, cleared his throat, and whispered. "You don't remember this?"

The vein in Casey's temple pounded.

Like a fog clearing, Casey saw himself, looking down through the beams in the attic of the barn. The dust and grit from the hay around him hurt his hands as he tried to pry open the doorway to the loft. His mother was laughing below him, staring out the open door. She was slowly removing the plastic from a package of cigarettes she'd brought home from the grocery store earlier that day. They were the type Billy smoked, and she had bragged to him and Sam that she'd picked them up for him because he had loved to smoke so much.

Casey had made the mistake of telling her that Billy had smoked Dunhill, not Newport. He remembered her eyes, how like a growling dog they'd become before she had picked up a china plate and thrown it into his forehead.

"No, Mama," Casey had cried, as she'd dragged him out of the house.

He remembered her snarl as she had pulled him along. "After all the good I do, you make it look like I'm stupid. Well … I'll teach you not to talk back to me."

He had felt the gravel gouge and sting after he'd fallen and bounced. She hadn't stopped to pick him up. She had just pulled him along, his bare knees grinding over the ground.

"You ruin everything I do; you do." She had yanked harder on him.

He remembered how he'd cried out, already knowing the Gran was off at the library. Billy had been gone to the cattle-sales barn, and Sam had been … Sam had been with their father—out on the tractor.

He remembered wondering why they were going to the barn. She'd hated the barn. She had said nothing good ever came out of a barn. He remembered how relieved he had been when she stopped, just up inside the barn, right under the ladder to the hayloft. He'd stared at the bales of hay behind her. If he could get to them, he might be able to hide in them. She had hated bales of hay and straw. She'd always said they were sharp and gave her pinpricks.

"Give me your hands," his mother had ordered. "Put 'em out."

"No," he remembered saying to her, pulling them behind his back.

Her eyes had narrowed, and he'd turned to run. But she'd been faster than a wildcat, and she had grabbed his shirt and hung on. She'd pulled him backward and twisted him around.

"You little jerk," she had said, her voice, now strangely calm. She'd whipped out the belt and had leaned down to him so close that he could smell the bitterness in her breath. "You've got a choice. You can go up to the attic and lock the latch. You can disappear into that hayloft for a while, or"—she held up the belt—"you can take the belt. Oh, I'd say ten per hand would be proper."

Casey had looked up at the mow. She'd thought the mow was a punishment? The same as a whipping?

She had jerked the belt over in front of his face, so close he could smell the leather.

"The mow, please," he had said, thinking he'd won.

She'd slowly smirked. "Fine. Off you go."

He had hesitated. Something had been wrong.

"Go."

He hadn't argued, but he had climbed the ladder faster than Sam ever could have. Jumping into the mow, Casey had grinned and pulled the door over the hole. He had crossed his legs and had sat down on the beams. He'd just wait for her to go and then climb back down and hang out until Billy came home. The mow had been full to the roof with green grass hay. It had smelled sweet, and with the sun streaming through the slats of the roof, it had been as pretty as the pictures in his book about farm life. Dust had sparkled around him like snowflakes. He had thought he might even stay in the loft until Billy got home or even until his Dad came back with Sam. He had thought he could jump out and scare Sam. That would be fun, he'd thought.

Then his mother had moved.

He had watched her through the spaces between the beams in the attic floor. These spaces had allowed air to move through the hay, keeping the mold from forming and ruining the bales. His dad and Billy had always been telling Sam and him to get out of the mow, so this had made him feel like a grown-up. Still, what had his mother been doing? She had grabbed a rake pole, and she had been holding it up to the attic door. The sound of the outside latch shutting had made Casey lean closer.

"Mama?" He'd called down to her. "Why did you lock the door, Mama?"

He remembered how her laugh had made him tremble. He'd heard her laugh so many times before.

"Mama?"

He had watched her turn. She had looked up at him, her face, snarly and mean. She had been still angry with him.

The fog, still clearing, Casey remembered. The belt had been no longer in her hand but on the ground below her. She had pulled the cigarettes she'd purchased for Billy out of her apron. Next, she'd pulled out a package of matches. Casey had known they were matches because of the bluish-green of the tiny book with "Salem" written on the top. They'd had a box of these matches near the stove. Why did she have matches? Maybe she had been going to give them to Billy too.

No. She had been opening the cigarettes. She had tossed the wrapper on the straw-covered floor. "You know, I haven't had a cigarette for so long." She'd said and had stared up at him.

"You can't smoke in the barn, Mama," Casey had said, feeling his hands tremble as he watched the chickens peck around cellophane on the barn floor.

She hadn't even bothered to look at him. He had watched her shake her head, and then she had pulled a cigarette out of the package and placed it in her mouth.

"You shouldn't smoke," he had cried. "Billy says." Big fires start small, his teacher had said, teaching the class not to set fires of any kind.

He had known, from Billy's fear of open lights and his father's reminders, never to bring matches near the barn.

She had opened the book of matches and had torn out one. Scratching it across the sparking strip, it had flared and then had burned down to a small flame. She had watched it burn and then had turned and had looked up at him. Still burning, she had placed it up to the cigarette and had taken a deep drag in.

"You can't smoke in the barn," Casey had pleaded with her.

She had dropped the still-burning match on the floor. It had gone out before it had hit the straw.

"Let me out," Casey had yelled out. He had pushed on the door. "Please, Mama."

His mother had laughed as if it had been an amusing greeting card at the pharmacy in town. She had lighted another match and had tossed it over to the hay.

"It's what you wanted, you pathetic child," she had said and then had taken a long drag on the cigarette. She had flicked the ash onto the floor. Casey had seen the straw on the floor flare into red and then die out. The tendril of smoke had risen in the air. She had lit another match and had tossed it into the hay. It had flared and then had gone out.

Casey had pulled his arms around his legs. He remembered rocking back and forth, watching the matches his mother had been dropping. Then, as fast as the flame on her final match, she had been gone.

"Please …" Casey remembered how he cried as he rocked. What if the matches were waiting to set the dust on fire? What if she had dropped the cigarette, and it was just burning slowly? How long did it take a cigarette to burn to the hay? He didn't know how long he cried. He only knew he was going to be blamed for the fire. The dust was so hot. Billy had told them how the dust in the mow had caused many a barn to burn. One match. That was all it took. He rocked and wept. He tried to be so quiet so she wouldn't come back.

"You tell anyone—anyone—and I'll do it again," she had told him, her face as scary as any monster he'd seen drawn in his books.

It had been dark outside when Billy had come running into the barn, calling Casey's name. At first, Casey hadn't answered. He'd be blamed for the fire. He hadn't been able to move. If he had moved, he'd have fallen through the cracks in the boards. If he'd moved, the dust would have exploded. The fire would have started. Billy had to reach up and had pulled Casey from the loft.

"Billy caught her doing it, setting matches on fire. She just laughed and told him she was kidding."

Lester was short of breath as if it was all too heavy to carry anymore.

"She was good at it. The bruises were rarely visible. She said she'd take you away from me. She said they'd never believe us, that she'd already told her doctor how I'd beaten her." Lester looked over at Sam. "You were so young. Strange. You talked early, walked early, and seemed to know just what to do to make your mother happy. At least most of the time." He paused and a sob wracked him as he tried to focus.

"I filed divorce papers." He reached out to Casey. "I really did. I was away at the mines, and I wanted to be home when she got served. She must have found out, because the next thing I know, they tell me from the office I've got a phone call, to come quick cause my son's on the phone."

He looked at Sam. "I thought it would be Casey who would call for help, but it was you. You were five years old, and you called me, crying, wanting me to come home and make her stop hurting Casey." He groaned and looked away. "Five!" He turned his eyes to Casey.

"She waited until I walked through the back door. She was holding Sam back, and you were standing, at the top of the stairs. I remember that. You weren't holding onto her. You were standing there, right where she'd told you to stand, too terrified to move, right at the top of the cellar stairs. She was ranting, all red in the face, right there in front of you, going on about how it was all my fault and, if I didn't leave, you'd end up dead, Casey."

"The night she threw Casey down the basement stairs," Sam said as if he understood completely. He tightened his hold on Kathleen. Lester seemed to relax a little.

Casey turned and looked up at his brother. "She didn't throw me down the stairs. He did."

"Well?" Sam stared at Lester. "You gonna tell him?"

"You already know?" Lester looked at Sam. "How could you know? You were just a baby."

"For me, it happened last night." He tightened his hold on Kathleen.

Casey stared at his brother. "What the fuck?"

"Tell him," Kathleen said. Sam gripped Kathleen's hand more tightly as he sighed and shook his head. "Tell him what happened. Thomas isn't here to do it!"

Lester stared at Sam in disbelief. "Thomas told you?"

"For the love of God!" Casey stood up.

"Sit!" Sam pushed him back down. He faced Lester once more. "Tell him!" He smiled slowly, as if relieved. "You tell him, and I'll tell him if it's the truth."

Lester faced Casey. "I don't know how Sam got the number or how he managed to call, but it took me two days to get back. It wasn't that I didn't try. I dropped everything when I heard your voice." Lester glanced over at Sam. "You were terrified." He turned and stared out the window, and Kathleen could see genuine torment in his eyes.

Casey stared at the man as if it was beginning to register.

"You don't remember?" Lester reached out across the table as if wanting Casey to take his hands. "She wanted to let me know she was serious. She set it all up, even had the gall to tell me she'd kill you."

Casey turned slowly to his brother, the gray haze of memory growing brighter as he stared. "You knew this?"

Kathleen wrapped her arms around Sam as his eyes glistened with tears. He turned to Lester. "Thomas showed me last night." He grunted, as if not believing it himself. "That's why I was asking questions about the stairs." Sam leaned over, his eyes boring into his brother. "Casey, from the angle Dad was coming and where the Beast was standing, there was only one way you went down those stairs." Sam leaned back. "He didn't throw you down. She did."

"I figured that out ages ago," Kathleen said. "You wouldn't listen to me, would you?" She poked Sam. "It makes sense."

"The hell it does." Sam was shaking his head. "Why did you leave? You didn't have to leave us with her."

"Yes, I did." Lester looked down and, for the first time, ashamed. "She said she'd take you boys. The way things were back then, the things she'd set up, she'd have gotten custody, and God knows what she'd have done then. It's not like the big city here. I couldn't prove anything, what with all the Kluggs in the county. She swore she'd kill Casey. She had me. I had a better chance saving everything by leaving. It was our deal. I knew Gran and Billy would look after you, and someday when you got older, maybe I could … could …"

"Waltz right back?" Casey said. "What about the farm?" He leaned closer to his father. "What's made the Beast stay all these years? What did Melissa want so badly she'd die for it?"

Lester Brennan smiled for the first time, slowly, almost a grimace. "Gold, lads." He sat back in his chair. "The farm is sitting on a good-sized vein of gold. Billy knows and your mother found out when I tried to divorce her. I had to make a full disclosure of assets. My guess is her lawyer informed her."

Casey's eyes skewed up in a suspicious arch. "You tried to divorce her?"

"Yes, but she told me she'd kill you if I did."

"Gold?" Sam said.

Lester's face changed completely, blossoming into pride. "Haven't you boys read up on the history of Killkenny County? Mining's what made these communities. That quarry should be enough to tell you that something of interest was underneath it all."

"Gold? Granite maybe. But gold?" Sam chuckled. "Right. I've read those reports. They don't say anything about gold … something about luminous something or other."

Lester raised his eyebrows and chuckled. "You haven't been digging enough, Sam. I've done studies. We're sitting on top of a fortune. Thing is we have to destroy a lot of good farmland to get it. I'd prefer to sit on it, save it for the next generations, at least until they come up with a way of mining it that won't do too much damage to the land."

Gold? Utter nonsense. Kathleen snorted and turned as the bell on the door welcomed another coffee lover to the Hole. She grinned at the sight of Sadie's confident stride. Kathleen hadn't seen the vet truck pull up. Casey hadn't noticed either, not until Sadie walked over behind him and, leaning down, kissed him. She smiled and looked over at Lester. Then she blushed and stepped back.

Kathleen was ready. "Sadie Parker? This is Lester Brennan, Casey and Sam's dad."

Sadie, one arm around Casey's shoulder, reached out with her right hand. "I'm very pleased to meet you, Mr. Brennan. You have your mother's eyes."

CHAPTER 51

When Billy pulled into the parking lot of the Hole, he saw Lester's truck next to Casey's vehicle and Sadie's vet truck. Billy realized he couldn't remember the drive back into town, unaware of anything other than Rachel's final threat and the consequences it would have on everyone.

Sam is your son, your son, your son, your … It echoed in his head, and he couldn't get past it. Rachel couldn't have Billy, so she'd loved Sam instead. Sam had carried the whole family on his back because of Billy and Rachel's one night in a cheap hotel. Casey had taken all that shit from her for all those years, not because of Lester, but because of him. Billy hadn't gained a son. He'd only taken one from his brother. He felt naked, filthy, with no hope of redemption.

Now, staring from his truck through the window of the Hole, he watched them talking. Casey was smiling. Sam was talking, his hands moving around as they did when he was bragging about the horses. Billy realized that it was going to be all right for them, that they'd work out their problems. At least it was starting.

Billy couldn't do it. There was no way. Not after all those years Lester had lost. He couldn't take it away from him so soon. Sam turned and looked out through the window and saw him. Billy watched his son wave. He waved back and then turned off the truck. No. Rachel would make sure Lester knew. He'd have to tell his brother. Lester would know how to take care of it. If he was really lucky, maybe Lester would just kill him. Billy pushed open the door and tried to fix a smile on his face on the short walk from his truck to the Hole.

Though they were all pretty quiet, Lester looked like he had been run through a wood chipper. Billy played with the truck keys, not able to look at Casey and Sam. He focused on Lester. "You all need a break. Lester and I have some business. Legal stuff to take care of. We'll meet you back at the barn."

"What's wrong?" Sam asked, his eyes locked on Billy's eyes.

"We ain't hanging around here any more than we have to. Come on, Lester," Billy said.

Kathleen hopped off Sam's lap, and Casey rose, shrugging into his jacket.

"You takin' the day off, Doc?" Billy picked up her jacket and held it for her as she slipped into it.

"I work two shifts tomorrow." Sadie gave him a peck on the cheek.

Casey stopped and turned around to face his father. "You are staying, right?"

Lester cleared his throat. "That's up to the two of you. I won't come home if you don't want me there."

Casey took a deep breath and swallowed hard. "You owe it to Gran." He placed his hand squarely on Lester's shoulder. "Go home, Dad. Get some rest, Billy. You look like shit," Casey said as he walked out the door.

Sam gave them one more glance, put his arm around Kathleen, and then followed Casey and Sadie out to the truck.

CHAPTER 52

As Sam headed for Casey's truck, Kathleen was pulling on his arm, telling him to slow down, but he couldn't. His mind was moving faster than a mouse in a maze. Maybe Casey hadn't known what to believe, but Sam was certain.

"If it's about that nightmare last night ...?" Casey had said, also trying to slow his brother down. "You're having visions now?"

They had decided that Casey was going with Sadie in the vet truck, letting Sam take Kathleen back to the farm in Casey's truck. Sam didn't know why Casey didn't understand. "It was just the way he said, 'Dad didn't push you.' She did. There's more too, Casey. Did you see the look on Billy's face when he came in? I've never seen him terrified before." He turned on the truck as Kathleen clamored into the passenger seat. "Lookit. We'll talk about it at home. I have to stop off at the feed store for some salt licks."

Casey scratched his head. "Okay. You might want to pick up some mineral licks too. We put Libby and babes in the front field."

Sam grinned. "About time. What are you doing?"

"Sadie wants to stop at the clinic, check on a cat that got caught up in an engine."

"Oooh, poor little kitty. She was telling me." Kathleen glanced over at Sadie.

"Maybe I should go straight home." Sam wondered if anyone was getting the point at all. The danger they were all in. Their mother, the crackpot, was back there at the farm, and worse, she knew that her target had just waltzed back into town. What was wrong with them?

"Life as usual," Kathleen said, "or she wins."

"Don't take too long, Casey." Sam threw the truck into reverse. "All hell could break loose when the Beast finds Dad's back."

Casey rolled his eyes and shook his head slowly. "Right." He turned and started off to Sadie. "Let's all rush home to get murdered. Nope. Not gonna happen today."

Sam wasn't so sure.

Sam knew from the moment that he and Kathleen stepped into the feed store that they'd made a mistake. Everyone stopped and wanted some answers, grilling them. "What the hell happened at your place yesterday? How's the horse? When did you get married?" The questions didn't stop. Sam grabbed Kathleen by the arm and whisked her out of the store and back to the truck.

"Billy can get it later."

"That's not really fair, Sam." Kathleen climbed back into the truck. "They'll be just as bad to him."

"He'll be able to handle it."

Kathleen snorted. "I don't know. He was looking kind of rough."

Sam agreed. Billy looked as though he was carrying a hay bale on his shoulders. Something was really wrong at home, and now it was centered squarely on Billy.

* * *

Lester wondered what the rush was all about as Billy took him by the arm and hurried him out and over to his truck. "Come on. Ain't got time to kill. You can pick up that thing you call a truck later," Billy told him.

"What's wrong?" Lester climbed in, closing the door, watching Billy scowl as he came around the front. Then Billy hopped in beside him and started up the truck. "You gonna answer me, or do I have to guess?"

"We'll stop at the liquor store on the way." Billy reached behind him for his wallet. Lester smiled and felt the tension ease in his shoulders. Nothing had changed. Billy was acting as he always did when he had something on his mind. Usually a direct person, his brother stared straight into a person's eyes when he spoke.

Billy didn't say anything on the way to the liquor store. He glanced at his watch, repeatedly. It wasn't even one in the afternoon, and they were headed to buy booze. *Nope*, thought Lester. It was big, whatever it was.

"I'll be back," Billy called to Lester as he ran into the liquor store.

Lester looked around at the town he knew like the back of his hand. It was the only town he knew that had placed their one and only liquor store on a lot carved out of the local graveyard. Wherever you looked, there were headstones. It was still as funny as when he stood outside the doors, only sixteen, waiting for some twenty-one-year-old adult to illegally take his money and buy him and Billy a six-pack.

"To the farm?" Lester looked at him.

"Let's go home," Billy said, and they were away. Lester looked into the bag and pulled the bottle out of the wrapper. Remy Martin. Indeed.

"So? What now," Lester said as Billy weaved along the road out of town.

"Pour some of that fancy brandy you're always spouting off about," Billy said, lightly. "Figured I'd get you the fancy stuff you like."

Lester had always known the difference between cheap brandy and a fine cognac. Since they were young men, Lester had answered the same thing.

"It's cognac," he said, quietly, smiling. Lester hardly ever drank it. He liked to hold it, swirl it, and take in its aroma before he drank it down and savored the aftertaste.

"While we're driving?"

"If the cops stop us, so much the better. We're probably going to need them before the day is out. There are plastic cups in the door next to you."

Lester was concerned now. His brother was talking too fast, a trait that Sam seemed to have picked up.

"Your talk with the boys, it went okay?" Billy asked as Lester poured the cognac into the cups and handed one to his brother.

"As well as it could have. They listened to me. You did a good job with them, Billy. They're fine young men." He grinned and looked at the highway ahead. "To the lads!" Billy shot him a quick glance and then raised his cup and downed it. He handed his cup back to Lester.

Okay, Lester thought. He downed his.

"Pour another," Billy said with an eerie nonchalance. "Did you ever love Rachel, Les?"

Lester looked over at him. *Okay.* "Never. I suppose I cared for her for a while. That changed real fast. No. I was in love with Debbie Bradshaw."

Billy raised his eyebrow and glanced over. "No kidding."

"Weren't you?"

Billy snorted. "Hell, no. Ruthie Cooper." He slipped into a long lost dream. "Cripes, what a woman."

"Ruth Cooper? She was downright scary."

"She had strength. Still works in the hospital here, last time I heard. Intensive care."

"You keep in touch?"

"I see her now and then." Billy didn't look at Lester but smiled. "She never married."

"Why didn't you do something about it?"

Billy turned down Saint Jude Road. "I was no more free than you." He reached out for another drink. "Rachel chained us all." Billy took his next ration, and they drank again. Billy took a long, deep breath, and Lester knew it was time.

"Les"—Billy cleared his throat—"you know how when you went away for that long stretch when Casey was a few months past one, and then you came home and things were good between her and you again?"

"For God's sake, Billy. Have another drink and spit it out." He poured another and handed it to Billy. "The truth, I mean, not the cognac." Lester didn't need a confession. There was already too much shit happening. "So you slept with her, right? Is that it? Because if that's all it is, doesn't mean a thing to me."

"You'd better have another drink," Billy said as he swallowed the last of his cognac down. He crumpled the cup up and tossed it behind him. "I got to talking with Rachel when I took Mum home. I told her I knew she had killed the girl. I told her I was going to the police, to tell them everything, Missy, you, and me. I told her it was over. That's when she told me …" He looked at his brother, briefly, just for a split second. "I'm sorry for all of us Lester, especially for the boys." He paused and then spit it out. "It's about Sam … and me."

Lester had wondered for years, and now, he was getting to the heart of the matter now. "I always suspected, Billy. I just never knew for sure." He looked down at the brandy as it swirled in his cup. "She's hated Casey, more than she hated me. It wasn't the same for Sam," Lester said in a quiet voice. "I'd lie in bed, night after night, wondering, too scared to ask." He looked over at Billy. "It really doesn't matter who sired him. He's a Brennan. It doesn't change the four of us much. It might even bring us closer." He looked at the amber in his cup. "You've been there for them the whole time. You're their father. I saw the look in their faces when you walked in. You won't lose their love, and I might even get a chance to earn it. I want to try, Bill."

Billy blinked at the road ahead of him. "Maybe I'll have one more brandy."

"Cognac."

Billy smiled. "You've been gone too long, Les."

"Well, I'm home now, and we have each other and those boys," Lester said. "We have to agree they won't hear it from that Beast. If we stay together on this, maybe we can get her the hell out of here."

Billy nodded, trying to see the road beyond the mist rising in his eyes. "Rachel killed Missy. She won't hesitate to kill again. She's begun threatening Kathleen."

Lester took another long swig, catching a glimpse of the farm from the rise that led to its valley. "Billy? What do you give a blackmailer?"

Billy looked at him and smiled. "Absolutely nothing! It's time to talk to the boys."

* * *

As Sam and Kathleen drove at breakneck speed, Sam went through it all again, slowly trying to figure out the timing. It bothered Sam that Billy had seemed so pale, so shocked, when he'd walked into the Hole. Sam knew by the white of Billy's skin that Billy had heard something so terrible, so chilling, that everything else seemed unimportant. Billy had never reacted like that, not even when he found out Sam had married Missy.

Something had to have happened at the farm, and Sam knew it had to do with the Beast. Only she had that effect on people, only when she pounced, and Sam knew she must have pounced hard. He was missing something important, something heavy enough to shake Billy to the core.

Why the big change? Billy hadn't looked at him once at the Hole. He'd spoken to Casey, to their father, even Kathleen and Sadie but not to Sam. He'd avoided Sam's eyes. What could the Beast have said to him? She might have threatened Kathleen. That was possible, but surely, Billy was smart enough to know that Sam would never let his mother hurt Kathleen. And why now, when his father had come home?

A horn jarred Sam to reality. "Shit!" He yanked the truck back to the right side of the road, staring into the eyes of the horrified driver, terrified, angry as he whipped past.

"Will you slow down!"

Sam had almost forgotten she was in the truck. He looked at Kathleen, and a wave of guilt washed over him at the sight of the tears on her cheeks. "Why are you crying?"

Sam shot her a pitiful look of appeal, and his hand tightened around hers. She should have been happy. Instead, she looked like she was going to throw up.

She looked out the side window. "I knew yesterday. I heard Gran talking to Missy. Missy told her how she knew your father." She peeked around at him.

His hands became clammy on the wheel. "What?"

"Sadie and I were hiding in the back staircase. I wanted to tell you, but Gran asked me to wait."

"Gran? Everyone knew? Except me."

Kathleen nodded her head back and forth a little. "Not everyone. Casey didn't know either."

"MyKate!"

"Don't be mad."

"I'm not mad." The truck roared around a corner and bumped across a set of railroad tracks. "I'm worried about the Beast."

"How could he stay married to her, Sam? I don't understand. He left? Instead?"

"What's that old joke?" Sam blew his horn at a car about to pull out in front of him from a side road. "Marriage changes passion—suddenly you're in bed with a relative."

"Holy shit!" Sam crushed the brake with his foot! The truck screeched and twisted on the old highway, skidding to a halt. He let it roll off to the side of the road as he tried to breathe. That was it! The sudden crystallization of truth. That was the secret his mother had kept! All those years and she'd held on to her weapon until everything else was lost, and she needed Billy on her side. A horn jarred Sam to reality. "Shit!"

"Sam!"

That was the secret! That was why Billy was so shaken up. After all those years, Billy suddenly knew the truth—and so did Sam.

"Sam! You have to calm down!"

"Calm down? Think about it, MyKate. Billy …" He pulled onto the road and sped up again.

She glanced down at her hands as if she already knew. He slowly turned to her and waited, already knowing what he was about to hear.

She grimaced. "Thomas kind of let it slip."

"What?"

"He told me Billy was your father."

"And you thought you'd keep it to yourself?"

"Now, Sam. Don't be—"

"It would have been nice of someone to tell me!"

"Well, the way he told me wasn't exactly straightforward. He kind of let it slide in there, you know? Kind of vague." She tittered a little. "I suppose that's how ghosts work … all vague and wispy-like."

"This isn't funny!" He couldn't believe how cavalier she was acting. "The Beast knows. She's capable of anything. Didn't you see Billy's face? He was scared! Billy!"

"Slow down!" She reached over for him.

"If I slow down any more, we might as well get out and walk." The truck kept shooting down the road, occasionally hitting a bump that knocked the shocks badly. Sam pushed the pedal to the floor.

"Slow down for Christ's sake, Sam, or you'll kill all of us."

"All of us?" He gunned it. "What! Thomas is in here with us?"

"I'm pregnant!"

Except for the truck, everything stopped for Samuel Dominic Brennan.

She was staring at him. "Sam?"

Anywhere. He had to stop everything. Right. The Gas & Go. Slowly the truck began to decelerate. His foot wasn't on the brake, but it wasn't on the gas any longer as he glided into the yard of the station. Kathleen looked from him to the worn-down gas station he'd pulled into.

"Finally." She looked back at him and took a deep breath. "It wasn't the way I'd planned to tell you, but …"

Sam felt the cold hand of dread grab his heart, instead of the happiness he should have been feeling.

She put her hands on her hips. "Frig! Say something."

Sam took a long deep breath and removed his hands from the wheel. Leaving the truck running, he opened his door and stepped down onto the broken asphalt. He walked around to the back of the truck slowly. Opening her door, he helped her jump out. She was sprightly for being pregnant and all. He closed her door behind her.

They had an audience. Three older men and Norm Smith, the proprietor of the Gas & Go, sat on rickety old chairs outside the run-down gas station. The men were staring at them, curious, appreciative that there was a bit of action to watch instead of just cars whizzing by.

"Can I help ya, Sam?" Norm called over to them.

"No, Norm, thanks. Just having a chat here." Sam didn't bother to look at the man, hoping Norm would take the hint and go back to work or sitting or whatever he'd been doing before the little scene began playing out before them.

"How's your Dad?" Norm emphasized the last word, as he always did, knowing how it set Sam off.

"Billy's fine, Norm." Sam looked over at him, trying not to lose it, knowing that was always what Norm was implying. "You know, Norm, for someone as busy as you … ouch!" Sam turned back to Kathleen, the feel of her foot against his shin obviously smarting.

"Thanks, Mr. Smith. We're just fine here. You have a nice day." Kathleen gave them her biggest, warmest fake smile. "You should wear that shade of blue all the time, Mr. Smith. It makes you look ten years younger."

Sam wanted to throw up as Norm blushed, his head dropping for a moment. "If you need anything, Kathleen, you just holler."

"I will, Norm." Kathleen turned to Sam as Norm headed back to the older men. Sam could hear them laughing and words like "blue" and "eyes," but Sam wasn't paying attention to them anymore. He wasn't paying attention to anyone except Kathleen.

"Do you want to run that past me again?" His eyes were searching deep inside her eyes, so sweet he almost melted. He had to make sure.

She took his hand. "Sam, I've practiced this hundreds of times since … well, I took the test last week … and when it said … well, I screamed and jumped higher than ever. Oh, Sam! I …" She lowered her head and her voice. "Do you know what I did? Just like D. H. Lawrence, remember in high school, *The Rainbow*? I locked my bedroom door"—her eyes widened to saucers—"got naked in front of my mirror and stuck my belly out … and I danced."

Tears glistened in her eyes, and he wanted to scoop her up right there and ride off into the sunset with her. She placed his hand on the lower side of her belly, suddenly trying her best to be matter-of-fact.

"We really are. We're pregnant, have been for about … four weeks? Since that first night, Sam. That very first night."

He didn't say a word but took her chin and lifted her lips to his lips. Then he kissed her. "Thank you," he said.

She hesitated. "Thank you? That's it? Thank you?" she asked, starting to get angry, putting her hands on her hips again. "Lookit! I think I deserve a little more than 'thank you!'"

He grinned, touched her breast as if he might find a change there already, and took in a deep breath. She wasn't going to like what he was about to do next at all. There was no way he was dragging her and his child into God knows what.

"You"—he kissed her once more—"deserve much more than thank you."

Having said that, he reached into his pocket and removed his wallet. While she stared, repulsed, he removed a twenty, shoved it in the pocket of her jeans, and kissed her again.

"Go back to the Hole. I'll pick you up there." Sam moved as fast as he ever had, back to the truck and into it, knowing she was still staring at the bill. He leaned over, locked her door, and then slammed his.

"A twenty? What?" she yelled up at him, but the rest was drowned out by the sound of his tires twirling on the gravel, muted as the dust rose.

"No, Sam! You son of a bitch." She lunged for the truck, but she hadn't a chance. "Shit!" She spun like a dervish, her fist in the air, spitting, choking on the dust. "Come back here! You son of a bitch! Sam!"

He watched her in the rearview mirror, kicking at nothing, wailing in fury.

"You goddamned son of a bitch!"

She roared obscenities at the truck until she was just a spot on the horizon, and he wondered how he was going to explain it all away, later, after he took care of business.

CHAPTER 53

The men outside the garage were riveted. She could hear them laughing. One suggested that perhaps they should walk over and offer her a ride. The three other men all said a horrified no.

She almost snarled at them. "Go back to the Hole?" She pulled the twenty out and shredded it. "Go home!" She headed for the highway, knowing there was only one place she was going, and it wasn't to the Hole. *Hell!* He would be driving right past her home. He could have dropped her off there but no! No! He didn't want her anywhere near home, near him. He had something planned, and it didn't include her. He didn't want her there? *Nope. That wasn't going to happen!*

That's when she heard the oncoming vehicle. Kathleen wasn't past hijacking, not now. Someone was coming, and by God, he or she was going to stop. She headed for the highway.

"The Hole!" She marched right out into the middle of the road. No one would hit a pregnant woman she thought, and then realized she didn't look at all pregnant, but that didn't matter either. She'd be damned if she'd allow that Brennan knob to do this to her. She straddled the solid do-not-pass line and began waving. She wondered if her eyes were seeing things straight. What she was seeing was too good, too absolutely perfect. Kathleen recognized the white vet truck bearing down on her, and she started jumping up and down, determined to have them notice her.

They couldn't help but notice her. She was in the middle of the lane, focused on only one thing. She was going to kill Sam.

"Go home?" She began jumping higher, frantically waving, suddenly beginning to break a small sweat, wondering if perhaps she's been a bit rash. The approaching truck didn't seem to be slowing down. No. It was.

They were stopping for her. "Son of a bitch." She would not allow that jerk to get away with what he'd done.

* * *

Sadie had decided the clinic could wait. There had been no calls in and no animals needing immediate attention. Casey seemed so upset. Once they all calmed down, she could zip back and take care of the critters. They hadn't been going breakneck speed but had to screech to a halt when they saw a woman standing in the middle of the highway.

"My God," Sadie said. "Is that Kathleen?"

The truck swerved slightly as Sadie, her knuckles white on the wheel, stared at Kathleen.

"Katie?" Casey's mouth dropped open. Kathleen was jumping around the highway like a crow on roadkill.

"My God! What in hell are you doing in the middle of the highway?" Sadie cried as she leaned across Casey. "You could have been killed!"

The door opened seemingly on its own. "Move over, Casey!" Kathleen pushed then jumped in next to him and slammed the door. "Let's go!"

"Where's Sam? What happened?" Casey asked.

"Nothing." She turned and faced the window.

Casey looked at Sadie, his eyes arched quizzically.

"Drive, Sadie, or we'll never catch the son of a bitch!" she screamed at them.

Sadie felt Casey edge closer to her as she stepped on the gas.

Kathleen said little for the next few minutes except "I'm going to kill the son of a bitch!" which she repeatedly said until Casey began nodding, as if he believed Kathleen Egan might just do it.

* * *

Rachel's hands were shaking as she folded the whites and sorted socks. She had put all thoughts of Billy out of her head. She had laundry on the go, bloodied blankets and Sam's shirt, stained jeans that all needed second washings, needed to be hung out to dry.

"No. No one's worried about me, are they?" She tossed a balled-up pair of work socks into the empty hamper. "All my good life, I've given for them." She balled up another pair of socks, tossed them into the hamper, and then grabbed two more, "And what do I get in return?" Her lip curled up in a sneer. "Turncoat treachery. Betrayal." She tossed the third sock ball into the hamper. "Sam's a fool. That brother of his is a nasty schemer. That Egan slut! She's out for anything she can get, anything that will make her rich." She should have taken care of Kathleen years ago, but no, she was Sam's friend, and she couldn't risk hurting Sam. She started up the stairs with the laundry.

Her room was cold. It was always that way now. She walked over to the window and, pulling the lace back, looked out over the yard. She sank into her rocking chair and stared out over the barnyard and the fields beyond. Such a waste, all for the sake of the cows. The farm was worth a fortune, and it really galled Rachel that she couldn't get to any of it. She hadn't put up with all these years of hell to let it all slip through her fingers now. Oh no.

Casey would be dead. With Casey dead, Sam would gladly hand it all over to her. With the money from the gold, she and Sam could go anywhere. Get off this stinking farm. He wouldn't have the heart to stay there; that was for certain. She'd be rid of all the insects, manure, and filth, and let the quarrymen dig out the fortune that lay deep beneath the fields. As for Gran, how long could she last? She stared down at the farmyard below. She could hear Billy's truck slow down on the road and turn up their laneway. They were coming. She watched as the truck stopped next to the front field.

Rachel's fingers hurt more than her head hurt. They were shaking, raw, and bleeding again from splinters from the arms of her rocker. She sucked her left middle finger in the effort to remove a maple splinter she'd snagged just minutes before from the arm of her rocker as it creaked and moaned under her weight. *Out? No. Oh no! No way!* Anger coiled around her stomach like a snake and squeezed. They all thought she was dim, but they'd find out.

Figured it was safe, did he? Figured that with so much time having passed, she'd have gotten soft, would have forgotten her promise? *Oh no.* Maybe he'd forgotten the deal, but she hadn't. *No, no, no.* He'd broken their deal, and Casey would pay.

"Come on. Let's see your face, Lester."

No sooner had she said it than she watched Lester Brennan step out of his truck and set foot on the soil of the Brennan farm.

"That can't be him," Rachel murmured, staring at a visibly older man through the lace. He was so old. Hatred wriggled like a worm in her gut. How dare he! Did he take her for a fool? But there he was sneaking back. And the gall! He didn't even try to hide his return. He stood staring at the expensive cow Casey just had to have, talking to Billy as if he'd never left. Then he stared right at the house as if he wanted her to see him.

How to do it—that was the thing, how to get away with it. Rachel knew where the answer lay. It lay on the rafters above the basement stairs. It lay already loaded and ready to go. That's where the answer lay.

A calm tide washed over her as she watched the men go into the barn. She gripped the arms of the rocker and lifted herself up, never more certain, knowing it was the only way. Crossing the room, she took a long, deep breath and stepped over to the door. Checking that the hallway was clear, Rachel slunk her way along and down the stairs, doing her best to make not a sound.

The kitchen was quiet except for Gran, asleep in her chair. Rachel stopped, her hand on the banister, watching the woman, listening for the telltale signs that the old bat was asleep. Gran spluttered gently, and an evil grin spread across Rachel's face.

As quietly as she could, Rachel moved over to the drawer next to the sink and pulled out a box of latex gloves. She pulled out two, the lightest and smallest, a snug fit that would be supple enough. She pulled the glove onto her right hand and then the other.

Rachel crept across the kitchen floor to the door of the basement stairs. She wished she'd had more time to prepare. She would have oiled the hinges. Each creak made her shrink and look over at the old woman. So slowly that Rachel felt that time had slowed to a stop, she pulled open the door.

The smell of dank and must was overwhelming. Rachel felt her head pound as her eyes adjusted to the shadows and the image of the gun materialized. *Two can play at this game, Casey,* she thought.

She had planned on using the rifle in Billy's trailer, but this pistol was even better. Casey had given her the implement of his own death. Not to mention his fingerprints were all over it.

She had to lean out over the stairs, reach up, grab it, and drag the pistol back, all as quietly as possible so as not to awaken the old woman. It was heavier than she imagined. The gun caught for a second, and Rachel felt panic surge inside her, but she gave it a slight wiggle, and it resumed its reverse movement. Within moments, she had it in her hand and was inspecting it, releasing the clip, checking to see it was loaded and ready to go, just as Lester had taught her so many years ago.

She checked the safety. *Off. Good,* she thought. She peeked back out the door. Gran was still asleep on the rocker. She closed the basement door and took the two steps to the mudroom. With one glance over her shoulder, she went outside, closing the mudroom door as quietly as she could.

Chapter 54

"Limb from limb." Kathleen could think of nothing else. She turned to Casey. "I'm going to tear him to pieces."

"You going to calm down and tell us what's happening?" Casey said.

"Casey," Sadie said. He grunted as Sadie elbowed him.

"No!" He rubbed his arm. "This is too important! Sam isn't one to take off and leave anyone alone on the side of the road, especially Kathleen."

Kathleen closed her eyes to the countryside passing her by. How could she have been so stupid, she wondered, as to blurt it out like that? Sam was never one to take things calmly, and she'd just yelled it at him. No wonder he'd kicked her out. Still, he hadn't seemed upset by the idea. She'd never seen such calm joy on his face, the kind of gentle peace that happens just before all hell breaks loose. Oh crap, she thought. He's going to save the day, save the entire earth. What was worse, he thought he could do it on his own, alone.

"How's the cat?" Kathleen said, trying to focus. *Stupid! Lame! Tell them the truth.*

Casey reached over for her hand. "We didn't stop."

She tried to shake the fear out of her head and think clearly. "Casey, he knows."

Casey nodded slowly. "Knows what?"

"Something Thomas told me, that night at Sadie's when ... Casey, I think Billy found out too." She turned to him wanting once more to throw up. She couldn't throw up. Not right now. She began to rock, hoping it would pass. "Sam's figured it out, and I don't know what he's going to do."

"Kathleen." Casey was rolling his eyes and sounding a bit fed up with her skirting around the problems. "Stop rocking and tell me."

"It's Billy. He's Sam's father, Casey." She saw the shock register on his face and then disbelief.

"Katie, just because—"

"Thomas told me. Thomas doesn't lie. When I asked him why Sam's father had never been there for him, Thomas's answer was—and I swear, Casey, word for word—Thomas said, 'Billy's always been right there for him.' He didn't say for you. He didn't say he's been there as an uncle. And I think Billy knows and now Sam knows. Did you see the look on Billy's face when he walked into the Hole? I'm telling you, he knows."

Casey stared at the road, putting it all together. Sadie wasn't saying anything, and Kathleen was beginning to wonder if she'd actually spoken the words out loud. Kathleen leaned forward into the belt and wrapped her arms around her, trying to get warm. "Casey? Sam dumped me to protect me. You don't think …?"

Casey's face turned slightly angry and very confused.

She covered her mouth and took a deep breath. "I think I'm going to throw up."

"Kate, did you tell Sam?" Sadie pulled quickly over to the side of the road and slowed down.

Kathleen rolled down the window and took in two large breaths, trying to calm down.

Sadie eyed her suspiciously. Kathleen was amazed as she realized Sadie knew. How do women know these things? Her mother had sounded suspicious too, on the phone the day before.

"Are you all right?" Sadie asked.

Kathleen nodded.

"Did you tell him?" Sadie said to Kathleen.

"Tell him what?" Casey jerked his eyes over to his vet. "Would you spit it out? What's going on?"

"I had to tell him," Kathleen said to Sadie, tears springing to her eyes. "I know I shouldn't have, but he was driving crazy. I thought it would slow him down."

"Tell him what?" Casey's voice broke. "What?"

"Oh, for the love of God!" Sadie said. "It doesn't matter, Casey, only Sam matters. Where's he going, Kate?"

"Home." Kathleen hated it when her lip trembled. "Casey, I've never seen him like this."

"He's going after the Beast alone," Casey said, rubbing his chin. "Shit! You know … this is really my battle. Not his. I'm the one she threatened to kill."

"What?" Sadie turned and looked at him, and Casey seemed to shrink a little as if he realized he'd scared her.

"If my father ever came back. That's what the Beast told him. She'd kill me."

Sadie's eyes grew huge with alarm. "Casey, he's back."

Casey reached for her hand. "I was seven when she made that threat. I'm not seven anymore."

"No," Kathleen said, snorting. "Sam is! What in the hell is he thinking?"

Casey's head rolled sarcastically. "I don't need his protection, but does that stop him? No. He still has to protect you … me …"

"His child." Kathleen said it so quietly she wondered if he heard her.

"He's not going to do this alone. He doesn't have to protect me anym—" He turned and studied her as if he hadn't heard correctly. "His child? You're pregnant?" His eyes sparkled for just a moment and then narrowed. Casey grabbed Kathleen's hand with both of his. "I'm going to be a nuncle."

"Not if I kill him first," Kathleen said and gave him a faint grin.

* * *

The barn door groaned as Rachel inched it open and slipped inside. Once again, her eyes took some time to adjust, slowing her down, pissing her off. She couldn't breathe. She should have considered that and worn a mask. A mask!

"Hah! Who was that masked man?" She snickered to herself.

The dust and smell overwhelming, she'd put her arm up over her nose and mouth. Thankfully, there were no animals inside. That would have been unbearable. She heard the men, faintly, her targets, voices coming from Billy's trailer.

"I've never seen anything as pretty as those calves," Lester said, his voice relaxed, a little older, Rachel thought, but just as strong. She moved over to the walkway and started past the stanchions. She pictured Lester, stuck inside the stanchion, his head guillotined between the parallel, vertical bars, helpless to do anything but bawl like a mad cow.

"We'd better figure out how to solve this mess," Billy said. "The boys will be here soon."

"Is that a fact?" she said quietly as she moved in front of the pens, hugging them, her nose rising at the smell of manure and old hay. She had wanted to look down, to see where her feet were treading, but dared not. No. Oh no, no, no. Keep your eyes straight ahead. She had pulled the gun up and aimed it forward. The door to the trailer was open. So she hadn't been heard. She wouldn't be seen. Not until she was ready.

A little closer. She'd jumped as a cat screeched. The damn thing. Her heart began pounding. "Goddamned cat." The whole barn and she had to find its tail with her foot. Damned thing. "The devil's animal," she muttered. She didn't move, hardly breathing as she'd stared at the doorway and placed her finger on the trigger. *Just come through the door*, she'd thought. *Either one of you. Come on.* They were still laughing. But they weren't coming out. *Stupid. Stupid!*

Rachel slumped against the wall, listening. She'd have to take care of Lester and Billy first and then wait for Casey to come out to the barn. There were chores to be done. She knew Casey would be the first one to the barn, Sam usually the first one to the stable. Like always. *Yes*, she thought. *That would work.* She was ready. She would kill Lester, then Billy, and then she'd finally kill Casey. She moved out from the wall, tightened her hands on the gun, her hand slick from sweat. She stepped farther into the barn until she was in plain sight, a ninety-degree angle from the trailer. Then she turned and stared into the trailer doorway.

"Would you look at what the cat dragged in?" Rachel said, pointing the gun directly at Lester's head.

They both seemed so surprised.

Lester smiled over at her. "We didn't expect to see you so soon. You're just in time for a drink, Rachel."

* * *

Billy jerked as he realized what they were dealing with. Rachel's eyes were like he'd seen years before, crazed and cold. He stared at the tiny piece of metal, the trigger, so ready to snap. Billy knew he had no chance of moving, let alone grab the rifle he kept mounted on the wall behind him. The rifle was facing backward, away from him, an awkward position. If he stood and turned, he'd lose valuable time and probably get the first shot she fired in his back. Maybe Rachel figured the rifle wasn't loaded. She had a fifty-fifty chance of guessing correctly. She knew that Billy had always kept the bullets safely tucked in a jar in the back of the pantry, up high, where Sam and Casey couldn't get them as lads. Standard safety precaution. But the boys were men now, and he'd long kept the rifle loaded.

Rachel's eyes skirted the trailer. Billy knew she was looking for possible weapons. *Would she think about knives?* Billy had one, but it would be no use in a gun battle, and though Lester always carried one before, he'd had to go through customs and might not be carrying. There was nothing, short of the booze, they could use as a weapon, except time and negotiation. Like negotiating would work.

"Rachel." Lester tried a familiar smile. Lester seemed to be taking it better, considering she was pointing the Glock at him. They both knew the damage a weapon like that could do. *How did she find the Glock?*

"It's been so long. Come on. Take a seat. Have a brandy."

Billy's eyes jerked away from Rachel's hand and over to his brother. Brandy? Lester never called it brandy. It was his way of suggesting it to Billy as a possible weapon.

Rachel lowered her face, displeased. "More subterfuge. You must remember what I said, Lester," Rachel said, not having moved a hair from the trigger.

Lester reached out and pulled the bottle closer. "You used to like cognac, Rachel. Always had some for me when I got home."

Rachel stared hard at Lester and then sneered. "Don't touch the stuff. You're not going to throw it at me either, Les." She moved the pistol an inch closer to him. "Billy, if you want to see your brother live a few minutes longer, you'll take that rifle off the wall, gently, and slide it over here."

"Won't do you any good," Billy said quietly. "Not loaded." There was little he could do. "Can I stand? I have to stand to get—"

"Stand then. Slow. The rifle! Now!" Rachel said.

"Rachel," Lester said, "can't we talk about this? I'm not here to cause—"

"Shut up! You talk when I say."

"That's not very hospitable, Rachel. I just got home," Lester said.

"I told you what would happen if you came home."

"Okay, fine, it's just that that was a long time ago, and I've had a chance to think things through, Rach. This could be the best thing in the world for you."

Her face twisted into a contorted sneer. "The rifle! Now Billy!" Her eyes shot from Lester to him.

"I have money, Rachel," Lester said. "Surely Missy told you. That's what she was after. That's why I'm here. I couldn't let her have Sam. I had to protect him, Rachel. You can understand that. I can have the papers you need drawn up by this afternoon, Rach. I know you want the gold, but that could take years. I can get the money for you by tomorrow. You saw how fast I took care of Missy. How did you think all that happened so fast? Their Gran? She can't get out the laneway by herself, let alone organize a divorce. Billy here? All Billy did was call me. He was worried about Sam and you. That's all. I told Billy what to do. Between Billy and you, Missy's no longer a problem." Lester tried raising his glass to her. "You pulled it off so well. The police believed every word of it."

Rachel cackled bitterly.

"Afraid I can't take any of the credit for that, Lester. No. Not my doing." Rachel's head bobbed a bit as she tried to figure out his lies. "The horse did the job."

Lester took a swallow of the cognac and putting the glass down on the table, raised his eyes quizzically.

Billy tensed then as he watched her finger tighten on the trigger while she raised the weapon and pointed it directly between Lester's eyes.

"Have some Rachel?" Lester said.

"No. I don't think so, hon, but you go ahead. Give me a reason to blow you away."

He smiled and poured himself a cognac.

"The gun, Billy. I'm getting tired."

"The money, Rachel," Lester said as Billy watched his brother try again. "Think about it. Millions: gold, emeralds, stocks, cash."

She laughed. "Millions?" She aimed the gun again. "No, I don't think so, Lester. Don't put your hands near the trigger, Billy. Just lower it down to the floor and shove it across here."

Lester swallowed his drink. "No, Bill. Don't do it. If she kills us with one gun, it's murder. That's it, isn't it Rachel? This is a setup. You want it to look like we shot each other."

Rachel drew her head in. "Why all that bother when Casey has every reason to kill the both of you?"

"Jesus, Mary, and Joseph!" Billy moved slowly with the rifle. "Rachel, if you ever loved me, don't do this."

"You know, Billy, I did once. I wasted my whole life waitin' for you." Her finger twitched on the trigger. "All these years you've been helping him." Spit went flying at the last word. "The rifle! Now!"

CHAPTER 55

As soon as Sam saw Gran resolutely shuffling toward the barn, a sharp, hard object glistening cold in her hand, he knew the situation was already well out of control. There was no other reason Gran would be headed to the barn with a gun. Where would she have gotten a gun? Sam drove right past the house, knowing his mother wasn't there. She was already in the barn. That's the only way his grandmother would be marching toward it, armed.

"Gran!" The truck skidded to a stop, and he jumped out of the cab. "Gran!" He ran around the front of the truck. "Give me that!" He stared down at the revolver, studying the gun. "This belongs to Frank Egan. How in the hell did you get that? Is it loaded?"

"I loaded it. Oh, Sam." Gran lifted the gun, waving it at the barn. "She thought I was asleep."

Sam stared in disbelief at her. "Where did you get this old thing?"

She smiled like the cat caught with a canary in its mouth. "I found Casey hiding it."

The weapon was old and rusted, and Sam wondered if it would fire if he had to pull the trigger.

"Gran. Give me the gun, please." Sam wrapped his own fingers around it. "Please." He twisted it slightly, and she released her grip. "Is she in the barn?"

Gran nodded. "Thomas told me to wait. She's been there awhile. She has your gun from the cellar stairs. This is what comes from having guns in the—"

He stopped her as she started walking toward the barn again. "Where's Billy?" He placed the gun in his belt, praying it wouldn't go off, and then grabbed her shoulders. "Gran? Where are they?"

She looked up at him, confused. “I’m not sure, but I believe—”

“Gran!”

“Billy and your father. They’re in the barn too.”

“Shit! Gran get back in the house.” He twirled the chamber to make sure there were bullets in the gun. “Go on back into the house.”

“No!” She stepped back. “You’re as bad as Thomas.”

“I don’t care. Go back to the house!” Sam could hear a heavier, low-sounding truck coming quickly down Saint Jude Road. It sounded like Sadie’s vet truck. “Oh shit! Gran. You have to stop Casey. If he walks in there, God knows what she’ll do.”

“Casey is quite capable of taking care of himself.”

“No!” Sam didn’t mean to scream at his grandmother. “She’ll kill him! You know that. Gran, please. What did Thomas tell you to do?” He lifted her face and waited for her eyes to fix on his.

“That’s not fair, Sam.”

“That’s what I thought. You get Casey out of the way and Kathleen if she shows up.”

Gran shook her head. “When are you going to learn, Samuel Brennan, you aren’t in this alone?”

Sam threw his hands in the air. “Christ, Thomas, if you’re anywhere around here, help me!”

CHAPTER 56

"There he is!" Kathleen struggled to get her seat belt undone. Casey knew it wasn't easy for her, because he was sitting on it and not about to move.

"Kathleen! You get Gran inside! Get her the hell inside. That's all we need, her in the middle of the drive. I have to get the—"

"What? No. Casey." She screamed, rolling down the window. "Sam!"

"Get Gran inside!" Casey yelled at her as he reached over across her and opened her door, finally allowing her to undo her belt. Casey cast Sadie a help-me look.

He didn't wait, his belt undone, he almost leaped over her as he ran for the back door. He had to get the Glock from the rafters above the basement stairs. Across the yard, through the door, into the kitchen, the door to the basement, the abyss, nothing else mattered. He threw himself over the drop and reached. Nothing. There was nothing there. He slapped his hand around furiously. But that couldn't be. The gun was supposed to be right there. Jumping down, he tore upstairs to his room and pulled back the board. He stared in disbelief. The revolver was gone too. Casey looked down at his empty hands. The hayloft. The shotgun, right next to the calf pull. Christ! He turned back from his room and through the door. Casey had to get to the barn.

* * *

"Nice and easy, Billy." Rachel's eyes never left the men, and Billy knew she was capable of doing anything now.

"Did you hear that out there, Rachel?" Lester said softly. "That's a second truck out there. Maybe we should just call it off for today. We'll call it a draw, eh? You take the check and voilà … problem solved."

"The rifle! Now!" She shoved the Glock farther out at Lester.

Billy didn't hesitate, having heard the trucks pull up too. Rachel's plan was falling apart. Even if she killed them, she wouldn't get away with it now. Time was all they needed.

"Fine! Fine, Rachel," Billy said, and taking the end of the butt of the rifle, gripping it hard, he then grabbed the barrel. "There, Rachel. There." He turned and lowered it slowly to the floor. "They're out there, Rachel, right outside." He had to keep her talking. She always softened up a little talking to him … until today.

"Shut up!"

Try harder, Billy told himself. "There's no way you can make it look like a murder-suicide. It's over."

"Shut up!"

"It's over, Rachel, at least this plan!"

Rachel straightened her lurid, grisly face like a gargoyle, eyes popping out and tongue between her teeth. "Don't be so cocksure, Billy. Maybe I have nothing to lose now; ever consider that? Maybe I was just waiting, you know, to keep my promise."

Billy sank into his seat. *No.* He wouldn't allow that. He turned to Lester, who was staring at Rachel as if he'd seen the devil itself. Lester's head was shaking in denial.

"No," Lester growled at her. "I won't let you hurt Casey again."

"You don't tell me what to do!" Rachel swung the Glock up and fired.

CHAPTER 57

Pigeons rose in flock and scattered across the farm when the percussion shook the barn from its foundation.

"No!" Sam screamed and ran, trying to ignore the sound of Kathleen yelling at him. *How in the hell did she get back so fast?* He had no time to think about it.

* * *

Sam slammed into the barn, the door crashing behind him. He didn't care if she heard him. He wanted her to hear him.

"Mum!" he yelled. "Mum!"

The air was filled with bits of straw and dust and the smell of gunpowder drifting in the stale air around him. He spotted her. She was standing straight ahead in the barn walkway, five feet from Billy's trailer door. Sam knew from that angle she would have a better amount of elbow room, no chance of them rushing her, as they would have to get out of the door. She was directly between Sam and the bales of hay in front of the back door of the barn. Dust swirled around her, settling down on her from the hole she'd blown into the rafters above Billy's trailer. She hadn't shot anyone. He swallowed and tried to refocus. She'd simply fired into the ceiling. He felt the metal of the pistol in his hand, slick and cold and tried to quell his shaking.

"Mum, please." Both hands on his pistol, he moved out into the middle of the walkway. Ready to fire, he pointed the revolver at her. She didn't answer him. "Billy! Dad!"

"Right here! Both of us," Billy called back as stoically as was possible given the situation.

Rachel didn't face Sam. "Go back to the house, Sam. This doesn't concern you."

"The hell it doesn't! Mum, please. Put the gun down. We'll talk." He stepped farther down the walkway between the rows of stations and the pens on the other side.

Rachel's focus didn't shift. "Don't even think about throwin' that bottle, Lester," she said. "Your father is playing games, Sam. I can't concentrate with you here. Go back to the house. I'll be fine."

"I love you, Mama." Sam didn't know where the words were coming from. He took a step closer, his finger on the trigger. "Please, Mum. I'm scared."

Her face softened a little. "Don't be scared, Sam. I won't let him hurt anyone."

"Who, Mama?" Sam inched his way closer. He could only see her left side as she stood facing the doorway to the trailer. The gun was set in firing position, her finger near the trigger. Any shot, any scare, could cause her to fire if she jerked while holding the trigger. She was totally focused on keeping the gun trained on the men while she pulled Billy's rifle closer to her with her foot.

"No. Nothing. Oh no, no, no. Nothing I can't handle."

Sam had made it over halfway into the barn. He had to think.

Rachel, eyes barely leaving the kitchen, her gun still focused on Lester, picked up the rifle and, snorting, shook her head. She pulled the lever back. "It's loaded now. You lied, Billy. I shouldn't be surprised." The pistol in her hand never wavered as she tossed the rifle behind her. It landed with a rattling thud in front of the hay bales.

Sam swallowed hard, a cold chill running through him as he tried to quell the panic rising in him. "You don't have to do this, Mama. Billy has always been good to us."

"I'm not aiming at Billy." She hooted maniacally. "Well, not directly. It appears we have unwanted company here, Sam. Seems he was overly concerned about that whore who tried to trap you. Seems he knew her."

"I told your mother I had money for her," Lester called out to him. "Enough for you two to live very nicely."

"Shut up!" She waved the Glock.

Sam could almost hear Billy and Lester telling him to distract her. "Put the gun down, Mama. I know the whole story." Sam felt the barn door open slowly behind him and felt a wave of relief wash over him. "We have to talk. We can get through this, Mama."

"I'm right behind you," Casey whispered shortly.

The cavalry had arrived. He needed his brother there, even though he knew Casey was the one person who might loosen the first stone of the avalanche, even though Casey was the one she probably wanted to kill next. "Mum, no one's blaming you for Missy. We know it was just an accident."

"I didn't kill her, Sam," Rachel said with a tight smile. "We both know who killed her. Have to give credit where credit's due. That Kathleen's really clever."

Sam fought the urge to blow her away, right then and there.

"I'm going to the loft," Casey said, as quietly as he could.

Hearing Casey turn and head up the rail ladder to the loft. The hayloft? Why the hayloft? He forced himself to sound calm. "We don't have to wait. It's over with MyKate and me. We could move to Boston. Just the two of us." Sam heard Casey pull himself up into the loft like a seasoned pro. "You've always wanted to go. We'll get one of those big, modern houses you like. Life in the suburbs. That's what you always said."

"Be quiet, Samuel!"

"I'm sorry, Mum. I'm sorry. I love you, Mama." He wondered if she had even noticed his pistol. "I can't let you hurt them, Mum. I won't."

"Don't be ridiculous, Sam. I'm doing this for you."

"Mum, please. For me. I can take care of things. We'll sort everything out."

"You!" Her voice broke. "How could you do this to me? You turned on me. First, that clown, and then that Egan slut and now … I heard you, you know?" She didn't move her head. "I heard you talking to that brother of yours." Her head jerked, but she didn't move her eyes. "And now you've taken up with Lester. Why, Sam? Why couldn't you just let it go?"

Sam felt the vein in his temple pound. "Why? Why didn't you tell me Billy was my father? Why didn't you tell me you threw Casey down the stairs? I remember, Mum, all of it. You did some pretty good lying yourself!"

Then Sam remembered. The shotgun was in the hayloft. Sam wanted to cry with relief as he remembered. As long as she had her finger on the trigger, any shot could cause her to squeeze out a shot. He could get a clear shot from where he was standing, but he couldn't risk her shooting off a round and killing his father. Casey would be able to see from the hayloft. *Stall. Keep her talking*, he thought. *That's what you're good at. Just talk to her.*

* * *

Casey didn't hesitate. He took the back ladder to the loft in three steps. The mow was dark, and it was a labyrinth of hay bales and beams that stood in the way. Quietly, he made his way across the length of the barn, pulling and twisting the last bales from the year before, all the while doing his best not to be heard.

Working blind, he wasn't thinking about the dark or the height; he was thinking of the lunatic with the gun below. Winding his way in the black was more difficult than Casey imagined. It wouldn't be so hard if he didn't have to be quiet, if he didn't have to keep the hay from falling. He could hear it all below, and he knew Sam was playing with fire. He wanted to shout, *Shut up! What in the name of God are you thinking? The woman is nuts!* But he couldn't. He had to get to the shotgun, and then he'd have to stop her. Casey was almost there. Finally, he reached the other end of the mow, the end with the calf pull and the shotgun. Grabbing the gun, he turned and faced the hole, his mother beneath him, down and only a few feet forward. Casey leaned down and stared into the trailer.

* * *

Kathleen hadn't waited any longer than it took Sadie to relax. Kathleen had tried to stay as calm as Sadie was, but the phone call had been made, and the police were on their way. Gran was safe, but she was left behind, twiddling her thumbs, while Sam and Casey were out there in the barn with the Beast. As soon as Sadie had gone off to get Gran a blanket, Kathleen had slipped out the back door.

Kathleen headed out toward the stable and the field beyond, checking back at the house to see if Sadie was coming after her. She managed to make it to the side of the barn, zigzagging in and around machinery, before Sadie ran out to the driveway, looking around frantically, searching for her.

Leaning down under the grimy barn window, panting from either the running, the adrenaline, or maybe both, she wasn't sure, she knelt by the back door and listened. Voices. It was just as she suspected. Billy and the boys' father sounded like they were in the trailer. The Beast sounded like she was not far from the doorway. She could hear Sam pleading with his mother. He was farther away, probably by the stanchions.

A diversion. They needed a diversion. She peeped through the dust and cobwebs. From what she could see, the large bales Casey had placed there three weeks before were just far enough away from the door that she could slip through if she really sucked it in and wiggled. If she could just crack the door open and go down low, she'd figure out what to do after that, when she got inside. Kathleen put her hand on the latch and slowly lifted.

CHAPTER 58

Sam wasn't getting anywhere with his mother, and Casey knew his brother was tired, his heart pounding too, probably beating harder than Casey's own heart was. Sam's breathing would probably be too fast. Sam needed to relax his shoulders, maintain his control.

"I have a gun, Mum," Sam was yelling, "and I'll use it if you make me."

Rachel laughed. "Now that's the spirit, Sam! See, Lester? Maybe I won't have to shoot you at all. Maybe Billy's son will do it for me." She waved the weapon around.

"Listen, you crazy old bat!" Sam screamed at her, his voice shaking with impotent fury. "I'm talking about you. Put the damned gun down, Mum, or so help me God, I will blow it out of your hands."

Casey heard his mother laugh again below him as he jerked the shotgun open to check and see if the shells were still there. Then he snapped it closed. "Shut up, Sam, for Christ sake." He murmured, crouching over the hole. All he wanted was a good sight.

Casey lowered himself onto his belly and shimmied to the edge of the opening. He had to be careful as he whisked and pushed the shavings and straw away from the hole. The last thing he needed was loose hay falling behind her. He peered down. She was below and about ten feet ahead of him, and she was staring straight into the trailer, her gun pointed directly into the trailer. He couldn't see Billy and Lester seated at the table.

Casey studied his mother. He had a clear shot of her back. Could he do it? After all the years of abuse, could he do this? When did it stop being self-defense and become murder? The thoughts ran through his mind, but he pushed them away. He really didn't care anymore. She wasn't going to hurt anyone else.

* * *

Kathleen could hear them, but she couldn't see them because of the hay bales. She'd gotten where she wanted to be; now all she needed was a plan. She sank against the bale of straw, hardly feeling the sharp prickles as they dug into her skin. She wasn't any better than Sam was. Wasn't she the one who had bitched about him charging off without thinking? She scanned around her, searching for anything she could use to distract the Beast, short of offering herself up to appease the monster.

Peeking between the bottoms of the bales, she saw what looked to be Billy's rifle. What was it doing there? Better yet, could she reach it?

Listening, she knew Sam was losing it. What was he thinking, yelling at her? He'd only make it worse. A diversion. Maybe just a noise. Thomas was good at that kind of thing. Maybe if she threw something, the Beast would startle and jump away.

Kathleen peeked between the two large round bales again. *Oh shit*, she thought. Sam was directly across from her, with the Beast right in between them. Kathleen slumped against the straw again. If he fired and missed his mother, he could hit her. Nope. It didn't matter. She needed a weapon, and she was running out of time. Her eyes went up to the wooden slats around the door—anything, dusty bottles, half-empty cans of paint and oil, and a bag of elastic bands used for castration. Kathleen's eyes lit up.

"Keep her talking, Sam. Keep her talking," she muttered as she reached up for the wide elastic bands and started searching the floor, her hands running everywhere around the dirt. "Keep her talking, Sam."

* * *

Sam stepped closer. "Put the gun down, Mum. It's over."

"We're not all here yet." She swayed and seemed to be talking to someone. Sam felt fear burn in his stomach.

"The cops are coming, Mum. You don't want to be standing there with a gun in your hand when they get here."

She snorted and then gasped a strangled cry. "Do you think I care anymore? They won't let me go." She stared into nothing for a moment, her eyebrows raising and then lowering as if listening to someone. "Oh no. They won't. No! I won't be here anymore. None of us will."

"Mum, I read all about it at school. You're sick. The police will understand that. We'll get rid of them, Mama. Please."

"I am not crazy!" she screamed at him. "Where is your brother? That's who I want! You get him!"

"You're not going to hurt Casey anymore, Mum." Sam felt his hands wet against the gun. What if he slipped? What if he missed? "I won't let you hurt him anymore. I won't let you hurt either of Gran's sons. You've done enough damage already, Mum." He stepped closer. "And I'll kill you myself before you destroy any more lives."

Rachel stepped back one step. Her side was directly in his view. "Stay where you are, Sam. Don't you move!"

"Put the gun down, Mum." Sam took another step closer. "I'll shoot, Mama." He stressed the word *shoot* and glanced up to the hayloft, hoping Casey would catch his reference. "I've never been so ready to *shoot*."

* * *

Kathleen knew. Rachel's finger had dropped away from the trigger. That was her moment. She whirled, spinning out into the open. Pulling the elastic band as far back as she could, she let go and launched the pebble straight at Rachel's head.

The elastic band snapped, and the projectile hit Rachel in the head. Kathleen dove behind the straw as the Beast jerked.

* * *

Casey watched in horror as Sam pulled the trigger. The revolver misfired. "Shit!" Sam said as he struggled with the gun to get off a shot.

Casey fired once as the Beast was turning from the force of the pebble.

Casey's shot hit her in the shoulder and twisted her. She struggled to stand, and then Rachel raised her gun again, pointing it directly at Sam. She fired.

Casey fired once more. He saw his mother drop and then heard Kathleen's horrified screech.

* * *

Sam gave a brief coughing noise as his chest exploded in pain. A millisecond later, he heard the blast of the shot. Why was he unable to hold onto his useless revolver? All he felt was the crushing impact of the slug as it tore into his upper chest. Surprised by the searing force, he found himself twisting in midair. Then all breath left him as he slammed into something behind. Everything went black.

* * *

Casey lowered his shotgun and saw Sam sprawled out on the cement in front of a concrete stanchion. *No!*

Lester and Billy rushed out of the trailer. Lester pulled the gun out of Rachel's hand as Billy ran to Sam.

"Ambulance," Lester said as he jumped for the phone. "Where the hell are the cops?"

Billy was at Sam's side, and Sadie suddenly appeared, running toward them, taking charge.

"Christ, no!" Casey dropped the rifle and jumped straight down from the mow to the main floor, landing hard but hardly feeling it, smelling, instead, the harsh sting of cordite. He grabbed Kathleen. She'd stopped screaming. She was frozen to the ground, fear shaking her completely. Sam had collapsed on the cement, lying there with bright red blood pooling on his shirt.

"Oh God! Sam!" Kathleen lunged toward him again, trying to free herself from Casey. "Let me go!"

* * *

As soon as Sadie had realized that Kathleen had taken off, Sadie knew all hell was about to break loose. She had turned to Gran.

"Promise me." She'd pleaded Gran. "You need to be here for the police."

Gran nodded, and Sadie had started out the door and had headed to the barn. But as soon as she'd entered the barn, she realized that the situation was well beyond her control. That is when the shooting had begun. When the smoke began to clear, Sadie had known why she was there.

"No!" Kathleen struggled. "Sam, no!"

"Jesus Christ." Sadie cried as she reached them. "Get out of the way!" She moved in closer and physically pushed Kathleen. "Casey, get her back."

Sam opened his eyes and looked up at Sadie, his chest jerking as he tried to get his breath. "Can't br—"

Kathleen collapsed on her knees beside him while Sadie knelt and ripped open Sam's shirt. The dark, hissing puncture hole was tinged blue, but brilliant red blood was pouring out with each beat of his heart. Sam groaned, and his eyes rolled back.

"It's a sucking wound, Sam," Sadie said, examining him. His entire body was shivering. "You have to relax. You can breathe. Just take it easy. Breathe easily." She was trying to speak as calmly as she could, but her teeth were chattering, and she knew she wasn't doing him any good by being upset. She had to stop the bleeding. If she could do it to an animal, she could do it to a person. She told herself that once more. She had to close the wound in his chest, or at least cover it so that he could breathe until the ambulance got there. His pulse was rapid and thready, and she knew he was only minutes away from shock. She was surprised he was still conscious.

She looked up at Billy and said, "I need plastic, latex gloves maybe, scissors, tape …?"

"Tape?" Sam gasped and tried to raise his head, shivering, his teeth rattling together, pink froth, forming at the crease of his mouth.

"Casey. Blankets. He's going into shock." She looked squarely at Sam. "Don't you go into shock!"

Billy was over to her with scissors, a thin latex glove, and a tattered roll of one-inch masking tape, and then he ran over to Rachel. Leaning down, he pushed the rifle away and checked her for a pulse.

"Is she breathing?" Sadie called back as she tore the bag open and slammed the glove down over the wound. Grabbing the tape, Sadie began tearing long strips off. Lester was shaking as he yelled into the phone, frantic to make them understand the situation had gone beyond a *possible* shooting.

"Come on, Sam," Kathleen said, grabbing a blanket from Casey, trying her best to wrap it around him.

"Don't try so hard to breathe. Sam, I want you to listen to me." Sadie placed the latex over the wound. "The bullet's in your lung. It hasn't gone through; must have hit a rib. I'm going to plug the wound and stop the bleeding." She taped the top side of the latex to his chest. "You'll be able to breathe better then."

Sadie didn't know if Sam could hear. He seemed to be drifting in and out of consciousness. "Sam, you stay awake for me, right." She taped another side and then taped the third, leaving the bottom side loose. "I'm plugging it so you'll be able to breathe, okay? It might hurt, but breathe for us. Breathe in. It'll be easier now."

Sam jerked up and gasped. The gasp was a good one as the latex took over and acted as skin, holding the air inside where it was needed. He was breathing again, at least a little easier. With the help of Billy, Sadie started in with the bandages, rolling them over and around, under him, placing them as tightly as she could over his wound, making sure the latex stayed where it had to be. Sam's eyes rolled in his head.

Kathleen got down on the ground as close as she could to Sam.

"My fault. This is all my fault." She wiped the pink spittle from his mouth. "Sam." She took his hand in hers. "Don't worry. You're going to be fine. I know this. We have so much to do. The baby, Sam. What do you think, boy or girl?" Kathleen said, rubbing his hand, and Sadie saw how hard Kathleen was trying not to cry.

"More blankets." Sadie wrapped another blanket around him. "Keep talking to him, Kate. Billy, get something under his legs to raise his feet. Shit! I have supplies in the truck. Casey, get behind him and push him up about a forty-five-degree angle. Lester, give him a hand. Back to back, Casey."

"MyKate," Sam rasped, raising his head. He tried turning to her.

"Right here. I'm right here." She raised his hand, locked in hers. "See? I'm holding your hand. I know it hurts right now, but you're breathing and Sadie's taking good care of you."

"She's ... a ..." He coughed, a new rush of blood coming from his mouth. He groaned. "She's a vet."

"I heard that," Sadie said. "I'm not used to my patients talking back to me. It won't be long. You hang in there for me. I want to put your picture up on the clinic wall with all the other animals." She placed her shaking hands on her knees, gripping them hard to stop the trembling. "What do you think? We'll put you in the middle." She grabbed Casey's hand when he laid it on her shoulder.

"Where's the damned ambulance?" Sadie had done everything she could.

Chapter 59

Kathleen curled up on the couch, leaning into a pillow propped up against the hard arm of the sofa, a blanket wrapped around her. She'd never felt such paralyzing fear, not when she heard that Casey had fallen down the stairs or when Gran had taken ill with kidney failure or even when Sam married Missy.

Every now and then, she'd try to catch a nurse's attention, but there was nothing they could tell her. And on the phone, she kept repeating to her mother, no news is better than bad news. One nurse, Ruth, when told by Kathleen that she was four weeks pregnant, had procured the blanket and pillow and had kept her supplied with water. Kathleen had filled in all the paperwork and marked an *X* in the *Wife* box, but she didn't think they'd fallen for it. They were just being kind. She'd tried to keep busy by talking to her child, telling her or him—it changed from minute to minute—all about her father or his father, almost everything she could remember from that first day when Sam popped up with her red crayon to how great he looked in the saddle, taking a rail fence like an Olympic athlete.

She hardly noticed the ding of the elevator. The sound blended into the ordinary workings of the nursing station, and she jumped a little when Casey touched her cheek. He and Sadie were standing in front of her—Casey, drawn and older than she'd ever seen him, and Sadie, small travel bag in hand, looking like a mother hen as she sat down next to Kathleen. She snapped open the bag and whipped Mr. Rumples out from inside.

"Figured you'd need him until it's Sam's turn."

"Oh, Sadie." Kathleen's eyes stung with embarrassing tears.

"We brought you some clothes and a few other things. Have you heard anything?"

Kathleen shook her head as she wiped the tears away and sniffed.

"How did you manage to get away?" Kathleen said, grabbing his arm.

"I'm not here for long." He gave her a grimaced smile. "I have to go to the station in about an hour. They just let me … well … I'll go find out what's going on," Casey said with what Kathleen thought was mildly misguided enthusiasm, but it was useless to try to stop him.

He stood up, scooped up Mr. Rumples, and started over to the desk situated kitty-corner to where they sat. Sadie laughed a little, but then Kathleen knew Sadie was no stranger to hospitals either. Those nurses were tighter-lipped than a five-year-old with a sour gum ball.

Casey plunked Mr. Rumples down on the desk and leaned across the counter. Kathleen watched the nurse behind, going over paperwork, a force that up to that point had been immovable.

"Excuse me. I'm Casey Brennan, Sam Brennan's brother. Could you tell me where he is, how he is?"

"Casey, eh?" Kathleen watched Mavis—the name on her tag was as much information as Mavis had given Kathleen—sit passively, not moving from her seat. She didn't even look up at Casey. "He's in surgery. When we find out anything, we'll let you know. Try not to upset his wife. She's pregnant."

So much for secrets, Kathleen thought.

Casey blinked a few times. "That's it?" He laid Mr. Rumples on the counter and leaned over. "How long has he been in the operating room?"

Mavis didn't look up from her charts. "Don't know."

"You don't know."

Kathleen could hear the frustration in Casey's voice, and he'd only been there a few moments.

"Look, lady, my mother shot my brother, and I shot my mother. It hasn't been a bonus day. Now! How long until—"

Kathleen pushed the blanket aside. "Come on." She scrambled to her feet and, with Sadie, walked over to the booth.

Ruth, the older nurse who'd taken care of Kathleen, stepped out of the office and interrupted him. Ruth was a big woman, with hair teased into a ramrod-hard mesh below her cap. Straight out of the fifties.

"You're Lester's boy?" Ruth said to Casey.

Kathleen smiled at the expression on Ruth's face as she studied Mr. Rumples. "Nice bear," Ruth said. "Sam looks more like Billy."

"That's because he *is* Billy's son," Casey said, tersely.

Kathleen recognized the pain in Casey's voice when he said it. "Do you have any news?"

Ruth reached for Mr. Rumples. "Billy's son, eh?" A slow smile spread over Ruth's solid face. "I wasn't wrong after all."

"You know Billy?"

Ruth's face, as she studied the bear, softened into a smile. "This guy's really old. I have one just like it." She looked up at Casey. "Sam is out of the operating room. In ICU now." She gave Mr. Rumples back to Casey. "He came through with flying colors. He'll be out for a while yet, but as soon as we can, we'll get you in there with him." She paused and looked at Casey. "I knew Billy a long time ago. Say hello to him."

"I will. He'll probably be here later." Casey gripped the bear and took a deep breath of relief.

Casey handed Mr. Rumples to Kathleen and took hold of her, just as her feet sort of gave out on her for some annoying reason she couldn't figure out.

"Come on, beautiful. You have to sit down." Together, they were moving her back to the bench.

"No. Wait." Ruth came around to the front of the desk, her white shoes squeaking on the floor. "You might as well come with me now, Kathleen." She took Kathleen by the elbow. "Just Kathleen."

Kathleen watched Casey's face dissolve into disappointment. "I'll tell him you're here." Kathleen hugged him. He held her tightly and then took her hand and smiled.

"The ring."

"I've been carrying it around for a few days," Kathleen said and then leaned against him.

Ruth waved him away with her hand. "He'll be in there soon enough." She arched her eyebrows questioning Kathleen. "You want to go or not?"

Kathleen didn't hesitate. "Let's go."

"Give him back the bear," Ruth said, her head shaking as if the stuffed toy was out of the question. Kathleen handed Mr. Rumples back to Casey and then let Ruth lead her down the hallway to wherever it was they were headed.

"He'll be in ICU for a day or so. He's serious now but stable." Ruth talked as they made their way down the gray hallways.

Why did hospitals always smell the same? It wasn't even a clean smell, Kathleen thought, too much antiseptic. Ruth was talking, and Kathleen was only half listening. She knew she should be paying more attention.

"It would have been critical if he didn't get that help right away. He's responding well. His lung collapsed, and he'll be on a ventilator. He's not awake yet."

Ruth stopped her in front of a large double door. "Don't be alarmed at the darkness and the machines that *bing* every now and then. He's hooked up to almost every machine we could find, and he's being constantly watched by people who know what they're doing." She turned and faced Kathleen. "There'll be lots of tubes. They're there for a reason, and they need to stay there. When he wakes up, he's going to want to remove them. Don't let him. Go on in." She opened the door.

Kathleen knew Ruth had tried to prepare her, but she wasn't prepared. It was a scene out of a bad science fiction movie. Sam looked small and frail, a child controlled by an octopus of machinery. Yet another nurse was adjusting something or other in front of the curtain. The nurse pointed to a large, gray chair, next to a drab bedside table on wheels.

"You, sit and talk to him."

"What do I say?" Kathleen asked, studying Sam's poor gray face.

"Just normal chatter."

This wasn't her Sam. Kathleen heard the ventilator and saw bags of what appeared to be blood hanging from him.

"Drainage bags," the nurse—tagged Frances—said, watching Kathleen as if waiting for her to pass out. "They're normal. His color's better. You comfortable?"

Kathleen nodded and took Sam's hand, trying her hardest not to jar the IV that was taped there.

"Good. We won't be far away." Ruth grabbed the drab drapery and, giving it a yank that ripped the room apart, pulled it around them, blocking them both out from the rest of the world.

At least for a little while, Kathleen thought.

* * *

Casey stood, clutching Mr. Rumples, as Ruth came marching down the corridor toward them. Maybe they'd get some answers now, he thought, something he could phone home with. He was thankful he was there at all. If it hadn't been for his father taking charge, Casey would still be at the police station, justifying his actions to a bunch of overzealous cops trying to do the right thing. He knew he'd have to eventually leave and go to the station, probably sooner than later, and he wasn't looking forward to it.

Lester Brennan had seemed to know everyone, and anyone who didn't know him knew of him. Except for Kevin, who was strutting around the station, out of earshot of his partner, proclaiming how he'd known that something was wrong, that he should have been left to investigate the young woman's death further, despite Klugg's directive. Kevin hadn't seemed all that impressed with Lester Brennan.

But Lester didn't seem to care. He'd marched right into the office, wrapped his arm around the detective, shook hands with the coroner, and began the tedious job of explaining the whole situation. Casey had hardly uttered a word. He'd simply written and signed a statement and agreed he'd be back for more paperwork and another statement. They'd told them there would be an investigation, standard procedure. They had said it would take time.

Ruth looked past Casey. "You're the vet, aren't you?"

Sadie stared at the woman. "Yes."

Ruth smiled. "I remember you from when your mother was here." She stopped and eyed Sadie as if wanting to say something. "The medics told us what you did this afternoon. You saved his life, you know?"

Casey took her hand as Sadie blushed.

"Good work," Ruth said.

Sadie thanked her.

Ruth looked back at Casey. "You okay?" He turned his head and gave her a wary glance. She grabbed a chart from the desk and looked down at it. "From what I hear, you had quite the situation there." She looked hard into his eyes. "I suppose it could have been worse."

Casey nodded. "He's going to be fine, right?"

Ruth's mouth turned up ever so slightly at the edges. "Should be. If he's anything like his brother, he'll be back on his feet in no time." She placed the chart back down and turned away. "I do remember you, Casey Brennan. You were a lot smaller then, but you turned out okay." She headed back to her office. "Now, I have work to do."

Casey felt the room begin to spin. Then Sadie took his arm. Her hands and the feel of her body against his gave him strength that he never knew he had.

"Let's sit." She pulled him over to the couch.

The shock of the whole ordeal must have been taking hold of him as he tried to get the room to stop spinning, to get his teeth to stop chattering. Sadie laid her hands on his hands—he guessed to stop the shaking—but she stopped long enough to wrap the blanket around him.

"Sorry," he said as she wrapped her arms around him and pulled him back into the sofa.

"He's going to be fine. They promised me. They won't let him go," Sadie said.

Casey was numb to everything but the feel of her against him. "There must have been another way. I can still smell blood, Sadie."

"You're still covered in blood." She ran her finger lightly down his face. "You had to shoot. You have to know that."

"Nobody kills their own mother." He'd committed matricide. *Christ!* He couldn't close his eyes, but he saw her twisting in front of him, saw her drop like dead weight to the concrete. One moment she was there, the next gone, and he hadn't even done a good job. He'd been trying to take her down without killing her. What the hell was he thinking? He should have pushed that thought aside and just shot her dead before she had the chance to fire again. "It's my fault."

"You had to, Casey. Hell! She shot Sam. She killed Missy. She wouldn't have stopped with your father, she'd have killed you too, or Kathleen. If you hadn't shot her, I sure as hell would have."

He snorted. "Right."

"You don't know," Sadie said, her voice rising in a way Casey hadn't heard. "I've killed before."

He snorted but looked over at her, suddenly concerned. Sadie was crying.

"Casey, I know exactly how it feels. I killed my mother too."

Casey stopped rocking her. "With a shotgun?"

She chuckled a little, but the tears didn't stop.

He was grinning as he pulled her closer. "I love you. Trying to cheer me up and—"

"I did!" She pulled away, her face angry.

"Your mother died of cancer."

"I made a chemical cocktail and injected it into Mom's line." She stared at him and then looked around as if someone might have overheard.

She looked down, and he realized she wasn't just being nice. He pulled her in tightly, his chin on her head, and let her finish.

"She wouldn't let me stay. Casey, she was in so much pain, and she didn't want to waste away, and she knew that my father would never allow it." Sadie was shaking from the crying. "I knew what drugs I needed. She kissed me and told me to go home. Then she simply went to sleep. Dad was on the phone, hearing she'd passed as I walked back into the house."

"And you've never told anyone, have you?" Casey didn't know what to do. She'd never cried, never said a word, and now, the floodgates had opened.

"No. How could I?"

For a long time, Casey didn't say a word. He just let her cry. He knew how it felt to keep a secret bottled up inside and how it felt to finally let it go. She'd done that for him, and now he was there for her. After a while, the crying eased, and they just sat together, their hands locked.

"Casey?" Sadie looked up at him. "I love you."

He shook his head then kissed her again. "I don't think I'll ever get used to how good that sounds."

"You won't make any jokes, will you? Or tell anyone?"

He kissed her eyes. "Never." He kissed her lips. "I can keep a secret."

"Will you trust me enough to marry you and not do you in, in the middle of the night?"

He grinned. He hadn't thought of that. Casey grinned. "I'm supposed to ask you."

"I've never been one for convention."

Casey Brennan felt warmth he'd never known. He wanted it to stay forever. He wanted her to be with him forever, and he couldn't believe that she felt the same. "Can we live at your place?"

"Wherever you want, Casey." She snuggled in closer to him. "I wasn't kidding about Sam's photo."

Casey laughed out loud. "We'll have to sneak one. Kathleen maybe. She's good at that kind of thing."

CHAPTER 60

Sam had been popping into and out of consciousness. The first time, there had just been darkness and brightly colored stars, jagged lines of light and muffled voices he couldn't understand. Something hurt his throat, and he couldn't move. The second time he was aware of pain when he moved his arm, and he'd felt the sheet hard against him. He heard Kathleen calling him. When he managed to open his eyes a little, nothing seemed clear. He could almost touch Kathleen, but the machinery was in the way. Gradually, he realized he was in the hospital, and Kathleen was right there with him. Her hand was on his forehead, and she was talking to him. He remembered someone removing a tube from his throat and nurses and doctors coming in and out, talking to him, and touching him in places he'd rather not be touched. His throat felt as though he'd walked the Sahara, but there was always a sliver of ice in his mouth. More and more, Kathleen was there, and it began to dawn on him that he was conscious and alive. The pain was a staggering reminder of what had happened and what he couldn't remember; Kathleen grudgingly filled him in on everything.

"You're going to be okay. The nurse said all your vitals are fine, and you should rest and not worry about anything because there's nothing to worry about anymore."

"Stop." He muttered and this time she seemed to hear him. She seemed to know.

"I'm fine. We're all fine," she said again.

"Why can't I breathe?" He knew he could breathe. It just hurt. It was a struggle.

"That's normal, I guess." Kathleen leaned over, kissed him, and stroked his forehead. "You took a ricochet slug to the chest."

"Mum never could shoot straight. Good." It was all right to go back to sleep.

* * *

The next week was one of small accomplishments and large readjustments. Sam was making a rapid recovery, and that was part of the problem. He wouldn't rest, especially when Kathleen was anywhere near him. The respirator didn't last long, and the drainage bags were disappearing, one by one. He was even complaining about the orange sunflower drapes in his hospital room. People were coming and going, but no one was mentioning anything more about his mother than that she was dead and it was probably self-defense and a closed case.

When Gran came to visit, she watched him as if he was going to break. The men had gone home to do the chores, and Kathleen had fallen asleep in the big gray chair in the corner.

"It's going to hit you, Sam."

She told him about the memorial service being planned for his mother. The Women's Institute was holding it. After all, she'd been a Klugg, and Kluggs honored their dead, even when they came from the black side of the family.

"Don't wait for me. All the Kluggs can go to the memorial for the Beast. I'm not going," Sam said.

"That woman was your mother." Gran leaned forward and took his hand. "If only to say good-bye, to let go of your anger; if you don't, it will stay with you forever. She was sick, you know. She couldn't help what she was doing."

"You know, Gran? There are lots of mentally sick people out there who don't do what she did. She would never have changed. Even if she had meds. She didn't want to change." He shook his head. Sam found tears in his eyes suddenly and fought them back. "Did we do the right thing, Gran?"

She ran her hand through his hair. "You did the only thing you could. You and Casey aren't responsible. Lester and Billy and I should have taken charge years ago."

He couldn't help the anger rising in him. "Why, Gran? Why did you let her stay?"

Gran lowered her head. "Sometimes you make decisions that you think are right. What if we did make her leave, Sam? What if she demanded you boys? She could have you know, what with all the Kluggs around her, and then what would have happened to you? More importantly, what would she have done to your brother? Lester did what he had to do. He's the one who's suffered the most."

"Gran, you know I love you, but I don't agree. I'd never allow that to happen to my child."

Gran turned away from him. "Thomas told me the exact same thing. I thought I could look after it." She smiled a little. "Maybe you're not like Thomas at all? Maybe you're like me?"

Sam squeezed her china-doll hands. "So that's where the good stuff comes from."

Sam saw Kathleen stir. "This baby, Gran, do you think, what with MyKate and me, well, there's got to be a good chance the baby will be able to see Thomas."

"I'd say more than a good chance, Sam. Much more than a good chance."

* * *

The week had been a rough one for Casey, and it seemed to be getting worse instead of better. It shouldn't have been, he thought as he stood over the spot where she died. If his father or Billy had known he was in there, they'd have pulled him out and sent him straight over to Sadie's. She was the only reason he got up each morning. He should have been on top of the world. But his dreams were filled with horror, not the horror of Sam lying in the barn bleeding, but the horror of his mother's form. He shot her, repeatedly, so many times that he could draw it out now, and each time her reaction was different. One time, she got back up and shot Billy, one time Lester; two times, she shot Sam, laughing, and the last one she turned and aimed at him. What scared him was that he wanted her to shoot him.

He didn't dare tell Sadie. It would just bring back all her misery. It had taken her days to get over her revelation, days of her grief, her shame, and her fear of the truth coming out. Everyone one was putting her strained mood down to the shock of the shooting, but Casey knew better. She was only beginning to grieve the loss of her mother.

Most of the stain was gone from the floor of the barn, but Rachel's image was present, almost laughing at him. What if she came back, like Thomas? Casey stood there, resting on a pitchfork. He hadn't wanted to cry in a long time, but he wanted to now, anything to feel more than shame. He didn't notice the sun coming through the barn window or the tiny dust particles as they swirled and danced. He didn't feel the breeze change, too busy looking at a half-stained square of concrete.

"You did the right thing, Casey."

Casey snorted at Lester's voice and then looked over and paled. His heart took off in double time as he stared at the figure. It wasn't Lester. It was a vague form in dancing dust.

"Thomas?"

Thomas seemed to move closer as Casey studied him. He reached out for him, trying to touch his grandfather.

"You did the only thing you could, Casey. She'd have killed everyone."

"Is that why you came, you know, to me, now?"

Thomas smiled. "What are you going to think of the next time you're standing here? Her or me? She won't be back, Casey. Not from where she's gone. There's nothing she needs from here anymore."

Casey smiled. That made sense. There really was a hell. "Good point." He stared at the specter. "You're a good-looking guy."

Thomas laughed. "You've been a hard one to reach, but well worth the effort."

Casey saw Thomas start to fade. "Thomas … Gran. You won't take her too soon."

"No. Not with our great-grandchildren to look after."

Casey stepped closer, his hand reaching out through vapor. "Thomas, I always thought you were … ah … kinda terrific."

Thomas was almost gone when he said it. "I always knew you were terrific." Then Thomas was just sun on dust.

Casey stood, staring, hoping, but knowing that Thomas was gone. Then he let out a whoop and jumped around like a maniac.

"Yes! Yes! I'm terrific!" He spun around, knowing just where he was going. He was going into town for an engagement ring. And then he was going to pick up Sadie. And they were going to start making great-grandchildren. Well, after the wedding and if Sadie wanted it, but that's what he was going to do. He pitched the fork and strutted out of the barn.

CHAPTER 61

Kathleen drove her Mustang right past her house and up the lane, sending autumn leaves scattering everywhere. So many people in her house, and though she should have expected it, the crowd overwhelmed her. And the fuss! She knew that if she so much as slowed down, she'd be stuck there in the middle of the living room, exhibit number one. And though she loved her mother, she didn't have time for that. They'd have plenty of time to chat with all the relatives at Gran's birthday party and then the wedding. Three days! Only three days and then the wedding. She grabbed at the red shoe box on the seat next to her as it began to slide, pushed by the gray garment bag hanging on the clip above the door.

A whale, she thought. *I'm going to look like a big white whale.* She tried to remember the name and then saw the sun catch her engagement ring. She realized that her size didn't matter. Her ring was perfect. Her life was perfect, and her wedding would be perfect. She screeched the tires to a sliding stop as the dust followed and engulfed the car.

As she got out, she noticed Gran and Casey over looking at the Tennessee walking horse Billy had picked up. It was a pretty dapple with plenty of spirit, Billy had said, and perfect for the little cart, just the right size for a driver and Gran. Gran and Casey waved, and she waved back as she grabbed the shoe box and the gown, slammed the car door with her foot, and made her way into the kitchen.

The smell of wallpaper paste and paint was everywhere, and though they had hoped to get it done by the time of the wedding, it was still, unfortunately, a work in progress. Everything else had been taken care of. The wedding would take place in town. They had wanted an outside wedding, but they couldn't trust Thanksgiving. October in Killkenny County could be sunny and wonderful one day, freezing the next. The local Women's Institute ladies were taking care of the spread. It would be big, one of the biggest in the area, as it had been a while since they'd had a double wedding in Killkenny.

"Is that it?" Sadie stopped icing the cake immediately and reached for the bag as Kathleen hustled inside.

"Yes, and I don't need icing all over it."

Sadie grinned. "The icing would only be on the outside."

"Too close." Kathleen turned to Lester, who was seated at the table reading the local advertising rag. "Could you hold this, please?" She handed the dress to him. "It will be safe with you." Lester put his hand out and accepted the gown without so much as a look up from his paper.

"Now," Kathleen said, looking down at the shoe box. "Not the pantry. Not the mudroom. She'll go right by there."

"The living room," Sadie said. "No one ever goes into the living room. Get your hands off, Billy." She shooed him away from the cake.

"Can I lick the bowl?" Billy said.

"My turn," Lester countered.

"What's that?" Billy asked, staring at the garment bag Lester was holding.

"Don't know," Lester said. "I have to hold it till Kathleen takes it."

Kathleen came bustling back in and grabbed the gown. "Where is he?"

Billy nodded upstairs. "Finally getting around to taking them down."

Kathleen's face sobered instantly. Then a gentle smile crossed her face. "Someone should get Gran and Casey in here. We want to get this done before—"

"What's that?" Casey stuck his head around the pantry door, wallpaper paste and goop hanging from his face. "I'm right here."

"You were just out with Gran." Kathleen's mouth dropped.

Instant pandemonium broke out as all four of them made a dash for the window, bobbing and straining to look out into the yard. The mudroom door opened, and Gran stepped in.

"My goodness! Whatever is going on?" Gran placed a pot of crimson mums on the counter.

One by one, they groaned.

"Is that it?" Gran walked over to Lester. "Don't let it touch the ground, darling. Why not take it to my room and hang it in the closet?"

Lester glanced over to Kathleen as she grabbed the dress. "No, thanks, Gran. I'll take it straight upstairs." Kathleen could hear them all laughing as she climbed the stairs and headed down the hall to Sam. Her back hurt, and she was more tired than she liked to admit, but she'd rest after the wedding. This wasn't just her wedding; it was Sadie's too, and it was going to be perfect, even if she was the size of a small white whale.

The emptiness crushed Kathleen as she stared into his room. The walls still held the ghosts of the posters he had removed. She hung the gown on the door and came inside. "Hi."

He was sitting on his bed, curling a poster into a tube. There was only one remaining—hers. He grabbed her hand and pulled her down on top of him.

"Oof!" He clutched his gut and moaned.

"Give me a break!" she said with a laugh. "You know we're all getting pretty tired of that oh-poor-me-I'm-so-injured bit. One minute you're moaning, the next you're out in the barn. Casey told me he caught you carrying buckets."

"But—"

"No buts. You can't do chores." She snorted. "You're 100 percent, for everything else," she said and giggled. "And I would know." She looked over at the stack of tubes. "You know … we could put them back."

Sam pulled her back onto the bed and into his arms. "No, MyKate. It's done now. I'll keep yours out for the nursery. God! Look at that ceiling! It really needs a coat of paint."

"Not your concern, Samuel Brennan. Your only concern is to get strong enough to be a super daddy."

He grinned and peered over at the dress. "Is that it?" His eyes widened.

"Don't touch it. I only brought it up because Sadie couldn't take her eyes off it, and you aren't allowed to see it." She looked away, furious at herself but unable to stop the tears from overflowing.

"MyKate." He was back down, his arms around her. "What's wrong? Did they make it the wrong color?"

She kneed him. "No!" She snuffled. "It's just … I look huge in it. I look like one of those big white whales."

"Belugas?"

She kneed him again.

"I should have known better. Gran warned me—pregnant women are temperamental, but this is crazy," Sam said with a grin. "You'll don't need sequins to sparkle."

She kissed him. "Sam."

He looked over suddenly concerned. "What?"

"Oh, nothing, really!" She reached over and touched his face. "It's just the scan I had today ..."

His face degenerated into worry. "What?"

"Well, they saw something they didn't expect to see." She let it hang there for a minute enjoying his concern. "Seems there are two babies ..."

* * *

There was a whoop from upstairs.

"Can we hurry it along?" Billy said, looking at his watch. Then he stopped as Gran caught his eye.

"Why, William! It isn't every day your mother turns seventy-five." Gran did her best to look shocked as Sam and Kathleen came bounding down the stairs. Casey had done his best, short of a shower, to clean up, but he still had some sticky substance holding his hair together in one spot. Sadie was standing behind the cake, the one candle propped at an angle, the lighter in her hand. Lester hadn't moved from his chair behind the table.

"But Ruth told me to pick her up at four," Billy said.

"Already it starts." Lester snorted from behind his paper.

"You didn't show him that dress, Katie?" Gran asked as she sat in her birthday-decorated rocker of honor.

Kathleen grinned then turned woeful. "I'm going to look like a big white—"

"Beluga," Sam said with a straight face. "She thinks she's going to look like a beluga."

"Belugas are so sweet!" Sadie said, grinning. "They're my favorite, and so gentle, and I swear they're the smartest."

"All right!" Kathleen put her hand out to stop them. "I won't look like a beluga. Okay? Is everyone happy now?"

"Show me the dress later, darling," Gran said. "I'll tell you the truth."

Kathleen snorted, knowing Gran would never say that she, Kathleen Abigail Egan, soon to be Brennan, would look anything other than beautiful.

"Are we all here?" She saw Gran look toward the stove.

"Thomas says we should hurry a bit. Company coming."

Kathleen cuddled into Sam.

"Well?" Gran asked them. "Thomas tells me you two have something to announce."

Casey's mouth dropped as he stared at his brother. "You're not pulling out of the wedding now."

Kathleen giggled. "You tell them." She poked Sam.

"No … you …"

"Don't start!" Sadie grunted and looked at Sam. "Well?"

"Well, it seems—"

"Twins!" Kathleen blurted out as Sam sighed. "We're having twins. Do you believe it? I'm going to be huge! Bigger than a beluga."

It took a few minutes for the backslapping and congratulations to ebb. Gran told everyone how she already knew, how Thomas had told Casey months before, but Casey didn't believe him, which left Casey scratching his head, trying to remember what Thomas had said.

"He did." Casey's face ballooned into a smile as it came to him. "He told me great-grandchildren. I thought he meant, me, us. Hey! I knew first."

Then Gran told them she wasn't certain she should say anything, but Thomas had told her there was a baby boy and a baby girl, and they were only the beginning. "Only the beginning!" She leaned over to Sadie.

Billy glanced at his watch. Lester was back into his paper. Sadie stood up and reached behind the stove.

"We should get started before everyone starts arriving. There are more of these." She handed a box about the size of a shoe box to Gran. "Eleven others … just like this one."

"Oh my," Gran said as she removed the wrapping from the box and stared down at antique candle scones. "Oh my. These are genuine." She looked over at Sadie. "They are lovely, darling."

Sadie leaned down and gave her a kiss. "We'll have this place up to scratch in no time flat."

"Easy for you to say." Casey grinned. "You're not the one with wallpaper paste in your hair." Sadie grinned at him and removed a strand of limp wallpaper from his shoulder. "I love you, Sadie Parker."

She nodded. "I know."

"Okay. My turn." Lester put down his paper and moved forward, tugging and twisting, pulling a rather large box from under the table. "Billy tried to outdo me with that pretty horse out there. But I upped him real good."

Billy snorted.

Lester leaned and pushed the heavy box closer. It was the size of an ottoman and had been under the table for the better part of two days, taped up. But now the tape was gone, and it was slightly open. "Go ahead, Mum. The box isn't sealed."

"Goodness, Lester. The way you're acting, you'd think there's a fortune in here."

He didn't say anything but shrugged. Turning, Sadie whispered to Casey, "In cash, as a piece or two, not a lot, but as heritage and love, it's priceless." He reached over and grabbed her hand.

Gran's fingers shook when she removed the wrapping from the first plate. "Oh, Thomas, look here." She held the plate up and ran her fingers over the textured weave. "Country Heaven. Oh, Lester."

"Your set was rather … well, … diminished, and I have this friend who has …" Lester looked confused as everyone broke into laughter. "The whole set is there, but I can get extras when you ladies tell me what goes with it. Sadie there seems to be a bit of an expert at those old things."

"Okay." Sadie quieted them all down with her hands. "Before we cut the cake, we have something special for you, Gran," Sadie said. "Go ahead, Katie. You picked it out."

Kathleen's face took on a new glow as she whisked past the group and into the living room. She came back with the red box she'd taken from her car. "This is from all of us, Gran. Hope you like it."

Gran took the box from her and peered up at Kathleen. "Kathleen Abigail Egan. Is there a new hope in this old house again?" Kathleen didn't have to answer as a tiny white form mewed and stuck its whiskered face out of the box. "Oh my. What a beauty too."

Sam leaned over and kissed Kathleen's tear-covered face.

"Did Thomas tell you?" Kathleen said.

"No, darling. I was rather hoping." She grinned coquettishly and held the little fur ball up to her cheek. "And she's perfect."

"The pick of the litter," Sadie said.

Gran held her up in front of her, the kitten's little eyes as blue as the water in the quarry, its whiskers as white and pure as the winter fields around the farm on a sunlit day. Gran pulled the kitten close to her cheek.

The kitten looked up into Gran's eyes. "It was well worth the wait, Thomas. Well worth the wait."

The End

ABOUT THE AUTHOR

Pamela Shelton is a forty-year survivor of mental illness, having been diagnosed as bipolar at the age of twenty. Since then, she worked as an outreach worker for mental illness in Ontario, Canada. She was editor of a monthly newsletter and had numerous letters to editors published in Canadian newspapers. She studied writing at WritersStudio, New York, under Phillip Schultz and many other prominent authors, such as Joel Hinman, Michelle Herman, Lucinda Holt and Cynthia Weiner. Pam has published three short stories: *Obsession (Mobius: The Journal of Social Change)*, and was awarded honorable mention for two stories, *The Wife and The Tenpenny (Canadian Writers Journal*, White Mountain Publication). Although Pamela spent over fifteen years on a productive beef farm, she now lives near the Gulf of Mexico, just south of Houston, with her husband, two English Springer Spaniel and 5 cats.

Printed in the United States
By Bookmasters